FAVOUR THE DEAD

Mackenzie Smith studied English Literature at university. A serial entrepreneur, pilot and big-game hunter, he lives in Wiltshire with his wife and four children.

Praise for Mackenzie Smith

'with great verve and an eye for detail, it crackles first page to last, and makes Smith a name to out for.'
Daily Mail

pace and content of this gripped me from the I found myself thinking: where's he got all this ? Is this about us and the early days of Executive omes? To me it read "for real".'
Simon Mann

n to earth and dirty like it is. Mackenzie Smith res what others miss. People need to know.'
Colonel R. Hoare

writing is good, the characters strong . . . I would nmend this to anyone who likes a good thriller.'
Soldier Magazine

Also available by Mackenzie Smith

Who Pays the Piper

MACKENZIE SMITH
FAVOUR THE DEAD

arrow books

Published by Arrow Books 2013

2 4 6 8 10 9 7 5 3 1

Copyright © Mackenzie Smith 2013

Mackenzie Smith has asserted his right under the Copyright, Designs
and Patents Act 1988 to be identified as the author of this work

Arrow Books
Random House, 20 Vauxhall Bridge Road,
London SW1V 2SA

www.randomhouse.co.uk

Addresses for companies within The Random House Group Limited
can be found at: www.randomhouse.co.uk/offices.htm

The Random House Group Limited Reg. No. 954009

A CIP catalogue record for this book
is available from the British Library

ISBN 9780099576754

The Random House Group Limited supports the Forest Stewardship
Council® (FSC®), the leading international forest-certification
organisation. Our books carrying the FSC label are printed on
FSC®-certified paper. FSC is the only forest-certification scheme
supported by the leading environmental organisations, including
Greenpeace. Our paper procurement policy can be found at
www.randomhouse.co.uk/environment

Typeset in Palatino by Palimpsest Book Production Limited,
Falkirk, Stirlingshire

Printed and bound by
CPI Group (UK) Ltd, Croydon, CR0 4YY

To Arabella

Acknowledgements

With thanks to: Tony, Gryller, Blofeld, NRC, Simon M, Simon T and Ben.

Prologue

March 1982

Corporal Daniel Raglan had hardly moved a muscle for approaching six hours yet he was still soaked with sweat. His eyes ached from peering through his binoculars and his elbows were rubbed raw from propping himself up where he lay beneath a camouflaged groundsheet. By any standards, it had to be an odd way to spend a birthday.

The late afternoon sun shone brightly and in some respects the scene was reminiscent of his home in Wales. Before him lay a wide green valley, flattening out onto a plain. Beyond, the South Atlantic glinted a deep blue. Sheep grazed right up to the high barbed wire fencing that surrounded Rio Gallegos, the largest military airbase in Argentina.

Each time an aircraft took off, he noted the type and

time. Every fifteen minutes he transmitted a compressed high frequency BATCO message on a short-wave radio which would be picked up by HMS *Spartan*, the British Hunter Class submarine sitting just beneath the swell about a mile offshore. Within seconds this information would be relayed to the Admiralty in London. From there, it would be passed on to the RAF, who were now flying combative sorties over the Falkland Islands from the aircraft carrier, HMS *Ark Royal*.

Since the invasion of the Falklands three weeks before, all leave had been cancelled and all British forces had been in a high state of preparation. The SAS had been tasked with delivering an early knock-out blow against the Argentinians. The plan was a full-blown airborne assault on their largest airbase to destroy their fighter aircraft on the ground. Without fighters, British air superiority was a given and the invasion more or less over.

But there were bad feelings at Hereford. People had been openly discussing the fact that it was a suicide mission. They had no doubt they could successfully 'crash land' a Hercules full of troops on the main runway, take over the airbase and take out a load of MiGs on the ground. Piece of piss. But then what? They could even hold the place for a few hours. Still OK, but then thousands of enemy troops would turn up with armour and butcher the lot of them. Not OK. The evacuation strategy was to disperse into small groups and walk out to Chile, over 400 kilometres away through hostile country. Utterly mad. Even senior brass were likening it to the infamous St Nazaire Raid in 1942 where 400 British commandos blew up the dry docks under the noses of the Germans in Northern France and five, *five,* men evaded capture and made it home via Spain. The objective was achieved but at hideous cost.

The valley looked peaceful and it was hard to imagine that in about nine hours the 114 men of A and G Squadrons 22 SAS combined would be hitting the tarmac. However uncomfortable his birthday had been, it was certainly going to be a memorable one.

Raglan knew that any minute he was likely to hear one of the other three members of the patrol approaching the forward OP to take over the next six-hour shift. They were positioned the other side of the ridge behind him. As he wiped the sweat from his eyes and raised his binoculars for what he hoped would be his final look around, he noticed sheep scattering to avoid several four-tonne military lorries driving at speed along the road that hugged the perimeter fence. His senses kicking into gear, he heard distant shouts coming from away downhill to his left. The lorries had stopped at intervals and troops were spewing from the back of them.

Raglan's body pumped with adrenalin as he transmitted the development to HMS *Spartan*. He rubbed his hand nervously through his short, black, curly hair. The troops had formed a line and were making their way towards him through the thin fir trees that peppered the valley sides. He slowly rose to his knees and folded away the groundsheet. He looped his arm through the carrying strap of the radio and lugged it onto his back. As he turned to start his retreat over the ridge, several shots rang out and echoed around the valley. The line of soldiers half a mile below him stopped momentarily in their tracks.

He quickened his pace uphill through the trees. More shots rang out; this time bursts of automatic fire. It meant one thing. The other three members of the patrol must have been compromised at the lying-up point. They would be retreating with covering fire along the adjacent valley.

By the time Raglan reached the crest of the ridge, he was breathing heavily. Taking care not to skyline himself, he crawled forwards and looked down into the next-door valley. There was now almost continuous fire with intermittent grunts from large-calibre machine guns. He struggled to hold his binoculars still as he surveyed the long, steep expanse. Within a couple of seconds, he spotted the other three members of the patrol lying 500 or 600 metres away towards the valley floor. They were huddled amongst a pile of rocks firing their weapons. Raglan's eyes followed down the line of the valley. Then he gasped.

There were too many enemy troops to count. They rattled off suppressing fire up the valley while more edged up towards higher ground. The patrol were pinned down in the rocks with a steep open area behind them. As Raglan grappled to assess the position, one of the patrol broke cover and started a zigzag run uphill. Within twenty metres, he fell and lay motionless.

The rocks had become largely obscured from view by dust kicked up from the mass of incoming rounds. Enemy soldiers were within a couple of hundred metres of their target. It would be grenades next. They surged forward and several fell.

Once they made it to the rocks, the firing ceased. Raglan grimaced as he saw a figure hauled from among the stones. He could not identify which of his comrades it was, but the man was forced to his knees and held in position by two soldiers. Raglan flipped his binoculars to one side and rested his M16 on the rocky ground before him. He peered into the telescopic sight. A tall soldier in a peaked cap drew a pistol and shot the kneeling man in the back of the head. A lifeless body flopped forwards.

Having witnessed how he could expect to be treated if he was captured, Raglan knew he had little to lose. He fixed the cross hairs of his sights square in the middle of the tall soldier's chest. Conscious of the distance and the slight cross-wind, he adjusted his aim and squeezed the trigger. Momentarily, he lost sight of his target as the rifle jerked up, but he regained his view in time to catch the lasts wisps of dust disperse into the air just to the right of the Argentinian officer.

Raglan watched for a moment as soldiers darted in all directions, desperately seeking cover from the unseen sniper. He emptied the rest of his magazine in the general direction of the rocks and then sprang to his feet, knowing this was the moment to get going.

1

October 1999

Christian McKie felt relief as he hung up the telephone in the High Commissioner's office. Even hearing Colonel Deveral's voice made him feel better and reminded him that there was still an ordered and real world out there. The last time they had spoken was moments before the assault on Geri Bana in Sierra Leone. After this conversation, his life had imploded.

He had been shot, left for dead, captured and imprisoned. He had been tortured, witnessed his friends being killed, turned into a gangster, nearly been killed again and lived in a parallel universe, allowing his family and Regiment to think he was dead.

It was hardly surprising that he had become a

properly committed smoker in the process. But making the call to Deveral had ended his dual existence. He had achieved what he had set out to do. He had risen from the depths of human existence as prisoner of the demonic West Side Boys to being a British Army officer again with a bright and exciting future, as well as a colourful but secret past.

Deveral had told him not to contact anyone else and to await details of his repatriation to Britain. He thought it would be later that day but could not say for sure. Christian was brought breakfast by the High Commissioner's wife and spent the morning dozing on a sofa watching Sky News, which was still dominated by the failed terrorist bombing of the Egyptian Embassy in London. Whilst his plan had worked well, he still felt unnerved by the intense media frenzy about the identity of the perpetrator. Sure, he had framed Sam with total precision, but no plan was ever completely watertight. His 'Dick Turpin' style alibi would be hard to challenge, as no court or lawyer was ever going to be able to check the date of his escape with the West Side Boys or al-Qaeda.

Thinking about his conversation with Deveral, it was the use of the words 'pure genius' that worried him. Something about this choice of words hinted that Deveral knew. It was possible, but he would not have long to wait and find out. The High Commissioner came in and told him that Deveral was on his way to

Morocco personally to collect him. They would be going to a nearby military airport about an hour's drive away to meet his plane.

Christian watched the white puff of smoking rubber as the wheels of a familiar Gulfstream 4 met the baking tarmac. The aircraft manoeuvred against a backdrop of rusting barbed wire fencing towards a row of sandy-coloured concrete buildings, where Christian waited under the suspicious gaze of two plain-clothed Moroccan military policemen. He felt uncomfortable standing there in slightly too tight borrowed chinos and baggy blue short-sleeved shirt.

Deveral's head appeared before the steps had fully lowered. The noise of the engines forced Christian to mouth his words of thanks to the High Commissioner. He walked forwards and started up the steps towards a casually dressed Deveral waiting at the top. Christian tried to read his expression but could not pick up anything except a wide and delighted looking smile. The outstretched hand added to the sense that even if he did know something, he was still on side.

Christian glanced down the empty cabin and saw that two seats had been screwed into the floor at the back of the plane. As he followed Deveral and sat down, the steps lifted and the G4 began to taxi.

'No point hanging around for anyone to start getting any bright ideas,' said Deveral, turning sideways to look at Christian.

'Quite right, sir,' Christian replied. 'I'm pretty keen to get going too.'

'Well, you've had a fairly busy time of it by any measure,' Deveral responded.

Christian pondered on another of Deveral's odd choices of words. People held in captivity could hardly be described as 'busy'. Of course, Christian *had* been busy, ultra busy, covertly sneaking in and out of the UK to deal with Sam.

The powerful engines pushed them back in their seats at they sped down the runway. It was not until they had taken off and levelled out that Deveral restarted the conversation. Christian was happy to let him lead.

'You know what, Christi, whatever happened to you and whatever you had to do in there, you will always have my unwavering support and respect. We all go through the training and, sure, it's the best preparation anyone can get, but we all know nothing can prepare you for when the shit really and truly hits the fan. That's the real test. No chance of a tap on the shoulder and a friendly RTU. No trucks waiting to pick you up at the end of the exercise. You've done it for real and you've exceeded any possible expectation that even this Regiment could ask. Most unusual, Christi, most unusual.' Deveral looked straight ahead as he spoke, with just an occasional glance in Christian's direction.

'Well, sir, kind words, sir, but let me assure you . . .' Christian began.

'There's no need to assure me of anything,' interrupted Deveral. 'The facts speak for themselves. Play it down as much as you like but, take it from me, you've done very well.'

Christian nodded and looked at the floor of the aircraft in front of him. He knew that his motivation to escape had been to get back at Sam, who had shot him in the firefight in Geri Bana and left him at the mercy of a sadistic militia rabble. He had been spurred on by a deep-seated thirst for revenge, nothing to do with any sense of patriotic duty. He had robbed and deceived, killed and duped, albeit rather successfully. Perhaps that was what Deveral meant? Maybe that was what *was* expected? He didn't know, but it didn't feel strictly heroic.

After several minutes of silence, Deveral spoke again.

'Is there anything you'd like to know about Barras or the operation in Mauritania, or about Jamie and Tim? Or, dare I mention, Sam Carter?'

Christian shrugged and turned to Deveral. His pained expression answered the question. Deveral read the signs and continued.

'No, I thought not. Let's just leave it there. I guess you must be looking forward to getting home and getting back to normal?'

Christian took a breath then paused.

'Sir, to be honest, I'm absolutely bloody dreading it. No one's going to understand what happened and quite why. Things broke down, people broke down, the whole show broke down. Not sure if it's really for me any more. It's hard to explain, but it's just how I feel at the moment.'

Deveral shifted in his seat and turned to face Christian, his foot starting to tap slowly.

'No, no, I get where you're coming from one hundred per cent. Things did go wrong, and, I agree, people went wrong. You don't need to explain yourself to me. I can guess roughly how you must feel. But may I run something past you? It'll probably be a no, but there's someone I'd like you to meet before you make any decisions and before we announce your return. It's just an idea and may be totally misguided. On the other hand, it could be very much up your street.'

Christian met Deveral's gaze.

'Who? Who do you have in mind, sir?'

Deveral glanced up the aircraft towards the cockpit, then lowered his voice.

'Well, I don't want to put too fine a point on it, but, on certain occasions, we've lost people, or to be more accurate, thought we've lost people when in fact we haven't.'

Deveral looked awkward, knowing he was not explaining himself very well.

'What I mean is that on more than one occasion, people have been presumed killed in action when it turned out that they were only in fact *missing* in action. Two very different things as it turns out.'

Christian felt his interest aroused by Deveral's inability to explain himself with his usual precision. This man tended not to beat about the bush. He opened his mouth to speak when Deveral continued.

'Well, this is a tricky one to set out, so bear with me. The point is that on several occasions, people who have been officially killed have, in fact, made it back from operations alive and well. And, if you think about it, it doesn't take too much imagination to work out that someone who is officially dead has certain advantages.'

Deveral paused and searched Christian's face for signs of interest. Christian nodded slowly, his eyes narrowed.

'Go on, sir,' he said quietly.

'Well, the fact is that we run, or to be more accurate, allow to exist, a unit made up of people that are officially dead. They work in parallel to the rest of the security forces. They are not soldiers, not civilians, not even British citizens any more. They don't have names, National Insurance Numbers, et cetera, and really don't exist except in the form of an alias. They can draw upon the full resources of MI5, MI6, us obviously, the Navy, pretty much whoever they need and whatever they need. They can do things no respectable government can. They operate in a hinterland, more or less outside the law. Now, you know, inadvertently, you've just qualified. That is if you would like to consider it?'

Deveral was now turned fully sideways on his seat, looking directly at Christian. He continued.

'You can either think about it or simply forget everything I just said. The fact is that being dead can have some quite meaningful upsides. Why not come and meet this person I have lined up for you?'

2

Sam Carter sat on the floor with his back against the door of his prison cell, his knees tucked up under his chin. Every ten minutes someone flipped up a metal disc that covered the small peephole into his cell and looked inside. Sam felt his position below the door offered him some small vestige of privacy, being the least visible part of the cell.

He clasped one hand in the other to stop his fingers from shaking just long enough to identify a tiny scrap of remaining fingernail to bite at. His teeth met and he tasted blood. The briefest moment of satisfaction passed in a fraction of a second.

He heard footsteps and then the familiar metal on metal scratch above his head. The sound meant another ten minutes had passed. He calculated that he was likely to hear this noise about another twenty times before they came for him.

He thought back to the last moment when he had led a normal life. He remembered the shock of answering the door one Sunday morning in the middle of breakfast and a wall of armed police invading his house. He had been bundled into a van, taken to Paddington Green police station, then extradited to Egypt and charged with detonating a bomb outside the Egyptian Embassy. He was certain that he had been framed by Christian as the most devious act of revenge he could possibly imagine.

Sure, he had shot Christian, but he had never set out to do so. Things had got out of control in the heat of the moment and it had just happened. There was no malice of forethought. It could almost be described as an accident. But Christian, on the other hand, had brooded over this vile act of revenge. He would have known Egypt still implemented the death penalty for acts of terrorism and he would have known precisely that the Egyptian Embassy in London was considered sovereign territory.

The first few weeks in Mahmood Prison, six miles to the south of Cairo, had been a blur. He had been held in the relatively comfortable 'International' wing. For up to fourteen hours a day he had been interrogated by a series of Secret Police officers. They had threatened violence but not given him anything more than an open-handed slap around the face. All within safe limits, he had thought, for this part of the world.

But then came the hammer blow. On the day of his

appearance in court, the day Sam was sure the charges would be dropped, things went from plain old awful to terminal. Despite the bomb he had been accused of detonating not actually killing anyone, he had been charged with attempted mass murder. Ordinarily, he was told, this would result in a death sentence that would be commuted to life imprisonment. But Sam's refusal to reveal which terrorist organisation had hired him to do the job had made things worse for him. The fact was that he had had nothing to do with any bombing, but the evidence was irrefutable. He had the option to confess and grass up the other parties involved, but how could he? There was no one else, otherwise he would have sung like a canary.

Now with the added indignity of being on suicide watch, he had even been stripped of his standard prison overalls and sat in a white paper robe. He stared around the filthy, greyish cell walls as if expecting some imaginary door might appear from nowhere. He envied the solitary mosquito that buzzed in and out of the small barred window through which he saw a tiny sliver of night sky.

His body jerked as he heard metal on metal once again. He did not think it was possible for his state of extreme tension to get any worse but it just had. A key scraped in the lock just behind his head. As he processed the implications, he heard the sharp clank of a lever and then voices. It suddenly made sense. Of course, they would come early and catch him off guard. Or was it some tiny act of kindness to spare him from a couple more hours of hell? It didn't matter, the room filled with a blur of prison guards wearing helmets and riot gear. They were clearly not taking any chances and Sam knew he had two choices. Either be beaten to pulp and then executed or just be executed. Before having time to decide, he found himself pinned to the floor and his arms twisted up and backwards. A hood was yanked down sharply over his head and he felt a drawstring tighten around his neck.

Despite not understanding a word of Arabic, Sam detected tension in the clipped bursts of language he heard around him. But one voice, noticeably deeper and calmer than the others, snapped instructions that were obeyed. Whoever it was, he was in charge and had done this before. This was routine.

Sam felt hands and arms pass around his body and the sensation of restriction as straps tightened around his waist, upper arms and knees. If he were planning on putting up a last-minute struggle, he had missed the chance. Next there was a moment of weightlessness as he was hoisted into the air. He heard the scrape of the cell door open and then felt a sharp burst of pain as his shoulder hit what had to be the concrete door frame.

He knew the execution chamber was only at the end of the row of cells. He had been cruelly shown inside on his way to the holding cell the day before. Still Sam clung to the microscopically minute belief that someone was about to intervene. The whole thing would be explained away as one big misunderstanding. It was just a matter of when, but it would happen.

Through the hood, Sam noticed an increase in the level of light. He must be out of the gloomy corridor of cells and in the brightly lit execution chamber. He heard a couple of the men carrying him exhale as they hoisted him higher in the air. His next sensation was his foot hitting something that sounded like a chair and his flip-flop falling off. He heard it land softly on the floor.

His mind swirled in a horrendous mixture of adrenalin, exhaustion, fear, disbelief and anger. This was Christian's fault. It was outrageous and light years out of proportion to what could be deemed justifiable revenge. Then a thought more terrible than death occurred to Sam. Was Christian going to be one of the official observers? He had been told twelve members of the public had to witness all executions. If Christian was capable of arranging all this with such precision, perhaps he could have got himself a position in the execution chamber too?

This was a thought too far. Every muscle in Sam's body ripped with tension as he hauled his legs up into his chest and then lashed out. The men holding his feet let go as he bellowed with rage. He twisted sideways and writhed like a wounded buffalo. The guards were only taken by surprise for a fraction of a second before regaining their grip. More hands held him more tightly, then a hand pushed between the back of his thighs and grabbed his scrotum. The hand twisted and Sam screamed with pain. The message was clear. 'You fuck with us and we make this a whole lot nastier than it has to be.'

Thud. He landed hard on the heavy wooden table he had seen before. The hands busied themselves with buckles and straps. Before the paralysing pain in his balls had subsided even infinitesimally, he was utterly immobile. His left arm had been released from behind his back and was strapped down to a protruding section of table.

A shock of white light followed as the hood came off. Sam craned his head forward for a momentary glance around the room. There were two rows of chairs against the wall. No Christian, just anonymous men in darks suits and a couple in Arab dress. They chatted quietly to one another. He had seen enough. He rested his head down and stared at the strip light above. He felt a prick just below his elbow. The token jab of anaesthetic was followed almost immediately by a much sharper pain. Sam strained against the straps as he felt cold run down his forearm towards his hand. His fingers tingled.

A voice read something out loud in Arabic. Sam blinked away a mixture of sweat and tears in time to see an expressionless doctor stepping back from him.

If he could believe what he had been told, he was in the last eight to twelve seconds of his life. He could expect his heart to fail, quickly followed by unconsciousness and death.

No one was coming for him, and even if they were it was too late now. Christian had succeeded. He had been utterly crushed. How could it have been worse? A lethal injection from an anonymous doctor in front of a bunch of bored looking Egyptian businessmen. Not even the offer of a firing squad that might have in some way reflected a degree of the military respect he deserved. No burial in an immaculately maintained British military cemetery. It would be a cheap wooden box and then probably a stinking rubbish dump roamed by rabid dogs and rats.

Through closed eyelids, Sam felt the intensity of the strip light above him increase. The sound around him faded to silence. His head rolled to the right and his lips mouthed his last thought. 'Fucking, bloody, bastard.'

3

Having been awake for more or less forty-eight hours, Christian slept from the moment Deveral had stopped talking to the point where the G4 met the tarmac at Brize Norton. He peered through the window and caught sight of familiar green hangars passing by as they taxied down runway eight.

Deveral pushed some papers into a folder which he then shoved into a battered brown leather briefcase.

'Well, that was pretty painless, I suppose. Shits on the C130 every time,' he muttered as he stood up and looked at Christian.

'Yes, sir, certainly does,' replied Christian with an awkward sideways smile.

As the aircraft came to a standstill, Deveral's grey Vauxhall Senator appeared at the bottom of the steps with its hazard lights flashing. A man wearing orange ear defenders and a yellow high visibility waistcoat got out and held the driver's door open. Deveral popped his head into the cockpit and nodded some words of thanks to the pilots before heading down the steps with Christian immediately behind him.

Despite having been out of the country for less than twenty-four hours, Christian glanced down at the tarmac and felt a sense of homecoming he had not experienced as he had piled into the back of Armalite's Land Rover when he had been smuggled back in a couple of weeks before. This time, he was setting foot on British soil for real, as a returning British serviceman, not as a fugitive packing illegal firearms, millions of pounds' worth of blood diamonds and a pile of cocaine. The RAF ground staff were now on side, not there to catch him. He could look them in the eye. That felt better.

Christian walked around the side of the car and got in the front passenger seat next to Deveral. As the doors closed, conversation became possible once again.

'Feel free to stop me any time and I'll drive you straight home to Lymington,' said Deveral, slightly too loudly, as if still speaking over the noise of the engines of the G4.

'Thanks, sir. Of course, I appreciate that,' answered Christian.

'We're heading for a little place near Llangorse – you know, the big lake where we do the canoeing stuff. Shouldn't take more than an hour or so. Think you'll like it. It's a pretty nice spot,' continued Deveral, still in sales mode.

As the A roads gave way to smaller and twistier Bs, Christian began to wish he had not ditched his packet of cigarettes in the sand in Morocco that morning. He had assumed that once he got home for real, he would automatically resume his ardent anti-smoking views. But this element of his parallel existence seemed to have followed him back through the rabbit hole into the real world.

'Sir, forgive me, but I picked up the odd bad habit down there. Any chance we could pick up some fags? I am going to kick it but . . .'

Deveral smiled.

'Open the glove pocket. For God's sake don't tell Mrs D, but I keep a packet in there for special occasions. Sorry they're Rothmans, but that's what Cornwallis smokes, and I need to be able to pretend they're his if she ever looks in there.' Deveral began to laugh, and pressed on the car cigarette lighter.

'The guys would love to hear that, sir,' Christian said as he rummaged in the glove pocket.

Christian found the packet and flipped open the lid.

'Only two left, sir.'

'Well, let's face it, there have been quite a few special occasions recently, largely on your account, Christian. Not to mention the light-fingered Cornwallis, who uses this car too,' said Deveral, grinning.

Christian reached for the lighter as it popped up and lit the first cigarette. He offered it to Deveral.

Deveral took the cigarette in his fingers and took a drag as Christian lit the second.

'The problem with this job is that it's a pretty bloody special occasion more or less every day. How is anyone meant to quit properly? Anyway, the thing we need to think about is what we say to your family if you decide to have a go at this,' said Deveral.

'In theory, everyone is meant to think you are well and truly dead, but I can see that might not sit all that comfortably with you. If it helps, we could always bring your parents in on things. Parents tend to be pretty reliable when it comes to their kids. It's brothers and sisters where it wouldn't work, but that's not a problem for you, being an only child,' Deveral continued.

'Yes, sir, that's critical to me. I couldn't have my folks wandering around putting flowers on my grave while I'm alive and kicking. Wouldn't really feel, you know . . .' Christian pulled hard on his cigarette.

'Leave that to me, Christi. I'll sort that. Now, we'll be there in ten minutes if I can find the place. You're about to meet a most unusual man.'

4

With low drystone walls lining the road and a mohican of mossy green down the middle, they continued in silence. Deveral slowed the car and pulled into a gateway to allow a small grey tractor to pass. The sun was still bright but low in the sky as Deveral exclaimed, 'Ah! This is it here. I normally drive straight past, but this is it.'

They passed between two weathered stone gateposts and drummed over a cattle grid. The drive looked like it had once been tarmac but now consisted of two lines of potholes falling away across a field dotted with grazing sheep. Christian saw a white farmhouse with woods to one side and a lake on the other. The Brecon Beacons provided a backdrop.

'Told you you'd like it,' said Deveral, leaning forward over the steering wheel as he tried to avoid the worst of the potholes.

'Yes, sir, this is what Wales is all about,' replied Christian, smiling.

'Now, it's less of the sir, please, Christi. From now on, it's Nigel. However odd that may feel. Not Nige, though, if you can manage that?'

Christian nodded, still looking around and taking in the place.

Deveral parked the car next to a battered green Land Rover with thick red mud splattered down the sides. There was a small porch with numerous pairs of walking boots piled in an old wine box. The front door was ajar and they could hear a U2 track playing inside. As Deveral raised his hand to push open the door, it was pulled wide open.

'Hey, hey, hey, the Devil's here!' boomed a voice with a tinge of a Welsh accent.

Standing immediately behind Deveral, Christian could not see the source of the voice but guessed whoever it was had to know Deveral pretty well. Arms in a woolly blue jumper with hairy hands appeared around Deveral's back and squeezed him.

'Rags! Good to be here. Looking good. Always love this place!' Deveral exclaimed, just as loudly.

The arms patted Deveral on the back a couple of times and pulled him inside. Finally he was released.

'So you must be Christian McKie,' said the owner of the arms, now pushing a hand in Christian's direction.

'Yes, that's right,' Christian replied, nodding awkwardly and smiling.

'Well, I'm Danny Raglan and it's a very great pleasure to meet you. The Devil here has told me quite a few things about you, but maybe it's what he hasn't said that I find most intriguing,' said Raglan, grinning.

Christian looked at Raglan's ancient blue jumper and faded DPM shorts. He wore no shoes. He was medium height with curly black hair dropping down into bushy sideburns. Christian felt his piercing blue eyes assess him and suddenly felt self-conscious of his too-tight cotton trousers and too big, rather bright blue shirt. Bad enough in Morocco but even worse in the Welsh hills. Like some kind of tourist.

Deveral detected his discomfort and came to the rescue.

'Christi, the first thing we need to do is get you some kit. Come on, Rags, you must have something that isn't either worn out or covered in sheep shit you could lend the lad?'

'That will narrow things down somewhat, but I may be able to find something less . . .'

'Less blue,' suggested Christian, starting to smile.

'Less blue indeed,' Raglan agreed. 'You guys go in the kitchen and sort out a brew and I'll be down in a moment.'

Raglan turned and set off up the stairs two at a time. Deveral turned to Christian and raised his eyebrows.

Christian then took his first opportunity to look about. They were standing in a generously proportioned hallway with a flagstone floor. There was an oak table against the wall, scarcely visible under a heap of outdoor coats. Above hung a framed large-scale Ordnance Survey map of the area.

Deveral jerked his head in the direction of the door to the rear. They stepped through into a large farmhouse kitchen with evening sun pouring through French windows in the back wall. Deveral lifted the lid of the Aga and slid a metal kettle onto the heat. Christian's eyes were drawn to the Parker Hale M85 sniper rifle resting on its bipod on the kitchen units by an open window. As he picked it up and squinted down the sights, he heard a voice.

'I haven't had a fox problem here for years, but all of sudden I'm inundated. Losing chickens even in daylight. Soon, they'll be at my lambs and then sleeping in my bed,' said Raglan, chucking a pair of jeans and a red chequered shirt on the table.

'But, from in here, I get a good wide arc and I've had a couple of headshots at nine hundred metres, which is always reassuring. Tempting to use something a little bigger, but mustn't upset the neighbours,' Raglan continued, sitting down on a kitchen chair.

'Neighbours, Raglan?' interjected Deveral. 'Surely you must have scared any of them off years ago!'

'You just hurry up and make the tea,' replied Raglan, lifting his feet onto a chair.

Christian looked at Deveral, keen to see how the Commanding Officer of 22 SAS would take the comment.

'To be honest, Rags, I call this drinks time not brew time. How about something sensible like a beer or a dram?' Deveral slid the kettle off the heat and moved towards the fridge.

'Beer's in the outside fridge through there.' Raglan pointed at the back door.

Deveral returned and put a four-pack in the middle of the kitchen table. He sat down opposite Christian and opened a can.

'Rags, how about you tell Christian what this is all about? Be honest, let's hear the bad bits too. We've got all evening and all night if necessary, so start at the beginning so Christi knows the whole story.'

'Well, OK then. I'll start at the beginning, I guess.' Raglan took a slurp of his beer. 'I'm a Welsh lad, born down the road in Abergavenny. I left school in the late Seventies, and as you can imagine, South Wales with no qualifications wasn't exactly opportunity city in those days. So, like quite a few of the local lads, the Army was just about the only option other than to start nicking. Mind you, there wasn't even much to nick round the valleys in nineteen seventy-eight. I signed up as a trooper in the Monmouthshire Regiment and found myself freezing my arse off on Selection. Scraped through by the seat of my pants in nineteen eighty.'

'No one exactly passes with flying colours, Rags. A pass is a pass,' Deveral chipped in kindly.

'I guess so,' Raglan agreed, shrugging. 'Anyway, the next thing I know, I'm badged and through Continuation. Then the Falklands kicks off and Maggie has declared war on Argentina. I'm on a sub about to be inserted into South America. You may have heard about that nutty plan to take out the Argentinian air force on the ground? I was in the OP watching the airbase when the guys in the lying-up point get compromised. As you can imagine, the shit hits the fan big time.'

'Shit. I can imagine,' said Christian, nodding.

'Well, from what Dev tells me, I reckon you can.' Raglan laughed.

'By the time I get my arse from the forward OP back up and over the ridge, the guys are well exposed. Fuckloads of enemy troops surging up the valley. The guys didn't stand a chance. They loosed off what they could but had nowhere to go. That was all fair enough and part of what we sign up for, but they got hold of Mark Pierce and drilled him in the head at point blank.'

Raglan paused.

'I had a go at the fucker that did it. Long shot. Missed the bastard. Still replay the shot in my mind. Put it down to windage and my breathing.'

Deveral nodded and looked at Christian. Raglan carried on.

'Anyway, so there I am. Three mates down and half the Argentinian Army pissed off and on my case.'

Christian saw through Raglan's easy-going manner. His face showed pain. His fingers tapped the side of the beer can and his eyes narrowed.

'Anyway, to cut a long story short, I made it out through Chile but it took me a year. By the time I made it home I was dead and buried, a bit like you, Christian. The Argies said they had killed all four "spies" and did a pretty good job proving it. They weren't going to tell the world that one got away.'

'The fact is,' Deveral said, 'we're talking about one of the most, if not *the* most, historic walk-outs in the history of the British Army. Other than Chapman after the fall of Singapore, I don't think anyone gets near this. Of course, nobody knows about it but that's not the point.'

'Come on, Dev,' replied Raglan. 'You can't compare these things. I was fit as a fiddle, tooled up and had all my kit. Other guys have set off at death's door in their underpants. All I did was drill a sheep every couple of days and keep walking west. Also, the general population weren't exactly on the lookout because the authorities said all the *spies* were dead.'

'Whatever, Rags, I know you don't give a shit, but one day I will tell the people who ought to know. You deserve it.'

'Kind words and I'm grateful. But there's plenty

more to do before tea and medals,' laughed Raglan, tipping back in his chair.

'So, Christi, I get back and I hear about a little group of so-called dead folk who go around doing bits and pieces for Queen and Country that's a little bit outside the usual rules of engagement, shall we say.' Raglan grinned. 'As far as everyone is concerned, I am just a simple Welsh sheep farmer, and, to be fair, that's really where my heart lies, here in this valley tending my flock. So in many respects I'm not kidding anyone. I'm a farmer first and foremost, but I supplement my income, as many farmers need to, with a bit of work on the side.'

Deveral burst out laughing.

'Heavens above, Danny. You really do have a way with words. You've shot more people than you have foxes.'

Raglan also burst out laughing, followed by Christian. 'Come on, guys, you stay where you are. I'll get the beer.'

Raglan flicked his legs off the chair and disappeared out the back door. Deveral glanced over his shoulder and whispered to Christian.

'Don't be fooled. He likes to play things down. He loves the Farmer Giles thing. Makes him feel better, I think.'

Christian nodded his understanding as the door opened and Raglan reappeared with a four-pack in each hand.

'Come on, Christian, that's enough about me. How come you wound up dead?' he said, sitting back down.

'Well,' said Christian, 'in my case, ending up dead was a pretty simple story. I take it you know what happened on Barras in Sierra Leone?'

Raglan nodded and Christian continued.

'When I look back, I could tell something funny was going on in the OP when we were watching the hostages in the jungle village. It was Sam Carter, and my two mates Jamie Baxter and Tim Symonds. The guys were up to something. Couldn't see it at the time, though. You know – knackered, stressed, couldn't fart we were so close to about two hundred and fifty drug-fuelled thugs. Anyway, once the rest of the Squadron cabbed in for the main assault on the village . . .'

Christian looked at Deveral.

Deveral spoke.

'Listen, Christi, we've come beyond any secrets. We're at the next stage now. The others are dead and I've joined the dots with just a few blanks along the way.'

'I know, sir. Sorry, Nigel. I get that,' Christian said. 'So the assault takes place at the crack of dawn on day four, I think. The West Side Boys are taken by surprise and scarper, but then regroup and bounce back out of the jungle harder than we think. No real problem, but suddenly we've got a hole in the perimeter. Sam Carter, Baxter and Symonds are all beating the shit out of the head West Side Boy in the hostage house, trying to find his stash of diamonds.'

Christian paused, took a swig of beer and continued.

'One of our lads gets overrun while reloading and the perimeter starts to fall in. I get pushed back into the hostage house and break up the party. It's not the looting of a few diamonds that's bothering me – it's the fact that Andy's dead because they weren't there supporting him. Macheted by a bunch of psychos. Fucking Carter realises the implications of what they've done and rips off my mouthpiece. Next second, he shoots me.'

'What?' interjected Raglan, sounding more Welsh all of a sudden.

'Just as he's about to finish me off, an RPG caves in the wall and covers me in rubble. He legs it and I have to listen to him telling everyone I'm dead.'

Deveral shook his head slowly.

'So he just snapped off your mouth stick but your ear-piece was still working?'

'Yes, exactly,' Christian said. 'I could hear everything. I heard him telling Major Day I was dead. I heard the order to pull out of the village. Bloody everything.'

Raglan's fist hit the kitchen table and he sprang to his feet.

'That's the worst thing I have ever heard in my whole life!' he roared. 'That's un-fucking-believable. I can't believe it!'

'I'm afraid it's true,' interjected Deveral in a resigned tone.

'So what the fuck happened next? No bloody wonder you're dead!' he boomed, pacing up and down the kitchen.

'Well, the next thing I know, the West Side Boys are pulling the debris off me. Just at the point where I think I'm dead for the second time, some guy comes in who's in control. He gets me out and puts me in his cellar under this old French-style house. I managed to break out but screwed up when I turned his .50 cal on the place trying to cause a diversion.'

'That's starting to sound a bit more like it,' said Raglan, sitting back down at the table.

Deveral offered Christian a reassuring nod.

'But I didn't get far. They soon got me again. The reason I had to make a break was because they barbe-cued some poor sod in the next-door cell to me and put his burnt head down there for me to look at.' Christian gave a nervous grimace.

'Fairly motivating stuff, I would have thought,' muttered Deveral.

'I thought they might turn on me any second. But in fact they had other plans. The head guy passed me on to another group based in a desert village in Mauritania. It was a kind of terrorist training camp. It didn't seem too bad at first, but it was a bluff. Their plan was to torture me and film it. You know, break an SAS man and get me to blow the whole myth wide open. Of course, they weren't going to show on video what they were going to do to me, just show me crumbling,' said Christian, looking at the table in front of him.

'This is where the rack thing came in, isn't it?' asked Deveral.

'Yes, that's right. They rigged up this medieval-style rack and demonstrated what they were going to do to me on a live pig. You know, apparently their anatomy isn't that different from people.'

'You mean, a bit like when we shoot a pig to show people how men behave with bullet wounds?' said Raglan, sounding confused.

'Same idea, I suppose,' said Christian, nodding. 'Anyway, this is when it gets really weird. The night before, I'm in my cell and I hear a noise. It's Tim tapping on the bars with a commando knife. Get the surprise of my life. It turns out he's come looking for me with Jamie Symonds.'

'What, the same guys that stitched you up back in the jungle?' asked Raglan, still sounding confused.

'Yes, the same guys. Don't forget these are good guys. My mates. They got hustled into the diamond ploy by Sam Carter. Nigel here had an inkling as to what was going on and gave them a few clues as to where the intel. people thought a hostage was being held. They took the bait and came to find me.'

'OK,' said Raglan. 'I follow, so proper guys after all.'

'Yes, totally. Their plan was to find me and somehow report back, but the next morning my captors were going to tear me apart on the rack. So suddenly a recce became a full-blown hostage rescue. Problem was, there were only two of them with an old .375 buffalo rifle, a couple of machine pistols and a few antique grenades.'

'Starting to like these guys,' grunted Raglan, looking at Deveral.

'This is when they called me,' said Deveral gravely. 'We mobilised D Squadron into the G4 and headed on down there, but only in time for last orders.'

'So what on earth happened?' said Raglan.

'Well, basically, Jamie and Tim took on the whole village. I guess there were over a hundred guys. Some amateur idiots, but a few trained operators. Properly armed, too, with some fairly Gucci kit.'

'And?' said Raglan.

'They were ripping the pig apart on this raised platform with a crowd all going wild. Tim came in close to get me and Jamie sniped from a ridge. All hell broke loose and I managed to get away in a pickup. Tim went down in a hail of gunfire and they got Jamie too,' said Christian quietly.

'The dirty motherfuckers!' hissed Raglan. 'And all thanks to Sam Carter wanting to pay off his mortgage a bit faster than the rest of us.'

'Anyway, I made it back to Sierra Leone, where I managed to find the West Side Boys' diamonds. Then

I got back to London without anyone knowing and framed Carter for an attempted terrorist attack on the Egyptian Embassy in London. I rigged it so only the detonator would go off, but he ended up being extradited to Egypt as, technically speaking, an embassy is sovereign territory.'

Raglan sat in his chair and looked at Christian, then at Deveral.

'He then got back to Africa,' chipped in Deveral, 'still undetected, and turned up at a High Commission saying he'd only just escaped from captivity. Meanwhile, Carter's starting a good stretch in some filthy foreign nick. Of course, my problem was then trying to explain why D Squadron shot the shit out of some backwater in Mauritania. Ongoing, shall we say.'

'Christian McKie,' said Raglan slowly. 'When the Devil said he was bringing someone special, I believed him, like of course I would. But I had no idea I was about to meet a man who lived to tell a story like that. It would be an honour if you would consider joining what a few of us call the Regiment of the Dead.'

5

Sam Carter opened his eyes and blinked. Receiving a lethal injection in a dingy underground execution chamber somewhere in the suburbs of Cairo in front of a group of uninterested local businessmen had been bad. In fact, very bad indeed, particularly as it had been arranged by Christian McKie. He had resigned himself to death and, worse still, complete and utter defeat. With no religious belief at all, Sam's expectation was that the lights would go out and then that would be it. All over. Being dead would at least offer some form of release.

He blinked again. He saw light and could make out dark shapes. This was not meant to happen. He had been executed. Fear engulfed him once more. He was conscious and the implications were terrifying.

He tried to move. His legs worked but his hands were stuck behind his back. His next sensation was vomit surging up from his stomach. He could taste it and feel it in his mouth and nose. He moved his legs around in front of him and manoeuvred himself into a sitting position with his back against a wall. He shut one eye and tried to focus. There were chairs and a man sitting at a desk.

As each minute passed, Sam became more aware. He spat lumps of vomit from his mouth and took a deep breath. He cleared his throat and dislodged more vomit and acrid-tasting saliva.

Sam was not sure how long he sat on the floor looking around, but the vomit stuck down the front of his white paper suit had congealed into a thick crust. He no longer felt sick but had developed an acute headache. His vision was nearly clear and he looked around. He was in a small, windowless office. There were two office-style chairs and a wooden desk. The man behind the desk was thin and balding in a light grey suit. He wore thick black-rimmed glasses and had papers spread before him.

'Mr Carter,' he said, cocking his head to one side in a pseudo kindly manner. 'Please take a seat here.'

He gestured to the chairs in front of the desk. With his hands secured behind his back, Sam struggled to stand. He took a couple of steps forwards and sat down heavily in one of the chairs.

The man glanced at his watch and spoke quietly.

'Your funeral is scheduled for two-thirty p.m. That's

in about twenty minutes from now and there is still plenty of time for you to make it.'

Sam assessed the man more carefully. He looked like a down-market Egyptian accountant of retirement age. But then Sam spotted his eyes. Hard, pale grey and confident. They were the eyes of a tough, experienced bastard who held all the cards.

'You may be wondering what's going on?' he said.

As Sam nodded his head, he continued.

'There is only one reason you are not swelling up in a cardboard box, about to be dropped in a hole in the ground. That reason is very simple. We have a use for you. You were injected with hospital grade anaesthetic as opposed to a paralytic barbiturate. Everyone in that room, with the exception of the doctor, believes your heart stopped on that table. To all intents and purposes you are dead. You have a death certificate, a time of death, and soon you will have a grave too. The world believes you are dead.'

Sam looked down at his vomit-stained paper suit and thought back to the last few minutes of his life. He had been crushed in an unspeakable way. He had been put through the ultimate mock execution. This was not some guy pointing an empty gun at the back of his head and pulling the trigger. This was on a whole new plane. He had been put through the worst. He envisaged Christian's face through his pumping headache. Surely, Christian had not orchestrated this final twist?

Sam cleared his throat and spoke, inadvertently imitating the man's quiet and confident manner.

'Yes, sir, thank you. So what happens now?'

'You have a choice to make. We know who you are and what skills you have. Eleven years in the British SAS gives you some value. You are also a convicted terrorist and have been condemned to capital punishment under Egyptian law. We have extradition in place with every civilised country in the world. That means we own you. Sure, we might have to agree to commute your sentence from death to life to keep your own country happy, but believe me, we can always bring you back,' he said in a matter-of-fact tone.

Sam's mind focussed on certain words. 'Commute your sentence' and 'bring you back' stood out. A glimmer of hope ignited in his mind. He assumed an earnest expression.

The man looked down at the papers in front of him and continued.

'So, Mr Carter, I'm offering you a way out. There are certain operations that are unsuitable for an Egyptian national and too complex for hired foreign thugs. You will probably be aware that my country has troops based in Somalia assisting Government forces to keep basic peace.'

Sam nodded.

'Yes, sir, I am aware there are Egyptian troops serving in Somalia, working alongside the Americans, I believe.'

'Working alongside the CIA, that's correct. No US troops there since the Mogadishu Black Hawk episode. The fact is that certain influential factions in our government oppose the deployment of our troops there. My task is to demonstrate the necessity to continue our military presence in the region for reasons that don't concern you.'

Sam continued to nod and adopted a concerned expression which he hoped suggested he understood and sympathised.

'Yes, sir, I understand,' he said.

'So,' the man continued, 'we need as much conflict in the region as possible. We need a war down there, a reason to deploy more troops and more military infrastructure. We need to dominate the country and control the Government. We need them fully dependent on us. That is all you need to know at this point. Now, you decide.'

Sam stopped nodding and paused for the slightest moment as if to weigh things up. If his arms had not been handcuffed behind his back, he would have hugged the diminutive bastard of a spook that sat before him.

'Sir, I am happy to accept your proposal,' he said stiffly.

'Very good, Mr Carter. That does not come as a surprise. Before you are released, a colleague of mine will brief you fully.'

Sam nodded in agreement as the man gathered his papers and left the room.

6

'So, do you want to eat in, or do you fancy popping out to my local?' Raglan slid a couple of cans across the kitchen table towards Deveral and Christian.

'That's a tricky one,' said Deveral, snapping his hand shut around his can. 'What are our options on eating in?'

'Well, the options are mainly reheated shepherd's pie. Tend to make big ones and then they last all week.'

'Let's give that a go,' said Christian. 'We aren't exactly going to be able to discuss much down Danny's local, are we?'

'McKie has spoken,' replied Raglan, standing up. 'I'll do the scoff, but you two need to watch for the fox, now that it's nearly dark. That scope's got an infrared setting, too. Just flick over.'

'You sort the food. We'll sort the fox,' answered Deveral, winking at Christian.

Twenty minutes later, Raglan pulled a large dish out of the Aga and served dinner. As they sat around the table eating, Deveral prompted Raglan into telling stories from his eighteen years in the shadows. Each one, however audacious, ended with the retort that it was nothing close to Christian's venture and that none of his adversaries, however violent and grotesque, came close to Sam.

'I don't care how bad these guys can be,' said Raglan, wagging his finger, 'but what gets me is the treachery. That's what I can't get to grips with. Fine, *be* a bad guy, *be* my guest, that's OK. But don't be one of us and be one of them at the same time. That's when I get pissed off.'

'Quite right,' replied Deveral, 'no one likes a bent copper. Now, Rags, would you like to let Christian know what the latest brief is and how he might be able to help you?'

Christian sat up straighter in his chair as he saw Raglan visibly switch from relaxed raconteur to focussed professional soldier.

'Christian,' Raglan began, 'I suppose looking at me sitting here all wild and woolly on my sheep farm, it must be hard to imagine me as a servant of HM.'

'No harder than for you thinking of me dishing out wads of fifties to a high-class hooker in a five-star hotel for Queen and Country,' replied Christian.

'Well, I guess so. They don't teach that at Sandhurst,' answered Raglan, smiling. 'Perhaps that's the basis of it then. But, like everyone else, I follow orders of a kind, although the brief tends to be very vague. This time it's probably the vaguest operation I have ever been assigned. As you know, there are certain parts of the world that lie outside the jurisdiction of any government, however basic and corrupt.'

Christian nodded. 'Like certain parts of Pakistan, Afghanistan, Mauritania,' he said.

'Yes, those sorts of places. So they attract a certain type of organisation. Sometimes it's just hardcore organised crime, like in parts of South America and certain parts of Afghanistan, but very often it's terrorists needing somewhere to hide out and train. Still watching for the fox?'

'Fuck the fox for the moment,' said Deveral.

'Sure,' replied Raglan, glancing over his shoulder towards the window. 'OK, so in the Eighties, it was Libya; in the early Nineties, Mozambique; and now the real hotbed is Somalia. There's absolutely no rule of law there once you step outside the central part of Mogadishu. The Yanks pulled their troops out and handed over, kind of, to a bunch of NCOs and African troops mainly supplied by the Egyptians.'

'Starting to sound familiar, Christian?' chipped in Deveral.

'Basically Stone Age, but with AKs and RPGs instead of spears and clubs,' Christian agreed.

'That pretty much sums it up,' said Raglan. 'But the problem is that it affects us back here. It would be fine if you could keep it all down there, but MI6 reckon the majority of terrorist activity aimed against the UK is orchestrated from abroad. A lot originates from Pakistan, but more and more is coming out of Somalia.'

'The whole bloody lot, according to some departments,' said Deveral.

'Our brief, Christian, if you're interested, is to get down there, infiltrate and neuter,' said Raglan.

'I reckon getting down there is probably the easy bit; infiltrating and neutering might be a bit more challenging,' said Christian.

'I think we have the infiltrating bit more or less under control. Or at least, we have a plan. It's definitely the neutering bit that might be the most demanding phase.' Raglan started to smile. 'But I do have some ideas, in basic outline.'

'Well,' said Christian, 'I'm OK for a bit of this but don't really want to be dead for too long. I can handle it for a while, but I . . .'

'Being dead really isn't as bad as it sounds,' interrupted Raglan. 'I have been dead since the early Eighties and have got quite used to it. No tax is absolutely marvellous, you know. I'd never have a farm half the size of this if I were properly alive. Honestly, lad, it's not all bad.'

Deveral burst out laughing.

'It sounds so good, I'm going to top myself right here and now, join you guys,' he said, reaching for the M85. 'Actually, on a more serious note, I will end up dead if I don't head off home. It's half ten and I really need to make tracks. Christian, you and Danny work it out. You'll have my full support whatever you decide to do. Maybe try it for a bit. Stay here for a day or two and see how you feel.'

'That's right, suck it and see,' said Raglan. 'Stay here and we'll go through the operation in proper detail. The only thing is, there's an external influence that might mean we have to move very soon.'

'I've decided,' said Christian. 'I'm in. I'll give it a try; see how it goes. I'll help on the Somali thing and then we can work it from there.'

'Good man,' said Deveral, moving towards the door. 'I'll call you tomorrow.'

7

Raglan knocked on Christian's door at 06.30 the next morning.

'It's a nice looking day and I was wondering if you fancy a workout before breakfast. Just a quick forty minuter, nothing too frantic.'

Christian rolled over in bed. His sixth sense had warned him that Raglan was likely to be an early bird.

'Do you have a word for lie-in in Welsh?' he shouted.

'Not that I am aware of myself,' answered Raglan through the door. 'I'll ask around, but most of my neighbours are farmers so they won't know either. By the way, don't have a shave. I'll explain later.'

'I'm coming,' said Christian, opening the door. 'Need some kit, that's all.'

'All sorted.' Raglan pushed a bundle of clothes at Christian.

Two minutes later Christian found himself on an

area of mossy paving stones overlooking the shimmering expanse of Llangorse Lake. Despite the first rays of sun breaking over the hills, a fine drizzle hung in the air.

'Beautiful or what?' said Raglan, smiling. 'OK, so we work out here for a bit, decent breakfast, whip round and check the sheep, then I'd like to run through some weapons and kit with you.'

'Sure.' Christian nodded.

'Later on,' continued Raglan, 'we've got my clever chappie coming up from Cheltenham to meet with us. You see, another good reason to be dead. Everyone has to come and see you. Can't be seen too much out and about.'

'What? A GCHQ spook?' Christian asked.

'Yes. Good lad, this one. Even does what he's told.' Raglan dropped into a press-up position.

The drizzle gathered momentum and became gentle rain. Raglan turned to Christian with a grin.

'Like I always say, if it ain't raining, it ain't training,' he puffed.

By the time they had finished breakfast and walked round the farm, it was late morning. They wandered back into the farmhouse and stood in the hall by the stairs. Raglan kicked off his muddy boots, bent down and slipped his finger through a D-shaped metal eyelet in the wooden floor. He lifted up a trapdoor and flicked on a light. An extractor fan whirred.

'Now this is what Dev likes to call my Bat Cave. Personally, I call it the bunker. Whichever, your mate Armalite would feel pretty much at home down here.' Raglan started down some stone steps.

Christian followed close behind Raglan as he descended.

'It's pretty much half the size of the ground floor of the house,' said Raglan proudly. 'Got everything I need down here and more.'

'Heavens above!' replied Christian, staring around. 'You really do.'

The room was well lit with strip lights. The walls were painted white but largely covered by a mixture of maps, framed photographs, metal lockers and racking hung with all kind of military equipment. The floor was rush matting. The tang of mothballs hung in the air.

'This end is where I do my research and planning,' said Raglan, pointing at a desk pushed up against the wall with a computer on it. 'The middle bit there by the table is my secure comms department. That's posh speak for sat phones, really.'

Waving his arm, he continued, 'Then the good bit is the armoury back there in the caged off section. Obviously, I've got all kinds of clothing, bergens, climbing stuff, webbing and all that crap in the lockers. Not bad, eh?'

'Not bad at all,' replied Christian, still looking around. 'Kind of reminds me of those underground IRA ops rooms in Northern Ireland.'

'I know what you mean. I always think weapons and kit stored underground has a subversive feel, but it's safe down here and out of the way. Let's sit down and start going through this Somali thing before old clever clogs gets here.'

Raglan sat at the table with Christian opposite. He unfolded a map of Somalia and oriented it towards Christian. Handwritten notes and circles were scribbled along the coastal section.

'It's just one big sandy dump really,' said Raglan. 'Most of the focus these days is on International Aid.'

'Or ripping off International Aid,' exclaimed Christian.

'Exactly, it's about the only industry they have except piracy. To be fair, there was some agriculture, but it's more subsistence farming.'

'If we were a bunch of starving Somalis, we'd be knocking off super tankers, wouldn't we?' Christian asked.

'Yep, we sure would. But that's not our problem for the time being. We need to knock out the leadership of a group called al-Shabaab. Or to be more precise, get them under control, as we can't exactly knock them out, just the two of us.'

'So what's the plan and what's the end result we need?'

'The main issue is that no one has any boots on the ground outside Mog. It means al-Shabaab have total and utter freedom to roam the whole country. That's from Kenya to the south right up to the Ethiopian border in the north. They have a thousand miles of coastline, endless mountain ranges, deserts. And of course, anyone that doesn't help them, comes to a sticky end.'

'I can imagine they do,' Christian said. 'Basically, it's lawless, and the guys with the biggest guns rule.'

'That's about it. And our job is to get there, bullshit the lot of them and get hold of the top man.' Raglan pushed back in his chair.

'Piece of piss then,' said Christian, starting to laugh.

'Well, it won't be easy and may take a while, but I think I have an idea,' Raglan said.

'I'm all ears,' replied Christian, trying to suppress any trace of exasperation in his voice. 'What I want to know is, how we find the boss without getting rumbled. It's not as if we can just grow our hair long, start smoking Lambert & Butler and put on an Irish accent like in Belfast. You can't fake being black. So we can't operate undercover.'

'I quite agree.' Raglan smiled. 'It's more subtle than that. Of course, we can't just turn up with a suntan and hope to fit in. Let me explain. My guys in MI5 have been working on this for a while with a department at GCHQ. We've been tracking a group of militant Islamists based in Leicester.'

'Leicester? Christian echoed.

'Yes, Leicester,' continued Raglan. 'It's a conduit for young men who have been radicalised to be trained in the dark arts of terrorism in places like Somalia. These are pretty harmless guys who think they're answering the call of Jihad and doing the right thing, but when they come back, they pose a threat – a very serious one. But my point is that these guys are British, sound British and behave British.'

'OK, I'm starting to see where you're coming from,' said Christian.

Raglan's mobile rang. He picked it up, looked at the screen, smiled and answered.

'Ah, David, hello.'

There was a pause. Raglan raised his eyebrows.

'It's on the right – you'll see the stone gateposts and the drive. If you end up in either the farmyard or the lake, you've gone too far.'

He pressed a button and put the phone back on the table.

'IQ of about two hundred and still can't read a map,' he muttered. 'He'll be here in a moment and I'll let him explain how we can insert. This guy knows a certain amount of what we do, but let me do the talking, if that's OK.'

Christian nodded and followed Raglan up the stairs to the hall. They stood by the window and watched a blue estate car approach down the drive. It parked by the Land Rover and the door opened. A balding man in his fifties got out wearing a Welsh national rugby shirt and jeans. He looked around and then walked quickly to the front door, a sports bag in his hand.

Raglan grinned. 'That'll be his idea of not drawing attention to himself in the Welsh countryside,' he said, pulling at the front of his shirt.

'Reassuring then,' Christian said.

There was a gentle knock and Raglan swung open the door.

'David! How're you doing? Thanks for coming all the way up here. Really appreciated!'

'It's a pleasure, sir. Always nice to leave the doughnut once in a while,' replied the man in the doorway.

Raglan smiled, knowing that Christian would have been surprised to hear him addressed as Sir.

'This is David Antcliff,' he said. 'We go back, us two. Done a fair few things together over the years.'

'Hi, I'm Chris,' said Christian, shaking hands with Antcliff.

Raglan and Antcliff talked for a minute or two before the three men walked through to the kitchen. Sitting at the table, Raglan wasted no time.

'David, I've given Christian a brief heads up on the radical lot in Leicester. What I need you to do is explain what you've been doing and how it all works. It's beyond me, really.'

Antcliff took on a more assertive note.

'Sure. We've been on these guys in Leicester for months now. Internally, it's been easy because we've got plenty of good reasons to deploy resources on them other than for your requirements. The fact is we've been tracking their communications in microscopic detail. We know who they are, where they are, what they do, who they speak to, who they email. We intercept absolutely everything. They fart, we know. I know them better than I know myself.'

Christian nodded, feeling reassured by Antcliff's confidence.

'We know that any day now two men will be leaving and heading down to join a Somali based training group. It's the classic formula. Head down, get trained, come back and wait for instructions. You know, "sleeper cell" style.'

'Sounds interesting so far,' replied Christian.

'Well, let me continue,' said Antcliff. 'These two guys will fly from Heathrow on tourist visas to Addis Ababa in Ethiopia. Then they'll quietly drop off the radar and make their way overland to Somalia. They'll be heading for a place in the mountains in the North. Now, what we can do is help you switch with them.'

'OK,' said Christian. 'How does that work exactly?'

'These guys are pretty savvy and they operate ultra carefully,' replied Antcliff. 'The way they talk to the people in Somalia is by email. But the clever thing is that they never actually send one.'

'Told you he was good, didn't I?' said Raglan enthusiastically, looking at Christian.

'What they do is simple but very effective,' continued Antcliff. 'They set up an email account on something like Hotmail or Yahoo, then create a file as an attachment to an email. They then log off, leaving the file attached to a draft email in the Drafts folder. With me so far?'

'Yeah, yeah,' said Christian.

'The guys the other end in Somalia,' Antcliff continued, 'or wherever in the world, simply log onto the Hotmail account and look in the Draft email file. They open the attachment and there's the information. The file never leaves the server and therefore cannot be intercepted. It's very, very effective. Usually the file is deleted and the account closed within thirty seconds.'

'Sure, that does sound crafty,' said Christian. 'So they set up another account, leave something in the Drafts file and move on.'

'That's the process. It's virtually impossible to crack unless you have another form of surveillance running in tandem, and, of course, we do with these guys. We watch the internet café they use and pick up the email details. Which brings me on to the next stage. Once they land safely in Addis, someone will add an attachment to an email with a photo of the two guys. The people the Somali end will then know exactly who to expect. We simply hack in and switch the file to photos of you. So when you turn up, it's you they are expecting.'

'I follow,' said Christian. 'It actually sounds quite simple too.'

'That's what I like about it,' said Raglan. 'All we need to do is get down there, intercept the two radicals in the desert before they make contact with the al-Shabaab people. We then turn up as the legitimate pair who match the photos. It means we're instantly accepted and pushing our way towards the inner circle.'

'We then infiltrate and win trust. We find out who's who and how they operate. We bide our time and strike,' said Christian. 'It's starting to make sense now.'

8

By early evening, Sam found himself gazing out of the window of a hotel room somewhere in central Cairo. A sprawling sea of flat roofs lay before him covered in a jumble of air conditioning units and satellite dishes. Car horns beeped and sirens wailed almost incessantly, but they didn't bother him.

He was thinking back to the holding cell. He saw the tiny slit window and remembered looking at the night sky outside. He had been so, so low. Unbearably low. But he had confronted death. Stared it in the face. He had handled it. He had not broken down or begged for mercy. Most people would have caved in and pissed themselves or freaked out somehow. He had coped with it, and that showed balls.

He flipped open the mini bar and pulled out a cold bottle of beer. He flicked on the TV and lay on the bed. It was hardly surprising the Egyptian Secret

Service needed him. They knew who he was and would have been told how he had dealt with being executed. They knew he was special.

Now he had to play the game. The moment he ceased to be useful, they would kill him. That was a no brainer. He would have to toe the line, keep useful and then give them the slip. It might take time but the moment would come. He reached for the bedside table and slid open the drawer. He squeezed the envelope containing a wad of US dollars. Then he pulled out his passport and examined it. It felt strangely new in comparison to his battered British one. Part of him liked the idea of being a Turkish national. He had been to Turkey once on holiday and had quite enjoyed it. His biometric details were correct, but he looked grim in the photo that had been adapted from his mugshot taken on arrival at Mahmood Prison.

He took a swig of beer but part of his mind remained on high alert. Even making allowances for the impact of the anaesthetic, he still thought what he had been told rang true. He was right to be suspicious, but it did make sense. He was well placed to stir up trouble in Somalia. Once the older spook with glasses had left the room, two younger men had spent an hour or so with him. They had immediately uncuffed his hands and helped him out of his filthy paper suit. They had been friendly and helpful, creating a feeling that they were on his side. Now he had money, a passport and a remit. All he had to do was take a flight to Mogadishu, where he would be attached to an Egyptian private security company responsible for operating security at the international airport and other high security installations. He would look out for areas of weakness and exploit them. It was basic stuff and he could see that it might lead to some potentially interesting opportunities.

Sam finished the beer and opened another. It was cold and refreshing and made him feel better. After an hour of channel hopping, he closed his eyes and fell asleep.

An alarm call woke him at 06.45 the following morning. He answered the phone and heard a polite male voice telling him his taxi would collect him at 07.15. He thanked the receptionist and replaced the phone gently, wondering if it really was the front desk. He showered and dressed quickly in a dark blue T-shirt and grey tracksuit. He stuffed the dollars in one pocket and the passport in the other. He glanced around the room needlessly to check he had everything.

He took the lift to the ground floor. Two women sat behind the large curved reception desk. Clearly neither of them had made his alarm call. He pushed through the revolving door into the warmth of the early morning. There were a number of cars parked along the front of the hotel and people were milling about, but Sam instantly clocked a middle management spook hovering by a new-looking SUV. He walked along the front of the hotel towards him. As he got close the man opened the door of the car.

'Taxi to the airport for Mr Carter,' he said.

Sam looked at him and said nothing. He stepped into the car, writing off any notions of an early getaway. Twenty minutes later they pulled up at Cairo International Airport. As Sam opened the car door, the driver turned to him.

'Here are your tickets. I'll be here for a while if you need anything.'

'Thank you,' snarled Sam, taking the envelope.

9

Antcliff looked at his watch and pushed back in his chair.

'I think that's more or less everything,' he said, tapping a buff-coloured folder on the kitchen table. 'There's the profiles of the two target operatives, photos and more background detail on them. Obviously, we'll update you on anything else of relevance we pick up.'

'Eternally grateful as always,' replied Raglan, shaking Antcliff's hand.

Standing in the hall, Raglan and Christian watched Antcliff's car meander its way at little more than walking pace back down the drive.

'I thought the whole point in having a company car was so you could trash it,' muttered Raglan.

'Mind you, I guess some little prick down there in Cheltenham might wonder why he's been rally driving when he's supposed to have been off at some training meeting,' Christian answered.

'I wouldn't last thirty seconds in that world,' said Raglan. 'What we need now is the green light to go. Sounds like the guys are about to move. We'll just have to hold on.'

'It would make sense for them to book their flights at the last moment like Antcliff said. Gives us less time to get organised, doesn't it?' said Christian.

'Yes, but I don't think for one second they really think anyone's properly onto them. They're just following procedure, you know, doing what they're told,' said Raglan. 'I'll tell you what, let's get outside and have a proper walk around. I'll show you some of the best views in Wales and tell you about someone who might be able to help us. Could be the final piece of the jigsaw.'

Christian followed Raglan out of the back door. They crossed an area of mossy lawn and climbed a post and rail fence. Raglan set a fast pace, and within ten minutes they were through the fields and into rough grass heading uphill.

'Fox holes everywhere up here,' grunted Raglan despondently, pointing at a clump of fir trees.

'Fuck the foxes,' said Christian, grinning. 'I'm much more interested to know who else you've got up your sleeve.'

'OK, well, I think we're going to need someone with a bit of local knowledge. That's what we're lacking. Also, someone to diffuse you and me looking too British, someone to gel the team and help with language, customs and behaviour. That kind of thing.'

'Not exactly that easy, then,' Christian suggested.

'Not at all easy, and normally I would rather have no one than the wrong one, but there is someone who fits the bill.'

The path steepened and narrowed. Away to their left Llangorse Lake glinted in the afternoon sun. Christian tucked in behind Danny as they pushed on fast uphill.

'The person I have in mind is a native Somali. Obviously, you need to be happy about this, so let me explain,' continued Raglan. 'Since al-Shabaab kicked off about five years ago, the geeks down there at GCHQ have been keeping tabs on their comms. But there's endless dialects and languages, so it wasn't that easy. They had to find native Somali speakers that could be relied upon.'

'Again, not easy,' Christian commented.

'No, not at all. But this person has a very good reason to support us, to be well and truly on our side. Three or four years ago her father did something to upset the boss man of al-Shabaab and came to a very, very unpleasant end. She had to flee Somalia along with the rest of her family, otherwise they'd have been killed too. Usual story – they make it to Europe, God knows how, and end up in a lorry coming through the Channel Tunnel.'

'I think I can see where this is going,' interjected Christian.

'No, it's worse than you think,' said Raglan. 'She's in the back of the lorry and for some reason it all takes longer than they expect. The air runs out and she has to sit there and watch her whole family suffocate. Mother, siblings, kids, the lot. Imagine it, them all banging on the sides of the lorry and gradually giving up, one by one. She was the only survivor. She sneaks away somehow and ends up working illegally in some call centre in South London that specialises in foreign languages. That's where MI5 found her.'

'That is really, really grim. But I suppose it makes her allegiance pretty clear,' said Christian, shaking his head.

'It most certainly does,' replied Raglan. 'The point is that she hates al-Shabaab more than we can even imagine. And she's a tough little cookie too. She grew up in some place just outside Mog, for fuck's sake. Makes Belfast look like an upmarket Chelsea kindergarten.'

'OK. I get that. So, she knows the place, does the lingo and is on our side.'

'And, of course, she's just as dead as you and me,' said Raglan. 'Mind you, she doesn't say much, but I've read her MI5 evaluation. Mostly psycho guff, but, reading between the lines, it says she lacks confidence but is bloody marvellous under pressure.'

Passing the tiny hamlet of Llangasty on their right,

they crossed the main road bringing them officially into Brecon Beacons country. A path of soft red mud led them steeply uphill and onto a ridgeline. They followed a left-handed circle and by early evening found themselves looking down on the lake once again.

10

Dharia Shomate removed her headset and rested it carefully on the computer keyboard in front of her. She caught the attention of her manager sitting at the end of the block of desks.

'Comfort break,' she mouthed. The manager nodded and smiled.

Dharia turned and walked purposefully down a corridor lined with motivational images of happy teams of young people roped together on mountains, rowing in eights and white water rafting. She bit her lip as she swiped her card to access the ladies' washroom. Inside, she looked at herself in the mirror and quickly turned away. She pushed open the door of the end cubicle and lowered the lid of the loo. She sat down with her back against the cistern and tucked her knees up under her chin. Tears streamed down her face.

It was not long before there was a click as the outer door opened and someone else entered. Heels clinked on the tiled floor. She closed her eyes and concentrated on breathing. She had to hold it together, her job depended on it and her job was all she had left. Any display of psychological problems or depression could jeopardise things. She had come too far and suffered too much to mess things up now. She breathed through her mouth and clamped a tissue round her nose.

The loo next door flushed and the lock slid back. The heels clinked again, stopped and a tap was turned on. The heels sounded and the outer door clicked shut. She stood up, breathed deeply and blotted her eyes. It was 5.30 p.m. Another hour and a half of trying to pick out words and phrases in the jumbled hiss of intercepted telecommunications from the listening systems in northern Kenya and she could go home.

Dharia made her way back down the corridor. She picked up her pace the moment she came back into view of other people and sat down at her desk. With her headphones back on, she keyed her password and used her mouse to scroll across the spectrum of frequencies. From time to time she liked to pick up local Somali radio stations and would listen for a minute or two. Part of her loved hearing the talk and music of her own country; another part of her found it hard to bear. The more she blocked the memories, the less miserable she felt. But how *could* she block the memories of home, working on the Somalia desk at GCHQ?

Shortly before 19.00, Dharia spotted the first of the evening shift drifting into the office. She would hand over her notes and another day would be over. She logged off and unplugged her headset and by 19.05 was walking down the stairwell to the car park.

As she reached the ground floor, she heard steps behind her. David Antcliff produced his access card and pushed open the door for her.

'Any day now,' he said to her quietly with a smile.

Dharia smiled back and nodded. She was pleased that he set off in a different direction across the car park from her. She could not risk him detecting so much as a tremor in her voice. He had confidence in her and it had to stay that way.

She approached her car where she always parked it under the glare of the security lighting. Automatically she glanced through the rear windows to check no one was hiding behind the seats. Of course, it was paranoid. She knew she was in one of the most secure car parks in the world. She unlocked the door and slipped inside. She reached into the door pocket by her right knee. Her hand brushed the handle of a kitchen knife. It was still there.

She approached the exit and a metal bollard sank obediently into the tarmac. She nosed out and joined the flow of traffic. After a few hundred metres, she braked for a red light. The cab of a lorry eased past her and came to a stop. She glanced through the driver's window and saw from the lights of the car behind that it carried a large blue metal shipping container.

The effect was instantaneous. Her head filled with tormented screams and pleading cries. The image of a battered shipping container with faded UN markings filled her mind. It had been dumped in the middle of her village by the al-Shabaab militia. They had arrived in the night and rounded everyone up. By the early morning, they had been forced at gunpoint to kneel in rows. They watched as men and boys were pulled randomly from amongst them. The militiamen formed a circle around the unfortunate group and beat them with wooden clubs and the butts of the their AKs until those who could not take it any longer crawled willingly into the sanctuary of the shipping container. Once there was no more room inside, they closed and locked the heavy metal doors.

The container had already been strafed with bullet holes. Not for ventilation but to allow the screams to be heard as a lesson to those outside. Terrified eyes peeped from some; rotting fingers from the piles of decaying bodies already inside poked through others, and swarms of bloated black flies buzzed in and out. Worse still was the putrid black sludge that oozed from the holes nearest to the ground.

Dharia's head echoed with the sound of the militiamen laughing and shouting taunts to the people locked inside. Within two hours the sun had risen and the heat of the day had begun. The screams from within had become more desperate as the temperature soared. Louder and more chilling. Last messages were shouted from inside what was rapidly becoming an oven.

She gripped the steering wheel and accelerated away through the lights. It was impossible to forget the screams and sobs, the smell and the flies. All day they knelt there and listened in the scorching African sun. By evening the screams were over. The decaying fingers poking from the holes had been replaced with fresh ones with bleeding nails.

Dharia's hand banged against the button to turn on the radio. The car filled with music. She just had to stop thinking and get home.

11

By the time Christian and Raglan had checked the sheep and closed up the chickens, it was dark. Christian detected frustration in Raglan's face when he played the answerphone in the kitchen. Nothing from Deveral and nothing from Antcliff.

'Well, I suppose, that gives us more time to read the files and learn a bit more about these guys.' Raglan reached for the folder Antcliff had left on the table.

'Let's just use the time. We'll head up to Leicester tomorrow like you said and get a feel of the place, hang out in the Asian part of town,' said Christian.

'OK with shepherd's pie?' asked Raglan.

'Shepherd's pie and the Let's Go Somalia is fine by me,' answered Christian.

The next morning, they were up early and down in the garden doing Raglan's daily workout. Still sweating, they got in the Land Rover and bounced off down the drive. Raglan wore blue shell suit trousers and an old grey anorak. Christian looked equally rough in paint-splattered jeans and an old hoody. Neither had shaved.

The drive to Leicester took the best part of three hours. Just like the day before, they chatted some of the time along with periods of relaxed silence. They hit the ring road and picked up signs to the town centre.

Raglan fumbled in his pocket and pulled out his phone.

'Better find out exactly what they're up to before we go bumbling on in,' he said to Christian. He pushed the phone to his ear.

'Hello there. Basic sitrep on A and B is all I need, David.'

A couple of minutes later, he thanked Antcliff and ended the call. They drove towards the east side of the city and parked the Land Rover just off London Road.

'They live two streets over. It's all Asian round here.' Raglan jerked his thumb at a row of red-brick Victorian terraced houses.

'Looks pretty reasonable,' said Christian, looking around.

'That's the whole point,' answered Raglan. 'These guys are second generation in the UK. Their folks are decent, respectable community people. Haven't got a clue what their kids are up to. They'd be horrified.'

'That's the scary thing,' said Christian. 'The

question is, why on earth they want to fuck off down to Somalia for a course in mass murder.'

'It will have been dressed up as exciting. Off on a big crusade to save the world from the decadence of the West.' Raglan opened the door.

'Less exciting when we drill them fifteen seconds after they leave the airport terminal.' Christian shook his head. 'You'd think we could just have a chat and sort them out. You know, just tell them they're being a pair of pricks and send them home.'

'Must give the Landy a wash,' said Raglan, kicking off a clod of mud from one of the front mud flaps. 'It's only when you see it in town you realise just how filthy and muddy it really is.'

'OK. I suppose not,' sighed Christian, following Raglan down the road.

'We need to get a feel of the place,' said Raglan. 'We need to make a mental note of little details that could get thrown at us. Things like the colour of their front door. The colour of the neighbours' front door, where the local shop is, what it's called, boring little things like that. The sort of things some smart-arse might ask to check us out.'

'We should probably buy some clothes while we're here too,' said Christian. 'Good, convincing local stuff. We wear it in a little bit over the next few days so we don't turn up with the labels still on. Might as well try some local grub, too. See what that's like and pick up on a few names.'

Christian watched Raglan for a moment as he strode off down the street. Sure, he looked like any scruffy slob of a guy, but he walked like a soldier, at the pace of a soldier, and his chin stuck out like a soldier. His nasty grey anorak hung unevenly across his back from the weight of the SIG Sauer pistol in his right-hand pocket. No wonder Deveral called him Rags. He was undeniably an oddball, but Christian felt himself starting to like him. He knew the Regiment was full of characters and eccentrics; it was part of it, the reason why it worked and the reason why they could do things other units could not. Not many people could cross the whole of Argentina at the age of twenty with several thousand enemy troops in hot pursuit. Then Raglan had spent twenty-five years running cover operations on his own from a farmhouse in the Welsh hills. He was hardly going to be normal.

Christian set off down the street, wondering how Raglan would react if he told him to ease off on the soldier-style walk. He would have to pick his moment. It might be best to turn it into some kind of joke. Passing off as Islamic converts was going to be difficult, even of the British born and British raised variety. If they screwed up and got rumbled, the consequences would be utterly horrendous. He thought of the pig being racked by the South African bastards in Mauritania to demonstrate how they were about to torture him. He heard the pops, snaps and tears of the ligaments and tendons as they stretched it. He saw the blood pouring from its anus, ears, mouth and nose. They could expect something similar if they screwed up in Somalia. They would be treated as deceiving spies. At least in Mauritania he had still been a soldier. This time, he did not know what he was. He was working for the British Government, kind of. It certainly did not feel very Queen and Country. It was so unofficial that the unit only had a nickname. It would be him and the scruffy guy in the grey anorak versus al-Shabaab. On their turf, too.

'So it's local details, local landmarks, nearby streets and shops. We need to find the mosque that Antcliff mentioned and get a handle on that area too,' said Raglan, counting on his fingers.

'Ideally without running into A and B,' replied Christian quietly, now walking parallel with Raglan.

They wandered the streets for most of the day. By late afternoon, they were testing each other on local details. They knew the street names, the order in which they ran off the main roads and what they looked like. They had sat on a bench outside the mosque and watched people come and go. They bought several long sherwani shirts and cotton trousers. Finally they entered a café with its name written in Arabic along the front. Raglan pushed open the door and stepped inside. A small, elderly man with a grey beard and long brown shirt greeted them with a surprised but friendly smile.

Raglan gestured towards an empty table close to the door.

'Alright here?' he said with a grin.

As Christian pulled back a chair, Raglan's mobile phone rang. His hand moved fast to his pocket. He pulled it out and looked at the screen. His eyes widened as he pressed a button.

There was a pause of some seconds before he spoke. Whoever had made the call was doing the talking. Raglan pushed a finger into his ear as if the line was bad. He nodded a couple of times and looked at Christian.

'That'll be fine. We'll be back later this evening. Should give us enough time. OK. Talk soon,' he said. The call ended and he dropped the mobile back in his pocket. He sat down opposite Christian and started fanning himself with a plastic menu.

'Looks like the birds are about to fly. Bought tickets on Ethiopian about an hour ago. Fly tomorrow night, apparently,' he said quietly.

'OK. Let's talk and walk.' Christian got to his feet.

'Shame,' said Raglan, now looking at the menu. 'Shepherd's pie it is, then.'

12

Christian had got the hang of Raglan's workout routine. He liked the view of the lake and agreed with Raglan that it was a great way to start the day. They finished by 07.00 and walked back to the house through a thin autumn mist. Raglan then disappeared off in the Land Rover to see his neighbour, who would be looking after the farm while he was away. Christian stood alone in the front hall looking at the kit they had assembled on the floor the night before. They had rations for a week, two sets of civilian clothes, sleeping bags and two 9mm SIG Sauer P226 pistols with spare magazines. They had a couple of sat phones, spare batteries and hand-held GPS. There was no point bringing anything else, as once they had switched with the two young wannabe militants, anything military or too professional looking would give the game away. Compared to the normal kit for an operation in a hostile desert theatre, it did not look like much.

After a few minutes' fiddling around getting familiar with Raglan's choice of GPS, Christian wandered back into the kitchen. He had already made the decision to make the call and reached for the telephone. His pulse quickened as he dialled the number. It only took three rings for his father to answer. Christian knew his routine and knew he would be just back from walking his pair of Irish terriers along the beach at Lymington. More importantly, he knew his mother would still be in bed.

It was not a long call – it didn't need to be – but Christian had spoken to his father. Deveral had already called them as promised, but this made things better.

'Come home for real next time, Christi,' his father said. 'And no more funerals, please. I doubt the Minister of Defence will come again if he finds out you weren't really there last time.'

Christian hung up the phone, feeling like he had just slipped off a 120-pound bergen that he hadn't known he had on. Things felt clearer. He felt sharper. Of course he had to phone home. Surely the point of being part of the Regiment of the Dead was that there weren't any rules. No code of conduct or anyone to tell you what to do. His father would tell his mother. Sure, she might tell his aunt, who might blab to her husband, who had a big gob. So what. He would probably end up being killed in Somalia anyway. At least he knew he'd had a decent funeral and some bigwigs had shown up.

Christian heard the latch of the front door clunk open and Raglan's voice singing the opening verse of 'Men of Harlech'. He burst into the kitchen conducting the song with a large, smoking cigar.

'I only smoke these things on live operations,' he said, grinning at Christian. 'And I'm pleased to confirm Deveral is on his way here. We're off. He's going to take us to the airport and we'll pick up our Somali friend on the way.'

'The third musketeer,' said Christian with a hint of sarcasm.

'We should be grateful for female company,' replied Raglan, puffing on the cigar.

It was early afternoon by the time they had their kit packed into the boot of Deveral's car. Raglan's upbeat frame of mind had given way to a subdued look of melancholy as they set off down the drive. He looked longingly into the fields and up into the hills. Christian saw a farmer torn from his land, not a warrior hastening to battle. No one said much during the hour it took to reach Cheltenham.

They pulled up at a bus stop outside a grim-looking concrete tower block adorned with seemingly pointless multicoloured panels. Christian saw a diminutive figure perched on a small fold-down seat with a green backpack resting against her leg. She wore jeans and a short coat. She looked at them anxiously then stood up and approached the car. Raglan opened the front passenger door and greeted her. She was no more than five foot five, slim with shoulder-length black hair. Christian thought she looked a mixture of races – Somali with Arab blood too. She opened the back door of the car before Raglan had a chance and slid in beside Christian. Raglan winked at Christian and got back in the front seat.

Deveral put the car into gear and they moved off. Christian smiled and pushed an open hand towards her.

'Hi, I'm Christian,' he said. There was a momentary pause before she replied.

'I'm Dharia Shomate.' She shook Christian's hand firmly.

A few seconds of awkward silence followed. Christian found himself looking at her with a fixed smile on his face. He was about to say something when Deveral came to the rescue.

'Good to see you, Dharia. We are all so grateful to have you with us.'

'Absolutely. We're pleased to have you on the team,' added Raglan, pivoting around in his seat. 'I don't know how much detail Antcliff will have given you, but the plan is to fly out of Brize later on this afternoon. We'll hop out over southern Ethiopia about midnight local time. So it'll be nice and dark and give us time to settle in before first light. You'll be tandem with me, and Christi here will have the kit. All sound OK so far?'

Dharia nodded and looked sideways at Christian. She had big brown eyes. Christian wondered if they were sad eyes or whether they just looked sad because of what he knew of her. Probably a bit of both, he thought. He tried to imagine the scene inside the lorry as her family slowly suffocated one by one. He had been through some pretty serious shit recently, but at least it had not involved his family. Knowing they were OK had been a source of comfort during the dark days in the filth of the West Side Boys' cellar. The comparison was pointless. Whereas he had teetered on the edge of the abyss, Dharia had base-jumped.

'So what's your story?' she said.

Christian saw the corner of Raglan's mouth twitch into a smile.

'Well,' he said, 'I guess I'm just a pretty regular middle-class kid who decided to join the Army.'

Dharia did not reply. Obviously she expected a more detailed answer.

'I'm twenty-eight and joined up after university, which was six years ago now.' Christian continued. 'I've got a shitty little dump of a flat in London and my folks have a place near the coast in Hampshire. I went to a decent-ish school and . . .'

'It's not fucking *Blind Date*, Christi,' said Raglan, laughing. 'Tell her the real stuff. Not that you like sailing, snowboarding and spending time with your friends. She's one of us.'

'OK, OK, OK,' said Christian, talking over Raglan.

Dharia looked at them both, clearly surprised to have caused such a reaction with her question. Deveral laughed too.

'Heavens, I so wish I was coming with you guys! Al-Shabab aren't going to know what's hit them when you lot turn up. It's going to be spectacular. You'll be able to talk them into submission.'

Christian looked at Dharia and said simply, 'The reason I'm sitting here in this car with you guys is a fairly long story. Not a very nice one and maybe best left for now. How about I tell you on the plane?'

Dharia nodded and Christian detected an expression of relief pass across her face. The journey continued for another forty minutes, during which Deveral let Raglan run over the insertion plans again.

'Almost there,' said Deveral, turning into a narrow country lane.

'You're going to like this, Christi,' said Raglan, twisting around.

'Like what?' Christian looked out of the window of the car.

Deveral parked the car on a square of concrete next to a metal fence surrounding a small red-brick building with various pipes and pumps around it.

'Looks like one of those Water Board places to me, a pumping house or something.'

Raglan opened the car door and produced a small key.

'That's exactly what it is or was, and about a mile over there is Brize Norton. And about seventy miles that way is Southampton.' He pointed over the roof of the car.

They unloaded the car quickly and Raglan used the key to open a padlock securing a metal gate in the fencing. They entered the small enclosure surrounding the brick building and followed Raglan around the back. He unlocked a door and they went inside. The place was full of industrial-looking plant machinery. Raglan gestured to a manhole cover in the corner.

'Like I said, Christi, you'll like this.' He bent down, slipped his finger into an eyelet on the manhole cover and lifted it up.

'OK, so what's the big deal?' Christian asked. 'Do you need to take a shit or something?'

'Not at this precise moment,' said Raglan, looking into the hole. 'Sure to later, though. Will keep you informed.'

A metal ladder set into the concrete wall dropped down below them into semi-darkness. At the bottom there was a glint of metal.

'This is an old Cold War secret,' said Raglan, a hint of seriousness in his voice. 'This is the pipeline that runs from Brize Norton right down to the fuel terminals at Southampton docks. It was built in the nineteen fifties as a way of making sure the RAF got the fuel they needed in the event of war. We're going to pop along the inspection way right into the airbase. Just as a precaution.'

'And because *you* think it's fun,' said Deveral.

Christian laughed. 'Sounds fun to me too. Where do we pop up? In the NAAFI?'

'Sadly not,' replied Raglan. 'In a hangar between the fuel depots and runway eight. Ideal really. You'd be amazed if you knew who's been in and out of the base through here. Saves questions.'

'Time for me to say goodbye,' said Deveral. 'Good luck, folks.' He shook each one by the hand. 'I'll lock up. Anything you need, just let me know somehow. Dharia, you're in good hands. Rags and Christi, no smoking down there.'

Raglan flicked on a torch and climbed down the ladder. Christian passed down their kit and climbed down too, followed by Dharia. Deveral clanked the manhole cover back into place.

'How long are we down here for?' whispered Dharia.

'It's no more than a fifteen-minute walk and there's no particular need to whisper for the time being,' said Raglan, his voice echoing.

They set off along a raised walkway that ran parallel to a massive, rusting steel pipe. The air was cold and smelt like a cellar. Christian had a sense that the operation had started for real.

13

Sam dozed for most of the three-hour flight to Mogadishu. The aeroplane was half empty and most of the other people on board looked like either foreign aid workers or security personnel. He had picked up a few things at the airport, including more clothes, toiletries and some decent desert boots. Approaching Mogadishu military airport, he looked through the window and caught a glimpse of a cluster of taller buildings which formed the central part of the city and a sprawling, low-level ring of shantytown surrounding them. As they banked into the final approach, the windows on the other side of the plane blinked the turquoise-blue of the Indian Ocean, which lay just to the east of the city. He wondered if anyone dared spend any time on the beach.

They touched down on a long, relatively new runway. Sam guessed it would have to be one of the last remaining legacies from the Americans. Runways were hard to steal and sell on. He stepped out of the aircraft into a wall of heat. He paused at the top of the steps and looked around. The airport had a double security fence all round the perimeter, with guard towers at intervals, giving the feel of a super-max prison or POW camp. At one end, several acres of freight containers were stacked three or four high. Faded images of oversized beach umbrellas decorated the walls of a rundown terminal building, a reminder of happier days.

Sam slipped on a new pair of black wrap-around sunglasses and barged down the steps. He set off across the runway following the line of passengers towards the terminal building. Ideas were already forming in his head. For the first time in weeks a smile cracked on his face. If the Egyptians wanted hell raised, they had come to the right man. How about a full-blown civil war? That would really piss people off. The little turd of a spook in the nasty suit might regret his condescending tone and sit up when his boss kicked his arse from one side of the Nile to the other. He'd realise treating Sam Carter like some piece of shit pawn in his small-time career plan might not have been quite such a smart move. Not so very clever when the UN moved in again and took full control of the country. Egypt could fuck right off and it would be back to patrolling the car park for the smug little bean-counting twerp.

He walked into the terminal building still scheming and brooding. A flutter of nerves focussed his mind as he pushed his new Turkish passport through a small hole in a glass window. A bored-looking man in a sweat-stained blue shirt decorated with epaulettes flicked to the back page and passed it back without looking up. Sam strode through some shattered glass doors held together by strips of brown parcel tape and looked around. A yellow sign still hung on long wires from the ceiling saying 'Arrivals' in English and Arabic.

A big, dark-looking guy in security-style clothing approached Sam. He pulled a pen from behind his ear and used it to guide his eye down a list of names on his clipboard. Sam stood with his legs a little wider apart than usual and assessed the man and his kit. Sure, he looked quite hard with his shaved head and stubble, but the paunch hanging over his belt was enough to give the game away. Soft ex-squaddie, thought Sam, subconsciously relaxing his stance and looking over the top of the clipboard to catch a glimpse of a small photograph of himself.

The man looked up and said something in a language Sam had never heard before.

'Sorry, I don't understand,' Sam replied. 'Do you speak English?'

The man looked surprised.

'It says you're a Turkish national. Why don't you speak Turkish?'

Sam had the response ready.

'Sure, I'm Turkish, but my parents left for London when I was a kid. Always made me speak English.'

The man seemed satisfied with this explanation. 'I'm Tariq, security supervisor for the airbase. I've been asked by the boss to show you around the place and then he'll talk with you.'

Sam nodded and followed Tariq out of the terminal building into what he guessed might once have been a car park. Now it was a village of dark green Portakabins partitioned by square-shaped blocks of Hesco barrier.

'Everyone has to live here within the compound of the airbase. It's the only safe place, like a green zone,' Tariq muttered.

'Great till someone zeroes in a mortar,' Sam responded.

'We don't get much shit round here,' Tariq told him. 'Al-Shabaab control ninety-nine per cent of the country, so why bother taking on the one per cent that's full of armed security?'

Sam grunted an affirmative reply. He could understand the status quo. The security people got paid and never left their one per cent, and al-Shabaab free-ranged the rest of the country – an unspoken détente that worked for everyone except the actual people of Somalia.

Sam kept up a steady stream of questions as they wandered around the airbase. As the only link with the outside world, it was critical. Everything came and went by air. Any link by road would involve crossing hundreds of miles of desert through al-Shabaab country, and sea freight was at risk from pirates. Knock out the airport and the umbilical cord would be chopped, leaving a few hundred people holed up in the secure part of Mog. That would mean an airborne evacuation in helicopters. And how vulnerable would that be? It would be *Black Hawk Down* 2. Sam raised his hand to his mouth to cover his grin. Things were genuinely looking up. In the mayhem, he could slip away. Maybe fake his own death and then set to work on his own agenda.

14

Raglan flashed his torch over his face and held a finger to his lips.

'Nearly there, folks. Better be quiet from here,' he whispered.

They carried on for another minute in silence until they stood beside a short metal ladder secured to the concrete wall. Raglan looped his bergen over his shoulder and climbed the ladder. At the top, he slowly slid back a couple of bolts and raised the manhole cover above his head. Slipping it to one side, he turned and looked down.

'All ready and waiting. Shits on Heathrow,' he said.

Christian followed Dharia up the ladder. As his head emerged from the manhole, he saw a familiar sight. The white G4 stood in the middle of a large, empty hangar, its door open and steps down. Raglan slid the manhole cover back in place with his foot.

'Yup, certainly does,' Christian agreed.

'We just get on and wait for the pilots,' said Raglan. 'There'll be parachutes and a few other bits and bobs inside. We'll lie down during the taxi outside, just until after take-off. Don't want ground staff getting too clever.'

They climbed the steps and moved to the seats at the rear of the aircraft. Christian noticed Dharia clasping her hands together. He knew it was to stop them shaking. Of course, she had never parachuted before – she would be shitting bricks. Everyone did. He remembered having nightmares about the prospect of his first jump. He caught Raglan's eye and discreetly trembled his hand. Raglan picked up on the sign.

'Dharia,' he said, smiling. 'Did I tell you that you and I'll be doing a tandem jump? No one's expecting you to jump out of this aircraft on your own.'

'What's a tandem jump?' said Dharia, a hint of suspicion in her voice.

'It's very simple,' Raglan told her. 'I strap you on my chest and we drop together with the same chute. All you have to do is enjoy the view.'

As Dharia opened her mouth to speak, there were voices followed by the sound of rubber soles squeaking on the painted concrete floor of the hangar. Two pilots stepped into the cabin wearing the standard issue green flight suits. One held a battered brown leather map case and a Thermos flask. Christian looked up. He knew most of the RAF guys attached to Special

Forces through his friend Oliver, who ran the Hercules C130s, but he didn't recognise these two.

'Five minutes and we'll be off,' said one of them, turning into the cockpit.

'Don't worry, Christi,' said Raglan quietly. 'These guys are attached to MI6, not SAS. Once I flew a dead body out of here in a body bag, and even then they didn't raise an eyebrow.'

'Must have made for an interesting tandem jump,' said Christian.

'There's a reason why they call them stiffs.' Raglan grinned. 'Mind you, by the time we put him back in bed in his house in a posh part of Warsaw, he wasn't quite so stiff. All floppy again by that stage.'

'Lovely,' said Christian, casting a glance at Dharia.

The engines kicked into life, sending a shudder through the aircraft. As they started to taxi, they slipped off their seats and lay side by side on the floor. The huge green hangar doors slid open like curtains and the aircraft accelerated into the sunlight. They turned left and swept across the apron of 08. A fraction of the way down the runway, the wheels left the tarmac.

The moment the G4 had levelled out, Raglan pressed his face to a window.

'There we are. What a beautiful sight to behold,' he said, his finger tapping the glass next to his cheek. 'The Welsh hills in all their glory. It's hard to make out exactly, but that'll be Pen y Fan right there in the middle.'

Christian had no problem reading the expression on Dharia's face. She had known Raglan for less than two hours but was clearly already struggling with his eccentricity. She would not have been told his full story, though she would have been briefed to some extent on his credentials. But looking at him now with his nose squashed against the window like an excited schoolboy, he knew how she felt. She glanced his way and caught his attempt at a reassuring smile.

'How about we go through the kit and then get some kip?' Christian suggested.

'Good idea,' said Raglan, turning round to face them. 'Realistically, we want to jump at about midnight so we can get some time on the ground before light. That way we can settle in gently and not be in a rush.'

Christian knew he meant it kindly, but he hoped Dharia would not pick up on Raglan's inadvertently condescending tone. Her helpful nod suggested he had got away with it thanks to the language barrier.

They spent the next forty minutes or so sitting on the floor of the aircraft going through their kit. Feeling sure he would make a better job of it than Raglan, Christian took it upon himself to tell Dharia that over half the kit she had pulled out of her bag was surplus to requirement. He helped her decide what to ditch. Once they had finished, Christian strapped the three small bergens together with para cord. He would jump with the equipment and Raglan would look after Dharia.

Back in their seats, Raglan pulled out the remains of a half-smoked cigar.

'Nobody minds if I smoke, do they?'

Christian shrugged and reached inside his shirt pocket. He flipped the top of a packet of Marlboros and thrust them towards Dharia. Contrary to his expectation, she took one, and Raglan was at the ready with his lighter. As Christian lit up too, there was a pinging sound as the 'No Smoking' sign illuminated at the far end of the cabin. One of the pilots turned around in his seat and looked back down the cabin with a grin on his face.

'Oi, yoi, yoi!' He wagged his finger at them.

'Shut up and fly!' Raglan barked back, crossing his legs and taking an exaggerated puff on his cigar.

Both the pilots laughed, setting off Dharia and Christian. Raglan chuckled and blew one smoke ring through another.

15

Sam had spent the best part of an hour and a half touring the airbase with Tariq before being shown into the security office. Dusty and hot, they climbed some metal steps to access the higher level of Portakabins. Tariq quickly closed the door behind them as they stepped into an air-conditioned environment. Despite the relative cool, Sam instantly caught the acrid tang of BO. There were two groups of four desks with computers sitting on them, and large whiteboards hung on the walls displaying what looked like staff rotas. At a larger desk at the end, sat the likely source of the smell. A small, toad-like man in a white civilian shirt placed his palms on the desk and pushed himself into a standing position. He looked out of place in the macho, ex-soldier security world and Sam's instinct sounded alarm bells. There was no need for the boss, particularly an older man, to get to his feet to welcome just another security bloke. He rounded the desk and stretched out his arm. As their hands squelched, the man spoke slowly.

'Welcome to Mogadishu.'

Unlike Tariq, this man knew to address him in English. Sam nodded in reply.

The toad grunted something to Tariq, who turned and left the Portakabin. He then gestured towards a desk.

'This can be your work station. We have three security levels and you will have access to all,' he said, leaving a glistening spot on the computer screen as he tapped it with his finger. He then rattled the mouse on the desk with his hand and a box appeared demanding a user name and password. Sam rested one hand on the desk and leant forward as the man typed with one finger on the keyboard.

'We all have the same user name,' he continued as the word 'security' appeared in the top half of the box. 'It's the password that determines level of access. This will be your password.'

Sam felt cold run through him as the letters spelling 'Mahmood' changed one by one to filled circles. The toad glanced sideways to assess the impact. Sam set his jaw and stepped back from the desk. The fact that this little man knew the name of the prison in Cairo meant something, but it didn't mean he knew everything.

'Thank you, sir. That's very helpful,' he said gruffly.

'That's alright,' said the toad. 'Now, Tariq will show you the living accommodation and canteen. I'll see you later.'

Sam closed the door to the Portakabin behind him and rejoined Tariq, who was leaning on the handrail at the bottom of the steps. Other people wandered past them as they set off again. Sam thought they fell into two obvious categories: regular operational personnel, and security people. Clearly in the security category, two dark-looking men in desert DPM trousers and black ops vests swaggered by. Sam eyed them through his sunglasses without moving his head. They carried new Heckler & Koch G36 assault rifles, and holstered pistols gripped their thighs. No sign of handcuffs or anything to make an arrest. Both smoked. Twats, he thought. Thirty K across the Beacons with weight and sideways rain; that's what they needed. That would sort them.

They ambled past a couple more Portakabins and then pushed through a narrow gap in the Hesco. Tariq opened a door and Sam followed him up a couple of breeze block steps into the sleeping accommodation. He was not surprised, but he had been hoping for better. Clothing, boots and general personal clobber spewed from under six camp beds which formed a row against the back wall. Multicoloured drapes suspended from strings attached to the ceiling divided each sleeping area from its neighbour. Better than his cell on death row, but certainly an incentive to get a move on.

He dropped his bag of recently acquired kit on the vacant bed at the end and sat down next to it. Instantly, the leg supporting the end section of the bed gave way. He had no problem reading Tariq's expression: surely you didn't expect the last guy in to get a working bed, did you? Sam felt his neck redden with anger. He wiped the sweat from his face and stood up. He wasn't going to suffer the indignity of sticking his arse in the air to fix the bed for the benefit of a gloating wannabe who wouldn't even get to drive a truck for the SAS. He managed a smile and walked slowly back towards the door. It was only the soothing effects of the plan for utter carnage already bubbling in his mind that prevented him from breaking Tariq's jaw.

16

At 23.45, one of the pilots called down the cabin.

'South west of Addis. Forty minutes to the drop zone. We'll start a gradual descent in twenty minutes, OK?'

'Fine'. Christian swung his feet off the bergens where they had been resting. He had not been able to sleep but had had his eyes shut for the past hour or two. It was better than nothing. Raglan sat up and stretched.

'Let's get sorted,' said Christian, standing up and smiling at Dharia perching on the front of her seat. 'Final weapons check. Confirm twenty-four and forty-eight hours RVs and then I'll help you two get your parachutes on.'

Dharia pressed her face to the window and looked out into the black of the night sky. Christian felt sure it was her way of hiding her expression of fear. For a moment, he tried to put himself in her shoes. It was pointless. The leap into the darkness two miles over the ground attached to an eccentric, smoke-ring blowing Welsh hill farmer was probably the easy bit for her. It would be crashing back into the world she had fought so hard to leave behind that would be the daunting part. She had made it out once against the odds and at massive personal cost. Now she was diving right back in. That took nerve.

Once they had pulled on black overalls, Christian lifted the larger of the two parachute packs onto Raglan's shoulders and then slipped into his own. They fastened the thick Velcro straps of their altimeters to their wrists and adjusted the elastic straps on their plastic goggles. The aircraft, now at a slight incline, shook as they hit the top of the cloud base.

'I reckon there's just about time for a smoke,' said the pilot, twisting around in his seat. 'Then we'll drop the speed down to about a hundred and eighty knots. Any slower and this thing will stall. You'll jump at about eight thousand feet. All OK?'

'Roger that,' said Raglan, allowing Dharia first go at Christian's packet of cigarettes. The three of them sat in a row against the fuselage by the rear door. On cue, the No Smoking sign pinged to life. Faint smiles broke all round.

'Right, folks, time to stub out and stand to.' Raglan got to his feet. He clipped two carabiners on the front of his harness, then two on the back of Dharia's. Winking at Christian over Dharia's shoulder, he manoeuvred her into position by the door.

'If I were you, I'd just shut my eyes and think about something nice,' he said.

'Such as?' Christian asked.

'I can't think of anything nice offhand, can I? Not just like that.' Raglan sounded more Welsh than usual.

'OK, you think of something nice, while I open the door.' Christian turned to look at the pilots.

'Anytime now,' called the pilot, walking down the cabin. 'I'll lock up after you. Good luck.'

Christian pulled the door lever up and round. Just before he slid the door back on its rails, Raglan spoke to Dharia.

'OK, I'll count to three and then we go.'

Dharia's arms gripped either side of the door frame, her elbows locked and her body flexed backwards. Raglan had to shout his next words over the howling roar of the engines and blasting wind.

'OK. One, two.'

Dharia's body braced backwards. Raglan snapped his arms around her, knocking both her hands free of the door frame. He surged forwards and they disappeared into the darkness. Christian lost no time. He nodded to the pilot and stepped out of the aircraft. The deafening roar of engines was replaced immediately by an intense rush of wind as he started the free fall. He released the bundle of bergens that swung beneath him on para cord and they flicked out into a star shape. He counted to twelve and reached for the D-shaped metal release pull on his chest. Crack! went the parachute above him and then came silence.

He released his grip on his harness with his left hand and held the altimeter within a couple of inches of his face. He had dropped a full 4,000 feet in free fall. He looked down, hoping to catch a glimpse of Raglan and Dharia, but all he could see below was darkness. Even in Wales, there was always light from some distant town or village, but in this part of Africa the darkness was unspoiled. He hung in his harness, knowing that the moment his feet hit the ground, the risk started for real. So far, it had all been hypothetical. But below him and getting closer by the second was a land where little, except the weapons, had changed since the Stone Age. Sure, there were pickup trucks too, but that was it. Subsistence farming, tribal law and piracy.

Christian held up the altimeter again: 1,000 feet. He gripped the harness with both hands and pulled down strongly with his right arm. The parachute responded, twisting into a right-handed turn. He glanced at the altimeter one last time as he straightened up. At 100 feet, he flared the parachute into the wind. A few seconds later, the bergens scraped the ground and he planted his feet in soft sand. He tilted forwards, fell to his knees and heaved again with his right arm to collapse the chute. With the adrenalin of the jump still pumping, he got to his feet and hauled in the parachute.

As he wrapped it into a bundle, he heard a noise in the darkness behind him. Instinctively, he reached for the SIG Sauer but found himself-grasping at it through his jump suit. Then came a familiar and reassuring waft of cigar smoke.

'Rags?' he said quietly.

'Hey, Christi. All OK?' came the reply.

Raglan and Dharia appeared in the darkness.

'Touched down just over there. You nearly wiped us out with your fancy display landing. Honestly,' said Raglan, his face glowing a ghoulish orange as he dragged on the cigar.

'Things have come on a bit at parachute school since the Seventies,' said Christian. 'It's not the good old days of static line and leap any more. Anyway, Dharia, are you OK?'

'Freezing cold but fine, thanks,' replied Dharia.

'You'll soon warm up once we get moving. But it must be nice to be home again,' said Raglan. 'Not quite as you imagined, I suppose.'

Christian knew he meant it kindly but imagined the glare on her face.

'No,' came the reply.

Christian felt himself tense as Raglan started to speak again. Fortunately, he set off on a different tack.

'OK, let's stash the parachuting clobber and get out of here. I'd like to get fifteen K between us and any point along the flight path before we hole up. Then we can get some kip before we check in with Antcliff and see who's got where.'

By 01.15 they were off at a fast walk, Raglan in

front, Dharia in the middle and Christian bringing up the rear. Moonlight broke at intervals from behind the cloud cover, allowing them glimpses of the surrounding country. Christian took the chance to look around. It was flat, open and featureless with soft, dusty sand underfoot. There was the occasional tuft of grass and the odd small bush; a cross between desert and scrub. The ideal choice for a night-time parachute drop with nothing nasty to land on. He tucked his thumbs under the shoulder straps of his bergen and locked onto Dharia's silhouette five metres in front.

To his surprise, they stopped after half an hour. Raglan dropped to one knee and pressed his GPS to the ground. Shielding the green glow with his hand, he checked progress and they were off again.

'Very orthodox,' hissed Christian.

'For heaven's sake, don't tell Dev,' Raglan called back over his shoulder. 'He'll have me as staff on the Troop Leaders course. I've got to keep up the unemployable maverick wheeze as long as possible.'

'Well, it's pretty convincing so far. I don't think you've got too much to worry about. What do you think, Dharia?

'What's a maverick?' she asked.

'It's a rare type of goat only found in certain mountainous parts of South Wales,' replied Christian quickly.

'So, he is a special goat with a cough that does not like work,' she said sounding both confused and amused.

'That's me all day long,' laughed Raglan.

17

They trudged on across a soft, open expanse for the best part of two hours before Raglan consulted his GPS for the last time.

'Anywhere from here onwards,' he said to himself. Then he turned to Dharia and Christian. 'We're a decent way off the flight path, so no one will come looking, even if they did pick up on the plane.'

It was a further twenty minutes before Raglan stopped. The first glimmers of dawn were sufficient for them to see they were a few hundred metres from the bottom of a series of rising valleys.

'Good,' said Raglan. 'The problem with this place is that everything looks the same on the satellite imagery, but this is better than I thought. We can hole up in one of these valleys and get some shade. May need it later.'

'And some elevation will mean we can see right

out across the plain we've just been crossing,' said Christian.

'It will be forty degrees or more today,' said Dharia. 'Too hot for lazy goats.'

'Much too hot for lazy old goats.' Raglan smiled at her. 'Come on, let's get on up one of these valleys and find a nice, cool, north-facing slope. Technically speaking, we'll actually be in Ethiopia.'

'I can't see that making much difference if we get rumbled by an Egyptian military patrol,' said Christian.

'The al-Shabaab militia don't care about borders,' said Dharia. 'They don't even know where the borders are. No one does.'

'I think we're pretty much fucked whoever and wherever we bump into,' said Raglan.

'Might be best to keep our heads down then,' said Christian. 'Come on, it's going to be light soon.'

Christian looked around and set off towards the steepest valley with Dharia and Raglan following. The ground underfoot soon changed from dusty sand into hard, rocky terrain. They meandered uphill around large boulders and heaps of loose rubble from landslips. Despite the relative chill of the night, Christian felt the first beads of sweat form on his forehead and temples. He slowed the pace – not for his own benefit – and turned to look behind him. They were not far behind, walking side by side, Raglan with Dharia's bergen looped over his shoulder.

Christian smiled and pressed on up the side of the

valley, running over in his mind the criteria for a lying-up point or OP. He scanned around in the half-light for somewhere that would be shaded and protected from the wind. They needed a vantage point, and somewhere that led to nowhere so there would be no reason for anyone to stumble upon them. Ideally, they needed a back door too. He moved higher, towards a collection of rocks heaped at the bottom of a small ravine that dropped from a ridgeline above.

He reached the rocks, slipped his off his back and pressed on up the ravine. By the time he had recced around at the top, he saw Dharia and Raglan sitting below by his bergen. He dropped back down and joined them.

'All fine up there. Just another valley behind, which would be as good as anything for a hasty retreat,' he said, wiping sweat from his face. 'How's the lazy goat?'

'Not so lazy now,' answered Raglan, gesturing at the bergens.

'Good goat,' said Dharia, smiling at Raglan. 'In this country, women do most of the work.'

'It's the right spot, Christi,' said Raglan, looking around. 'I think we could hole up here for a couple of days, at least till the water runs out, anyway.'

'So what do we do then?' asked Dharia.

'Well, we can be resupplied by parachute whenever we want, but that shouldn't be necessary. We are about thirty kilometres south of Balbalaiar, which is the major town in southern Ethiopia. It's the only realistic route from north to south, unless you've either got a plane or a camel. Our chaps will be coming through there by bus, and I reckon it's about a twenty-four-hour drive from Addis, where they'll be landing in the next few hours.'

'That's assuming they make the right bus and it doesn't break down,' chipped in Christian.

'Believe me,' said Dharia, 'everything takes twice as long in Africa.'

'Of course it does,' Raglan agreed, 'but we have to plan on the basis that they don't screw up and that they make it. Antcliff will confirm they made the flight from the UK and what time it landed. He didn't say exactly, but I wouldn't be surprised if between him and Dev they've got someone from MI6 or maybe MI5's G6 section sitting in the row right behind them on the bus. The fact is, we're going to know precisely when and where they turn up.'

'So we just sit here and wait for joining instructions.' Christian offered his packet of cigarettes about. 'Good old traditional British Army stuff; sitting about for days either freezing your butt off or being roasted alive. These guys will probably get homesick after half an hour and fuck off back to Leicester.'

'More than likely,' Raglan agreed, lighting up. 'Mind you, I'll be dying to kill someone after a couple of days sat on my arse here.'

'Sure,' said Christian, grinning. 'And the insects

haven't even started yet. Just wait till the sun gets up.'

Dharia laughed out loud. 'Sounds like you two don't like being in the Army?'

'It's not all bad,' replied Raglan. 'There are a few good bits, now and then.'

'That is if we *are* in the Army,' added Christian. 'Anyway, how about you guys settle down and get some kip? I'll do the first stag. Probably best if I'm up on the ridge.'

'Sure thing,' said Raglan. 'We'll get sorted here and swap over at oh-six hundred.'

Christian looped his bergen over his shoulder and set off uphill again. Careful not to skyline himself, he settled at the top of the ravine just below the line of the ridge. He rested his back against a rock and found it was pleasantly warm in contrast to the air temperature. Nice now, he thought, but it did not bode well for later.

He took a long drink from his water bottle and unclipped the top of his bergen. He fumbled around inside and pulled out a clear plastic ziplock bag. He studied the contents. It was depressing to be back on army rations, but at least it wasn't shepherd's pie. He took out a white plastic sachet, tore off the corner and squeezed some soft brown gloop calling itself spaghetti bolognaise into his mouth. It tasted familiar in a neutral way and reminded him of being on exercise in Wales. He thought of sitting in the middle of forestry block trying to shelter from the wind and rain. At the time, it had been pretty grim. Cold, wet and utterly knackered. Sore feet and feeling like shit. But at least he had known what he was doing. There had been a structure and, above all, light at the end of the tunnel. However long and miserable, exercises would always come to an end. Eventually, there would be a lorry waiting, even if they occasionally moved off at the last moment.

He looked back down the ravine and saw that Raglan had laid out a groundsheet between the rocks and rigged up a poncho over the top like some kind of miniature Bedouin tent. Bashing down in hills felt normal enough, whether it was in the Brecon Beacons, a jungle in Belize or in the Ethiopian Highlands, but despite some touches of regular soldiering, things felt pretty bizarre. He remembered Deveral talking to them a few hours after the end of Selection. Nine of them had sat informally in his office. He had told them that life would never quite be the same again. They should prepare for the extraordinary, where the training would seem meaningless. They would be asked to give more than they could possibly imagine. Not to expect reward or the recognition they deserved. It could be a lonely life, separated from family and friends and often away even from the Regiment itself. Death would more likely be a hail of Third World bullets, not flying through an embassy window in a cordoned-off street in Mayfair. Nothing glorious, and probably an empty grave at the Hereford military cemetery. Did anyone still want to quit? Last chance.

Christian had not believed it at the time. He didn't think anyone had. He didn't even think Deveral had. It was just part of the process. One more barrier to crash through before laying hands on the elusive sandy beret. But tucked in below the ridgeline watching the sun slowly rise to the east, Christian found meaning in those words. Maybe they had been passed down from Deveral's predecessors, who would have commanded the Regiment in more desperate times. Whatever the origins, they resonated now.

Next came a squeeze of more brown slop labelled Beef Stroganoff and Pasta. It tasted the same but different. The important thing was to get the calories down. That was all that mattered. He had lost so much weight in captivity in Sierra Leone but had at least started the operation in reasonable shape. He folded the empty sachet twice and pushed it back into the ziplock bag. He had deliberately not allowed himself to think of Jamie and Tim but he knew with tiredness came the slip in self-control. It was 5 a.m. and bar a bit of power nap on the G4, he had been awake for nearly twenty-four hours. Thoughts of his fallen friends crept from the restricted part of his mind. He saw Tim standing calm and alone amongst the baying militia mob as he knelt and witnessed the demonstration of the barbaric torture that awaited him. He heard the crack of Jamie's suppressing sniper fire from the nearby ridge and recalled the chaos as over a hundred frenzied extremist fighters hit the ground. His friends were outnumbered fifty to one and still they had piled in with just a couple of souvenir AKs smuggled back from Gulf 1, a buffalo rifle and some antique grenades.

Christian's hand trembled as he pulled a cigarette from his packet. Holding one hand in the other, he sparked the lighter and lit up. Tears formed in the corners of his eyes. What the fuck was he doing?

Sitting alone in a wire cage in the dark cellar under the West Side Boys house in Sierra Leone, he had promised himself two things. One, he would nail Sam, and two, he would leave the Army immediately and lead a boring and comfortably middle-class life. Sure, Sam was nailed, well and truly, but he certainly had not delivered on the second part of his promise. Maybe there would be time one day for walks by the sea and a pension plan, but there wouldn't be for Jamie and Tim. They had died fighting like lions to save him, proving Deveral's words had not been so wide of the mark.

The first rays of sun cast a contrasting shadow across the valley. He looked out to the south across the wide open plain towards the lawless vacuum of Somalia. Turning his head, he surveyed the ridges and peaks of the Ethiopian Highlands. A world apart from the lush green cradle of Raglan's hill farm. He finished his cigarette and lit another.

18

Shortly after 06.00, Christian made his way down the ravine. He dropped to one knee and poked his head under the poncho to see Raglan and Dharia sleeping side by side. Raglan lay on his back, partially propped up against his bergen. His hand rested on his chest, gripping the stock of his SIG Sauer. Dharia lay on her side, wrapped around her bergen, a black woollen jumper tucked under her head as a pillow. Knowing how hard it was to sleep in the field, Christian slowly stood and turned to leave them to sleep. Before he had taken a step, he heard a movement. Raglan was awake and looking at his watch.

'No you don't, Christi,' he said. 'Otherwise this lazy goat thing might start to stick.'

Christian smiled. 'Nothing going on. Happy to hold on an hour or two more if you want.'

'No, no, I'm cool. We'd better sitrep with Cheltenham.

Don't want to sit here and cook for two days if they missed their bloody flight.'

'Sure.' Christian nodded. 'Stranger things have happened.'

Raglan produced his sat phone, twisted the aerial into position and dialled.

'Get on with it, yer slag,' he muttered in response to the automated voice recording from the sugary American lady informing him of his remaining credit.

'Easy, Rags. I think she sounds quite nice. Closest thing you get to a woman sometimes,' said Christian, raising his eyebrows.

'Actually, you might have a point,' said Raglan. 'Might give her a buzz more often. Do you reckon it's a real bird or just a machine?'

There was a cough from within the Bedouin tent. Raglan and Christian looked at each other.

'Perhaps you could make your,' short pause, 'telephone calls somewhere else,' said Dharia.

Raglan pressed a button to end the call. Christian looked on anxiously as he crawled back under the poncho.

'No, really, is it a real woman or a computer thing trying to sound sexy and intelligent?' Raglan said seriously.

A couple of seconds later, there was a peal of laughter from Dharia.

'She sounds really hot to me. And I think she must like you guys.'

'You goats, you mean,' replied Christian, also laughing.

Raglan emerged from the tent with the phone pressed to his ear.

'Over five hundred dollars left and it's ringing now,' he said, looking at Christian.

Raglan sat on one of the rocks , listening, then he spoke. 'Send.' Half a minute or so later, he spoke again. 'Yes, situation normal and on task.'

He nodded twice, glanced at Christian and nodded again. 'OK. Roger that. On task.' He lowered the phone.

'That's all good. The *assets*, as Antcliff likes to call them, have made the flight and landed. They're on the bus and very much on schedule.'

'OK. So, it doesn't look like we're going to have to sit here for too long then,' said Christian. 'In theory that gives us twenty-four hours here and then we move to the intercept.'

'Exactly, so you get some shut eye, and I'll get some scoff. Swap over about midday,' replied Raglan.

Christian ducked under the poncho beside Dharia and pulled off his boots and socks. He turned on his side with his back to her and rested his head on his forearm. He had done his thinking and was not going to do any more. He focussed on the pleasant and soothing feeling of the gentle breeze on his feet. Then a jolt ran through him. He could smell his own feet. They stank. And if he could smell them, that meant she could too. In theory, it didn't matter. Of course people smelt on operations. They took shits into plastic bags and carried them round in their bergens for days. That was part of it. There was an unspoken understanding. On ops, you stink. Fact. But there weren't any women on ops. That was the fundamental difference. Particularly, quite attractive ones. He straightened his legs and pushed his feet as far away as possible. That was all he could do.

When Christian woke it was around midday. Despite the shade of the poncho, he was soaked in sweat. His hand had moved subconsciously, for a reassuring feel of his pistol. He pulled his boots on and looked around for the others. They sat at the top of the ravine looking out to the south. Christian moved up to join them and sat down.

'Just telling Dharia about an operation in the early Nineties,' said Raglan. 'I was tasked to nick a working example of the latest type of Russian battle tank. Apparently a shitload better than Challenger Two and giving the MOD the fear.'

'So what happened?' interrupted Dharia.

'Well, we ended up bribing a Russian army major. They were moving some of these tanks across the Caspian Sea on some landing craft, and he agreed to accidentally drop one off the back. It was in about six hundred feet of water, so as far as they were concerned, it was a goner. But we knew exactly where it was and got the Royal Navy engineers to fish it out. We got it back to the tank training place at Bovington.'

'The lads down there must have been chuffed,' said

Christian. 'I was there for a couple of weeks on a demolition course.'

'Like dogs with two cocks, they were. Couldn't believe it, and the best bit was the Russians had no idea.'

'So what did they do with it?' Christian asked. 'Endless tests, I suppose?'

'Exactly,' said Raglan. 'It gave us a big insight into their armour and ballistics. The irony was that it wasn't that good anyway. Otherwise we'd have been in deep shit and couldn't have defended Germany against a ground-based invasion.'

'Listen, guys, nicking the tank was good, but let's not spoil it and get all nerdy,' said Dharia, rolling her eyes.

'That's not nerdy by military standards, I can assure you,' Christian told her. 'I did Sandhurst.,' He lit a cigarette.

'Sandhurst? Yes, I've heard of that,' said Raglan. 'Something to do with officer training, I think. Is that where you learnt to use a garrotting wire?

'Don't think becoming a diamond-nicking gangster was on the course either,' replied Christian, taking a drag on his cigarette.

'You two are weird,' said Dharia, looking at them both in turn.

As the afternoon wore on, the breeze eased and the direct heat of the sun turned down a notch due to the formation of a helpful layer of thin grey cloud.

The trade-off seemed acceptable until the still air filled with a buzzing melee of mosquitoes. Christian brushed the first few off his wrist and rolled down his sleeves. As dusk fell, they agreed the advantage of the view from the top of the ravine would be lost as darkness fell and that they might as well decamp back to the rocks below. They sat on the ground and Raglan pulled out the sat phone. He dialled and held out the phone towards Christian and Dharia. They all craned forward in anticipation.

'Your remaining credit stands at four hundred and sixty-nine dollars and ten cents,' purred the voice. 'Please hold the line while your call is connected.'

'What's so funny?' said Antcliff in response to the chorus of laughter.

'No idea,' lied Raglan, 'but send anyway.'

'Situation normal,' Antcliff continued. 'We anticipate the intercept within twelve to twenty-fours hours, so be prepared to move. Likely to be the asset plus one. Will have coordinates tomorrow.'

Raglan ended the call and folded the aerial away.

'So it's plus a guide of some kind,' he said.

'Might be a bit more than a guide,' replied Christian. 'It could be someone a bit less rookie who knows what he's doing.'

'Yup,' Raglan agreed. 'More than likely. So we'll do the guide first and then nobble the asset.'

19

When it came to his turn to get some sleep, Christian had no problem dropping off despite the hard ground and the itching mozzie bites on his hands and shins. Within forty minutes he was awake again. He found the smell of Raglan's cigar smoke hanging in the night air strangely reassuring, but the prospect of a cold-blooded kill within the next twenty-four hours weighed heavily on his mind. He had killed in close quarters before. But that was in the heat of the moment, fighting for his life. He had been spared the agony of premeditation. He shut his eyes and tried to close out the thoughts, but images of the quiet suburban street in Leicester formed before him. Knowing where they lived made it a whole load more personal. The respectable middle-class parents who had no idea what their kids were up to didn't help either.

He had grappled with putting his own parents through news of his death. It was the hardest thing he had ever done. He understood the thought processes. Sooner or later there would be a knock on a front door in that pleasant Victorian row. There would be initial disbelief and then the gradual acknowledgement and the start of the suffering. Christian rolled over and shut his eyes again. Either he had to forget it or focus on the bigger picture. These guys were heading to Somalia to train in mass murder. Sure, they might be misguided, but try telling that to the parents of a kid blown up on the London Underground. Christian adjusted the position of his holster to stop his pistol sticking into his leg. He consciously switched his thoughts over to walking along the banks of the River Beaulieu which ran through the fields a few hundred metres from his home in Hampshire. He would follow it down to the sea like he had so many times. The cigar smoke was no substitute for fresh sea air, but overall it felt good. If he made it to the sea, he would hang a right and have a wander round the harbour at Lymington.

Christian was just passing the sailing school when he felt a hand on his shoulder. For a moment he thought it was his father's hand, steadying him or pulling him back.

'It's four a.m., Christi. Hate to do this to you, lad, but we need to get moving. Had Antcliff on. They're ahead of where they should be,' whispered Raglan.

Christian rolled over and looked at Raglan in the darkness.

'Don't know why I'm whispering,' Raglan continued in his normal voice. 'We've got some coordinates of where they're meeting the al-Shabaab lot in about forty-eight hours.'

'Sounds OK to me.' Christian sat up. 'So what's the plan then?'

'Well, we know where the bus terminates and we know where they RV. So, that means we know they'll be travelling in a roughly straight line between the two. Antcliff has worked out an approximate half way point which is about thirty K from here as the crow flies.'

'OK, so we'd better get going then,' said Dharia, standing up. 'No one walks around Somalia in the heat of the day.'

'Except mad goats and Englishmen,' replied Christian.

Within less than five minutes, they had squeezed rations into their mouths, taken a glug of water and packed up the groundsheets. Dharia had ripped her bergen off Raglan's shoulder and they were moving fast downhill, aided by intermittent moonlight. As they hit the plain at the bottom of the valley, the ground turned from rocks and gravel back into the soft, dusty sand. They pushed on, keeping the high ground to the right. Christian leant forward into the straps of his bergen and felt relieved that Raglan was in charge of navigation. It was not long before a more consistent light from the first glimmers of sunrise lit up the plain. In some respects it made things easier but their tracks were now uncomfortably visible.

Christian knew from experience they were covering four K per hour. Fine in the relative cool of the dawn but not a sustainable pace for a thirty-K tab that would end up being nearer forty in reality. Raglan led the way with a confident stride, with Dharia tucked in behind him. Christian noticed her adjusting the position of her bergen more and more frequently. At first she tightened the belt strap to take more weight on her hips and to give her shoulders a break. Within ten minutes, she had loosened it again and was pulling on first one shoulder strap and then the other to spread the weight across her back. Christian knew the signs. He upped his pace and came parallel with her. He gripped her bergen and without eye contact or a word said, she released the belt strap. Christian slung it over his left shoulder and eased back to the rear.

Despite the sun not having fully risen above the horizon behind them, the heat was already building. Christian raised the dusty blue and white chequered shemagh from round his neck and wrapped it round his head. Sweat dripped down inside his shirt. The extra weight made a difference.

Raglan looked down at his GPS, raised his hand and stopped.

'Let's take a break here,' he said, taking off his

bergen and sitting down on it. 'We'd better get some fluids in.'

Christian lowered Dharia's Bergen to the ground and they sat facing each other.

'Pretty fucking same old round here,' continued Raglan, looking around. 'Dust, dust, and more dust. It's not even real sand like in a desert.'

'It's not always so dry here,' said Dharia. 'When it rains, it rains for real.'

'We need a bit of wind or a section on hard ground,' said Christian. 'Don't like leaving ten miles of tracks. We really should work in a snap ambush at some point.'

'What on earth's a snap ambush?' said Dharia. 'I thought we were meant to be undercover?'

'It's just basic procedure to make sure you're not being followed,' said Christian. 'When you want to stop, you walk round in a big fishhook-like circle and come back nearly onto your tracks. It means you can ambush anyone that's following you.'

'Think we'd better go for the hard ground option,' said Raglan between gulps of his water bottle.

'I don't fancy ambushing a bunch of tooled-up tribesmen with a couple of Siggy's and a garrotting wire anyway.' Christian swiped a tsetse fly from his forearm. 'There weren't any of these little fuckers on the ridge. Must have been the wind or the height.'

'Well, they've started now,' said Raglan, smacking at one with his hand against his thigh. 'And if they can bite through proper kit, we don't stand a chance in this clobber.' He tugged at the cheap cotton trousers from the shop in Leicester.

'Why don't you guys both get jobs in the call centre where I worked?' enquired Dharia. 'All the clever secret stuff and none of the flies and nasty guys with guns.'

'That's actually not quite as stupid as it sounds,' replied Christian. 'In fact, that was exactly what I was going to do.'

'Until he met me,' exclaimed Raglan triumphantly, leaning forwards to pat Christian across the back. 'A couple of doses of my shepherd's pie was all it took.'

'That's right, hook, line and fucking sinker,' Christian laughed. 'What a twat I am.'

Fifteen minutes later, they were on their feet again and moving. Initially, they continued to hand-rail along the line of valleys dropping from the high ground to their right, but as the morning wore on, their direction took them further into open country. They passed the occasional heap of rocks randomly dumped in the otherwise flat and featureless plain. They plodded on and, hour by hour, the outline of distant mountains crept into sharper focus.

Raglan raised his hand and they all sank to the ground. No one spoke for a couple of minutes. As Christian stuffed his water bottle back into a side pouch on his bergen, his eye caught a movement over Raglan's shoulder. His raised a hand to shade his narrowed eyes. Raglan and Dharia spun round and stared in the direction Christian was pointing.

'We've got company,' said Christian. 'Can't see what, but it's moving this way at speed. Look at the dust.'

'Bloody marvellous,' muttered Raglan. 'Well, we had to move in daylight. There was no alternative.'

'Sure.' Christian stood up. 'Dharia, get a decent drink into you. If the shit hits the fan, we'll twenty-four-hour RV back at the ridge. After that, it'll be personal best back to the UK.'

Dharia stood up and took a defiantly tiny sip from her water bottle. A small black speck at the centre of an expanding dust cloud became identifiable as a pickup truck. At about a kilometre away, it veered sharply to the left and began a circle around them, the dust cloud now a trailing wedge shape behind it. Having completed the best part of 180 degrees, it turned inwards and drove straight towards them.

Christian pulled at the Velcro strap and released the holster containing his SIG-Saur. He pushed the holster into his bergen and tucked the pistol into his belt with his shirt covering it. The pickup approached, still at speed. Three men stood in the back gripping a roll bar running over the cab, which contained the silhouette of a driver.

'Here we go,' said Raglan sideways to Christian.

'Terrific,' he replied without moving his mouth.

The pickup screeched to a halt, metal on metal, the

front bumper less than a metre from them. Despite the thick crust of greyish dust, Christian saw the word Toyota written in white lettering across the bonnet. The driver's door opened and the three men in the back scrambled down. Each held an AK 47 assault rifle and wore a mixture of military and civilian clothes. Out of the cab stepped a tall, young-looking black man. With slick sunglasses pushed up on his head and without a weapon, he was obviously the boss. His trousers were new US issue desert DPM and his black ops vest covered a long striped shirt. He eyed Christian first, then Raglan and finally Dharia. He walked around behind them like a triumphant hyena sizing up a wounded impala.

Completing his tour, he stood in front of Christian and reached forwards for the strap of his bergen. Christian took half a step backwards and brushed his hand aside.

'No,' said Christian quietly.

The expression on the boss man's face changed in a nanosecond from the amused and relaxed 'we're just going to rob you idiots and probably let you go' to a 'don't you fuck with me and make me look stupid in front of my men; now we're going to murder you too'.

The three heavies from the back of the truck surged forward, bristling with aggression. The hand reached forwards again, this time faster and more purposefully. Christian held his ground, his right hand snapping up to catch the approaching hand. In one smooth movement, he gripped it and twisted it up and round into a goose-neck. By the time the AKs were raised and pointing his way, he had his man's arm bent up behind his back. Christian used his leverage to yank the man around, forming a precautionary human shield. He then slammed him forward, smashing his face into the bonnet of the Toyota. Pulling him back into a standing position, he snatched the SIG-Saur from his belt, regained his grip and shoved it in under the man's chin.

Raglan moved in beside Christian, his pistol raised. Semi-dazed, the boss man flapped both his palms wildly in the air as signal for calm. Christian arched backward and tightened his grip.

'Put your fucking weapons down now!' yelled Raglan over a barrage of incomprehensible shouting.

With his men becoming more incensed by the second, the boss waved his hands still more desperately. He shouted something but no one heard.

'Put your weapons down!' yelled Raglan again at the wall of noise and jabbing AKs.

'We're all going to die,' Christian growled in the boss's ear. 'You decide. You control them.'

'No, no. We stop,' gasped the boss, his eyes bulging.

'Shut the fuck up!' yelled Raglan, with his pistol almost muzzle to muzzle with the closest AK.

Dharia darted forward and squeezed into no-man's land. With her hands raised, and staring directly at the ground in front of her, she screamed something in her native language. She continued to yell, looking first at Christian and Raglan and then at the three frenzied heavies. Slowly, her high-pitched wail won the war of sound and she scaled back to audible and coherent language. Christian and Raglan had no idea what she was saying, but the boss's desperate efforts to nod suggested she was having some effect.

She carried on, speaking quickly, her head turning from side to side. Christian detected a fractional decrease in tension and relaxed the pressure of his pistol under the boss's chin. Raglan released one hand from the butt of his pistol and held it open in the air. Dharia continued, her voice slowing and becoming more deliberate as the AKs eased in the shaking hands of the heavies. Dharia placed the palm of her hand on the muzzle of Raglan's SIG Sauer and the other over the end of the middle AK. She pushed slowly back and down. Raglan obliged and lowered his aim from horizontal to a conciliatory forty-five degrees.

'Right, Dharia!' barked Raglan. 'Tell them to get back in the truck and we'll let matey here go. Then they can drive off.'

'And waste us with those AKs the moment they're out of range of our fucking pea-shooters?' snarled Christian.

'Dharia,' said Raglan. 'Tell them I'm swapping my brand-new SIG Sauer for one of their rusting, heap-of-shit AKs.'

'Tell them!' yelled Christian in the boss's ear as Dharia turned and spoke.

The boss grunted and the exchange was made. The heavies clambered aboard the truck and Dharia leant across the bonnet to retrieve the boss's sunglasses from where they had landed by the windscreen wipers. She pressed them into his hand as Christian manoeuvred him round to the driver's door.

With Raglan leaning into the stock of his newly acquired AK, the engine started and the wheels of the truck spun in the dust.

'Surely they'll be back with reinforcements, won't they?' said Christian, watching the truck speed away.

'They are humiliated,' replied Dharia. 'This never happened. They never saw us and will never speak of this moment again. Let's move. The Udedi Mountains are still far away.'

20

Dharia set off at a fast walk, her thumbs tucked in under the shoulder straps of her bergen. Raglan and Christian exchanged looks and shrugged. She had not got far when Raglan called after her.

'Come back here now, please.'

She stopped, but a couple of seconds passed before she turned around.

'I said come back here.'

She walked back to them and stood in front of Raglan.

'You did very well just then. Without you, I expect there would have been a bloodbath. Thank you. But you will not just walk off like that. I lead this operation and you will follow me, even if you do know where we're going.'

Christian saw Dharia's jaw move from side to side. She had saved the day, but Raglan was right to bring her back in check. He prayed she would take it. She seemed about to speak, but then she slipped her arms out of her bergen straps, smiled and pushed it at Raglan.

'And you were going the wrong way,' said Raglan, smiling too. 'Probably only out by ten degrees, but over fifteen or twenty K that makes quite a difference.'

He looped her bergen over his shoulder and set off. Christian caught her eye as she fell in behind him.

'Impressive,' he said quietly.

They trudged on through the day with the sun right above them. Walking became easier as the ground changed from the soft dust to a harder version where their boots left little imprint. Raglan periodically consulted his GPS and made minor adjustments to their route. By late afternoon, Christian found himself squinting at the foothills of the Udedi Mountains, which made up the southern aspect of the Ethiopian Highlands. They pushed on through dry, knee-high grasses and then stepped from one large stone to the next as they crossed a dry river bed. Either side of them rose steep valleys dotted with small bushes.

Christian felt relief as Raglan raised his hand to signify the next stop. Dharia instantly flopped to the ground and started pulling at the laces of her walking boots.

'Blisters?' said Raglan, sitting down next to her.

'Nope,' Dharia lied.

Christian sat down too, wondering if he looked as

knackered as Raglan, whose sweating face was caked with greyish dust that emphasised the lines across his forehead and around his eyes. He rubbed his fingertip down his cheek and, on examining the grey mush under his nail, guessed he probably did. Dharia, on the other hand, appeared not to have broken a sweat.

Once they had consumed the next round of rations, Christian reached for his cigarettes. Raglan broke the silence.

'Let's have a well-earned smoke. Might get rid of some of the mozzies.'

'So what's the plan for finding them in all these valleys?' said Dharia. 'Surely they could just walk straight past us and we'd never know?'

'Well, that's certainly a risk,' said Raglan. 'But Antcliff's people say there are a couple of obvious routes through here. In fact, the valleys are to our advantage.'

'How come?' Dharia looked confused.

'If we were out in the desert or in the bush, there could be a hundred possible routes. They could be within a mile or so and we might not see them. In the hills, it's different. They'll be funnelled along the bottom of the valleys. Far fewer routes available unless they start hopping over ridges.'

'Which they're not going to, I suppose,' said Dharia.

'So,' Raglan continued, pointing at the ground beside him, 'we need to cover off this valley and the one next door. That should do it.'

Christian took a drag on his cigarette and blew the smoke at the tower of mosquitoes hovering above them.

'Pass me that AK,' he said to Raglan. 'I'll give it a look over. Better make sure it actually works.'

'Cheers, Christi,' said Raglan, passing it over. 'Dharia, you and I'll stay around here and Christian will be over there watching next door. We'll get visual on them and then link up again and work out where best to knock them out.'

'Probably best if I get going then,' said Christian. 'It'll be dark in an hour and I might as well get up and over the ridge in daylight.'

Raglan nodded as Christian hauled himself to his feet.

'Looks like you'll have to restore this antique yourself,' said Christian, passing the AK back to Raglan. 'Let's turn on the sat phones for five minutes on each even hour.'

'Sure thing. We'll talk later, but no grabbing them both for yourself.'

Christian pulled his bergen onto his back and set off north across the valley. Initially the ground fell away beneath him, but soon he felt the burn in his thighs as he powered his way up the incline of the far side. He navigated between rocks and piles of hard-baked chunks of landslipped earth, looking for the best route up. Working at his own pace felt good. He had a rhythm and only half the weight he had been carrying for most of the day.

Being careful not to skyline himself, he quickly crossed the top of the ridge. A pang of irritation shot through him as the terrain in front of him came into view. He dropped down thirty metres or so and squatted next to a clump of thorny little bushes to think. Despite the fading light, he could see the supposedly tight, narrow and funnelling valley was at least three kilometres wide with a complex network of gorges, gullies and river beds dissecting at all angles. Worse still, there was enough vegetation along the bottom to hide a herd of elephants.

He glanced at his watch and saw it was 19.57. Just enough time to calm down before calling Raglan. Halfway through a cigarette, he made the call.

'Fucking geeks,' he muttered as the call connected.

'What's that?'

'Hannibal could come through here in broad daylight and I wouldn't have a clue,' Christian went on.

'Harry who? said Raglan, his voice switching from concerned to confused.

'Hannibal. I said Hannibal could come right through here with his whole bloody great army.'

'What, the Roman geezer?'

'No, well, yes, that's the guy. But he wasn't actually Roman.'

'Yes, he was.'

'OK, Hannibal, the Roman geezer then, could come right through here with his whole bloody great army.

Either way, the geeks have fucked up. The satellite imagery must be from a different time of year or something. There's vegetation and cover galore, so anyone could come through here and I wouldn't have a clue. Forget the funnelling concept.'

'Oh, fucking hell,' groaned Raglan.

Christian had a moment to think as he heard Dharia's voice in the background and Raglan summarising the situation.

'OK. I'm going to keep up high tonight,' said Christian. 'Then, at first light, get down onto the flat and check out any obvious pathways. You know, the obvious route through. I can then hover about and do my best to pick them up.'

'Roger that,' answered Raglan. 'It's going to be much more obvious this side, which probably means they'll go your way. I'll contact the Ant and update him. They might be able to help. Get a drone up or something.'

'What I need is eight of my guys from D. Boots on the ground, not more intel from boffins in an office the shape of a frigging doughnut.'

'You know we can't do that. The slightest whiff of boots on the ground and they'll be spooked to shit round here. They'll just go to ground and we'll never get inside.'

'Sure, sure, I know that,' answered Christian. 'Sorry, just not quite used to doing things this way. I'll do my bit this side.'

'Roger that,' said Raglan. 'They should come right past here under our noses in the next twenty-four hours, but if we miss them, we miss them. Shit happens. Simple as that. Comms on again at oh-four hundred and then two-hourly.'

Christian pressed the button to end the call, twisted the aerial back and stowed the sat phone in his bergen. Taking advantage of the last of the remaining light, he followed a contour along under the ridge to the point where he felt he had the broadest view of the valley. He settled himself down between some rocks and tried to get comfortable enough to have a sleep. After an hour of fidgeting and moving from one side to the other, he made it into a light doze. What felt like every few minutes, he awoke for no apparent reason. Sure, he was far from comfortable, but he was not either wet or cold nor especially hungry. This was relative luxury compared to the hell of the OP back in Sierra Leone. Also, for the time being, he was not in particular danger but still his sleep was fitful.

21

Around midnight, Christian's eyes opened, but for a legitimate reason. He heard a scratching noise followed by something brushing through bushes. His hand moved slowly for the cold, metallic reassurance of his SIG Sauer. He turned his head in the direction of the noise and his eyes searched the darkness. More scratches and now a growling came from a little distance downhill. Growing in awareness, Christian moved his hand from his gun to the handle of his commando knife. He gripped it hard, feeling tightness in the skin around his knuckles from the swelling of insect bites. If it was just an animal, he would not risk the noise of a bullet.

Slowly he rose to a crouching position, his head cocked to one side. More scraping but from a different direction. Maybe several creatures? A pack of some kind? He had no idea what roamed at night in the

Ethiopian Highlands. On a normal operation, someone would have briefed him as to what to expect. Likely story now. He looped his arm through his bergen and stood up. He would slowly back off uphill.

He felt the electrical jolt of adrenalin before his brain had time to rationalise what he had seen. An orange eye winked in the darkness. Christian drew the SIG Sauer and looked again more carefully. It was not an eye but the flicker of a fire. A campfire away down in the valley. He took a deep breath, unsure whether he felt relieved or not. He focussed and tried to revisualise the area before him from memory. As far as he could remember, it had all looked roughly the same. Trees, scrub and a network of river beds.

Forgetting all thoughts of prowling carnivores, he pulled out his compass and took a bearing on the tiny glow. He set off downhill and within a few hundred metres he was pushing through a waist-high wall of tiny, tugging thorns. He eased a few degrees off the bearing and, taking sideways steps, inched his way forwards. Clear of the bushes, he found himself ducking below the lower branches of trees, his left hand holding the compass, the SIG Sauer in his right. Wiping what felt like cobwebs from his face and hair with his sleeve, he edged along, keeping as close to the bearing as the terrain and darkness permitted.

The faintest scent of wood smoke caused Christian to freeze. He dropped silently to one knee and turned his head to listen. Over the occasional soft sigh of wind gusting through trees, he identified what he thought was a human cough. He glanced up at the night sky, wishing for a crack in the cloud base to alleviate the intensity of the darkness. Now hearing nothing bar the night-time call of insects, he crept forward, increasingly aware of the crunch of each step. With sweat glistening on his forehead and dripping a dusty solution into his eyes, he raised his shemagh from around his neck and wrapped it round his face and head. Whoever was sitting out in the bush at the dead of night in the no-man's land between Somalia and Ethiopia was hardly going to be friendly. The best-case scenario would be an abandoned fire. He could pick up some tracks and follow whoever it was from a safe distance while he assessed what to do. Equally OK, it might be local tribesmen out on a hunting party, but more likely, and less OK, patrolling militiamen or people on the run from them. Or, of course, Antcliff's theory might be right. It could be the asset.

Christian pushed the compass back into the pocket of his shirt and buttoned it up. Taking a couple of seconds to listen between each step, he moved forwards. He paused as his nostrils signalled a more defined smell of woodsmoke. A metre further, his eyes narrowed as they locked onto a tiny chink of orange light directly in front of him. Anticipating some form of tripwire or early warning mechanism, he took over a minute on his hands and knees to cover the next ten metres.

He had no need to part the vegetation before him. He could see enough. Illuminated by the glowing embers of the final stages of a small campfire, sat a bearded man with an AK silhouetted across his knees. Next to him, either side of the fire, two men lay sleeping. Christian craned his neck to get a better view of the man facing his way. It was a young face, cradled in the palm of a hand and clearly unaccustomed to sleeping rough. It was also one that Christian had etched into his mind.

He waited long enough to make sure that no fourth man was taking a shit behind a nearby tree before taking advantage of a noisy gust of wind weaving through the trees to cover any possible sound of his retreat. Fifty metres back, he got up from his hands and knees and sat against the trunk of a tree. It was 12.45 a.m. and he had the mother of dilemmas. He had agreed with Raglan not to turn the phone on again till 4 a.m. This made sense, otherwise they would have had hardly any sleep. Every even hour was fine in the daytime. This meant Raglan would not be back on air for over three hours, by which time it would be almost light and the asset might well be on the move. It would certainly be daylight by the time Raglan and Dharia caught them up. Much harder to strike and much more likely to be rumbled.

With his knees tucked up against his chest and his chin resting in the palm of his hand, Christian tried to think. The one thing that he knew for sure was that his usual power of analysis was shot from lack of sleep. He remembered from the endless duress training that the default position was to make safe, unambitious and flexible decisions. But there might only be one chance. He could walk back to Raglan, but what if they got back and found the fire covered over with earth and no tracks?

Looking up through the branches of the tree at a patch of stars that had appeared through the clouded sky, he ran his fingers around the edges of the packet of cigarettes in his shirt pocket. Cigarettes were for moments like these but he couldn't risk the smell of tobacco. Not for the time being. But the quicker he did the job, the quicker he would be lighting up. He unclipped the belt of his bergen and slipped out of the straps. He stood up and, with adrenalin already pumping, rolled up his sleeves and tucked his shirt into his trousers to make sure nothing could get between his hand and his pistol. Back on his hands and knees, he started back in the direction of the fire.

The insect calls and wind in the trees played second fiddle to the pounding thump of his heart as the orange glow came into direct view once again. His grip on the handle of the commando knife in his right hand felt inadequate and weak. Sweat leaked from his pores and his damp shirt sucked against his upper arms as he crawled into position.

Christian observed the same scene except from a different angle. He saw the face of the second man lying on the ground: young, chubby and thinly bearded. Knowing that hesitation was his greatest enemy, he manoeuvred around in the undergrowth to within a metre of the sitting man with the AK. Silently, he raised himself from his hands and knees into a crouching position. He pounced forward, grabbing his target around the head with his left hand. In one fluid movement, he yanked the man's head up and backward while sinking the commando knife through the larynx. Pulling the knife back through ninety degrees, he felt the resistance of tearing muscle tissue confirming that he would have severed the jugular.

With nothing but a stifled gasp and a kick of his legs, the dead man flopped sideways. Christian sprang forwards into the orange glow and landed both his knees on the chest of the closer of the sleeping men. The man's eyes were already wide open and his body rigid with fear. His arms flapped up to shield his face and he twisted sideways. Christian gripped one of his forearms, pulling him back and flat on his back. Then came the scream. High-pitched and desperate. Not a scream for help, a scream of terror and finality. Christian felt himself pause for a fraction of a second as his victim wrapped his free arm around his neck to protect his throat. Christian changed his grip on the blood-soaked handle of the knife and plunged it down into the man's heart. The scream continued as Christian shifted his weight from his knees onto his toes, thereby increasing the pressure on the knife. Feeling the blade penetrate another couple of inches and stick, he twisted the handle. The blade responded and tore in further, to the point that Christian's fist pressed against the entry wound, momentarily stemming the volcano of blood. He hauled back on the handle of the knife, the scraping of serrated metal on bone audible over the subsiding scream.

The third man had flicked off the coat draped over him and had made it to his feet. Wobbling like a newborn giraffe, he plunged headlong into the darkness. Christian leapt over the remains of the camp fire and took off after him. Within less than ten metres, Christian's outstretched hand gripped cloth. He clenched his fist and jumped, wrapping his legs around the man's hips. The effect was instant and they crashed to the ground with Christian on top.

'Please don't, please, please. I'm a British citizen,' wailed the man, twisting round.

Christian was aware of a Midlands accent, but the words themselves washed over him. He reached forwards with his left hand and pinned the man's head against the ground. With his right, he plunged the knife into his neck a couple of inches below the ear. Beneath, he felt the body stiffen and heels drum against his lower back. Christian pulled the blade towards him and felt the warmth of blood gushing across the back of his hand. The heels stopped and the man's arms made a final movement, as if attempting front crawl.

Christian straightened up and found that he had to wiggle his knife out. With a sucking noise, he pulled it free. Still sitting astride the body, he cocked his head to one side. It took him a couple of seconds to realise that the moaning noise from beneath him was caused by his own weight slowly squeezing the remaining air from his victim's lungs up through the vocal cords. He stood up quickly and the death groan sounded its last.

Tilting his wrist towards the sky, Christian looked at his watch. He squinted and adjusted the angle further, hoping to see the luminous hands. A feeling of nausea churned in his stomach as he found himself having to spit on the face of his watch and wipe the blood off with his finger. But knowing the time would at least provide him with some tiny connection with the ordered world. It was 01.05 and three hours until Raglan would turn on the phone.

He bent down, grabbed hold of a leg and dragged the body back towards the campfire. He stepped into the ring of orange and looked around. The embers glowed sufficiently to reveal the head of the first man at an impossible angle, his ear resting on his shoulder. Christian stooped and took hold of the feet. As he pulled the body towards him, the head lolled and twisted around to face backwards. Christian dropped the body and used his foot to push the head around the right way. His final task was to roll the last body over once. He hauled on an arm and all three lay side by side. Seeing the discarded coat on the ground, he laid it carefully over their faces.

Taking a couple of steps back, Christian reached for his cigarettes in his shirt pocket. He fumbled with the button and realised his hands were shaking too much to undo it. A surge of anger coursed through him and, before he had time to think, he had torn the button off and was scrabbling at the packet. He pulled out a cigarette and, holding his lighter in two hands, lit up. Dragging hard, he picked up the AK from the ground and stepped forward to kick some earth onto the last of the embers. If he had seen the glow from a distance, someone else might too. The orange gave way to darkness and Christian turned away and pushed his way back through the trees to find his bergen.

He sat down heavily under the tree. Reaching for another cigarette to light off the remains of the first, he found his fingers sticking to one another. Thankful for the darkness and knowing he did not have the water to spare, he rubbed his hands in a mixture of dead leaves, grass and earth in an effort to get rid of the congealing blood. His hands and arms were still filthy but it did not feel quite so bad.

Christian looked up at the same patch of stars through the same crisscross of branches and listened to the breeze still gusting through the trees. Somehow he expected the natural world around him to be up in arms in reaction to the heinousness of the triple murder. The branches should have turned to witches' fingers with the last cries of dying men hanging in the rustle of the wind. But it was not like that. The stars didn't care and nor did the wind or trees. It was only inside his head that the sounds of steel puncturing ribcages and slicing through human flesh still echoed.

He lit his third cigarette from the stub of the second. The moment he took a drag he realised he did not really want it. He snuffed out the end and slid it back into the packet. He lifted the AK onto his knee and started to strip it down. It would take him twenty minutes to go through it. That would be twenty minutes' less thinking time.

Having done his best to loosen up the working parts of what he guessed had to be a thirty-year-old rifle, Christian tilted back against his bergen. He shut his eyes and slipped in and out of a light doze. Each time he woke, he held his wrist to his face to check the time.

At 03.40, he decided to stay awake for fear of missing the 04.00 call slot. He lit the end of the partially smoked cigarette, and positioned the sat phone against his leg. On the nail of 04.00 he made the call.

'Hello, lad,' said Raglan purposefully. 'Take it you're calling for a reason?'

'You could say so,' replied Christian, lowering his voice and looking around.

'Go on.'

'I'm about an hour's tab from you. I expect you saw the direction I took. Just head over the ridge, like I did, and slight left down the other side. I'm in an area of trees and stuff in the bottom of the valley. Call if you need exact coordinates.'

'What's happened? You OK?' Raglan asked.

'On mission. Job done. Your man Ant was right. Just think Macbeth.'

'Macbeth?'

'Yes, Macbeth. Surely . . .'

'Heavens, sounds serious, lad. We're on our way.'

22

Christian leant back against his bergen and tried to shut his eyes. Once Raglan turned up they would be off and into the next phase of the operation. So far, things had not been too far removed from regular SAS soldiering. From here on in, though, things would be hanging on a thread of bluff, bullshit and luck. A lot of it. The bluff and bullshit felt reasonably OK, but it was the luck element that was most worrying. The other bits could be managed, but if luck was in short supply, that would be it. A brutal and protracted death at the hands of some ultra experienced sadists.

With the peaks along the ridge on the far side of the valley turning a bright, sun-washed pink, Christian knew that any further sleep was likely to be wishful thinking. He sat up in the half light and resisted the need for another cigarette. He took off his watch and concentrated on using the fastening pin to push little cylinders of dried blood out of the holes in the strap. How would his parents cope with being told he had been killed for a second time? Would they believe Deveral? In the unlikely event his body ever made it back, would they quietly slip it into the grave he already had in the Regimental Cemetery? Would they change the date on the gravestone? Having two graves would be a bit odd. Also, if he did make it back alive, would it be too weird to go and have a look at his own grave?

At 05.00, Christian guessed Raglan and Dharia had to be close. He had just decided that he would wander slowly back towards the ridge in an effort to find them, when he heard a whistling tune. He waited a second and then called out.

'Hello! Over here.'

There was a movement in some bushes and Raglan appeared, shouldering Dharia's bergen.

'Christi!' he said, waving an arm. 'There you are. OK?'

Dharia emerged a moment behind him. As they drew closer, Christian saw the looks of concern across their sweating faces. Raglan's forehead furrowed and he reached out to rest his hand on Christian's shoulder.

'Bit of a scrum down, was it?' he said, tugging at Christian's shirt.

Christian looked down at himself in the dawn light and realised how shocking he appeared. The right-hand side of his shirt was stiff with dried blood. Mixed with dust and sand, it was all down his trousers too and congealed into the laces of his boots.

'Kind of, I suppose. Come on, let's deal with the guys. Then I'll get sorted,' he said, directing a small nod of greeting towards Dharia.

Christian led them through the trees to the site of the camp fire. They stood together without speaking. Several dark brown rings of blood contrasted with the dusty earth. Raglan stepped forwards and had to stretch over a headland of crimson a metre wide that surrounded the three outstretched bodies. He caught hold of the coat covering the faces and pulled it slowly away. They stood in silence for several more seconds before Raglan spoke.

'Shitting hell, Christi. Looks more like a mortar strike.'

Christian stared down at the bodies. Dharia raised her hand to cover her eyes and turned away into the bushes. Flies crawled all over the faces of the dead men, looking for the easiest way in through the eyes, noses and mouths. Worse still was the head of the bearded man, whose lips appeared to have fallen prey to some kind of small, gnawing carnivore, leaving his long tobacco-stained teeth exposed in a permanent grimace.

'Guns for show, knife for a pro, as they say, Christi,' said Raglan. 'Come on, let's get through their kit as fast as we can before they start to bloat.'

Christian nodded slowly, feeling the cogs of his mind start to turn once again. Trying not to breathe too deeply, they went through the pockets of the dead men, pulling out a bizarre assortment of personal effects, including letters, family photos, notebooks, strings of coloured beads and rolls of US dollars.

'Didn't think these lads would be into footie,' said Raglan, holding up a Leicester City cigarette lighter.

'It's the photos that do my head in. Anyway, Leicester are crap, aren't they?' said Christian.

'That's not absolutely true,' Raglan countered. 'They've had their moments. I think they've had some very reasonable players over the years but have always been let down by shitty managers.'

'Are we going to bury these guys or what?' said Christian, watching Raglan emptying the contents of various bags onto the ground.

'Yes, we'll bury them. We'll put the two Leicester supporters together and we'll put the guide in his own grave a few hundred metres away. That means if someone comes looking and finds the two bodies, they'll assume it was the guide that killed them and vice versa if they just find the guide's remains. Make sense? All together and there would have to have been a third party.'

'Yeah, yeah, I get it. Also, we should probably load up with as much of their clobber as we can and stash any of our obviously military kit.'

'Sure, but let's get these guys in the ground first. Beardy here's starting to freak me out. But we'll do it properly so they face the correct way and lie on their right sides.'

'The burial is important and we must do it the right way,' said Dharia, reappearing. 'I will show you how it's done.'

It was 07.00 by the time the bodies were buried. Pouring in sweat, they kicked fresh earth across the large, reddish brown smudge that was the only remaining evidence.

'Couldn't leave it looking like the surface of Mars,' muttered Raglan. 'Let's get moving and I'll call Antcliff and check everything's OK from his perspective. We'll get some rations later on. I couldn't eat right here anyway.'

They hoisted their bergens onto their backs and set off in the usual order. After about a mile, Raglan pulled out his phone and held it to his ear. Christian could not hear what he was saying but saw him punching away at the buttons of the GPS with his other hand. Once the call was over, Raglan called back over his shoulder.

'There's been no change to anything their end, so in theory all we have to do is rock up to the RV which is about twenty-five K from here.'

'And then start being convincing wannabe militants,' replied Christian.

'And explain who the fuck I am,' added Dharia.

'You didn't use language like that three days ago,' said Christian.

'It's all your fault,' retorted Dharia. 'You've changed me.'

'If they buy us, they have to buy you too. Otherwise you wouldn't be with us. It'll be fine,' continued Raglan confidently.

'That's assuming al-Shabaab aren't quite as sexist as you two,' retorted Dharia.

They followed the line of the valley for the next couple of hours before turning left and into the next. Christian had started to notice the weight of the extra kit when Raglan drew them to a halt in a shaded area of vegetation. They sat in a circle and ate as much of their remaining rations as they could. It was not until Christian passed round his cigarettes that conversation started.

'We'll stash any leftover rations here along with the guns and the sat phones. From now on we have to be fully legit,' said Raglan. 'I'm Aashir, and Christi, you're Husam, which, according to Antcliff's notes, means sword or long knife in Arabic.'

'I know,' replied Christian, sighing audibly. 'I was waiting for that. So, what did Aashir mean? And shouldn't it have a T on the end of it?'

'Probably,' said Raglan. 'Can't actually remember. Think it meant servant of someone or other. But on the subject of names, obviously I know who Macbeth was, but what did he actually do?'

'He was a Scottish nobleman that killed the king with a knife and tried to nick his kingdom.'

'Even I know that,' chipped in Dharia, rolling her eyes.

'And he made a bit of a mess of it?' asked Raglan.

'Well, he killed him OK, but the whole thing was a bit bloody, let's say.'

'That's what I meant. Didn't his wife put him up to it?' said Raglan, grinning at Dharia.

'On the subject of blood and guts, Christi, you really need to change,' said Dharia.

'I will, I will,' said Christian. 'From here on, it's got to be full-on militant.'

While Christian changed into a long brown and red striped shirt and baggy black cotton trousers, Raglan busied himself separating their kit into two piles.

'Right, Dharia,' he said with a tone of exaggerated authority. 'That's the kit we're taking and that's what we're stashing. I've deliberately left one small telltale item in the pile we're taking. See if you can find it?'

'Missing the Army, are we?' said Christian.

'Just making sure I haven't missed anything. And, yes, I am, rather. Anyway, at least it gives me a decent excuse to finish off my last couple of cigars. Right, I'd better get into some civvy clobber too.'

'This,' said Dharia, holding up a curled piece of grey plastic. 'It's from the top of a ration pack. An army one.'

'Nice one, Dharia. No flies on you,' said Raglan.

'Shame we can't say that about me,' growled Christian, scraping dried blood from the laces of his boots with a twig. 'I still feel like a walking abattoir.'

'Relax, Christi,' said Raglan. 'By the time we hit the RV, which should be later this afternoon, you'll have sweated it off you.'

'That makes me feel a whole lot better then,' said Christian, not looking up. 'Come on, let's stash this lot and fuck off.'

Raglan stuffed the kit they were not taking into his bergen and scooped a hole in the soft, crumbling earth in front of a rock. Once he had covered it over, he took a waypoint on his GPS. He read the number out loud several times and then scrolled through the memory and deleted it.

'This way, I think,' he said, gesturing with his hand. 'Sun on our backs first.'

Christian felt relieved to be walking again. It was time to get into the next phase. The whole operation depended on whether or not they could pull off the bluff. And with each step they took, they were that much closer to finding out. Antcliff's interception and manipulation of the email communication between the al-Shabaab handlers and Leicester might have been faultless, but one dumb comment could blow it. The language barrier would be their closest ally.

For the rest of the morning, they followed a network of dusty valleys, all strewn with rocks and the occasion flash of vegetation hinting at some form of moisture within the ground. They stopped once in a shaded spot at the bottom of a small cliff for a drink and a smoke. Christian watched Raglan puffing faster than usual on his last cigar and knew he was not the only one feeling tense. They were up and off again, walking a fraction faster than before. A black speck in the air above caught his eye. He glanced up and tried to identify the lone black bird gliding above them. Too big for a crow, he reckoned – it might be some sort of raven. Whatever it was, he was pleased when he looked up and it was gone.

Just after 16.00, Raglan drew them to a halt and dumped Dharia's bergen hard on the ground. Dharia immediately sat down on top of it and started pulling off her boots. From the way she had been walking, Christian was not surprised to see a thick flap of skin hanging off the ball of her right foot. She ran the side of her finger slowly over it, pushing out a mixture of blood and pus. She slipped her sock back on and replaced her boot.

'We're within five or so Ks of the place these guys are due to meet. The RV was set for any time today, not an exact time,' said Raglan, still looking at the screen of the GPS. 'So hopefully not too much more walking.'

'So in theory, we're pretty much in theatre,' said Christian, looking around.

'Guess so,' Raglan said. 'Not really sure if I'm pleased about that or not. But anyway, we're here, and so far so good.'

'There's nothing good about my foot,' said Dharia.

'Well, apart from that, it's been OK,' Raglan insisted. 'Now, we need to keep going a bit further north and then cut over some high ground so we can look down into the valley where we're meant to RV. That way we can see a bit of what's going on before we steam on in.'

'Sure,' said Christian. 'Makes sense.'

Christian's hand beat Raglan's to the shoulder strap of Dharia's bergen and he hoisted it to his shoulder. They continued slowly along in the same direction for fifteen minutes, then turned through ninety degrees and set off uphill. Christian watched Dharia's head bob to the right with each step. Her clenched fist said it all. He knew the pain.

With the terrain getting steeper, Raglan turned back and looked down.

'OK, folks,' he said quietly. 'In a moment, we'll be summiting over here and able to have a spy into next door.'

A couple of minutes later, they had crawled across a flat area of sharp, slate-like rocks and lay side by side looking down into a valley.

'I thought there would be something different,' said Dharia, breathing heavily and looking underwhelmed. 'Are you sure we're in the right place?'

Raglan smiled.

'Yup. This is it alright. Conspicuously mundane and ordinary, wouldn't you say, Christi?'

'I would.' Christi shielded the sun from his eyes with his hand. 'But what's interesting is that this valley has three easy ways in: each end, and that piece of low ridgeline in the middle.'

'So it does,' said Raglan. 'We'll just lie here for a while and get a feel of the place.'

'Suits me,' answered Dharia, twisting over and reaching for her boots.

'You know you should only ever take one boot off at a time,' whispered Christian.

'It's fine for me. My feet don't smell quite like yours.'

'It's not really about smell. It's more about being able to leg it at short notice' said Christian, still staring down into the valley.

'I won't be legging it anywhere with feet like this,' she replied, pulling her right foot up almost parallel to Christian's face.

'OK, OK, fair enough,' he gasped, recoiling away.

'Fucking hell, love,' hissed Raglan. 'You're not in a good way. You really need to get them seen to. If they get infected, we'll really be in the shit.'

'And they're what's attracting the flies now,' said Christian.

'Fuck it, folks, let's get down there,' said Raglan. 'Can't see anything happening. I reckon they'll be in amongst those trees down the bottom. That's if they're here at all.' He stood up.

Once Dharia had squeezed her feet back into her

boots, they made their way off the summit and took long, slow steps downhill. As the ground flattened out, they climbed through a waist-high maze of eroded gullies and found themselves brushing through tall grasses towards the area of trees. Christian felt his heart beating faster and noticed himself breathing deeply. He had prepared for this moment in his mind. He'd know if they were suspicious. He thought of the notes and silently repeated the names of the streets that ran parallel with the one where they lived in Leicester. He visualised the house, the front door and the mosque. It was the details that mattered.

Raglan walked slowly into the trees, his head turning from side to side. Dharia limped closely behind him. Christian paused, looked around, then down. In the dry earth on the ground before him, an unnatural shape had caught his eye. He looked more closely. The horseshoe-like imprint of a heel mark was clearly visible. He let out a quiet whistle and Raglan turned. Christian pointed two fingers towards his eyes and then at the ground. As Raglan nodded his understanding, there was motion to the right and the air was suddenly filled with shouting.

23

Christian spun around in time to see four heavily armed men in desert combats and ops vests appear from nowhere. They charged forward, waving assault rifles, all yelling. Three more soldiers spilled out of the trees in front of them and two popped up to the rear.

Raglan muttered something that Christian could not hear over Dharia's scream. Within a couple of seconds, they were encircled by a dozen soldiers all jabbing at them with their rifles and still shouting. Christian raised his hands and tried to assess the situation. These guys were real soldiers with matching uniforms and proper weapons. They certainly were not the militia-style rabble from the day before. The flash eliminator three inches from his nose was attached to a new M16 A2 assault rifle. It was what they used. Sure, they were shouting a bit too much for a 'hard arrest', but they had kept themselves pretty covert until the right moment. They had darkish skin but definitely were not African troops. No visible insignia.

Christian knew the procedure. He waited with his hands raised for someone to identify himself as being in command. Raglan had his hands raised too and was gesturing to Dharia to raise hers.

'Shut the fuck up,' yelled a taller soldier with broad shoulders and a moustache. He was so close that Christian had to blink the spit out of his eyes.

It took him a moment to work out that the accent was American. It was hard to tell, due to the pitch, but it sounded Deep South. Without thinking, he shot Raglan a sideways glance. Immediately, he knew it had been a bad idea as the American swung a gloved fist at the side of his face.

It was not a hard punch – just something to keep up the momentum and maintain the edge – but the effect was disastrous. Dharia sprang forwards and shoved the big American with her forearm. With her finger wagging in his face, she yelled.

'Back the fuck off him now. Back off. You don't know anything.'

There was a momentary pause when Christian allowed a tiny piece of him to entertain the thought that she was not about to be hit. But he was wrong. Twisting his torso sharply round, the American smashed the stock of his rifle into Dharia's side. She let out a gasp as the air rushed out of her lungs. One of her legs seemed to buckle and, as she dropped to one knee, he hit her again. This time it was more of a flicking movement, sending the stock of the rifle hard against the side of her face. She fell sideways onto the ground, clasping her head in her arms.

Christian felt his body shudder as a wave of molten lava pulsed through him. He inhaled deeply and felt the anger swell in his chest. Someone grabbed his arms and he felt himself being pushed down and forwards onto the ground.

'Fuck her,' grunted the American to the soldier next to him. 'It's these two streaks of militant piss we're after.'

The American's words were translated into what Christian could now identify as Arabic. He felt a knee crunch into the small of his back and for a few seconds a hand pressed his face down into the earth. There was a tug followed by a zipping sound as he felt flexi cuffs tighten around his wrists. His head was pulled up and a second later things went black as a hood was yanked down over his face. Hands rummaged in his pockets and patted down his clothing.

With the shouting now over, Christian found it easier to manage his fury and to think. It was an American in charge of what were probably Egyptian troops. Whether he was CIA or mercenary was impossible to tell. Definitely not Delta; they wouldn't smash up an unarmed woman. Maybe he wasn't American?

He didn't have to be. He might just have the accent. But why in that case would he have the Southern-style drawl? He *was* American and so far it had been pro. That meant it was CIA-led with Egyptian SF providing the manpower. It had to be. So, in theory, he just needed to start shouting the fact that he was British SF and after some initial disbelief this big Yank would eventually suss they were for real. Of course, it would be Raglan's prerogative. He was in charge and technically at least he was the senior officer. It would be his call.

Around him, Christian heard several conversations going on in Arabic and what sounded like sobbing next to him. Then came a long and desperate female scream.

'Get the fuck off me!' wailed Dharia.

Christian heard a kicking noise and laughter. Lumps of earth landed across his back. Dharia screamed again, followed by the sound of tearing clothing. Her scream was piercing and close to hyster-ical. He knew she was tough and had experienced unimaginable hardship by normal standards, but things sounded like they were moving up a level. She was sure to flip.

'Easy, lad, easy,' murmured Raglan, pressing his shoulder against Christian's arm.

Christian coughed in quiet acknowledgement and felt an element of relief. Raglan was there and somehow his words suggested there were options and he had some kind of a grip. They just needed to keep quiet and go with it. But the next scream changed all that. It came from further away, perhaps thirty metres or so, but carried a sickening note of outrage. There was more laughter and then slaps followed by uncontrollable sobbing from Dharia.

Christian pressed his ear into the sand. He did not want to hear. Despite the pitch black inside the hood, he still clenched his eyes shut. This was appalling. When would Raglan call it? It should not be happening. After twenty minutes or so, the sobs subsided and were replaced by the occasional gasp. Christian counted the number of soldiers in his head. He had not seen for sure but he knew it was over ten.

His thought process was broken by a flash of white as he felt his body flip over from the force of a kick to the side of his head.

'If your bitch wasn't HIV-positive before, she certainly will be now,' laughed the American in Christian's ear.

It took Christian a couple of seconds to register the words. He felt surprise. Not from what the American had said but by his own reaction. He was not hit by an obvious wave of rage. He was beyond that. He was cold, focussed and contained. He had felt like this at the moment back in Sierra Leone when he had promised himself that he would deal with Sam. He had honoured that promise, against the odds. He was good at revenge and this Yank would find that out.

Hands grabbed Christian by the shoulders and hauled him to his feet. Clipped, aggressive language cut through the conversations that Christian could hear around him. There was a moment of silence before the American spoke.

'Move it, now! You sacks of shit.'

Now that he was standing up and the hood was no longer pressing against his face, Christian noticed that he could see the rough outline of shapes through the material. He slowly looked around and thought he could see Raglan being pushed in front of him.

Something hard pushed against his shoulder blades and they were off. Christian tried to remember the last time he had looked at his watch. It had been on the ridge. It had been 16.00 then, which meant it had to be about 17.00 by now. They were walking in a westerly direction into the sun. He started counting his paces but before he had even got to a hundred metres, the shape in front seemed to drop.

'Arrrh, fuck,' muttered Raglan.

Christian twigged in an instant and walked straight into Raglan, who was scrabbling to get back on his feet. He stumbled forwards over what felt like one of Raglan's legs. He staggered to get his balance and fell to one side. Before he had made it to his feet, the hood had been ripped off and he was blinking in the sun. He shot a glance at Raglan, whose hood had been pulled off too, and glimpsed the fleeting presence of tiny laughter lines around his eyes.

Raglan tucked his legs under him and in the process of standing pushed himself as close as he could to Christian.

'They've let her go,' he mumbled.

Christian took a good look around as he got to his feet. Sure enough, there was no sign of Dharia. He had expected her to be with them. But how did Raglan know they had actually let her go and had not just left her dead or killed her? If he was right, it had to be good news. She would head back to where they had hidden the kit and call Deveral or Antcliff on one of the sat phones. That would mean help was at hand. Deveral would sort things. It would take just one call to someone senior in Cairo or Washington and they would be released back into the game.

There were a couple of grunts from the American and they were off again at a fast walk. They followed the bottom of the valley for what Christian estimated was about three kilometres and then swung around towards flatter-looking ground to the north. At every twist and turn in the path, Christian tried in vain to catch Raglan's eye in the hope of gleaning more information. It had not occurred to him before but now it seemed obvious that Raglan must speak Arabic. How else could he know about Dharia?

After what felt like the best part of an hour, they rounded a tangle of thorn bushes and dropped down a sandy bank with a dust road below it. Christian immediately spotted a military lorry in desert camouflage parked under some trees just outside the long lines of ruts. He struggled down the bank, finding it hard to keep his footing without the use of his arms. Raglan slowed his pace and they were parallel for the time it took to exchange fleeting looks. Christian took a smaller, faltering step and slipped back into line to digest Raglan's 'Hope you're OK. Let's go with this for the time being' expression.

As they drew closer, a large white Land Cruiser became visible in the early evening shadow cast by the lorry. Relaxed sounding conversation broke out amongst the soldiers. Christian knew the feeling. They'd done the job they had come to do and were about to get in the vehicles, have a smoke and head back to base.

Raglan was shoved against the back of the lorry and manhandled up and through the opening in the canvas cover. Christian was bundled up behind him and pushed along until he found himself sitting next to Raglan with his back against the cab. Eight soldiers climbed in and occupied the more airy position at the back. There was a stuttering screech from a distant starter motor, a shudder and then the sound of an engine. Almost immediately the back of the lorry filled with diesel fumes, confirming in Christian's mind the rationale behind the seating plan.

Christian's eyes had already adjusted sufficiently to the relative darkness in the back of the lorry to see that most of the soldiers were gripping onto the metal bars supporting the roof. A second later, he slammed into Raglan's side as the wheels of the lorry lurched into the first line of ruts. He pushed out his legs as wide as he could in front of himself just in time to control his body for the second bounce. This time Raglan piled into him, ending up lying across his lap to raucous laughter from the soldiers.

Raglan gave a quiet but clearly sarcastic sigh as he struggled back into position next to Christian. Over the noise of the engine and chat from the soldiers, Christian whispered without moving his lips.

'How do you know about Dharia?'

Raglan pushed his knees up higher in front of him in an effort to cover his mouth.

'Speak a bit of Arabic. They were there waiting for us. They knew we were coming. They don't take women seriously and thought she was just a guide or something.'

'So they just gang raped her instead,' murmured Christian, feeling his hackles rising.

One of the soldiers sitting closest to them glanced their way. His face stiffened and he reached for one of the higher bars supporting the canvas roof. He pulled himself to his feet and made his along the back of the lorry. Balancing himself with one hand on the floor, he squatted in front of Christian. He raised a finger and wagged it in Christian's face while talking in a slow, condescending way. Without warning, he slapped Christian hard across the cheek with the back of his hand. He carried on the lecture, punctuated with a series of intermittent slaps.

Unable to understand a word of it, Christian nodded submissively and muttered 'yes, sir' at what felt like suitable moments. The strange thing was the condescending tone. Back in Sierra Leone his captors had treated him with extraordinary brutality but with almost unashamed fear too. He had been a trophy captive who might have broken his bonds at any second and killed the lot of them.

On the fifth or sixth slap, Christian tasted blood in his mouth and guessed he had a nose bleed. The soldier stood up and reached behind him to where an arm was holding out the hoods. The lights went out and Christian found himself being kicked across the floor of the lorry to a position against the side. He felt Raglan's feet against his ankles and guessed they were now sitting opposite one another.

Christian tilted his head back in an effort to stop the flow of blood, which felt like it was coming from his left nostril. It dripped down his chin and he felt the fabric of the hood sticking against his face. His hands strained at the flexi cuffs as he tucked his knees up and pushed his face forwards to wipe his itching chin on his knees. He focussed on the fact that Deveral would most likely know by now what had happened. It was just a matter of time until there would be a tap on the shoulder and a friendly word in the ear. Just like at the end of an interrogation resistance exercise.

But people did not get gang raped in exercises. These guys might be as friendly as hell once Dev made the call, but he would see justice done for Dharia. That was for sure.

The lorry bounced along and Christian bounced too. His face felt sore and his nose was so clogged with dried blood that he could only breathe through his mouth. He postponed the moment as long as possible but eventually he took a deep breath and blew the gunk out of his nostrils. He could breathe properly again, but the mixture of blood and snot stuck all over his face, combined with the diesel fumes and motion of the lorry, made him retch. He could not control the boiling surge within him. He rocked forwards onto his knees and felt the hood fill with warm, acrid vomit. Panic pumped through him as he gasped for breath. A second later, the hood was pulled off by a disgusted-looking soldier. Christian spat vomit from his mouth and took a breath. He pushed himself back into a sitting position and wiped the foul mixture from his face on the sides of his knees. He sat back, feeling light-headed and faint.

Raglan's head moved from side to side, as if he was looking around. His boot pressed gently against Christian's shin. It made a difference. Despite the fact that Raglan was cuffed and hooded, he was still there. Christian was not alone like before. He was with a man that Deveral regarded as one of the most outstanding SAS soldiers of his generation. At the same time, he was an eccentric Welsh hill farmer who shot foxes out of his kitchen window at nearly a kilometre with a sniper's rifle. He was also dead, and, in theory, Christian was too. Maybe they both really were? It might just be a matter of these soldiers dragging them out of the back of the lorry and shooting them. It would be too late to start announcing who they really were.

24

The dusk had pretty much given way to darkness when an intense light filled the back of the lorry. Even Raglan, still hooded, turned his head. The monotonous desert scrub was now fully illuminated by ultra-bright floodlights mounted at intervals along the top of five-metre-high 'super-max' security fencing. Christian's eyes blinked as he struggled to get as good a look as possible. Through the fence he saw an old-fashioned fort, like something from the days of the French Foreign Legion. It was grey and crumbling and a large section of the outer wall had collapsed. Lights shone from some of the tiny windows, hinting that it was in use. The lorry swung around and the soldiers in the back sat up and readied themselves.

Christian caught a glimpse of the white Land Cruiser as they turned and drove into a barbed wire cage. There was talking followed by the screech and clunk of a metal gate closing behind them. After thirty seconds or so, there were more voices and the metal on metal of a gate opening in front. The lorry moved forwards out of the caged area and drove through a high archway into the central compound of the old fort.

Christian was manhandled out of the back, closely followed by Raglan. As the big Yank stepped out of the Land Cruiser and walked towards them, he clocked half a dozen Portakabins raised on concrete blocks, one of which had a tall communications mast protruding from the roof. There were several new-looking pickup trucks, an armoured personnel carrier and a sandy-coloured T-90 Russian battle tank. Green and red drums of fuel were stacked in rows against the rear wall of the fort and the silhouettes of sentries stood out in several watchtowers. Whoever was running the place was clearly not taking any chances.

The Yank snapped his fingers and Christian found himself frogmarched through a small wooden door into an empty room lined with new breeze blocks. A single strip light in a wire cage provided the illumination and playground for a swarm of mosquitoes and tsetse flies.

'Against the wall now. Chin up and eyes front,' croaked the Yank, not looking at Christian. A soldier raised a camera and there was a blast of flash.

'Now sideways on. Move.'

Raglan was ushered in, still wearing the hood, his

shoulder hitting the door frame. He was pushed up against the wall and the hood was pulled off. He blinked a couple of times and jolted as the flash went.

'Right, you two sacks of shit, my name is Colonel Lee and I am authorised to hold you here by the legitimate Government of Somalia,' said the American, pointing at Christian and Raglan. 'It's my duty to inform you that you are . . .'

'Bullshit,' said Raglan, drawing out the word to mimic the Colonel's southern accent.

Time froze in the room as the shock of Raglan's remark hung in the air. The three soldiers standing behind the Colonel gawped at Raglan and then at each other. The Colonel's mouth fell open and Christian prayed he had misheard. Surely this was now the moment that Raglan would blow the cover and reveal who they were.

The Colonel took a breath and rocked on his heels. He clasped his hands behind his back and gazed at Raglan. A sideways smile cracked on his face that looked like it was designed to mask any possible hint of confusion. There was a pause before he spoke again. Christian knew he was battling his natural urge to punch Raglan to the ground, but he would need to demonstrate control and cool to authenticate his status. Colonels did not bash handcuffed detainees. That was the job of NCOs.

'You're going to regret that remark,' he growled. 'I know exactly who and what you two are. Now, I don't have the time to sit around and let you *bullshit* me with your cooked up cover crap. We know who you are. That's why we were there to pick you two dumb fucks up.'

The Colonel paused again. Christian could see he had recovered from the surprise of Raglan's comment and was back in control.

'Now we're a little full here, which means you'll have to have your own private accommodation tonight. Well, until such time as I feel like seeing you again.'

The Colonel grinned through a sheen of sweat, and turned to leave the room. Halfway through the door he stopped and looked back.

'I don't reckon folk of your calibre speak much French, but they built this place a long time ago with facilities to deal with trash like you. They called them the boo tay noir.'

It took Christian a moment to filter out the accent and to hear the words. It was *bouteille noire*. He knew that meant black bottle in French. He shot a glance at Raglan, whose raised eyebrows suggested he did not speak any French. As if expecting some sort of reaction, the three soldiers still in the room raised their weapons and started to shout and point. Christian and Raglan were jostled out of the room and along a dimly lit corridor with a flagstone floor and flaking walls. At the end on the right, one of the soldiers unlocked a rusty metal door leading to a flight of steps. Before

Christian had even passed through the doorway, he was hit by the thickness of the air and the reek of body odour. A hand shoved him. He ducked his head and started down the stairs.

As they reached the bottom, the soldier leading the way turned to gauge the expression forming on Christian's face. His first thought was that they had dropped into the belly of an eighteenth-century slave ship. Down one side of a wide open cellar were a series of metal cages, each full to bursting point with men lying or sitting in neat lines. He could not see clearly in the gloom, but some were African and others were bearded men of Arab appearance. Each wore a simple grey tunic. Whilst most of them stared at the floor, a couple glanced up with fearful faces.

Once they had been allowed to survey the scene, they were pushed forward once again. Christian cast a look at Raglan and felt frustration turning to anger. It was time to blow the whistle and call time. This was getting stupid. But Raglan's imperceptible nod seemed to say 'just a little longer'.

As they walked the length of the basement, Christian realised why the men were all in such orderly rows. The shiny metal of leg irons connected to a pole cemented into the floor down the middle of each cage glinted in the glow of the two light bulbs that hung on wires from the walls. At the far end, two men in green military fatigues sat in white plastic chairs that would have looked more at home in a pub beer garden. They looked up and Christian detected a hint of glee in their eyes as one of the soldiers behind him called out.

'*Bouteille noire.*'

There was a murmur amongst the prisoners which sent a ripple of fear through Christian. Most looked up now. Some shook their heads but they made no sound. Something was happening, and they obviously were not yet in the so-called *bouteille noire* as Christian had assumed they were.

The men in the plastic chairs got to their feet. Both had pistols in holsters attached to their belts and one held a metre-long bamboo cane in his hand. They greeted the soldiers with familiar-sounding grunts and walked towards the other side of the cellar, which had four unusually narrow doors spaced evenly along the wall.

Christian felt his arms yanked up behind him and heard a sharp clipping sound. As his arms came free, the three soldiers raised their weapons.

'Drink from this now,' said one of them, picking up a metal bucket from against the wall and thrusting it towards Christian. Detecting hesitation, the soldier continued.

'Or you will die.'

Christian took the bucket and raised it to his lips. Overcoming the metallic taste of rust, he tipped as much water down his throat as possible before the bucket was pulled roughly away from him. Raglan took a moment to take hold of the bucket as it was shoved aggressively at his chest. Christian saw the minute act of defiance and hoped Raglan would not be his usual pig-headed self. As Raglan raised the bucket and drank, one of the doors was pulled open.

Christian shuddered as he looked at the tiny space behind the door. It was painted black and was less than a foot deep and barely two feet wide, the upper section narrowing still further at head height. He turned to Raglan. This was the moment, surely? Raglan stared straight ahead.

Christian felt the sensation of pre-battle adrenalin flowing into his arms and chest. His hands tingled. This was the moment when he would have acted. Sure, it would have been insane and he would most likely have been shot to bits, but, once the heavy wooden door clunked shut on him, a ninety-nine per cent chance of being cut down by a wall of bullets would seem like the soft option. All he had to do was get behind one of the soldiers, control his weapon and the others would not dare fire. There would be a stand-off and he could work from there. He just needed the sign from Raglan. What the hell was the problem?

There was a sudden increase of energy and noise from the soldiers, which Christian knew was to overcome any kind of last stand or effort to resist. The stock of a rifle hit him squarely between the shoulder blades and he heard the cracking sound of the bamboo cane. His back was already against the wall before he had any sensation of pain. Hands pressed him back and the door started to close on three sets of iron hinges. With the door almost shut, his last image was the outline of a head jerking back. Warm saliva hit him in the face, and the darkness was complete. One by one, three bolts slammed.

25

Christian pushed himself back against the wall and breathed in sufficiently to create enough space to manoeuvre his left hand up over his chest to wipe the spit off his face. He understood what was going on and he knew that the new enemy was panic. That was the purpose of the cell. Intelligence services, however brutal, did not want half-starved detainees with missing fingernails and scars. There were plenty of ways of breaking men without leaving any evidence. However resilient, any man would be sent into meltdown by the gnawing sense of claustrophobia.

An image flashed into his mind. He was arriving in a large clearing in a forestry block during the first week of Selection and people were pointing at a series of manhole covers dotted around. They were told to strip off their webbing and lower themselves into a network of pipes half-filled with muddy brown water.

The covers had been replaced and they had to find their way out. Christian remembered a guy freaking out after about thirty seconds. He had been a steeple-jack before joining the REME and had been supremely confident during the high ropes confidence test. He was ultra-fit and boxed with the ferocity of a lion during the milling, but the first whiff of a confined space had flipped his lid. Eventually, someone had found a way out and told the Staff, who dragged him out. Christian could see him being led away towards a Land Rover, his whole body shaking and his eyes wild with fear.

A voice spoke inside Christian's head. It was the soft Scottish accent of the instructor on the interrogation resistance course. 'There's nothing I can say that can take the pain away,' he said. Christian remembered the occasion. He was being debriefed after he had been tied in a kneeling position, bollock naked, to a wooden shipping pallet for about twelve hours and continually hosed off with freezing water. 'But you need to think through what's going on and why they are doing it. Get inside their thinking and you'll regain a sense of control.'

Christian did not have to think hard to work out that the purpose of the bottle cell was not to kill him. He had not been put inside to suffocate or to starve to death. It was a softening-up process, and a pretty effective one. He rested his face against the rough wooden door and thought of the misery that must have been endured in this minute space in the hundred years or more since the fort had been built by the French to suppress the Abyssinians. Back then, men might have been put there to die, not just to break them down before interrogation. Then a twist of nerves stabbed Christian in the stomach. He was working on the assumption that he was being softened up, but he might be wrong. Clearly, they had been rumbled somewhere along the line, and if this big Yank really thought they were jihadists from the UK, killing them might be the cleanest solution. No need for awkward, politically harmful machinations between friendly governments whose relationship was already strained enough.

The knot of nerves tightened and Christian breathed hard to fight against the lack of air. His mind jumped from an ordered and coherent analysis to a sudden and desperate need to get out. His mind flashed white and the panic exploded within him. He had to get out. He could not stand the feeling of confinement a second longer. He thumped his forehead against the wood and back against the bricks behind him. Sweat poured down his face and he chewed at his lips and tongue. It was intolerable, but he would not allow himself to scream. The phobia had broken out; the cruellest kind of psychological torture. He clenched his fists and flexed his body one way then the other. It was a nightmare and the door had been shut less than a few minutes. How long would they keep him inside? They would not have filled him up with water if it were just for an hour or two. He could survive twenty-four hours without any material harm other than to his mind.

Christian did not know long it took for the rush of panic to subside. He tried to concentrate on anything but the minuteness of the space around him. He knew he was not prone to claustrophobia and tried to imagine how someone who suffered from the condition would cope. Would they go mad? Or faint? The panic retreated to his stomach but he could feel its latent presence. Just one uncontrolled thought and he felt his nerves swell and fear run through him. In theory, he just had to stand there. He felt exhausted and hungry but he was not actually in pain. Eventually the door would open and he would be released. There was life on the other side.

He thought of Raglan. How would he be coping? At some point, he would find out, and this ordeal would be behind him. He would be looking back and the phobia would seem irrational. Until then, he needed to keep calm and not freak out again. He tried to listen and see if he could pick up anything in the basement. Not a sound. It looked like some kind of punishment place where no talking or noise was allowed. He guessed the two bastards with the cane would beat the shit out of anyone who broke the silence.

With his back starting to ache, Christian rested the

front of his knees against the door and his backside on the wall. It did not make much difference but did something to improve the feeling of stiffness. Raglan's game plan had become clear in his mind and he was surprised it had taken him so long to work out. If they had screwed up on meeting up with the original al-Shabaab people, ending up in prison with a whole bunch of them might be an acceptable plan B. The fact that they had been stuffed into the bottle cells would make it pretty clear they had not been planted. Perhaps Raglan's 'Bullshit' comment had not been quite as moronic as it had seemed at the time. Still, it was a bizarre and high-risk way of doing things.

Christian allowed his mind to bounce about from one thing to the next. It felt like the mental equivalent of channel hopping but he did not care; anything to keep a lid on the panic. He had no idea what he was thinking when he felt his brain kick into gear. He opened his eyes and straightened up as best as he could. He turned his head a little to the side and listened. Sure enough, he had just heard one of the bolts being drawn back. A feeling of relief washed through him, followed by a pang of doubt as he thought it might be his imagination. There was a second scraping noise. This time louder. It sounded like the middle bolt being slid back. He had not imagined this. He braced himself for release. The third bolt scraped and he guessed it was face height.

Then came a feeling of deep bitterness. The middle

bolt scraped again and so did the bottom one. Fucking arseholes, thought Christian. It was no surprise, and he knew he should have anticipated it. It was no different from the lorry moving off at the end of a long march before anyone could get in. Christian pushed back against the wall and took control again. At least they knew he was still in there and it might well signal the halfway point.

He set off from the back door of his parents' house, climbed the post and rail fence into the field and headed down the bank of the river on his walk to the sea. Seagulls called to each other and the wind blew in his air. He blinked and he was with Deveral in his office. They were not talking, just sitting there either side of his desk. Another incoherent change of scene and he stood in the little sitting room of Armalite's terraced house in Hereford. He was looking at the collection of regimental photographs which covered every spare inch of wall. He knew the faces. Some seemed younger then: youthful and confident. His mind's eye searched out Tim and Jamie. They stood next to each other. He pictured just how they had fought and just how they had died. Without warning, their faces blurred and faded, becoming black cut-outs.

He tried to stop it but it was too late. Invisible scissors cut more faces from the line-up. He heard Andy's voice shout 'reloading' to his right. A mob of West Side Boys broke from the jungle and stormed his position. Their rusting machetes hacked away in slow motion. He was in another of the black holes. He looked around for Sam Carter, the man whose greed had caused all the carnage in the first place. He was nowhere to be seen.

Christian did not hear the bolts slide the second time. The first he knew of the door opening was his knees hitting the floor just outside. Subconsciously, his hands flicked out in front of him and saved him from a full face plant on the stone floor. There was noise around him and he felt something impact on his back. He squinted in the relative brightness of the cellar and pushed himself into a sitting position. The cages opposite were empty, and for a moment he wondered if he had dreamed the scene from the slave boat. Raglan lay a few feet away, his cheek resting on the floor and his arms out in front, as if he was attempting some feeble form of front crawl.

A different group of guards stood around, their weapons slung casually over their shoulders, hinting that prisoners released from the *bouteilles noires* posed no threat. Christian sucked in the oxygenated air and struggled to think through his headache, which felt like an electric current passing from one ear to the other in time with his heartbeat. Phobic fear gripped him once again as he imagined for a terrifying second that they might be about to be shoved back in. A rational thought slipped through the pulsating fuzz. Why let two delirious zombies out of the cells just to put them back in again to die? There was no point playing mind games on dead men.

With the fear still twisting inside him, Christian was pulled to his feet. His legs functioned somehow beneath him as he was hauled towards the stairway. He swivelled around just far enough to catch a glimpse of Raglan. He hung more or less limp, his arms supported by two expressionless guards. His mouth sagged open and his head lolled like a corpse. They passed through the metal door at the top of the stairs and along the corridor towards the bright light of the courtyard where they had been dropped off from the lorry.

Feeling like a fossil pulled from the ground, Christian flinched in the direct sunlight. His senses were rebooting from the dark void of the cell. Shadows fell from the ancient walls along which soldiers stood at intervals holding incongruously modern weapons. It had to be late afternoon or early evening, and that meant they had been holed up for the best part of eighteen hours. Great for Raglan's grand plan, but not for his shrivelled brain. They were marched across the courtyard, past the Portakabins and through a wooden doorway into a passage. They were then steered into a small, empty room with dirty walls and a grey concrete floor. They had hardly been able to obey the instruction to sit down when Colonel Lee filled the doorway behind them.

Christian looked up and remembered something

about interrogators liking to stand while their inter-
viewees sat or kneeled in a lower position. Pathetic,
he thought, but it was all part of the process.

'Still a bit short on accommodation, so if you two
cocksuckers would like to stay on down there, I'd be
much obliged,' he crowed, resting his elbow on the door
frame. There was a pause as he leant backwards.

'The fact is that you two bore me,' he continued.
'There ain't no shit I need to kick out of your sorry
arses. I know you come from some shitty street in
Leicester, Britain. I know you're just a pair of numb-
skull pricks who think it's big to come down here and
learn to fire an AK. Like some sort of bullshit stag
night activity.'

Christian saw life forming in Raglan's face and
prayed his brain was not starting up just yet. Even in
his state of dehydrated delirium, he surely knew
neither of them could take another minute in the cells.
Raglan opened and closed his mouth, then nodded.
The Colonel's eyes narrowed as he searched Raglan's
expression for the slightest sign of sarcasm.

'So, you'll be facing a seven- to ten-year stretch
back in your country of origin once we've done the
paperwork here. But, as I said, we are underresourced
here, so things take a while – say three to five years.'
He paused again, a smile cracking on his sweating
face. 'Then, of course, it's possible you may not be
well enough to travel. That's happened before.'

Christian's eyes became fixed on the faint imprint

of a boot set in what he thought was a newish concrete floor. He wondered what kind of person it would have been. Who built secret prisons in the Ethiopian Highlands where people could be holed up in coffin-sized cells or chained to the floor in rows? He looked back at the Colonel. He was still talking but the room looked like it had filled with mist. He tried to concentrate, but the electrical pulse between his ears had increased to a constant surge. His hands shook and he felt his jaw tremble.

The Colonel ended the lecture with a nonchalant shrug and backed out of the doorway. There was a series of grunts from the three guards and one moved forwards to kick Raglan as he struggled to his feet. They were hustled through the door, along the corridor and down some stone stairs into a cellar that looked like a mirror image of the one on the other side of the fort. Four separate areas were divided along the right-hand wall by old-fashioned jail-style bars, each roughly three by four metres. Modern wire cages were bolted to the floor inside. Faces peered at them from the end two, the expressions both anxious and inquisitive.

The sharp odour of unwashed human bodies kicked Christian's mind into life like smelling salts. As he looked around, a grey bundle and a pair of blue plastic flip-flops were pushed into his hands by a bearded guard who gestured at him to take off his clothes. Christian stooped and struggled with his bootlaces, which were still stiff with dried blood, sweat and dust. He peeled off his cycling shorts and trousers in one. Keeping his back against the cage in an effort to hide the scarring on the back of his shoulder, he stripped off his shirt and slipped the grey tunic quickly over his head. The door of the first cage was pulled open and he stooped to get inside. Raglan stumbled in behind him and immediately slumped down on the floor against the dirty whitewash of the back wall. A plastic bucket of water was placed on the floor just inside with a red plastic mug floating in it. The door was closed and locked with a heavy chain and padlock. Once the guards had disappeared up the stairs, Christian immediately snatched up the bucket and moved over to Raglan. He scooped up the mug and pushed it into Raglan's hand.

Raglan straightened himself up and drained six mugs of water before Christian pulled the mug out of his hand.

'Easy, or you'll be wetting your pants next,' he whispered.

'I haven't got any fucking pants on, have I?' growled Raglan.

Christian sat against the wall next to Raglan. He put the mug to his lips and felt the water slipping down.

'I guess they weren't trying to kill us after all,' he said when he'd finished. 'You OK?'

'Fuck, that was nasty, and you're taller than me.' Raglan turned sideways to look at Christian.

'You look like death.'

'I feel like death. Anyway, you don't look so hot yourself, lad.' Raglan gave the glimmer of a grin.

'And you reek of piss.'

'Don't tell me you didn't piss yourself too.'

A loud clang sounded at the top of the stairs. Through the echo, there was a second clunk and the three strip lights overhead momentarily morphed to glowing rods of orange before extinguishing altogether, plunging the cellar into total darkness. Immediately chatter broke out from the men in the end cages. Initially, Christian thought they were talking amongst themselves, but as the pauses grew longer between exclamations, it dawned on him that they were asking questions.

After thirty seconds or so, one voice stood out, speaking aggressively in English.

'Who are you?'

Christian felt Raglan's hand rest on his arm and his face close to his ear.

'Let's be careful, they might not be real prisoners,' he whispered.

'Sure, but don't forget we aren't us.'

'Ignore them anyway.'

'Suits me.'

'Who are you?' demanded the voice again.

There was a pause. Christian could not see Raglan's face but knew he was looking at him.

'*Who are you?*' hissed the voice, each word separated by the sound of a hand slamming against metal caging.

'Who the fuck are you, more like?' snapped Raglan without warning.

Christian raised his hands to his head and massaged his temples with his thumbs.

'Is there anyone round here you *don't* want to piss off?' he whispered. 'It amazes me you aren't dead.'

Raglan's reply was drowned out by a tirade of incomprehensible vitriol, punctuated by the rattle of metal and fists smacking into palms.

'Getting any of that?' said Christian.

'Well, not much,' replied Raglan. 'Something about a slow, painful death involving, I think, a piece of agricultural machinery of some sort.'

'I didn't think they had any agricultural machinery round here. Anyway, I'm going to die of starvation long before any of these cretins manages to jump-start a stolen . . .'

Christian was interrupted by the blast of the lights flashing on. Silence reigned. The same clang echoed down the stairs, over the sound of multiple footsteps descending at speed. Christian pushed his face into his knees and hoped Raglan would do the same. There was a rush of movement past their cage followed by the unmistakeable swish of canes in the air. What sounded like protestations of innocence were replaced by screams and sobs.

The frenzied pace of the caning eventually slowed

to a few last, tortuous whimpers. A voice spoke and there was silence once more. Boots tramped back along the cellar. Christian pressed his face harder into his knees. The boots stopped outside the cage and the dreaded sounded of chain sliding though the wire reached Christian's ears. He felt Raglan move next to him and nudge him. He looked sideways, meeting Raglan's eyes. He could not see much of his face but he read the question in his expression: 'I can handle it if you can?'

Christian shut his eyes and raised his arms to protect his face and head. He braced himself and felt adrenalin flow weakly around his body. There was a bang just above his head and he automatically found himself crouching lower. Something bounced off his shoulder and landed on the floor in front of him. He heard the chain and then the boots padding back up the stairs. As the door clanged shut, he looked up to see a small square cardboard box on the floor in front of him. He reached forwards and picked it up. Turning to Raglan, he spoke quietly.

'Yank twenty-four-hour ration pack.'

'Happy days,' sighed Raglan as darkness enveloped them once again.

26

The night crawled past for Christian. Each time he closed his eyes and tried to sleep, he felt the oppressive presence of the wooden door immediately in front of his face. He could taste the fetid air and feel the roughness of the brickwork behind him. He opened his eyes and pushed his hand forwards in the darkness around his head. Raglan breathed heavily beside him on the cellar floor and there was the occasional mutter from the far cage. He moved from lying stretched out into a sitting position in the corner. He would sit it out and hold on until morning came. If what the Colonel had said was in any way true, there would be plenty of time for sleep going forward.

Hunched in his corner, Christian finally heard the sounds of activity above. The stiffness in his back and legs made him suspect he must have been asleep at least some of the night. He felt an unexpected sensation of relief as the door groaned open at the top of the stairs and the lights pinged on. Raglan sat up with a start and looked around like a bewildered old man. A number of unshaven guards descended in their usual green fatigues and unlocked the end cage. The dozen or so occupants shuffled out and a series of scowling faces, of Arab appearance, processed past. Last in line, came a tall, bearded man with a bald head, his raised index finger discreetly sawing at his throat.

Raglan looked at Christian and shrugged.

'Could do with a piss,' he muttered.

A minute later, they were making their way up the stairs too. They were hustled along the corridor in the opposite direction from the one by which they had entered, and outside into the cool dawn air. Christian felt the tips of his toes, which extended over the end of his flip-flops, dig into damp, dewy sand. He blinked in the sunlight and realised they had to be around the back of the old section of the fort, where a large exercise yard had been sectioned off with four-metre-high barbed wire fencing mounted on concrete posts. Behind and higher still, rose the outer layer of metallic super-max mesh. Beyond, the ground fell away in swathes of brown and yellow. Mountains, dark from early morning shadow, formed the horizon with hazy blue above.

A hundred or so men milled around, talking despondently in conspiratorial groups. All were dressed in their ill-fitting shabby grey regulation tunics. Some glanced sideways, checking out the new arrivals, but most did not even look up. Christian felt his hand move to his chin. His fingers crackling through grimy stubble, he realised that with his dark hair and suntan, he probably looked less like a British Army captain than he felt. Raglan's matted black hair, partial beard and general state of filth did not look too military either.

In the corner of the yard to their right, a lean-to section of corrugated iron roofing extended from the wall of the fort. Below, set on a square of concrete, four sections were screened off from knee to chest height with wooden panels to form the most basic of shower cubicles. Running parallel to a couple of dented metal water troughs, ran a series of rusting manhole covers. Each had a large hole cut through the centre with flies buzzing in and out.

'Ah, the wellbeing centre,' said Raglan quietly to Christian, laying on the slightly thicker Welsh accent that he reserved for sarcasm.

Christian scanned the yard carefully as he followed Raglan towards the washing area. Standing confidently among a group of men, the tall bald guy with the beard raised his hands to his hips. A smirk broke across his face. Christian's head turned instinctively to the top of the wall above him where three guards sat with their rifles across their knees and their legs hanging down. Immediately, he regretted it, feeling rumbled as the scared kid in the playground looking for the safety of a teacher.

Raglan planted his feet with a clatter either side of the hole in one of the manhole covers. He bent forwards and yanked up his tunic. Christian momentarily forgot bald guy as Raglan grunted and released a torrent of yellow diarrhoea. He stood up, scratched his head and used the hem of his tunic to wipe his arse.

'When in Rome,' he mumbled scarcely audibly, looking at Christian, a hint of laughter lines cracking around his eyes.

'Looks more like a loony bin than a nick,' said Christian.

'African nicks always do,' replied Raglan. 'Been in a couple.'

Christian rolled his eyes. 'Of course you have.'

'Look, here comes matey now.' Raglan raised his eyebrows.

'Why does it always have to happen in the showers?' sighed Christian.

'Nothing you can't handle, I'm sure,' said Raglan, turning his back and pulling open the door to a shower cubicle.

Christian took a breath and swivelled around to see the bald guy leading a wall of grey towards him. Fuck it, he thought, and shot a glance up behind him to see the three guards staring down like spectators at a game. One smoked and another bounced his heels to and fro against the wall.

Drawing closer, the bald man's hands formed fists and his torso tilted forward. As the smug grin twisted into a fixed stare, Christian heard the whoosh of cascading water behind him. Impossible, but Raglan was actually taking a shower. Christian grappled with the absurdity of the situation and could tell from the baffled expressions of some of the men descending upon him that he was not alone. With bald guy reaching out to grab his tunic, Christian stepped nimbly to one side. Somehow, he remembered the Arabic etiquette and used his thumb as opposed to a finger to point at Raglan in the shower cubicle.

'It was him,' he said quickly.

Raglan used both hands to wipe the water off his face and back over his head.

'Hold on, please,' he said cheerily.

The bald guy paused, his momentum temporarily stalled. Christian watched him as he assessed Raglan, clearly trying to evaluate whether or not he wanted to attack a naked man in a shower in front of his supporters. He turned back to Christian, his determination back in the ascendant. Christian stepped away again and raised his hands, gesturing once more at Raglan. The man snarled and muttered under his breath. His eyes darted from one side to the other and sweat glistened around his temples. It was touch and go, but Christian knew that every second of hesitation that passed was one step closer to some kind of climbdown.

Around them, the wall of grey, several men deep, snapped into focus. Men jostled forwards and necks craned. Christian saw inquisitive faces peering at him. Some spoke quietly to one another and raised their hands, suggesting some form of debate.

Christian drew air into his lungs in preparation for a worst-case scenario. The bald guy turned to him once more, his eyes now fixed and purposeful. He moved in close and pushed his face and chest forwards. Christian tasted his sour breath but held his ground. Using his slight height advantage, Christian looked down fractionally into the bald man's face. He reckoned he was only in his late twenties but the bags beneath his eyes belonged to an older man. With glasses, he might have looked intellectual: a scholar who had taken the wrong path.

Christian tried to guess when the blow would come. If it were him, there would be a tiny feint first. Just something to set his opponent off balance before the strike. But standing nose to nose, it would be hard to hit properly. He would hold his nerve and his ground too. Bald guy was breathing hard, the frame of his chest rising and falling. He was under pressure too. Of course he was. To the left, Raglan had rested his forearms on the side of the shower cubicle. To the right, the semi-circle of grey stood quietly. Bald guy pursed his lips and Christian felt him tremble. If there was ever a moment for a pre-emptive strike it was now, but Christian held on. He could take him down, he knew it, but that was the invitation the others needed. Right now, it was one man's battle. Knock him down and that would be it. And clearly the tosspot guards were not going to intervene. Raglan just needed to keep his trap shut and stay out of it.

Without altering his stare, Christian detected a glimmer of hope. Some men were drifting away. They had seen enough and were turning their backs. Conversations were breaking out. He could not understand the language but the tone sounded uninterested and like they had had their time wasted. Another second or two crawled past. Then, with a sharp backwards movement, bald guy pushed away and raised his hands in the air in a gesture that suggested Christian was not worth a fight. He turned to his acolytes and snorted sharply through his nose. The remains of the crowd parted for him and he walked away, blending into the crowd of grey.

Christian stood still, his eyes focussed on the space that had been vacated. Raglan was saying something but it felt like there was a delayed reaction before he heard the words. It didn't matter. For the time being, they were both OK. Just.

27

Raglan pulled his tunic over his head and emerged from the shower cubicle. He reached forwards and tapped Christian gently on the elbow.

'Come on, lad, have a scrub and let's just sit down in the sun for a while. Warm up, you know,' he said.

Without replying, Christian stepped into the shower and stood under the cold water in the hope that it might make him feel better. He realised his mistake immediately as every little nick, scratch and insect bite on his body seemed to come alive angrily at once. He scratched at his scalp with his fingernails, releasing what had to be flakes of forty-eight-hour hold vomit. Worse still, the hairs on his chest released a hint of crimson into the water. Shivering from the combined effects of the cold water and nervous tension, he yanked his tunic back on and flipped open the front of the cubicle. Avoiding eye contact, he navigated his way slowly across the yard to where Raglan sat with his back against the wall.

'Better?' asked Raglan.

'No,' said Christian, sitting down next to him.

'OK. Sorry, lad. To be honest, I never was much good at playing the, you know, man.' Raglan tugged at his tunic.

'And it's going to get us killed. Just a matter of when.'

Raglan paused, looked around and lowered his voice still further.

'Just hold on a day or two in here. We might as well. We can see what happens.'

'A week. That's the limit,' growled Christian, looking directly forwards. 'And don't forget, I've got a certain amount of experience of African prisons. Fairly fucking recently too.'

Raglan nodded.

'Any time you want to pull the plug, I'm right with you. The job sucks. Couldn't agree more.'

Scratching at an oozing insect bite on his knee, Christian looked sideways and saw both sincerity and concern in the furrows lining Raglan's forehead. Yes, he was a nutter, but a likeable one, and realistically, the job was going to take a nutter. In fact, probably two. Anyway, what right did he have to call Raglan unhinged? He was the one who'd set most of West Africa alight in the last month, become a diamond-dealing gangster and let off a bomb in Central London.

Not to mention the double-digit head count he had clocked up in the process. Who was he to point fingers?

They sat quietly against the wall in the sun for the best part of an hour before there was a hollow tapping sound. The prisoners looked up and began wandering slowly towards the door in the wall of the fort. Two men set up a trestle table and began laying out lines of white plastic bowls. An orderly queue formed and a runny ladle of rice was slopped into each bowl, along with a large dollop of stew on top. Christian exchanged a glance with Raglan as more men emerged from the door carrying brightly coloured carpets in rolls on their shoulders. Next came an old wooden bookcase and several large stacks of red plastic school chairs with no legs.

'Whatever next?' muttered Raglan.

'Fuck knows, but this place is getting odder by the second,' said Christian. 'You can see there's some kind of pecking order, can't you? There's guys hanging back.'

'I guess that's normal,' said Raglan, looking about. 'I reckon the mix in here's about fifty-fifty local hoods versus your genuinely committed militant.'

'Not much difference if you ask me, but it's not the locals we need to get to know,' answered Christian quietly.

'I see your mate's right up the front.'

'My mate?'

'Bloody hell. There's footballs now.'

'No wonder the chairs have had the legs removed. They'd be smashing the shit out of each other after each goal. They'll be digging a pool next.'

'I don't give a fuck about the swimming pool, but I could do with a smoke,' said Raglan, staring at a man dishing out packets of cigarettes.

'I guess it makes life a whole lot easier if you keep the punters happy,' replied Christian. 'Come on, let's get stuck in before these guys hoover the lot.'

Christian and Raglan joined the back of the queue and collected their allocation of food along with a packet of twenty Craven A cigarettes and a book of matches. By the time they were back in their position by the wall, the exercise yard was alive with colour and thick with cigarette smoke. Carpets had been looped through the barbed wire to form areas of shade like windbreaks on a beach. Men rocked back and forth on their plastic seats and dragged hard on their cigarettes. Conversations had broken out and the two posts supporting the corrugated iron roof over the washing area had become goal posts.

Some men sat alone with their thoughts and others pored over books taken from the bookcase. A guard sheltering beneath a faded red parasol flicked a cigarette butt down from the wall above. Sparrow-like birds hopped nervously near an elderly inmate, pecking at the grains of rice he tossed on the ground around him.

'What do you reckon old Hanniballs would have made of all this, then?' said Raglan.

'Hannibal,' replied Christian out of the corner of his mouth, in the middle of lighting a cigarette.

'I'm sure you said Hanniballs the other day. The elephant bloke.' Raglan cupped his hand around a flaring match.

'No. It's definitely Hannibal. Singular. You know, one ball. Think Hitler.'

'OK, him. *His* prisoners would not have got to sit around on their arses like they're in some kind of holiday camp.'

'I don't know what sort of holidays you're used to, but I didn't find my *boo-tay noire* all that much of a break. No rosettes or stars from me.'

'Well, I don't go on many holidays. Why would you when you live where I do? Anywhere else is a sideways step at best. Normally, I hate holidays.'

'People go on holiday to where I live, too.'

'Clogging up the roads and dropping litter everywhere. Asking directions back to the main road. Can't leave the car park without a ski stick in each hand. Drives me nuts.'

'Really,' groaned Christian. 'Oh, fuck. Here we go again.'

Two young black Africans were approaching. They both smoked and walked with the West Side Boys' rap-star gait. Christian felt vulnerable seated on the ground and stood up as they drew near. The closest man paused and looked down at Raglan, who still sat on the ground cross-legged. Several seconds passed with no communication before one gestured with a turn of his head that they should follow. Christian paused for a drag on his cigarette before following the pair across the yard.

As they pushed through a group of jostling football players, Christian looked back over his shoulder and saw Raglan sauntering along behind him. The players seemed to get out of his way. In the far corner, all on orange plastic chairs, sat a circle of men shaded by several carpets hanging through the wire above them. Christian noticed there was also carpet beneath their seats. By prison standards, they seemed to have all the gear. Most were Arab and all of them smoked. On the far side, looking at him, sat the bald guy tilting back in his chair. Christian held his stare but no longer saw the aggression. He looked different. The man was thinking, assessing and scheming. Maybe he had flashed earlier and lost control. Christian had thought he looked intelligent, but that might make him more dangerous. A clever man brimming over with violence was more of a worry.

The two young black men squatted down next to each with their backs against the wall of carpet, leaving Christian standing awkwardly in the gaze of the seated men. Recognising his tension, the bald guy allowed a few more seconds to pass before speaking.

'You, Husam, are the reason we are all in here,

aren't you? You and your friend there.' He nodded at Raglan, now standing next to Christian.

Christian kept his expression blank. If the big Yank Colonel knew who they were, it made sense that other people might too.

'I have no idea what you are talking about,' said Christian gruffly.

The bald guy smiled and started to shuffle sideways on his chair. The other men in the circle did the same, creating a gap.

'Why don't you come and sit down with us? Believe me, everyone needs friends in here.'

Christian navigated his way around the circle of seated men until he reached the newly formed space. He flicked the butt of his cigarette out through the wire and sat down. Raglan squeezed in next to him.

'So, you have come a long way to find yourselves in prison,' said Bald Guy, addressing the whole circle. 'How did you find the accommodation?'

Christian glanced around at the faces. There were eight in total, six bearded Arabs of varying ages and two older black men. The matching grey tunics engendered a cohesive look, like some meeting of village elders. These men weren't local hoods doing time.

Christian made the decision to communicate. If he'd been playing himself, he would have kept quiet, but, in theory, he was just a lad from Leicester. Sure, he would not have been chosen to be sent to Somalia to be trained by al-Shabaab unless he'd shown real ability, but now he'd resisted hard enough.

'Bad. Very bad,' he replied quietly, looking at the pattern in the carpet directly in front of him.

'They have a lot worse than that here. That's just for beginners. How do you think they picked you up so fast? It was no accident. We were intercepted on our way to meet you, Husam and Aashir. May I assume those are adopted names?' said Bald Guy, turning to look at Raglan.

Christian nodded.

'Given names. Chosen for us when we joined the community. It's customary.'

'We understand,' answered Bald Guy, gesturing around the circle. 'And I know your background. We have your photograph from a trusted source. That's all that matters. They said you have courage and I can see that for myself. I am Sha'inti and these men are my family and will be your family too.'

There were almost imperceptible bows of welcome from the seated men. Christian straightened up and spoke again.

'So why did you want to kill me this morning?'

Sha'inti smiled.

'Because you are the reason we are in here. Also, I wanted to see if you are worthwhile to me. To see if you and your friend were worthy of further compromise. I assure you, it was not pleasant how they extracted the details of the meeting place.'

'What happened?' said Raglan, clearing his throat.

'Well, it's simple. We were on our way to meet you at the agreed location when we were intercepted by so-called Government forces. They did not know our purpose. So they took us here, and after two days of brutality one of my men gave away details of our meeting with you.'

Raglan grunted a note of sympathy. Sha'inti continued.

'We were separated and each of us was told the others had confessed. After two days' illegal violence, there is no shame. So, here we are. All here together.'

Christian reached for his packet of Craven As, pulled a couple of cigarettes part of the way out and offered them around. There were a series of polite nods and several were taken.

28

Sam adjusted the position of the monitor and glanced around the empty security office. He reminded himself that he had finished his inspection of the perimeter fence and now had every reason to be using a computer to type up his report. There was nothing suspect about that. Anyway, he would hear anyone coming as they clumped up the metal steps. Still, his hands trembled and he had to concentrate to make sure his forefinger only clicked once each time on the little button on the front of the mouse.

His first couple of days at the airbase had been pretty uneventful. He had been tasked with assessing the security fencing, and he had wandered around the full perimeter noting down details of any holes in the wire and areas of salt corrosion on the supporting steel posts. Under normal circumstances, he would have been bored and fidgety, but it had given him time to settle down and get a real feel of the place. He had fixed his broken bed, and despite the constant comings and goings at night from his Portakabin, he'd had a couple of respectable nights' sleep.

He still found Tariq irritating, but he liked the fact that his immediate boss had picked up on his imperceptibly elevated status with the real boss. It made things easier. There was also a knock-on effect with the other security guys, who treated him ever so slightly warily. It reminded him of how regular soldiers behaved when interacting with their colleagues from Special Forces. He had decided he would keep his distance and remain the mystery man while he figured out the details of his plan. The primary objective had to be keeping his Egyptian masters happy, at least in the short term.

He positioned the cursor in the password box and sounded out the phonetic spelling of Mahmood in his head. He tapped the return key with his thumb, leant back in his chair and frowned at the symbol of a small spinning egg timer in the centre of the screen. A second later, the egg timer slowed, blinked twice and was replaced by a menu offering a series of reports set out in chronological order. Sam reached for the mouse and clicked on the most recent. The screen filled with data and various satellite images of what he thought was Mogadishu. He scrolled down and scanned through the text which set out details of cargo flight schedules in and out of the airbase.

He closed the report and clicked on the next most recent. The screen filled with Arabic text and he closed it down. Back in the menu again, and now with steady hands, he clicked on the third report and was pleased to see it was written in English. His eyes darted around a report detailing the arrest of a group of eight militiamen with likely connections to the al-Da'at, the militant wing of the Muslim Brotherhood and al-Shabaab. They had been picked up by an Egyptian patrol and interned at a secure unit referred to only as P1.

Sam scrolled down further, pausing to look at a series of prison-style mug shots of the detainees. Despite the poor quality, nothing could disguise the anger and disgust bubbling in their eyes. All radiating defiance, some stared at the camera like they were about to charge it and others gazed straight through it. Biting gently at his lip, Sam manoeuvred his chair closer to the desk. He carried on clicking through the reports but had already decided on his next move. It was just a question of how he approached the Toad.

29

Christian spent the rest of the day tucked in against the carpeted wall, drifting in and out of sleep. It felt strangely reassuring to be an accepted part of a group and no longer the outsider whom everyone seemed out to get. In theory, he could sleep peacefully under the protective wing of his new-found 'family'. Raglan wandered around for an hour or two before finally sitting down next to Christian with a tatty heap of *National Geographic* magazines which he had taken from the bookcase.

As the sun pendulumed slowly across the sky, various alterations were made to the positions of the carpets to ensure as much shade as possible. The guards on the walls changed every couple of hours and games of football of various sizes and standards came and went. Christian was awake but decided it was easier to keep his eyes shut as if he were asleep.

His listened to conversations around him and tried to ignore the sound of Raglan flicking through the pages of the magazines. Eventually, he sat up.

'Why don't you try actually turning the pages rather than just rubbing your hand across them?'

'Did you know that it only took a hundred and fifty Spanish guys with a few muskets to invade the whole of Mexico in the fifteenth century? They took on over five thousand Aztec warriors at once and still won,' Raglan informed him.

'Yes, I did know that.'

'Leaves your Macbeth man in the shade, doesn't it?'

'Yes, it does. Now, where are the Aztecs? I mean the cigarettes?'

'*The* cigarettes?' queried Raglan. 'Mine are here. And *you* can have *one* if you want.'

'Anyway, the only reason the Spanish managed to beat the Aztecs was because they all turned up with flu and the Aztecs had no resistance to it. Basically, they all died of influenza.'

'What, so the Spanish just turned up and sneezed all over the place?'

'That's right. They turned up, sneezed all over the place, nicked their gold and fucked off. Job done.'

'I suppose that shows a certain amount of style. Anyway, they're extinct now. A bit like these lizards might be,' said Raglan, tapping his finger on the magazine.

'If only we could add mosquitoes, the East African

tsetse fly and . . .' lowering his voice, 'religious fanatics to the National Geographic watch list,' replied Christian.

'Might as well add overweight Yank mercenaries.'

'Fast track, ideally.'

The afternoon wore on and finally the sun dropped below the far side of the fort. The tapping noise sounded and the trestle table was set up again. The prisoners drifted slowly into a queue to collect a large flat loaf of pitta bread stuffed with strips of dried meat and a couple of oranges. Once these had been consumed, the various carpets were pulled down from the wire and rolled up. Finally, an old dustbin was placed in the middle of the yard and a group scoured the ground for cigarette butts.

The walkway along the top of the wall filled with more guards. One spat his cigarette butt down into the yard. It had hardly hit the ground before it was seized upon and added to the dustbin. A dozen or so guards slouched into the yard with their weapons raised and began organising the prisoners into groups of ten. One group at a time they were marched through the door back inside. Christian and Raglan held back, watching the process before tucking in behind Sha'inti's group. Just as they reached the door, a hand was raised and they were pushed back into the yard.

Raglan wiped a glistening line of orange juice from his chin and shrugged at Christian.

'Don't think for one moment that I have not been

observing you two filthy sacks of shit today,' boomed Colonel Lee, emerging from the doorway. 'Causing trouble on your first day in the yard. Hanging around like a couple of cheap whores with the worst of the trash we have in here. What am I meant to do?'

Christian's eyes were drawn to a dark line of sweat which had permeated about a centimetre up the Colonel's olive-green shirt above his canvas belt. He knew where this was going. The thickness and weight of the wooden door of the *bouteille noire* groaning on its hinges filled his mind. He heard the finality of the closing clunk and the scrape of the bolts. And this wanker might just be about to put them back inside. He breathed hard and allowed the fear in his mind to flood into his face. Looking terrified might just give this guy what he needed.

The Colonel paused to assess the impact of his words. Christian risked a short, terrified glance at his face. It was impossible to read.

'I have no alternative,' he drawled. 'You leave me no alternative.'

The Colonel sighed and muttered something in Arabic to the three remaining guards. He glanced briefly at Christian, as if expecting some kind of acknowledgement of his language skills, pivoted around and disappeared into the gloom of the doorway.

Trancelike, Christian felt a tap between the shoulder blades. His feet moved and his legs conveyed him through the door, along the corridor, across the central courtyard and down the steps to the cellar with the four small black doors. The wire cages on the right were empty. Apart from a buzz from the strip lights, it was quiet and the temperature cool. Something pushed him towards the closest *bouteille noire*. The door was hauled open, grinding on its hinges. The space behind was a fraction deeper than the cell he had occupied on arrival but the height substantially lower: a crueller space where a man could not stand up straight.

The cold fingers of panic spread through Christian's chest. His heart took an exaggerated beat and his head swam. There was no way he could do it again. He'd done it once. And that had unleashed a primal fear that would stay with him to the grave. This was the moment. It was time to break cover. As he was pushed forwards he turned his head towards Raglan in desperation. But Raglan's face was set. They were going in again.

As Christian stooped to enter the hole, a chorus of sniggers broke out behind him. A guard poked his back and jerked his thumb over his shoulder, an amused expression cracking across his face. He was hauled backwards and frogmarched across the cellar towards one of the cages opposite. He ducked through the wire of the inner cage and flopped down against the rear wall. Raglan piled in behind him and the door was locked. The guards then tramped up the stairs and the sound of their high-spirited chatter came to an abrupt end with the clang of the metal door.

'It's all very well for a runt like you,' muttered Christian. 'It would be like putting you in a fucking shoe box.'

'You should think yourself lucky. They were built by the French to suppress the Abyssinians, and they are all about eight feet tall. It's why they win marathons these days.'

'Are you sure you don't mean the Italians?'

'No, they're all fucking tiny. You could have six of them in there. Anyway, they play football.'

'No, no, I thought it was the Italians who occupied this place. Actually, I don't give a shit who it was. Bunch of wankers either way.'

30

It was on the morning of day eight that Christian realised he was becoming used to prison life. He was sitting cross-legged in the carpeted corner of the exercise yard eating his breakfast when he found himself looking up. Several new arrivals, clearly identifiable by their clean tunics and bewildered expressions, were being bundled into the yard. Christian surveyed them in the bored and nonchalant way he himself had been viewed the first time he had been thrust into the yard. They hastily beat a retreat to the safety of the empty corner in the glare of the sun where nobody liked to sit. He knew the feeling. Not a nice one. But now he felt a part of Sha'inti's crew. They sat with them by day but were still confined to their own cell by night, apparently standard practice for the protection of Western prisoners.

'You know,' said Christian barely audibly to Raglan, 'I've just had a very bad thought.'

'What? Just the one?' Raglan exhaled a cloud of cigarette smoke. 'Is it me smoking while you eat?'

'No, worse than that.'

'Go on then, make my day.'

'Well, it's to do with Colonel what's-his-face.'

'Captain what's-his-face, more like. I'm the only fucking Colonel round here.'

'Not sure if I believe that, either,' said Christian, pulling the cigarette out of Raglan's mouth and using it to light his own. 'Anyway, I've been thinking.'

'Go on,' sighed Raglan.

'Well, we've been sitting here thinking that if the shit got too heavy, we could just "call time" and reveal ourselves to the fat bastard. But the reality is, he's not going to like the fact that he sanctioned gang rape and now has two highly credible, first-hand witnesses. I'd kill us if I were him.'

'Bollocks, he would. He's probably forgotten all about it,' replied Raglan, flipping a page of *National Geographic*.

'Well, it's something to bear in mind. We'd want to fess up with someone else senior around.'

'We just need to get on with busting out of this place with matey and his band of merry men. Then we're back in the game. He'll lead us up the food chain.'

'Just can't quite see how.'

'Something will come up. We'll see a chance, and every day we're inside, is one more day of credibility.'

A football bounced across Christian's lap and he found himself yielding to pressure to join in the game. He stubbed out his fag and stood up. A dozen or so of the younger inmates shuffled about in the heat of the midday sun until the ball caught an angle off the corrugated iron roof over the washing area and flew over the inner wire. An angry rumble of disapproval broke amongst the players, and some of the spectators laughed. The ball rolled across the dusty no-man's-land and came to rest against the outer fence, just below one of the yellow high-voltage signs.

Within a few seconds the angry grumbles had escalated into a full-blown row between the Somali who had had the last touch of the ball and the young Arab who had booted it hard into his shin. Christian knew it was time to sit down as two racial factions massed in the middle of the yard. As the first fist was thrown, there was a crackle of gunfire and Christian watched the walkway along the top of the wall fill with guards, their weapons levelled at the men below. He counted nine in total, two of whom were manning the massive 50 cal in the watchtower. Someone shouted down in Arabic and a guard appeared in no-man's-land. Running his hand gently along the line of the inner fence, he negotiated his way gingerly along until he was parallel to the ball. With all eyes on him, he looked up and, on receiving a signal from the top of the wall, stepped forward gingerly and snatched up the ball.

An hour later Christian saw it dropped back into the yard; a simple punishment and strategically short in order to keep the peace.

31

Christian spent the afternoon in what had become his usual position. He lay in the corner with Raglan sitting next to him reading magazines. The shadow cast by the sun dropping behind the fort reached the mid-point of the yard and, on cue, the table appeared with the evening scoff. Guards filtered in and allocated people to the various clearing-up tasks. Christian positioned a rolled up carpet on his shoulder and, with a grin, flicked his fag end onto the ground near Raglan, who was on cigarette duty.

They trooped inside and downstairs. The strip light buzzed and the air was cool. The new boys were in the end section and, for no apparent reason, the middle section contained six men too. Christian sat back against the wall and looked around, taking advantage of the last moments of light. The door slammed and, after the momentary orange phase as the strip light died, the cellar plunged into darkness. Quiet chatter broke out and he tilted his head back against the wall behind him to contemplate another night of concrete floor, snoring, coughing, whispering and men crying out in their sleep. It was depressing at best, but in real terms, utterly miserable. He had slept half the afternoon and would now have to sit in the dark for at least six hours before he had a chance of being able to sleep. Also, there was a degree of privacy in the corner of the yard where there was enough space around them that he could speak to Raglan. In the cellar, any conversation would have to be back in actor mode.

Without a watch or any view of the night sky, Christian had found himself depending on routine noises coming from the building above to provide some sense of passing time. Footsteps were hard to hear unless there was total silence, but chairs scraping in what he guessed was an eating area above were clearly audible and usually occurred what felt like a couple of hours after lights out. Then came a changing of the guard, which involved a certain amount of loud talking and sometimes the lights flicking on and off, as if someone did not know which switch did what.

Now, with nothing but the second change of guard to break the tedium, he set off from the back door of his house towards the river once again. He climbed the fence and was halfway across the field when he heard footsteps above. He opened his eyes in the darkness. This was too soon. In contrast to the rhythmic breathing of sleeping men, the metal door scraped open quietly and without the usual echoing bang as it clanged into the wall. The light did not go on either. Weird. Boots descended the stairs at a pace and torch beams cut the darkness. Christian sat up straight, his hand shielding his eyes. He could not see how many figures had entered the cellar but it had to be at least four. They grouped around his door as one fumbled with the lock. The cage was opened and a torch shone directly in Christian's face.

'You, move,' snarled a voice.

Christian's initial assessment that a new arrival, perhaps recently caught in the desert, was being dumped in the cellar, disintegrated into fear. Not the phobic fear he had experienced in the *bouteille noire*; this was rational fear based on potential outcomes that he could likely expect. At one end of the spectrum he could be about to be moved to a different prison, and at the other end, it could be a firing squad.

He made it to his feet just in time to be grabbed by the front of his tunic. He could not see the face of the guard but the man's fingernails scratched into his chest as he pulled him forwards. Raglan was halfway to standing when he was pushed back to the floor. One at a time, thought Christian. If they were to be shot, it would be together – why any other way? – but interrogation would be done separately. But why on day eight? The Colonel had said he knew everything and it sounded like he did. Something else had to have come up.

Christian missed the bottom step of the stairs and smashed his toes into the brickwork. Pain shot up his leg as he was bundled forwards and upwards. Gathering speed with every step, he was hustled along the dirty white corridor above in semi-darkness and out into the moonlit quad. Just as he raised his eyes and saw the stars, the pace slowed a fraction and a hood was slid over his head. He was spun round in a semi-circle and then moved on again. The gritty surface under his feet turned back to hard and smooth and he was climbing stairs. Twenty-two spiral steps up meant he was on the second floor. There was rough wood underfoot and one of the guards breathed heavily. Cigarette smoke permeated the hood. The chug of a distant generator. He was steered around an invisible obstacle and then pushed backwards onto a hard surface at waist height. Hands gripped him and yanked him into a lying position. There was a momentary jingling of metallic buckles and then leather straps tightened around his arms and legs.

Christian arched upwards in reaction to the feeling of straps securing his chest and stomach. An initial sense of confusion subsided into grim reality. This was bad. Desperately, he cast around in his mind for a benign reason as to why he might be secured like this. Only the blackest possibilities seemed credible.

There were a few words in Arabic and the sound

of boots tramping out of the room. A door closed and Christian raised his head slightly off the table in a futile attempt to look around. His fingers pulled involuntarily at the cloth of his tunic by his sides. Through the hood, he made out the brightness of a light above him. He breathed hard, fighting against the fabric that clung to his sweating face. The scratch of a cigarette lighter confirmed his feeling that someone remained in the room. A dark shape briefly eclipsed the disc of light above him and he tasted cigarette smoke.

Right up against his ear, an East London accent crackled.

'Hello, Christi. Forgotten all about me, have yer?'

Christian felt his body stiffen as his mind exploded into overdrive. He knew the voice. Or did he? Yes, he did.

'That's right. Stitched up like a lunatic in a strait-jacket. Nappy on, a tranquilliser up my arse and off to twenty-five years' hard labour in an Egyptian prison. That was your last thought of me.'

Christian felt his jaw twitch. This was impossible. He strained against the leather straps and raised his head off the table.

'I've got no idea what you're talking about,' he gasped. 'My name is . . .'

A hand slammed his head back against the table and then positioned itself over his mouth. Christian twisted his face sideways but to no avail. The hand gripped his face and, in combination with the soaking hood, made him gag for air.

'You're a scheming piece of shit, McKie. Think you're so fucking clever too. Thought you had got rid of me, didn't you? But I'm back. And you're here with me.'

'Get the hood off me,' spluttered Christian.

'Yep, why not?' replied Sam, pulling at the drawstring of the hood and yanking it roughly over Christian's face.

Christian blinked in the glare of the overhead light and flicked his head to one side in an effort to clear his eyes of sweat. Sam Carter took a drag on a cigarette and then moved his face in close to Christian's. He wore a grey T-shirt, the bottom of his Parachute Regiment tattoo just visible on his upper arm.

'Now then, have you noticed what you're lying on?' he growled as cigarette smoke escaped from the crack of his smile.

Christian pushed down with his fingers on a soft textured surface. It took him a moment to work out that it was rubber.

'No, not for your comfort,' Sam purred. 'You probably can't see much from there, but let me walk you through the various bits and bobs we've got to play with in here. It's a pretty nasty place, one way or another.'

Christian craned his neck as Sam pushed the overhead light to one side. The room was small with a dark wooden door to his left. Metal racking lined the side wall. He squinted and bobbed his head further forwards. The shelves appeared laden with what looked like garage equipment. Unable to support his head any longer, he rested it back down on the table and shut his eyes. He knew what he had seen and he knew what it was for.

'Basic in some respects.' Sam shrugged. 'But you're dead anyway. So it doesn't really matter how much of a mess I make of you. It may surprise you, but I'm here in a pretty unusual capacity. There isn't really anything I can't do.'

'For fuck's sake, Sam. Untie me, and stop being quite such a prick,' snapped Christian.

'Sure thing. Yes, of course. Right away,' said Sam, releasing the light. 'Do you think those nice Egyptian chaps on Death Row would have been quite so accommodating if I had asked them that?'

'What?' said Christian.

'Perhaps you don't know,' replied Sam. 'Well, let me fill you in. Your little wheeze almost worked. Except that the Egyptians, in all their wisdom, decided not to kill me after all. Sure, I went right through the whole process. The murder trial, solitary confinement, last rites and the lethal injection in front of witnesses, the whole fucking shebang. But they injected me with something else, and now I'm working for them. Which is why I happen to be here with you right now.'

'Bullshit!' said Christian, his body vibrating with

anger. 'I had no idea they would kill you, although you fucking deserved it. And have you forgotten shooting me at point-blank range and then leaving me to be finished off by the most savage bunch of psychos in the world? Who's the cunt round here?'

'Right, that's enough!' hissed Sam, spit forming in the corners of his mouth. 'I haven't been to hell and back to chat this through with you. No, that's not the plan at all. You're here to suffer for what you did. What you knowingly did to me. What you planned in the cold light of day. You dreamed it up and allowed it to happen. There was nothing impulsive or spur of the moment. I shot you because you asked for it. I did not plan it. It was a fucking accident. Totally fucking different and you know it. We both know.'

'Yup, and that makes a whole world of difference, does it? Was I meant to feel a whole load better as I was slowly torn to pieces on a medieval rack for a couple of days because *you* didn't *mean* me to be there?' roared Christian. 'When my guts were pulled out and burned? Oh, fine, absolutely bloody fine. Sam didn't plan it? Never mind me, it was just an accident. Something unplanned, so it must be fine.'

Sam leant back behind him and grabbed a rubber ball gag from one of the shelves.

'I had to pull this off a dead body earlier on. Had a feeling I might need to shut you up.'

'And Jamie. I'm sure he'd be fine about being racked now you've so kindly explained it was all just a misunderstanding. Yeah, you must let Tim's folks know too. Yes, and Andy's while you're at it. He got diced while you were busy with your little unplanned fucking plan. What planet are you on?'

Sam spat his cigarette on the floor and leant forwards with the gag stretched between his fists. He seized Christian's face in his hands and pushed his fingers into his eyes until Christian voluntarily opened his mouth to take the rubber ball. Sam pushed it hard between his teeth with one hand and pulled the straps around the back of his head with the other.

'Right. That should do it,' he said. 'Now for the good bit.'

Sam turned around, gripped the handles of a metal trolley and pulled it parallel to Christian's head.

'Not quite sure what they call this but I do know what it does,' said Sam, rubbing the dust off the window that protected a guage on the top of a large plastic box with two thick wires protruding from each end.

Sam flicked at a switch on the back of the box. A light appeared in the window and a line of green LEDs glowed. He unclipped two cables, one red and one black, moved around the table and snapped the crocodile teeth ends onto Christian's toes.

'You're going to have to bear with me on this, Christi, while I work things out,' muttered Sam, making his way back to the plastic box. 'Seems obvious enough, but I don't want to kill you in the first ten seconds.'

Christian turned his face to Sam and shook his head. He tried to speak around the ball gag but found it impossible to make any comprehensible sound. He rested his head back on the table, praying that this elaborate bluff would soon be over.

Sam lit a cigarette and bent forward to squint at the controls.

'Looks like it runs from ten volts up to a thousand. Let's try two hundred and fifty for starters. That's probably a bit like zapping yourself when you change a light bulb.'

He pinched the dial between his thumb and fore-finger and turned. The reaction was immediate. Christian's body bucked on the table and then writhed against the leather restraints. His eyes bulged and a stifled roar reverberated through the ball gag. Sam stepped back before reaching for the dial again.

'Crikey, Christi. You should see yourself. A couple of seconds on two hundred and fifty and you look half cooked already. We're really in for a long night. I don't want to peak too early but let's give five hundred a whirl.'

Sam squinted at the window and turned the dial. Just as before, the reaction was immediate. Christian's body bucked and writhed once again. His fingers formed twitching claws and his head shot forwards to the point that his chin touched his chest.

'This really works,' said Sam, dragging hard on his cigarette. 'Better turn you off for a moment.'

Christian's body sank back down on the rubber matting. His arms shook and his jaw juddered from side to side.

'Oh, look, Christi. I think your toes may be burning. Not to worry, I can think of plenty more places we can clip onto. Look at my nails,' he said, presenting his outstretched fingers in Christian's face. 'It's amazing what the stress of an impending lethal injection can do to a man.

'Now, Christi, budge over.' Sam pulled his hand away and rested half his backside on the table beside Christian.

'It's quite an odd thing being executed. You get to think some very weird thoughts. You could call it quite enlightening. They kid you on the exact timing, so the last moments come as a bit of a surprise. But it's the thoughts that go through your head, knowing you are about to die.'

Sam stood up again and walked around the table. He stopped by Christian's feet and stooped to examine the crocodile clips attached to his toes.

'I've never understood why burning flesh smells sweet. Anyway, where was I? Yes, I remember. Being executed. Yup, they come in and grab you. A little piece of you thinks there's a chance you might be able to fight your way out like something from a movie. But the reality's different. You've basically already half died in your head. Then you get picked up like a piece of meat, Christi, and taken through to the execution chamber. It's not far, just down the corridor, in fact. There were a bunch of witnesses waiting there to watch. And you know what, Christi? They looked bored. There was I in the last minute or so of my life and they were chatting amongst themselves. Probably discussing the price of kebabs.'

Christian breathed hard around the ball gag. Without the power of speech, there was nothing he could do to influence things. The only option was to make Sam think he was suffering. The more he suffered, the better Sam would feel. He let out an agonised groan and allowed his eyes to roll back.

'So there I am. Strapped down a bit like you are now. Obviously, one arm poking out to the side, and all I can see is you. That's right, Christi, all I could think about in my last seconds on earth was you. You. Then some pathetic little drip of a doctor comes trundling over with a syringe. He's wearing a little grey cardigan and his tie's at half-mast. The little cunt doesn't bother tapping the syringe to get the bubbles out. No need, is there, because I'm about twelve seconds off being dead. And still, I have to put up with seeing your fucking face. I thought I saw you sitting in among the witnesses for a moment. Are you starting to understand just how much you piss me off?'

Christian raised his head and, despite the searing pain down his spine, managed to nod.

'Oh, you are, are you?' Sam shrugged. 'I'm really

not sure you are, actually. Perhaps a full five minutes on six hundred before we swap toes.'

Sam swivelled the dial and Christian felt his mind turn white with pain. Pulsating ripples of agony tore down his left leg and fanned out through his torso. The source of the pain blurred and his whole body flexed and thrashed uncontrollably. His world had become an empty void without rational boundaries and dimensions, the only fixed points being the distance between the present moment and the time when the pain would subside. On and on, second by second the electricity flowed.

Once again, he became aware that Sam was speaking. This had to mean the power was off, but the pain was still there, at least most of it.

'So in goes the injection. I guess it was at that moment I really knew there was no last-minute reprieve. You know how people hope. You still think there might be some last-second intervention; some bloke from the Embassy or Amnesty International bursting in waving a letter from the Prime Minister or something.'

Christian shook his head and tried to think through his beating brain.

'But then it would be even more tragic to get the reprieve once the poison was already in. Can you imagine that? That's probably the only way you could have made it any worse for me, Christi. In fact, I'm surprised you didn't set that up too. You know, icing on top of the icing. Anyway, I felt this cold stuff going down my arm first. Weird, I thought. Perhaps it's going the wrong way? Surely it should be heading for my heart. Maybe there's been a mistake? But then I felt it grip me. It was all over me, Christi. Death was there, all around, gripping me; gently at first and then a tiny bit tighter. I should have been thinking of my mum and dad, or maybe playing on a summer's day when I was a kid. You know, something like that, but, no, oh no – I had your sniggering face hovering there. Yes, you looked all smug and chuffed.'

Christian shook his head and stared at Sam through widened eyes. He had somehow to convey some kind of empathy and contrition.

'I've never been a particularly religious man, Christi, but I have always felt a man deserves some kind of decent funeral, even if it's just a few mates in a churchyard. A couple of cans afterwards, you know, nothing much. But my body was heading for a shallow unmarked grave somewhere in the outskirts of Cairo. Odds on, I'd be dug up by dogs in a day or two, or they'd build some crappy discount supermarket over me. The sort of place without real shelves where you just help yourself straight off the pallet. Of course, when *you* died, Mrs fucking Thatcher turns up with Denis and half the bloody Cabinet. *You're* pushing up sweet little daisies in Hereford while I'm festering under aisle fucking three.'

Christian fixed his gaze on the light above. He tried

to guess what the time might be. He needed some handle on the world outside this room. Clearly Sam was here with some kind of mandate. He could not have just turned up and demanded a prisoner be dragged up to a torture chamber. Sam had to be on the inside. The morning would eventually come, and what then? Was the plan to kill him? Was the fat Yank Colonel involved? Surely, Raglan would do something if he simply did not come back. That was logical, but when had logic last played a hand in his world? Raglan was the most persistent nutcase he had ever met. He was prepared to get back in the *bouteille noire* for another night. What was logical about him? He could not rely on him doing anything. He'd just sit it out.

'Then, Christi, a weird thing happened. I actually died. Yep, my eyes closed of their own accord. I can remember the feeling. I didn't need to breathe any more. I was just swimming off.' Sam looked into space across the room.

'Anyway, I mustn't bang on too much. The important thing is that you're going to die for real this time. The last thing you're going to see is my face in this filthy little room. Burial wise, I'm not sure about the exact details, but they have a bit of a morgue downstairs where they keep bodies before they dump them out in the desert. So, it will be scavenging animals gnawing on your bloated, fly-blown carcass. There's one difference, though, Christi – lethal injections are more or less painless.'

Sam lit a cigarette and reached for the dial. Christian's body arched and convulsed. He gnashed at the ball gag and his eyes bounced about in their sockets. Pouring in sweat, his body strained against the leather straps and his hair stood on end.

'I think you may actually be on fire, Christi,' said Sam excitedly. 'I don't think you can see, but your toes are smoking. You'll have to take my word for it.'

Sam adjusted the dial downwards and perched back down beside Christian on the table.

'And then, Christi, I was coming to in some office with an Egyptian spook offering me a job. Imagine that. You think you're dead and you wake up again. The next thing I know I've accepted to work for these guys and my job is to come down here and stir up as much shit as I can to make sure the Egyptians have a reason to keep troops in Somalia. My kind of thing or what? Basically my own boss, their full backing, license to kill and to do whatever the fuck I want as long as it causes trouble. In fact, the more trouble the better. And then, joy of joy, whose ugly mug do I see on the computer in the security office where I was working? Could not believe my eyes.'

Christian heard the words but struggled to make sense of them. Anything to postpone the next wave of agony had to be good, though.

'So, I thought, if you need to whip up some shit, why not enlist some help? I probably would have transferred up here anyway. The idea's to set up a mass breakout. Can you imagine? There's about a hundred of the most violent militants in East Africa in here. Let them out and this country will be anarchy. Job done. So you being here is just a bonus. Win-win, that's how I see it.'

Christian tasted blood in his mouth and felt himself start to choke. Suddenly a foaming mixture of blood and snot shot from his nose. He gagged and gasped for air around the ball gag. Sam looked on for a moment, a frown forming across his face.

'Oh, no we don't,' he said, stepping forwards and reaching for the strap of the ball gag. 'There's no getting out of this like that. No choking or heart attacks for you.'

Sam yanked at the strap and pulled the rubber ball out of Christian's mouth. Christian instantly raised his head and spat a mouthful of blood and saliva onto his heaving chest.

'Sam,' he spluttered. 'There's something you need to know.'

'Like what?'

'Well, how do you think I got hold of that cash to hide in your attic? And the coke and those passports, and the guns?'

'I expect you nicked it all, knowing you.'

'Yes, I did, but it's what else I nicked that matters.'

'What then?'

'Like about eighty million pounds' worth of diamonds. I sold about three to get the cash I needed but I still have the rest. There's about two hundred of them, all sorted and in different sizes, including some massive ones.'

'And how the fuck did you find them?'

'When I was sitting in the tree by the OP, I saw Foday messing about in the bushes. I watched him through my binoculars. Never gave it a second thought at the time but I clicked when I was being held. As you point out, it's amazing what goes through your mind when you're on Death fucking Row. Once I broke out, I went back to Geri Bana and found his whole stash: the diamonds, all that coke, the passports. Think about it. Where else did it come from?'

'And where are they now?'

'Wouldn't you like to know? Kill me and you never will. Let me out of here and you can have the whole lot. You can live the life, you'll be so loaded you can't imagine it. Also, don't think for one second your new Egyptian pals aren't going to slot you the minute you've done the job. Being on the run as a penniless tramp won't be that much fun. Whereas bobbing about on a super yacht with more . . .'

'OK, Christi. Even if I believe you, what's to stop me torturing you so you tell me anyway?'

'OK, you torture me and I tell you some place in the hills. You kill me and then find your back to Wales and they're not there. Then what?'

'I think you're forgetting that you're not really in a position to negotiate,' replied Sam, turning the dial.

Christian's body bucked into an arch and his face contorted.

'Are you?' continued Sam, turning the dial back down again.

'I can do better than that, Sam. I can get them brought here for you.'

'Bullshit. How the fuck are you going to do that?

'Just one phone call. I won't say what's really going on. I'll just tell my man to bring them and he will. He'll know I'm in the shit but won't have a clue it's anything to do with you, will he? You can listen to every word. If I mess it up and start blabbing, you end the call and kill me. You could have them in less than two days.'

Sam dragged hard on his cigarette and looked at his watch. He stood up and walked around the table with his arms folded, his fingers drumming against his triceps. He opened his mouth to speak and then appeared to change his mind. He paced around the table again before dropping his cigarette and grinding it into the floor.

'OK. Who would you call? Who's sitting on the stash?'

'Before I tell you, you might as well know he's not the sort of bloke you could go and grab and beat the info out of him.'

'What makes you think I might do that?' grunted Sam.

'For fuck's sake, Sam. You can start by untying just

one of my hands and giving me a smoke. Isn't that traditional for a condemned man anyway?'

'No one gave me a smoke before . . .'

'Whatever, but I want one.'

Sam pulled at the strap securing Christian's right arm. As the buckles came undone, Christian raised his hand and rested it on his heart.

'Fucking hell. I think I'm about to have a heart attack,' he groaned.

'Not for the time being, you're not,' replied Sam, lighting a cigarette and putting it between Christian's fingers. Christian took a drag and wiped his sweaty hair out of his face.

'So do we have a deal, Sam?'

'Depends who you're going to call.'

'OK, it's Armalite.'

'Armalite? *Armalite?* He's got eighty million pounds' worth of diamonds? Why him?'

'Because he's a good bloke. Simple as that.'

'Did he have anything to do with stitching me up?'

'No, that was just me. He knew where I got the stash but he had no idea about you.'

'What about Deveral? What does he know?'

'He thinks you were paid to set off a bomb in London. Doesn't have a clue about you and me. I could hardly tell him what I'd done, could I? When I got back, he offered me a job working undercover, which is why I'm here.'

'Doing what?'

'Basically, I'm here with another ex-Regiment guy and the plan was to penetrate an al-Shabaab cell.'

'Fucking hell, Christi. Why do you bother?'

'Honestly, I really don't know. Now, are we going to call Armalite and make you a multimillionaire, or are we going to carry on sitting around in here like a couple of arse bandit S&M freaks?'

Sam retreated to a corner of the room and picked up a small green rucksack. He unzipped the top and pulled out a 9mm Browning and a sat phone.

'Right, it's about six forty-five a.m. in the UK,' he said, unbuckling Christian's feet. 'I hope for your sake Armalite answers his phone.'

Sam released the last strap and Christian rolled over slowly. He lowered his feet to the ground, wobbled and slipped onto the floor. Cursing, he pushed himself up with his arms and slid into a seated position with his back against the wall.

'Right, let's call him now,' said Sam, thrusting the sat phone towards Christian.

Christian took the sat phone and peered at the glowing green screen. He had committed Armalite's number to memory but that felt like a lifetime ago. He dialled the code for the UK and Hereford, then paused. Sam detected the hesitation and raised the Browning closer to Christian's face. Christian punched in the next six digits. A painful memory passed through his mind as a voice informed him of his remaining credit. Not the sugary American lady, but still he flashed to the joke he'd shared with Raglan and Dharia. Sam squatted by him, his head pushed forwards and his head no more than an inch from the phone.

32

Sergeant Frank Norman rested a hoe against the side of a wooden shed at the end of his garden behind his red brick terraced house in Hereford. Despite the apple trees around him having lost most of their leaves, there were still a number of decent apples left clinging to the branches. He stood up and, using his good hand, pulled one down. Early morning dew cascaded down his green jersey as the branch pinged back into position. He strolled back towards the house, assessing each of the raised beds with the eye of a Guards Officer inspecting troops. For the time of year, things looked pretty good. What he needed, though, was a frost to deal with the slugs.

As he bit into the apple, his mobile phone rang.

'Bit early,' he muttered to himself as he fumbled in his pocket of lightweights.

'Frank speaking,' he said, pushing the phone to his ear.

Christian took a deep breath.

'Armalite, it's me, Christian. Are you on your own?'

'Hey, Christi, bit early, all OK? Yes, yes, on my tod. You know me.'

'Good, well, listen, I need your help. I'm sorry, but I'm really in the shit.'

'Bloody hell, mate, not again.'

Christian felt Sam's breath on his cheek and the muzzle of the Browning press against his ribcage. For a moment he lost concentration as he noticed blackened scorch marks on his blistered toes.

'I'll explain when I see you. You know I wouldn't ask if it wasn't important.'

'Of course, go on. You know I'll help.'

'Well, I need you to bring me something.'

'What?'

'I need the diamonds. They're wrapped up in a sports bag in the back of my VW.'

'In the VW?' replied Frank.

The Browning pressed harder.

'Yes, in the VW. They're in the bag in the boot.'

'Yes, yes, I'm with you, Christi. I can bring them. Now, where to?'

Sam breathed in Christian's ear.

'Tell him to get leave on compassionate grounds. Fly to Addis and then make his way to Nanchinda. It's a town near here.'

'Armalite, I need you to get compassionate leave, fly to Addis in Ethiopia and then travel overland to

Nanchinda. Then you ring this sat phone when you're there. Can you see the number on your phone?'

'Fucking hell, Christi, yes, long number on the screen. Nanchinda, you say. Yes, I'm on my way. It'll be a day or two, mind.'

'Two days max,' mouthed Sam, raising two fingers in front of Christian's face.

'Thanks, thanks, I promise . . .'

Sam pulled the sat phone from Christian's hand and pressed the End button. He propped himself up against the table and tossed Christian another cigarette.

'So, what the fuck happened? How did you do it?'

Christian looked up towards Sam's outstretched arm. There was a click and a flame popped up from his fist.

'Well, you shot me as that RPG hit the hostage house. I came round under a pile of rubble but my earpiece was still working. I had the joy of hearing you telling everyone I was dead. Then a bunch of guys were pulling the rubble off me and ripping all my kit off my ops vest. Couldn't use my rifle, could I, so I thought it was pretty much all over when some senior guy rocks in and drags me out of there.'

'OK, so someone saved you?' interrupted Sam.

'Not exactly *saved me*. He chucked me in a cellar for a couple of weeks before moving me on to a terrorist training camp in Mauritania. That's where Jamie and Tim found me.'

'I still don't understand why they went charging in.'

'The reason they came charging in, as you put it,

is because they could see that I was about to be ripped apart on a medieval-style rack. They'd already torn a pig to pieces and burnt its guts so I could see what they had in store for me.'

'Nutters,' grunted Sam, shrugging.

'Not nutters, Sam, two deeply courageous men who were making up for a mistake they made under your influence when they abandoned their posts during the firefight to lay their hands on some filthy blood diamonds. They died fighting like lions against insane odds. They could have slipped away. They had choices and did not have to wade in. That's what courage is, Sam. It's different if you have your back against a wall.'

'So what happened then?'

They went down and I got out. Simple as that. I twigged where I thought Foday might have had his stash. You know the rest. What now?'

'I'll tell you what now. You're going back downstairs and you will stay put here until Armalite calls. Any fucking around from you and I'll make sure you die. So just stay quiet, and if Armalite delivers, you'll never see me again.'

Sam moved towards the door and lifted the latch, while Christian used his arms to pull himself onto his feet. The room filled with green overalls and Christian found himself hobbling his way down the stairs on his heels. They passed through the reddish glow of dawn in the quad and down to the cellar.

33

Raglan's face appeared momentarily in the gloom before the door at the top of the stairs slammed. Christian used the wire along the side of the cage to navigate himself to the back wall where Raglan's hands guided him to the floor.

Masked by chatter and movement from the other cage, Christian pressed close to Raglan's ear.

'Sam Carter's up there. He's working for them. Can't believe it, but it's true.'

Raglan's body jerked forwards in the darkness.

'Yes, he's out of prison. Not dead and has just been roasting me with electricity.'

'What on earth . . . Are you sure it was him? Did you see his face?' Raglan whispered.

'Yes, it was just him and me. He wanted to kill me but I've got Armalite coming down with the stones to buy him off.'

'Holy shit.'

'More later,' murmured Christian, pulling back from Raglan's ear.

The men in the cellar were all awake and the sounds of activity in the rooms above heralded the end of another long, dark and uncomfortable night. Christian rested his head against the wall and closed his eyes in the hope of finding some temporary form of peace. The image of Sam's smirking face had tormented him in the solitary days of imprisonment in Sierra Leone and now it was happening again. Against extraordinary odds, he had made it out and somehow managed to put Sam in a place where he could do no harm to anyone again. Yet the tables had been turned. Impossible, surely? And now, once again, he had placed his life in the hands of Frank Norman, the Regimental Armourer – or Armalite, as everyone called him since he had lost half a hand in a bomb blast in Northern Ireland. Sure, he'd served in Twenty-two as long as anyone else could remember, but was it fair to involve him again? Had he understood? Would Sam just kill him on sight?

Ping. The lights went on, the door scraped and then came the clang as it hit the wall. Down came the guards and the occupants of the end cage were ushered past. Eyes scrutinised Christian, some fearful, some inquisitive and some gloating.

Up in the exercise yard, there was none of the usual early morning quiet. Intense chatter made it clear word had already broken. Christian stepped into the sunshine, his eyes fixed on the ground, and made his way over to his usual corner, trying to walk as normally as his burnt feet would allow. The carpets had not been set up, so he sat down cross-legged and faced outwards through the wire. He looked at the distant mountain tops, where a flotilla of iron-grey clouds gently processed past. Raglan sat down heavily beside him but facing inwards.

'Anyone would think these people had nothing to do,' muttered Raglan out of the side of his mouth. 'No need to look, but the whole world's having a good ogle at you.'

Christian cast a glance over his shoulder at a wall of grey onlookers. Necks craned and fingers pointed at his burnt feet. He breathed hard and fixed his gaze on the horizon as a roll of carpet slapped down in the dewy dust beside him, followed by a light tap of a packet of Craven A landing in his lap.

'Hurts, doesn't it?' said Sha'inti's voice quietly, before snapping something in a Somali dialect at the crowd of onlookers.

Christian swivelled round slowly and looked up at Sha'inti, unsure if it was his sharp words or the arrival of breakfast that had prompted the crowd to start shuffling off. Sha'inti half kicked, half pushed the carpet roll with the side of his foot. It unrolled obediently, and he squatted down beside Christian. He tilted his long face forwards as if examining some ancient object of antiquity in a museum. His eyes wandered around Christian's face unhurriedly.

'You are an interesting man,' he purred. 'Perhaps our paths lie together. Perhaps not. We shall have to wait and maybe we shall see.'

Christian cocked his head to one side to meet his gaze, shrugged and fumbled at the cellophane that wrapped the cigarettes.

'You smoke too much,' said Sha'inti.

'Yeah, I know,' Christian replied.

Sha'inti paused before rocking forwards onto his feet and standing up. 'An interesting man,' he whispered in the direction of Christian's ear.

Sam gripped the butt of the Browning with his right hand and rested his left over the cool stream pumping out from the air-conditioning vent in the centre of the dashboard. He had been parked there for the best part of an hour, and it was now nearly four p.m. His eyes were fixed on the glass door of the café thirty metres away down the street. He had not been able to give Armalite the name, as its only means of identification were a series of unintelligible Arabic letters in swirling green plastic stickers across the front window. It did not matter; it was the only place in Nanchinda. The sight in his rear-view mirror of three dogs tearing at the flesh of a dead donkey, which had interested him at first, now made him feel sick.

Sam pushed open the door of the Nissan jeep and

stepped from the relative cool of the vehicle into an oven of heat. He pushed his sunglasses against the bridge of his nose and, subconsciously, his hand felt the outline of the Browning through his shirt, where he had tucked it into the front of his baggy canvas trousers. He would have preferred something heavier. He peered sideways through the corner of his glasses at a young woman in a long yellow robe and strolled past several two-storey houses built of white concrete with narrow alleys between them. Behind one, he glimpsed a battered corrugated iron workshop and piles of rusting farm machinery. On the other side of the dusty mud road that ran through the centre of town, an ancient bus idled and men in scruffy shorts piled large plastic-wrapped bundles held together with bungees onto the roof rack.

Glancing around, Sam raised a foot onto the wooden decking of the patio outside the café. He approached the door, grasped the handle, then quickly removed his hand from the scalding metal. Inside, there was a fractional drop in temperature, most likely the result of the two ceiling fans that spun awkwardly at different speeds. Clouds of steam from a doorway in the back wall carried a sweet, spicy smell of herbs. The place was empty, except to the left, where a young man in a long brown Arab shirt appeared behind a counter built of railways sleepers with a smooth glass top. He nodded a welcome and a sweeping motion from his hand told Sam he could sit at any of the tables.

'Thank you, a coffee, please,' Sam grunted as he continued to scan the room.

As the young man busied himself behind the counter, Sam navigated his way between the white plastic tables towards the entrance to the kitchen. He parted the multicoloured strings of beads, poked his head inside and flashed a quick smile at two women preparing food in a giant wok. Having clocked the position of the back door, he checked the men's toilet, then seated himself at the table under the faster of the two fans where his coffee now waited.

He took a sip of sickly sweet coffee and immediately realised why there was also a small glass of water on the table next to it. He reached for his cigarettes and watched the smoke being sucked upwards above him and dispersing against the oily yellow paint of the ceiling.

At exactly four p.m. a small, stocky figure appeared, silhouetted in the window against the brightness of the world outside. The shape paused and Sam detected hesitation. Was Armalite nervous? Of course he was, and that was a good thing. He had been astonished to get the call an hour before and hear Sam's voice when he had been expecting Christian. He had stammered in the most satisfying way. Like everyone else, he'd underestimated Sam Carter. The good thing was that with only an hour's warning, there was no way he could have mobilised any back-up. Not in this hick dump miles from anywhere.

Sam smiled as the door pushed open. Armalite stood and stared, framed by the doorway. Sam tried to read his expression. Was the look of disgust an effort to cover anger and shock? Shaking his head slowly, Armalite took a step forward and raised a red biscuit tin in one hand. With his other, he pulled up his navy blue T-shirt and slowly turned in a circle. Sam nodded and used his foot to push back the chair on the opposite side of the table. Armalite moved forwards, chucked the tin on the table and sat down with his hands spread wide on the table top.

Sam grinned through a mist of cigarette smoke. Of course Armalite was baffled. The whole world thought he was banged up in a high-security prison in Cairo. This would set tongues wagging back in Hereford. He knew he was not the most popular guy in the Regiment, but this would put him up there in terms of sheer ability and resource. People didn't just bust out in a matter of weeks. This was unheard of. People could fuck right off.

Armalite's top lip curled under his black handlebar moustache. Sweat trickled down his weathered cheeks.

'You do know you're a cunt, don't you? growled Armalite. 'Always thought so.'

Sam's grim broadened.

'Never were much good in the heat, were you? Or are you boozing too much again? Anyway, nice to see you too.'

'Dismal,' replied Armalite, exhaling. 'Anyway, I've got your nasty little diamonds. Why don't you count them up, weigh them or whatever the fuck you want, and then we'll talk about McKie.'

'You do know that it was McKie that framed me for that bomb in London?'

'Don't know, don't care. Nor does anyone.'

'Well, McKie's the cunt, people need to know,' snapped Sam, his grin narrowing.

'You've got the stones, now where is he?'

'How do I know they're real?'

'How the fuck do I know? Does the British Army run a gemmology course?'

Sam lifted the lid of the biscuit tin and groped inside.

'The deal is this. I take these away, and if they're worth what you say, I'll let him go. If not, I'll waste him, local style.'

Armalite raised his hand and rested it on top of the tin.

'No deal then.'

'Yes, deal, actually. I'm the one pointing a gun in your guts.' Sam tapped the bottom of the table with the muzzle of the Browning. 'And I can get away with it round here.'

'You probably don't know this,' replied Armalite.

'What?'

'Well, I was still only Lance Corporal at the time, but I was Staff when you were on Selection. You only got through by the skin of your teeth; a fluke, really. There was a big question mark over you.'

'Bullshit.'

'There was. People thought you were sloppy. Bit of a careless yob. Don't believe me, do you?'

'Is that really the best you can do?' replied Sam, rolling his eyes.

'Come to think of it, I can do better, yes.'

Although there was no accompanying noise, Sam was aware of movement behind him. Before he had been able to react, his eye caught the momentary glint of sunlight on metal a few inches in front of his face. His brain then caught up as he felt the gentle pressure of a serrated garrotting wire tighten around his neck.

The massive, sweating head of Trooper Grant MacDonald appeared over his shoulder.

'For a man of your size, you do move stealthily, Beasty,' purred Armalite.

'He's right,' rumbled the Beast in his thick Glaswegian accent. 'You are a sloppy cunt. Should have checked the Ladies' too.'

Sam's eyes darted sideways. He instantly recognised the bright ginger number-one cut and heavily pockmarked cheek. This was the Beast. Sure, everyone knew he had a gentle side, but revved up, he was the biggest, hardest and meanest killing machine in the British Army. A six-foot five, eighteen-stone brute of a man, he'd grown up on the toughest council estate in Scotland and passed into Para Mortars aged eighteen.

'And before you get any bright ideas, Carter, this wire is linked to my belt. Shoot me, and your head will hit the floor before I do.'

'Yes, a careless, sloppy yob,' continued Armalite. 'You let the Regiment down in so many ways.'

'What the fuck are you doing here?' spluttered Sam.

'If you must know, Carter, I'm actually on paternity leave,' the Beast replied.

'Paternity leave, what? *Paternity leave?* Who the fuck ever got that?' Sam twisted his head around very slightly to look at the Beast.

'Yep, you could even congratulate me.'

'Before you saw my head off?'

'Either's fine.'

'Right,' Armalite interrupted, pointing a finger in Sam's face. 'This is the deal, and it's actually quite good for you. Too good, in fact.'

'I'm still the one holding the gun.'

'Shut up,' croaked the Beast, increasing the pressure of the wire.

'The deal is you release Christi from the prison where ever you said it was,' Armalite continued, 'and once he's out, you can have the stones.'

'That is actually the deal I was offering you, you prick,' snarled Sam. 'There was no need to bring Trooper MacDonald here halfway across the planet to kill me when he should be at home changing nappies.'

'There's one slight difference,' replied Armalite, raising an eyebrow.

'Like what then?'

'Like you're going to stick to it,' said Armalite, getting to his feet. 'Right, we're off, and you can call when you've found a way of getting him out.'

'Yep,' the Beast snarled in Sam's ear. 'Anyway, it must be your turn on that donkey by now.'

34

Christian had only caught a brief glimpse of Sam that day. He had wandered along the top of the wall above the exercise yard and spoken briefly to the gunner manning the 50 cal. He had hovered about and then wandered back along the walkway. Three days had passed since that extraordinary night, which meant that Armalite could, in theory, have made it at least as far as Addis. The day had dragged past, hotter than before and with more flies buzzing around his scabby toes. Finally, the cigarette butt party was set to work and the carpets were rolled once again. They filed down stairs and off went the lights.

Christian pressed his back against the wall and the felt cold fingers of depression reach for him. Another dark and timeless night of concrete, muttering and waiting faced him. Surely Armalite would have hauled his arse down to Africa by now? Yes, he would have moved heaven and earth to get there, but what about Customs? Some over-vigilant, try-hard arsehole at Heathrow might have opened up his suitcase and found the diamonds. Around Hereford Armalite looked normal enough, but to a customs officer his missing fingers, massive tash and wild eyes would look pretty odd. Then, if he did make it through, had he twigged on the coded warning? Would he be ready to cope with Sam? He was a great soldier, but that was different from dealing with the likes of Sam.

Chair legs ground against the floor above and one tiny milestone moved into the past. Next, the guard would change and the lights would most likely ping on for a second or two. Then the long haul through to dawn. Miserable. And Raglan would snore and fidget the whole way through. The cold fingers gripped tighter.

Christian's eyes opened. Initially, he was not sure why. He listened, his head cocked to one side. He had heard voices first but now there was shouting. Doors were slamming and boots pounded in the corridors above. Raglan crouched beside him and the end cage buzzed with activity.

'Bit odd,' whispered Christian, using Raglan's shoulder to push himself up.

'Sounds like chaos up there,' replied Raglan. 'Probably some exercise to keep the lazy fuckers on their toes.'

The top door clanged open and crashed into the

wall. Boots clattered down the stairs and the darkness was dissected by an array of torch beams. A barrage of shouted orders echoed incoherently around the cellar and the doors to the cages were flung open. Guns jabbed, hands waved and guards yelled. Christian piled out with Raglan on his heels and felt himself thrust up the stairs. Seconds later, men spewed into the moonlit expanse of the exercise yard. Above them on the wall, a dozen or more guards stood silhouetted against a backdrop of glowing orange. Smoke billowed above them and swirled into the starry sky above.

More and more inmates surged into the yard and gravitated into their natural groups. Sha'inti grabbed the tunics of his men and hauled them together. Yelling instructions, he gestured to Christian. Without warning, the world lit up as the vast system of flood-lights they had seen on their arrival illuminated, forcing the guards on the wall to shield their eyes momentarily. Huddled in their corner, Christian felt a sense of order return with the lights. The guards were gaining control and any potential for mass disorder was fading.

As Christian stood and stared at the rising flames, two guards on the right-hand end of the wall crumpled and fell forwards through large puffs of dust. A split second later came the screech of inbound rounds and the rough grunt of large-calibre machine-gun fire. More guards toppled, some forwards, some backwards, and the top wall was consumed by a wave of dust.

'What now?' gasped Raglan through a bedlam of gunfire and screaming.

'Just hold on,' replied Christian. 'Fuck knows, let's see.'

'Sounds like a bit of a one-man band out there,' hissed Raglan in Christian's ear.

Sha'inti's face pushed in between them, shining orange and fixed with determination.

'I told you my people would come. Stay with me. Close, very close.'

Christian looked around and saw the inmates falling into two categories. Some had rushed forwards to seize the weapons of the fallen guards and some simply stood rooted to the spot. A siren sounded in the inner quad and the sounds of engines contrasted with the clatter of machine-gun fire. Christian was about to join the stream of men rushing back into the fort when a dark figure emerged on the wall. With the distant machine gun from the desert behind them focussing on the fortified emplacement of the .50 Cal, this man raised a rifle and fired a series of short bursts of fire, knocking out each floodlight one by one.

With the yard slipping back into relative darkness, the figure rotated his position and fired a series of single shots down into the central quad. A second later, he was sliding down the corrugated iron roof over the washing area and crashing to his feet in the yard. Pushing forwards through the seething mass of men, he made a beeline for the back fence and flashed a torch in circular movements above his head.

Even before he saw his face, Christian knew it was Sam from the short, sharp, well-aimed shooting. Regular troops never conserved rounds like that. Sam suddenly sprang backwards as the front half of a four-tonne lorry slammed through the wire. The front wheels spewed plumes of dust and sand into the air as the vehicle was momentarily gripped in the metal strands. The engine roared again and the canvas roof covering the rear section ripped into strips.

'Quick, before they turn it back on!' yelled Sam, pulling open the passenger door.

Christian looked on as the lorry lurched forwards into the yard. The driver swung the wheel to the left and slammed on the brakes. The wheels spun again, this time in reverse. As the lorry manoeuvred around, Christian caught sight of a familiar profile. Armalite pressed his foot back to the floor, sending the lorry hurtling back towards the tangled hole it had just created. With seemingly less momentum than on the way in, the lorry slowed as lengths of wire snagged at the remains of the roof.

After a moment of hesitation, a frenzied blur of grey swarmed around the rear of the lorry. Some squeezed down the sides and others clambered up into the back. Others pushed against the tailgate in scrum-like formation. Still the rounds screeched overhead, thudding into the walls of the fort and sending slabs of masonry cascading to the ground. The lorry lurched forwards and men surged through the gap behind it.

Sha'inti bellowed instructions at his men and gestured wildly to Christian. Kicking off his flip-flops, he bolted through the gap out into the desert. Christian ducked through the inner wire, his hands raised to protect his face from hanging strands. He leapt across the area of no-man's-land, past a swinging panel of the outer super-max mesh. Around him men bomb-burst in all directions into the darkness. Sha'inti was still shouting, calling the names of each of his men. He ran among them, goading them to increase the pace and to keep together.

Christian tucked into the middle of the pack with Raglan right on his heels. Behind them gunfire crackled and, although obscured now from direct line of sight, an orange glow hung over the fort. Sam would have known where to put the match. Most likely, he would have torched the fuel depot. That would have caused the panic and been the reason to evacuate the inside of the fort. In the minds of the guards, there would have been no difference in risk between emptying the cells at three a.m. and doing it at six-thirty a.m., and even they would not have wished to explain away over a hundred deaths in custody.

Around him Christian became aware of increased

puffing and panting. Raglan moved parallel to him but others were falling back. Sharp stones and invisible spiky plants underfoot made each step feel like Russian roulette. Men cried out as they pelted through an area of rocks that formed the side of a rising escarpment. Soft sand welcomed them down the other side. A mixture of staff sergeant and sheepdog, Sha'inti continued to bring up the rear, his tone alternating between stick and carrot. Without warning, he snapped an instruction and Christian found himself running into the back of the man in front. The group came to an abrupt halt and collapsed to the ground.

Lying in the dust, Christian soon realised why. Behind them and off to the right, engines revved. Headlights lit up the desert in V-shaped slices which elongated and contracted as pursuing vehicles bounced over uneven ground. Men shouted and shots rang out.

'Reminds me of lamping rabbits,' muttered Raglan between breaths.

Christian raised his head slightly.

'Keep flat,' hissed Sha'inti. 'They'll gun us down like dogs.'

'Where are your people then?' asked Raglan.

'Shut up!' snapped Sha'inti. 'You will see.'

The sound of men trying to catch their breath took over again as the vehicles bounced away over the horizon. Christian pushed himself up into a sitting position and tried to examine his feet in the moonlight.

'Better not look,' said Sha'inti. 'We need to move and then keep moving. Fast, fast, fast. South.'

Christian stood up and, as they set off, looked up into the night sky. Over his shoulder, he picked out the Plough and followed a line up from the vertical end to find the North Star. Sure enough, they were heading south. Still snarling words of encouragement, Sha'inti led the group from the front. The pace was no longer a headlong sprint but a steady jog. Within a few minutes, Christian smiled inwardly. Just like on any group exercise, the men were starting to spread out. The gaps were growing bigger. It always happened, from Boy Scouts jogging round a park to the fittest SF storming up Pen Y Fan on personal best. Christian resisted his natural instinct and positioned himself at number three, just behind the two young Somali lads who had approached them in the corner of the yard on the first morning. Further back, the older men huffed and puffed.

The pace slowed and, as the first glimmer of orange appeared to their left, Christian felt the sweat on his forehead start to dry. They continued at a fast walk across what could now be seen to be smooth baked mud. Soon they were picking their way through shale-like debris on the far side of a dry river system, ending the brief respite on their feet. With the rising sun, came the tsetse flies. Christian wiped the first few from his forearms. For some reason, they were slower and lazier first thing in the morning.

They trudged uphill in a line through crumbling yellow rocks. No one spoke. Even Sha'inti seemed resigned to the slow pace. Behind them, the ground fell away, revealing a wide open plain of brown and grey scrub, broken up by patches of shadow cast by the odd clump of bushes. Christian tried to think how far they had travelled. Having been going the best part of three hours, they should have covered about fifteen kilometres, but their route had been anything but direct. It was perfectly probable they were no more than eight kilometres from the fort. That would put them firmly in the inner circle of any search party. No wonder, now that dawn had broken, Sha'inti was leading them up into high ground which would be impassable to vehicles.

The strange thing was that they were now at the point they should have been at the moment they had been intercepted by the Egyptian troops. The last two weeks had just been a sideshow. They were now back on task. As usual, the 'plan' had gone to rat shit, like it usually did. So far, he'd been half tortured to death, half bored to death, and the only tangible outcome was that the bastard who had ruined his life in the first place was now likely to be a multimillionaire. Very, very wrong. Armalite must have played ball with Sam, otherwise the breakout would not have happened. Then there was Dharia. More wrong still. Grotesquely wrong. What had become of her? Would MI6 deny all knowledge and cut her loose? Perhaps she wouldn't even try and come in. What would she do? What *could* she do?

Sha'inti waved a hand in the air, muttered some words and pointed at the ground. Once the men had flopped down, Christian observed him lower himself slowly into a seated position next to them. It was impressive leadership. His legs and feet hurt just as much as anyone else's, but he didn't collapse like an exhausted mule at the first whiff of a break. This guy held himself out as a cut above his men.

'Ten minutes. No more,' he said, looking at Christian.

'Sure,' Christian replied. 'May I ask where we are heading?'

Sha'inti paused, his voice disconcertingly relaxed.

'Well, I think we'll go and visit my people. There, we, you, all of us will be safe.'

'How far's that?' chipped in Raglan.

'Not far,' said Sha'inti. 'We walk today. Maybe get a ride. Not far. We'll get water on the way.'

35

The morning wore on and the sun rose in a big blue sky. Scattered wisps of cirrus held out defiantly and speck-like birds rested in rising thermals. Around them, an array of insects buzzed and danced with increasing persistence. They filed through narrow rocky gullies, each man scanning the ground before him for the next safe place to put his foot. Sha'inti led the way, the back of his tunic a dark grey from sweat.

Christian plodded along behind Raglan, a part of him happy to be led. Sha'inti was the man worrying about the route and the fact that if they did not get a drink in the next few hours men would be falling down or, more likely, deserting first. He was the one having to keep up the bullshit of pretending everything was under control when very clearly it was not. It would be fascinating to see how he handled it. There

273

was already discontented muttering coming from the guys at the back. The drama of the escape was over and the reality of being on the run in the blistering heat of the Somali badlands had set in. Whilst it had been a mass breakout, anyone caught was likely to feel the wrath of the fat Yank. It had happened on his watch and he'd be feeling the heat too.

With the sun directly above them casting no shadow, Christian guessed it had to be around midday. The gullies had flattened out and the ground underfoot had turned to a dusty grey mixture of sand and baked soil. They shuffled along in dazed silence, each staring at the sweating back of the man in front. Christian had not noticed but Sha'inti was now nearly 500 metres ahead of them. He stood still, looking from left to right with his hands on his hips. As they drew closer to him, vehicle tracks became visible on the ground before him. Sha'inti squatted down and pushed his fingers into the ruts.

'Only Army vehicles have new tyres,' he said over his shoulder. 'These have no tread. Come on, let's go.'

Christian looked around and gauged a minor improvement in atmosphere. They had hit a dirt road and that suggested Sha'inti had some idea of where they were going. Looking back over his shoulder, Sha'inti stabbed at the air in front of him with his index finger and they set off again at a brisker pace, hand-railing from the track at a distance of fifty metres. An hour of sweat, thirst and grilling heat passed before a distant whine interrupted the suppressed chorus of painful gasps as raw feet padded as lightly as possible over scalding sand. Sha'inti froze, cocked his head momentarily to one side and dropped to a crouching position. Like a row of falling dominos, the line of men followed suit. A couple of seconds passed before the noise was clearly identifiable as an engine. A tiny lateral cutting movement from Sha'inti's left hand sent the men onto their stomachs.

The engine approached. A single sound, just one vehicle. Still no clue as to whether friend or foe. Christian peered forwards, his chin raised just above the sand. The track was less than fifty metres away. The ground rose and fell slightly between them, but not enough to offer any form of protection from fire. To the rear, there was the best part of 200 metres of open scrub before the beginning of a rising slope. Raglan caught his eye. He had read the terrain too. No chance. Sha'inti had fucked up. It would be either surrender, a massacre or a miracle.

Movement drew Christian's eye to a flash of white paint, the brightness of the light reflecting from the sand forcing him to squint. A moment later, a Humvee with UN markings clearly visible down the side came into view. In the armoured turret, a man in green gripped the handle of a 50 cal.

'Keep still,' hissed Sha'inti, his body rigid and lizard-like, supported a fraction off the ground on his fingertips and toes.

The gunner's head pivoted around and his hand thumped up and down on the roof in front of him. His torso lurched forwards as the vehicle came to a screeching halt. The 50 cal swung around and now pointed directly at the spot where they lay. The back door swung open and spat out a string of soldiers into a cloud of steadily expanding dust rising from the wheels. Weapons in arms and amid a barrage of shouting, the soldiers scuttled in an arc-shaped manoeuvre and threw themselves to the ground.

'Oh, for fuck's sake,' exhaled Raglan, turning towards Christian and resting the side of his head on the ground. 'Here we go again.'

The soldiers, all Somali in appearance, inched forwards in scruffy desert DPM, some leopard-crawling, some raised into a crouched walking position. At thirty metres' distance, the chorus of shouting and yelling condensed into one identifiable voice issuing a stream of orders. Sha'inti snapped something at the men closest to him and raised his hands in the air. Slowly and awkwardly, he stood, his hands above his head. Christian stared up at his face where streaks of sweat formed defined lines in the dust down his cheeks. His hands quivered visibly and a tremor seized one of his legs. He raised his chin, fixed his stare and stepped forwards. Christian had seen this expression before. It was the face that had pressed against his the first morning at the fort while Raglan had pissed about in the shower.

Sha'inti strode forwards. The soldiers paused their advance and swivelled their aging SLRs in concert to concentrate their aim directly at him.

'He's got balls,' whispered Raglan. 'One twitchy dickhead and he's toast.'

Two soldiers sprang forwards from the middle of the line and approached Sha'inti, their weapons still raised. Sha'inti slowly turned through a full circle on the spot, his hands still high. By the time he faced them again, the tension in their faces had eased to confident grins. Chatter broke out amongst the remaining soldiers and they surged forwards.

Sha'inti snapped something at the soldier closest to him, lowered his arms and pointed at the Humvee. The soldier paused, looked around at the other soldiers in confusion. As Sha'inti stepped closer to the soldier, the front door of the Humvee creaked open. An older soldier slid down from the front seat. To demonstrate he was in no hurry, he paused to light a cigarette. Taking a long, slow drag, he let his arm fall back to his side, revealing three stripes of authority on the sleeve of his shirt.

Sha'inti pushed through the thicket of rusting gun barrels towards him. The officer jerked his head and Sha'inti followed him around the far side of the Humvee. The remaining soldiers exchanged glances and stood awkwardly, their weapons hanging limply in their arms. Sha'inti's men clumped together, eyeing the soldiers with a mixture of suspicion and defiance.

The seconds ticked past with nothing moving except a plume of cigarette smoke winding skywards from behind the Humvee.

After a couple of minutes, the officer reappeared with Sha'inti behind him. He jerked his thumb in the direction of the rear door and muttered a couple of words to the driver, who remained at the wheel. The soldiers lowered their weapons, retreated and climbed one by one into the back of the vehicle. Next, Sha'inti was issuing instructions to his men and they were clambering up the side and onto the roof. A canteen of water was passed up, the engine revved and they bounced off down the dirt road. Christian gripped the roof rails and looked around at the men as they squatted uncomfortably on the scorching metal.

'Out of the fire and back into the frying pan,' grumbled Raglan, tucking the material of his tunic under his backside.

36

The rest of the day crawled past in a haze of heat, exhaust smoke and juddering discomfort. Even the tsetse flies which could tolerate the diesel fumes provided a welcome distraction. The canteen was refreshed in the early evening and after a short break spent sitting in the shadow of the vehicle, they were off again, winding through arid valleys hemmed in by steeply rising mountains.

'Eighty Ks south?' whispered Christian under the cover of the engine noise.

'Five hours at fifteen or so, yeah, roughly,' croaked Raglan.

Early evening came as a relief from the sun and the scorching roof of the Humvee. Sha'inti sat with his back pressed up against the gun turret. He leant forwards to offer around a packet of cigarettes that had just been passed up to him by the gunner. Morale cranked up a notch and quiet conversations broke out amongst the men. Christian watched the look of relief spread across Raglan's filthy, sunburnt face as he dragged hard through cracked lips. His mind flicked randomly back to his grandfather telling him that cigarettes were pushed through to the front lines in the trenches of World War I as a priority, even over food and medical supplies. 'Every General knows, cut off the fags and you're buggered,' he'd said.

The gunner's head suddenly popped up in the turret. He unscrewed the fixing pin, lowered the barrel of the 50 cal from its resting position at forty-five degrees and levelled it at the horizon. Sha'inti spun around and raised himself to a crouching position. The other men snapped out of their exhausted detachment and scanned the area ahead through squinting eyes.

Christian followed the direction of the outstretched arm of the young Somali squatting next to him. Initially, he saw nothing. Then, an oblong shape stood out, rippling in the heat-blurred distance. The Humvee rumbled on, closing in on what was fast becoming identifiable as a lone pickup, side-on across the track. Figures stood in the back, guns poking in the air. At a distance of about 200 metres, a second pickup, lurking out of sight immediately behind the first, peeled off slowly in an arc. Flanking them, it parked behind a lip of rising ground with only the rear-mounted gun clearly visible.

The gunner on the Humvee pivoted the 50 cal in one direction and then the other. Sha'inti rested a hand on his shoulder and said something that cracked a nervous smile. At fifty metres, the Humvee braked and came to a rest. There was a pause while the swirling dust settled before the passenger door opened and the officer stepped out. As Sha'inti slithered off the roof to join him, he pulled off his beret and shoved it into the side pocket of his combat trousers. He muttered something at the gunner, who instantly pushed the barrel of the 50 cal to a conciliatory angle pointing in the air. The two men turned and walked slowly towards the waiting pickup. Like earlier, they disappeared around the back.

Christian looked at Raglan and interpreted the frowning furrows ploughed across his forehead. They both knew it. This was the moment they were about to step into the Stone Age. So far, at least, their captors had worn uniforms and had some form of recognisable hierarchy. Sure, they had been brutal, torturing bastards, but even Third World rabble would probably prefer to shoot a prisoner than slowly decapitate him with a saw. From now on, there were no parameters. This was the void. The pack of photocopied sheets given out after Selection setting out how prisoners could expect to be treated by different regimes didn't cover these guys.

The gunner passed round more cigarettes. Christian saw his hands were shaking and felt tension radiate from him. One of the older Arabs pulled out a cigarette but kept hold of the packet. The gunner nodded apologetically as if he had been wrong even to expect it back. Next, the lighter came round and the Arab kept that too.

Christian felt a sense of relief as the two re-emerged smiling from behind the pickup. Whatever deal they had done seemed to have worked for both parties. Sha'inti waved his arm and the men were leaping down from the roof and making their way over to the waiting vehicle. Cries of greeting rang out and some turned to watch the Humvee make a three-point turn and lumber off.

Christian and Raglan were last to clamber up the back of the dusty grey Toyota. There was just sitting room for the eight new arrivals in addition to the four shemagh-clad men propped against a bull bar that ran along the back window of the cab. Each held an AK. Three were Arab in appearance, young men, bearded and with purposeful expressions. A tall African propped himself up on the end. His long brown shirt hung down over faded green, lightweight trousers. A netted pouch on the front of his dust-encrusted US Army ops vest contained a handful of dried tobacco leaves and two grenades. Christian tried not to stare but found his eyes drawn to the name badge on the upper left-hand side. It was a strip of green material with heavy black lettering sewn into it. All the letters of the name had been blotted out, leaving just three letters: RIP. Raglan had seen the sick joke too.

With Sha'inti sitting in the cab, they moved off. The other pickup caught up and hovered behind them. Wedges of pitta bread were passed around, followed by a damp muslin rag containing a block of white goat's cheese. Christian observed the protocol as the men bit open one side of the pitta and stuffed the space inside with a blob of cheese pulled with their fingers from the muslin. His turn came and he followed suit, desperate to ease the gnawing hunger in his stomach.

Once the pitta had been consumed, chatter broke out. Christian could not understand the language but the triumphant tone and body language said it all. The guys with the guns listened as the older Arab gesticulated with his hands, building up to his fist smacking into his palm. Christian's guess that this represented the lorry smashing through the wire was confirmed as the Arab's fingers flicked in all directions like running figures. The Arab continued with a series of hissing sounds and pointed at his feet. Christian felt a wave of fear pass through him. He could see these guys doing the maths. Who the fuck were these two oddballs in the back of the truck?

Raglan, with his curly black hair and his naturally dark skin made even darker by a mixture of sun tan and dirt, looked fairly passable as a man of Arab origin, but he felt exposed. With several weeks' matted beard growth, he might look as rough as a badger's arsehole, but the whole plan looked weaker than ever. Sure, he knew the cruel and manipulative hands of sleep deprivation could unravel any cover story given the chance, but the guys with the guns were looking fairly suspicious, to his mind. The only thing holding it together was the fact that he had evidence of electricity burns on his feet. Of course, they would hear about the stint in the *bouteille noire* too. No one, however committed to their government, would go through that to build a story. Christian slumped back against the side of the truck and closed his eyes. There was no way he could sleep, but it might afford him some kind of peace.

The pickup bounced on as darkness fell. The drop in air temperature combined with the breeze in the back made the heat of the day feel like a long-lost friend by the time they finally came to a stop. Christian sat up and looked around. In theory, he should have been noting speed, distance and passing landmarks, but in reality, he'd been a shivering wreck doing his best to close down the paranoid muddle of his mind. If Raglan's expression had been anything to go by, he was just as miserable and uncomfortable too. His head had hung to one side like a corpse, with an occasional twitch that seemed to bring him round reluctantly for a few seconds.

There was movement and noise all around. People were calling to each other and pointing. Figures milled around the vehicle, illuminated as silhouettes in the headlights of the pickup parked behind them.

'Get out and come with me,' said Sha'inti, appearing in the darkness.

Christian hauled himself to his feet and, using the top of the rear tyre as a step, lowered himself stiffly to the ground.

'So where are we?' he said gruffly.

'We have travelled about three hundred kilometres to the east. We are now in my village and not far from the sea.'

'The sea?' Christian echoed.

'Yes, the sea is fifty kilometres from here. That way.' Sha'inti pointed into the darkness. 'Now move it. You two come with me.'

Christian resisted his natural instinct to ask more questions. Grateful for the darkness, he followed Sha'inti through a sea of staring faces. One man gripped his tunic and twisted him towards the glare of the headlights to peer at him through wide, excited eyes. Christian held his gaze just long enough to wither the man's toothy grin. The hands released their grip and he pulled away.

Sha'inti led the way along a row of huts, the conical roofs forming dark triangles against the night sky. He bent down outside the last in the line and fumbled in the gloom. There was a squeaking noise followed by the metallic tap of a bolt snapping back.

'In here for you,' he said, stepping up and back.

Christian stooped down and through a doorway, the overhanging thatch scratching through his hair. Raglan pushed inside behind him.

'In the morning, you will have new clothes and food. Stay in here now,' Sha'inti called from outside.

There was a scraping noise followed by a click. Christian reached around in the darkness, his fingertips finding rough concrete walls rising to chest height. Above, wooden rafters supported thatch which rose to a central circle, through which an eye of night sky looked down on them. Raglan rested his hand on Christian's shoulder and guided him to a sitting position in the middle of the hut.

'If I were them, I'd have someone sitting outside that door with his ears on maximum,' he whispered in Christian's ear.

Christian nodded in the darkness.

'The weird thing is,' Raglan continued, 'that the smell of goats and animal manure round here makes me feel quite at home.'

Christian cupped his hand around Raglan's ear. 'Why on earth we bother with all this shit, I really don't know.'

'Well, we've got choices, haven't we?'

'Choices? Like what?'

'As I see it . . .'

'Like what sort of gun we'd like to be shot with? Back of the head or gut shot? Depth of grave? Endless choices.'

'For heaven's sake, I'm not worried about detail. Either we punch our way out through the roof and make for the coast or we sit it out here, hold our nerve and keep going.'

Christian pulled his head away and rested his chin in the palm of his hand, his mind grinding like an engine short of oil. It was impossible to make a good decision on three hours' sleep in two nights. He knew that. The secret was not to change plan and to have confidence in the strategy that had been formulated at a time of full clarity. It had made sense before. What had changed?

He felt the warmth of Raglan's breath against his ear once again.

'What would Macbeth do?'

'Macbeth? God knows. He was a delusional Scottish psychopath hellbent on violence and murder with a bitch of a wife. Our decision making shouldn't . . .'

'Sorry, I meant Hannibal. What would *he* have done?'

'It's hardly relevant. He commanded the largest and best-equipped army on earth at the time. That's called having choices. There're two of us. In bare feet and togas.'

'Well, if I had to pick one of them, I'd take Macbeth. Sounds handy.'

'He sounds like half the fucking Regiment. Anyway, I reckon we stick with it. In theory the story still stacks up, and if you factor in what we've been through too, it has to look better. Doesn't it?'

'I think so. But that Sha'inti's a slippery sack of shit.'

'OK. Here's the deal. If either one of us wants to pull the plug, we both go. No arguing, pulling rank, shit like that. We both go together. OK?'

'Sure, OK, that's the deal. I'm happy with that,' said Raglan, nodding his head slowly in the darkness.

37

When Christian opened his eyes, a bright column of sunlight dropped from the hole in the roof above. Flies appeared golden as they darted in and out of the light, and particles of glowing dust hung in the air. He raised himself onto an elbow and looked around. Encrusted animal excrement flaked from the stained concrete walls and piles of pellet-like dung littered the dusty mud floor. The bottom half of a blue plastic drum stood by the low wooden door. Christian got to his feet and peered at the array of drowned insects floating on the surface of the murky brown water inside.

'Hard to know if we're meant to shit in this or drink out of it,' he muttered lowering a finger into the water to allow a large black beetle to crawl to the safety of his finger.

Raglan opened his eyes and groaned.

'What's going on? I was having a perfectly nice dream about something quite pleasant.'

'Like what?' asked Christian, guiding the beetle off his finger onto the floor.

'Well, there's been this big dog fox in the valley for ages. Cunning as you like. Will take livestock in daylight, you know the sort of thing. Anyway, fortunately, one of the kitchen windows was already ajar, otherwise they make a noise when you open them and the foxes bugger right off.'

'Don't tell me, please,' said Christian, a smile cracking across his face, 'you were actually dreaming about vermin control?'

'Vermin control? No, no, I was just dreaming of being at home.'

'Same fucking difference.' Christian sighed, pressing his eye to the crack that ran along the top of the door. 'More to the point, get a load of this. I can see the back end of a brand-new Toyota Land Cruiser. Must be fifty grand's worth at least. Well pimped.'

Raglan hauled himself up, shuffled stiffly over to join Christian by the door and pressed his head into the corner of the doorway to get the widest possible view.

'So weird,' he whispered. 'Stone Age sitting side by side with twenty-first-century bling. Never a very healthy combination.'

'Kind of says it all round here. It's the classic case of the bastards at the top using religion to control the

Muppets at the bottom while they mop up and spank their cash on . . .'

'I always enjoyed the *Muppet Show*,' Raglan interrupted, twisting around to look in the other direction. 'I liked the one that played the drums. The one with long, shaggy brown hair.'

'Did you really?'

'I felt Animal had a lot more about him than Karl Marx,' Raglan continued.

'Well, there's nothing Marxist going on round here. Capitalism looks alive and well to me. I can see the top of a satellite dish over there,' said Christian, pointing upwards with his finger. 'Anyway, what was the big yellow chicken called that ran the show?'

'It wasn't a chicken. It was a bird,' sighed Raglan.

'Since when has a chicken not been a bird?'

'I'd have a better idea than you. I've got twenty at home. Well, at least I did when we left.'

'Well, here comes Big Bird now. I can see him coming this way.' Christian pulled back from the door and rubbed the blood back into the side of his face.

The scraping of a bolt followed the metallic jingling of keys. The door creaked outwards and the barrel of an AK appeared. The head and shoulders of the tall African guy from the pickup squeezed through the doorway. Inside, he straightened up and brushed pieces of straw from his hair. Initially he looked around the room as if it were empty. His eyes then settled on Christian before dropping to the floor, where he rubbed his boot through the dried pellets of dung. The message was clear: 'you sleep in shit'.

With a jerk of his rifle, he swivelled round and retreated back through the open door. Christian followed Raglan out and immediately raised his hand to shield his eyes from the blazing glare of sunlight. Sha'inti stood outside, the tails of his long white shirt rippling in the breeze. He wore loose brown cotton trousers with a Glock 17 holstered on a black canvas belt. Without a word, he walked off the way he had just come. The African jerked his rifle once again and they set off behind him. They passed through a gateway in the wooden fence that encircled the row of huts. White and brown goats wandered freely and women in brightly coloured dresses sat on the doorsteps of whitewashed breeze-block houses with glinting, corrugated iron roofs. Beyond extended a rough scrub of yellowy grey sand and soil.

As they came parallel to the Toyota, Sha'inti shot a glance over his shoulder. Christian guessed it was to gauge their reaction to the incongruously new and fully armoured vehicle. They turned a corner and passed a row of shipping containers, most still carrying the names of international transport companies down the sides. Christian counted thirty before his eyes were drawn to the barrels of an anti-aircraft gun poking up above a white Bedouin-style tent. Again, Sha'inti glanced back.

As they rounded the side of the tent, Sha'inti pointed to some white plastic chairs set up in a circle under an awning of grey canvas which formed an entrance way. He sat down and gestured to the others to do the same. Christian chose the seat directly opposite, his mind momentarily questioning how these plastic chairs must have been intercepted on the high seas somewhere between China and their intended destination on a patio in Europe.

'Right,' said Sha'inti, opening his hands wide in front of him. 'Tell me who you really are.'

Christian concentrated on keeping his face still. In theory, this was Raglan's turf. He was the senior officer and it would be his call. The tall African sitting next to Sha'inti adjusted the position of the AK in his lap. Raglan shifted awkwardly, his hands gripping the arms of his chair.

'And if I don't believe you first time,' Sha'inti continued, 'there won't be a second chance. We have old customs in this country and very modern ways of carrying them out. Do you understand?'

Raglan released the arms of his chair and leant forwards to speak.

'Well, we weren't told what you were told. All we knew was that we would be met in Addis and taken to you. They said you would have photographs of us and that would be enough. They said communications had to be kept to a minimum.'

'So who are you then?'

'Well, it's very simple. We're two guys from Leicester. We met through the mosque about six years ago and things went from there. Like a lot of people, we want to join the jihad and play our part. You can't do that sitting on your arse in the UK. There's so much talk but nothing ever happens. And in a climate of extreme suspicion, you need people that can blend with the crowd. Being of mixed parentage, we look British, speak British. That's why we got the chance to come. They said it was a big advantage and we would be useful.'

Sha'inti tilted backwards. His eyes narrowed and his fingers drummed on his thigh.

'It's possible you are who you say you are. You match the photographs, and no MI6 guys these days are stupid enough to end up in those holes in the walls like you two did. I appreciate you may have converted, adopted new names and become a part of the religious community. I understand that. But still, there is one little thing I need to verify before I will consider you.'

Raglan cleared his throat.

'We'll talk again tomorrow,' continued Sha'inti. 'In the meantime, you will have clothes and food. I need to speak with the boss first. It's for him to decide.'

'The boss?' said Raglan, unable to suppress his surprise. 'Aren't you the boss?'

'Me?' answered Sha'inti with half a laugh. 'No, no. I am nothing but a humble lieutenant.'

The tall African pushed his hand into the netting on the front of his ops vest and pinched a wodge of tobacco leaves in his fingers. He stood up and pushed them into the side of his mouth.

'Move, now,' he said.

'Thank you,' replied Raglan, looking at Sha'inti. 'We're . . .'

'Go now. See you tomorrow,' cut in Sha'inti.

The tall guy led the way back around the tent towards the containers. Halfway along the row, he paused and peered down the side of a large blue container. Muttering to himself, he yanked back two levers and hauled open one of the heavy metal doors to reveal an eight-foot-high wall of red shoe boxes. With obvious satisfaction, he stood back and gestured with his hand. Christian stepped forwards and examined the boxes, looking for something his size. He pulled down a box, lifted the lid and folded back some pristine white tissue paper.

'Bit fancy for me, those,' said Raglan, opening a box.

'Better than flip-flops,' replied Christian, pushing his foot into a pair of white Adidas tennis shoes.

Back in the hut, Christian cleared the dung pellets from an area of floor and sat down with his back against the wall.

'Feels weird to be wearing normal clothes again,' said Raglan, pulling at the sides of his new trousers.

'Normal clothes?' Christian queried.

'Well, not quite what I usually go for, but one up on a toga.'

'You'd fit in fine at one of those full moon parties on a beach in Thailand.'

'Is that what they wear? Stripy shirts and baggy blue trousers?

'I really don't know, but if we have to leg it, I'd rather not be barefoot. So what the fuck do we do?'

Raglan swept the area of floor next to Christian with the side of his shoe and sat down.

'I see it this way. He may not be the boss, but if he thought we weren't legit, we'd already be dead,' he whispered. 'Of course, he's got to be suspicious, and I reckon he's making more checks with whoever in the UK. In the meantime, he's got to play it reasonably nice in case we *are* on-side, hasn't he?'

'Well, he'll have plenty of time to make up for it if he changes his mind, and I don't just mean taking the trainers back.'

'So, it all depends on Cheltenham holding it together. They've done a good job so far.'

'I suppose so. And if you add the shit we've been through too.'

'Believe me, I am adding that in. A critical part of the equation.'

'So, do we stick with it and meet the boss? See what he's got to say? After all, he's the guy we need to get hold of. Or do we just bust the fuck out tonight?'

'I think we stick with it. One more day.'

Approaching footsteps brought the conversation to

a halt. The bolt slid back and the tall guy's head appeared. He dropped a wooden bowl on the floor just inside the hut with two plastic plates. A large plastic bottle of water followed with a similar lack of ceremony, and a packet of Craven A.

The column of light dropping from the hole in the roof tilted further and further towards the door as the afternoon wore on. By the time it began to climb the wall, the cigarettes were over and the bowl of polenta with chopped up dates had become a figment of the distant past. Raglan sat cross-legged in front of Christian, scratching a series of lines with his finger in the dust on the floor between them.

'To be honest,' said Christian, 'I'm really struggling to tell the difference between your knights and your bishops.'

'Really?' replied Raglan, frowning. 'But the bishops are taller. And the knights do lean forward like horses' heads.'

'I'll tell you what,' said Christian, reaching forwards and carefully singling out one of the little dung figures from the row in front of Raglan, 'if I just squidge him a tiny bit taller and thinner, then I'll know.'

'Fine, but do be careful. He's clergy, after all.'

'Sure, sure,' said Christian. 'He'll be fine once he's dried out.'

'Not too tall or he'll end up a queen.'

'Don't worry, I'm not going to let you get away with three queens.'

'Come on, then, we'd better get started, otherwise it'll be dark and then they'll all look the same.'

Raglan grimaced with concentration as he moved two small black balls of dung sitting one on top of the other forward two squares. Christian surveyed his pieces, largely the same in appearance as Raglan's except for an identifying tuft of straw poking from each of their heads. Pushing his chin into the palm of one hand, he used the other to advance a dung-ball pawn.

'We should have played a bit of this back at the fort,' said Raglan after twenty minutes' silence.

'Wasn't any goat shit,' replied Christian.

'You don't have to have goat shit to play chess,' Raglan said.

'Yes, you do.'

'There are other materials.'

'Such as?'

'I don't know. In extremis, I suppose you could . . .'

'Human shit?' interrupted Christian. 'That would be revolting. Quite a good deterrent, though.'

'My larger pieces would be quite safe. Anyway, we can't really see things properly any more. It's too dark. I think we should put it on hold and pick up again in the morning.'

'Sure,' said Christian, sitting up straight. 'And no cheating in the night. I know exactly how much dung I've still got standing.'

'Fine, I'm winning anyway,' Raglan retorted.

38

Lying on his back, Christian peered up at the circle of night sky. He had done his best to clear a smooth patch of ground, but however he positioned himself, something still jabbed into him. Wisps of cloud began to obscure the brightness of the stars and each time he woke, they shone with less clarity. Raglan snored next to him, his chest rising and falling, and outside, the constant night-time chorus of insects was occasionally accompanied by the gentle bleating of goats.

Christian's eyes opened and his body jolted. His subconscious mind had detected something out of synch with the calm of what was now the early morning. His brain caught up and kicked into gear. Engines were running nearby and people were talking loudly and calling to each other. Raglan sat up.

'Bit early for all this?' he said, looking around in the gloom.

'Sounds like the whole place is up and at it,' replied Christian, squatting down to press his face to the crack along the top of the door.

'Yup,' he continued, 'I can just make out a whole load of pickups and there's a bunch of people all milling about.'

'Quiet as a grave it was yesterday,' muttered Raglan, moving over to join Christian by the door.

'Can't see exactly, but it looks like they're piling into vehicles. Shit, look, here he comes now.'

'Who?' said Raglan, pushing his head against Christian's shoulder to get a better angle.

'Big Chicken. And he looks tooled up enough to storm an embassy.'

Footsteps crunched outside and the bolt snapped back. The door was flung open and Sha'inti's voice barked.

'Move, now, outside.'

Christian pushed out through the doorway first. Sha'inti stood there in desert DPM combats, a black shirt covering his arms and an ops vest with two grenades clipped to the front. The Glock hung from his belt and an M16 A2 looped over his shoulder on para-cord. Webbing around his waist bulged with magazines and the aerial of a sat phone poked from under a Velcro flap at his side.

He turned and stomped back past the row of huts from which goats were spilling out and trotting off in all directions. Christian swapped the briefest of looks with Raglan and set off behind Sha'inti at a fast walk. A row of pickups and other four-wheel drives were parked up by the nearer end of the containers. Each was crammed with people – men, women and some children. As they drew closer, Sha'inti pointed at a dirty white Toyota with a group of armed men in the rear, their weapons pointing skywards like the spines of a startled porcupine.

'That one,' he snapped, pointing a finger. Christian changed direction and found himself being pulled into the back by the tall, tobacco-chewing African. As Raglan was yanked up behind him, the engine revved and the vehicle moved off in a cloud of white smoke. Christian remained standing for a moment as most of the other occupants opted to sit down. Three vehicles were visible in front, seemingly following the pimped-up Land Cruiser. To the rear, a line of fourteen vehicles stretched out in convoy.

The Toyota gathered speed and Christian slid himself down by the tailgate with his knees tucked up under his chin from lack of space. The tall guy leant confidently against the back of the cab, a grey shemagh protecting his face from the wind and dust. His finger rested on the trigger guard of his AK and his nonchalant expression willed Christian to make a sporting jump from the back of the vehicle. Closer to him, sat the two young Somali men from the fort, older weapons in their hands and clearly lower down the pecking order. One nodded an uncertain acknowledgement. Raglan sat sideways in the back corner, with dust and straw from the floor of the hut still stuck in his beard. His eyes were fixed in a stare but Christian knew he would be counting vehicles and people, checking out weapons, clocking distance, time and landmarks passed.

With the sun rising, orange fingers of dawn light streaked between the hills behind them, seemingly pointing them on their way. Above, rose-tinted clouds curdled uncomfortably, swelling in size and thickness. Away on the horizon to the left, a skirting board of mountains rose from a featureless plain.

The talking died down and the men in the back of the pickup cupped their cigarettes in their hands to protect them from the wind. Christian pulled two from a passing packet and passed one over to Raglan. Next, a large copper teapot was unwrapped from an old white blanket and an assortment of plastic cups was handed around. Starting with the men leaning against the cab, each man poured a cup of steaming yellow tea for the person next to him. The last thing to be circulated was a white cardboard box with a colour image down one side of a smiling blonde woman working on a laptop computer. Christian reached inside and pulled out a piece of pitta bread.

Despite the cloud cover, the heat of the day began to build, turning the cold rush of wind over the top of the pickup into a welcome breeze. The vehicles behind, now a uniform grey, broke from the linear convoy and began to bunch up. Drivers sounded their horns and people began waving and calling to each other. Christian leant to the side in an effort to see what had triggered the carnival atmosphere. Ahead, a deep line of ruts curved away from the open scrub of dusty grey towards a harsher looking terrain. The vehicles slowed to walking pace and meandered their way through fields of broken rocks and shale.

A series of crumbling concrete buildings came into view, confirming Christian's sense that the journey was coming to an end. The roofs and window frames had disappeared, leaving dilapidated walls on which a series of military-style slogans had been painted. Christian's mind bounced back to Northern Ireland, where images of masked men with broad shoulders holding assault rifles adorned the end wall of most rows of terraced housing. Robed figures wielding rifles stood over the prostrate body of a soldier waving the Stars and Stripes, with more crawling away on their hands and knees. The last building they passed was taller than the rest, the criss-cross structure of a rusting crane rising from behind it.

The pickup slowed, for no obvious reason, to the point that the wheels were hardly turning. Finding himself sliding forwards, Christian gave up trying to work out why there would be a series of derelict industrial buildings in the middle of the desert and peered forwards to see that only the upper half of the Land Cruiser leading the convoy was still visible. They were driving steeply downhill into a narrow cutting hewn out of the rock. After a hundred metres or so, the rock wall to the right of them fell away into space to reveal the vast, empty expanse of an abandoned opencast mine. A track just wide enough for a vehicle gripped the near vertical walls spiralling down inside.

Having left their vehicles parked at the top of the cutting, a group of people on foot appeared behind them, eager to overtake. The driver braked gently and an arm appeared from the cab, beckoning them forwards. They slipped past one by one, then broke into a jog and surged on down the track ahead of the vehicles. Ten minutes later, the dozen or so vehicles that had risked the descent reached the bottom and began negotiating their way between huge blocks of yellow rock. The ground then opened out into a flat area roughly the size of a football pitch.

Before they had come to a stop, people were bailing out over the sides and rushing towards a long white shipping container. Sha'inti appeared from the melee, his M16 swinging at his side.

'Get out and come here,' he called.

Christian swung a leg over the tailgate and lowered himself to the ground. Two hundred metres above, he saw a couple more vehicles, toy-like in size, parked perilously close to the edge of the cliff.

'The people call this place hell and you will see why. This is where we bring the enemies of our people and our cause,' Sha'inti continued.

They crunched over to where people had crowded into a semicircle around the shipping container. Christian peered through the sea of heads bobbing excitedly in front of him. Squinting in the glare of the sun, he saw that the side had been peppered with machine-gun fire.

'Come forward,' said Sha'inti, the crowd parting as he raised his arm.

Christian shuffled forwards, braced by the acrid smell spreading from his nostrils down to the back of his throat. A thick, dark brown sludge oozed from the lowest holes, contrasting with the flaking white paint. It dripped to the ground, forming a congealed ring around the base of the container. A crawling crust of bloated insects gave the surface an impression of movement. Above, around waist height, skeletal fingers poked out, confirming Christian's worst suspicions. Flesh still hung from some, making work for busy flies, whilst others were bleached white by the sun.

'It can take several days to die in there. Longer than you think,' said Sha'inti, having to raise his voice. 'We have to keep a permanent guard here to prevent the relatives mounting any kind of rescue or taking back the bodies of the dead.'

Christian felt the cold rush of rage build in his chest and spill down his limbs. His hands tingled and his head fizzed from a shortage of oxygen. He'd known they would confront barbarism on a medieval level but now it was so close up he could taste it. Contrary to his instincts, he breathed hard, sucking in the foul air. He had to confront the scene before him and get a grip on himself. As he turned to gauge Raglan's reaction, a movement inside the container caught his attention. An eye had appeared at one of the holes. The crowed spotted it too and pounced forwards. Some banged on the side of the container with stocks of rifles while others stood back and called insults.

Sha'inti allowed the crowd to enjoy the moment before walking away in the direction of the base of the cliff some fifty metres away. The increasingly agitated crowd abandoned the container and moved en masse towards him. Christian moved with them, feeling the atmosphere harden. An engine revved and people turned to look. A pickup with a large rear-mounted 50 cal nudged through the throng. Bristling with heavily armed militiamen, it turned side on and pulled up. Several men jumped to the ground, whilst those remaining on board lifted a long bundle wrapped in what appeared to be a bandage-like funeral shroud.

As the men on the ground reached up for one end, Christian's hope that the whole thing might be nothing more than a funeral disintegrated. The bandaged bundle let out a muffled scream and twisted sideways. The men on the ground took the weight on their shoulders and marched off towards the base of the cliff.

All eyes now focussed on Sha'inti, who had stepped

up into the back of the pickup. Leaning on the barrel of the 50 cal, he waved his arms for quiet and the crowd obeyed. Half politician on the hustings, half preacher in the pulpit, he started quietly and soon held a willing audience in his hand. Within a few minutes, he began to raise his voice and thump his fist against his ops vest. The response was electric. The crowd roared with approval and clenched fists pumped the air.

Christian felt a prod between the shoulder blades. It was the muzzle of the tall guy's rifle.

'Move,' he hissed, prodding Christian again.

Further prods steered Christian and Raglan through the crowd towards the pickup. Sha'inti looked down, pointing at them, and continued with his rhetoric as if justifying a series of points.

Christian glanced at Raglan, searching his face to understand his state of mind. An imperceptible nod of the head said it all. They should keep calm and ride it out. With the crowd whipped up into a state of near frenzy, Sha'inti's address came to an abrupt end. He sprang down from the pickup and strode off towards the base of the cliff, where the group of armed militiamen who had arrived in the pickup busied themselves with pickaxes and shovels.

As the jostling mob drew close, they laid down their tools, gripped their weapons and formed a defensive ring around the white bundle, which had been half buried in an upright position in a hole. Sha'inti positioned himself between two of them, their rifles pointing at the feet of the front row of the crowd.

'Come forward,' he called to Christian and Raglan. 'This is your opportunity to prove your commitment to jihad. I give you the chance to show these people that you have the strength and courage to wage war. We need men of action. Not men of talk. Prove you are who you say you are. Otherwise, we have no need of you.'

Christian felt a hundred or more pairs of eyes bore into him. Whilst he could not understand the language, the expressions on the faces radiated a mixture of glee and disgust. Some pointed, some shrugged, and others taunted. Sha'inti swivelled round and approached the bandaged figure in the hole.

'Come here,' he called, gesturing to Christian and Raglan.

Christian found his legs transporting him through the ring of snarling militiamen as his eyes flicked up the towering cliff and back to the crowd. There was nowhere to go.

A large plastic toolbox was placed with a clatter at Sha'inti's feet. He stooped and released the catches, and as he flipped open the lid, the crowd roared.

'Let me explain a few things,' he said, speaking to Christian and Raglan. 'This hole is bigger and deeper now but it's always been here. For generations, the rejects of society were hurled in here from the top. They landed on this exact spot where we stand now.

'These stones contain the bones of thieves, adulterers, the insane, and, of course, liars too,' continued Sha'inti, tapping his foot on the rocks. 'You can't see much, because the rats and vultures cleanse this place just as we cleanse our society. Now, this woman here has committed grave crimes against her own people. She is guilty of the highest treason and, as a consequence, will pay the highest price.

'You may be asking, why do we wrap her like this?' Sha'inti continued. 'This will protect her modesty once the stones start flying. Also, it will stop her bleeding out too fast. We find the stones here are too big and sharp. Unwrapped, she would be dead in less than twenty minutes. Like this, the process can take nearly an hour. Her screams will be heard for miles around, such is the echo from this place. People hear, and people remember who runs this country.

'But before we start, you have your chance to prove your worth.' Sha'inti jabbed his finger at Christian and Raglan. 'Due to the severity of the crimes, it is customary to cut off her nose, her ears and her lips before the stoning. You will do this.'

Using the side of his foot, he tipped the toolbox over, sending the contents sliding onto the ground. Christian looked down. At his feet lay a rusty heap of tools that in a different context would have looked ordinary enough. But here, each one became a gruesome torture device. A pruning saw with a twelve-inch serrated blade stood out. The orange plastic handle was streaked with dried blood. Garden secateurs, pliers and a claw-headed hammer lay there, next to a chisel and a tangled ball of wire.

'And what if we don't?' croaked Raglan.

'Well, in that case it's going to be a better day than I hoped.' Sha-inti smiled. 'Right, get started. Nose, ears, then lips. In that order.' Stepping behind the woman in the hole, he untied a knot and pulled down the bandages covering her face.

Dharia's big dark eyes blinked in the light. Her body bucked forwards as she spat out a strip of sodden material which had been gagging her mouth. Her head tilted backwards and she gasped for air.

Time slowed for Christian. Giddy with adrenalin, he held Sha'inti's stare as his mind attempted to park the shock and grapple with the options. What options? What difference did it make if *he* mutilated Dharia or someone else did it? It would be just as agonising for her. If he did it, at least he could try and be quick. That would be better, surely? If he refused, they would all be stoned. The mission would be over and Sha'inti and his following would be free to continue training terrorists to commit atrocities in the UK – never mind the piracy and everything else.

'I'll start,' said Christian, reaching down for the pruning saw.

Sha'inti raised his eyebrows with surprise and Raglan's mouth fell open. Dharia gave a broken sob and flopped forwards to the extent her half-buried body would allow her. The crowd whooped with excitement and the militiamen turned inwards to observe.

Christian moved around behind Dharia and dropped to his knees. Leaning forwards, he grabbed her torso with both arms and hauled her upright. Releasing his grip with his right arm, he raised the pruning saw level with her face. As he pressed the blade to the bridge of her nose, he relaxed the pressure with his left arm and slammed her body forwards. Cursing over her screams, he yanked her back and repeated the process a second time.

Positioning her upright once again, he snapped at Raglan.

'Get me the fucking secateurs.'

Then he turned to the tall guy.

'You, help me hold her.'

Sha'inti nodded to the tall guy and beckoned him forwards. He sank to his knees and reached around Dharia's chest. Christian balanced himself and raised the pruning saw.

'On my command,' he growled, looking up at Raglan.

In the same movement as lifting his elbow to start the sawing motion, Christian raised the tip of the blade a fraction from Dharia's face and plunged it forwards into the tall guy's right eye. Pushing the serrated edge down and in, he released the handle and snatched a grenade from the front of the tall guy's ops-vest. In the fraction of a second it took for guns to be raised and pointed, Christian ripped the pin from the grenade and sprang to his feet.

'With this cliff, there's only one way for the blast to go,' he yelled, holding the grenade above his head. 'Your fucking way. Nothing to absorb it except you.'

Sha'inti snapped some instructions at the men closest to him and lowered the barrel of his M16. Raglan darted forwards and snatched up the AK from the tall guy, who lay writhing on the ground, groaning with pain. Positioning himself several metres to Christian's left to create two separate targets, he pressed the rifle into his shoulder and used his thumb to push the selector lever to the automatic fire position.

Sha'inti released his grip on his M16 and allowed it to hang by his side.

'So, I was right!' he shouted over the barrage of orders bouncing between the militiamen.

'Shut up!' yelled Christian and Raglan simultaneously.

'OK,' replied Sha'inti. 'So what are you going to do now with one grenade and one gun with one magazine?'

'That won't affect you,' replied Raglan, pointing his AK. 'You'll be getting the whole magazine to yourself. We're both dead anyway, so taking you down with us will be a bonus.'

Sha'inti shrugged. 'You're not going to get far.'

'Get her out,' hissed Christian.

Raglan swapped the AK over to his left and used the secateurs to snip away a line in the bandages down Dharia's back. With her hands free, she began scrabbling frantically at the rocks holding her in place. With every moment that passed, Christian felt the initial advantage of shock wearing thinner. The crowd were no longer cringing behind each other for fear of the grenade but pushing forwards, more confident by the second.

Dharia hauled herself backwards and used her arms to pull her legs free. Kicking the remaining strips of material away, she staggered to her feet.

'To the truck,' said Christian, striding towards Sha'inti. 'Now, we're going to drive out of here, and if anyone moves, my friend will shoot you first. You first. Got that?'

Sha'inti shrugged again and spoke to the militiamen, who nodded their understanding. Christian knew the words would have meant, 'Don't worry, we'll track these nutters down and kill them later.'

With Raglan keeping Sha'inti in his sights, they eased their way slowly away from the base of the cliff with the crowd reluctantly falling back. Just as they drew close to the pickup, Dharia gasped.

'They have two Europeans in the container. One tall one, very tall with red hair,' she spluttered.

'Fuck,' muttered Christian, pulling open the driver's door of the pickup. 'Get over there and open it up.'

Raglan planted a foot on the back tyre and managed to step up into the rear of the pickup without wavering from his aim. Still holding the grenade in one hand, Christian turned the ignition keys, slammed the gear stick into first and pressed the accelerator. They pulled up by the end of the container just as Dharia heaved back one of the large metal doors. A plague of flies poured out, followed by Armalite and the Beast.

'Get in, now,' Christian yelled.

The Beast leapt forwards, placed one hand on the side of the pickup and threw himself into the back. Armalite and Dharia scrabbled in beside him. With the cab buzzing with flies, Christian stamped down on the accelerator once again. The pickup gathered pace and he swerved one-handed through the slabs of rock following the tyre marks on the ground.

Using his knees to hold the wheel, Christian skipped second gear and pushed into third. The whine from the engine dropped a note and the pickup started the ascent up the side of the mine. With the front wing bashing against the rock wall, Christian realised he needed two hands on the wheel. He shouted 'GRENAAAADE' and lobbed the grenade down into the space below. Five seconds later, there was a massive boom and with the echo still reverberating, a barrage of gunfire erupted from the bottom of the mine. The détente was over and the chase was on.

39

Christian ignored the bullets slamming into the rock above him, knowing that the truck was largely protected by the angle their height afforded them. With debris cascading onto the bonnet and clattering on the roof above, he perched forward, straining to gauge the position of the track. They rounded the final bend and raced into the cutting at the top.

'Stop!' yelled the Beast, thumping on the rear window of the cab.

'What?' Christian called back.

'Stop at the top,' said the Beast. 'Let's block the cutting.'

'OK, OK.' Christian pumped on the brakes.

The Beast, Armalite and Raglan were already piling out of the back and running towards the vehicles parked along the top of the cutting. One by one, they released handbrakes and rolled them forwards, sending them crashing into the cutting below. The last vehicle remaining was a white Chevrolet van. The Beast appeared inside and pulled at the door. Unable to open it, he stepped back and kicked in the passenger window.

'These'll help,' he called to Armalite as he grabbed two M16s from a rack above the front seats.

'Let's go,' bellowed Christian, revving the engine.

'That'll slow them up,' puffed Raglan, sliding onto the passenger seat beside Christian. 'Now let's get the hell out of here. Towards the mountains.'

Christian's foot hit the accelerator, sending a cloud of dust into the air. They passed the derelict buildings, bounced across the rutted track and set off across the scrub.

Raglan slid back the rear window of the cab.

'Dharia, you first,' he shouted over the noise of the engine. 'What the hell were you doing in that hole?'

Dharia pushed her face halfway through the window into the cab, her hands clenched around the bottom of the frame for balance.

'Who are these two?' she asked, jerking her head sideways at Armalite and the Beast.

'Two very good friends of mine,' snapped Christian. 'Without them, you wouldn't be in a position to ask questions.'

'OK,' she said. 'You don't understand.'

'Well, make us,' interjected Raglan.

'Do you want the good news or the bad?' shouted Armalite, pushing Dharia to one side.

'Good news? Since when has there been any good news?' said Christian. 'OK, come on, let's have the good news first.'

'Well,' said Armalite, 'we got a lot of ammo back here for the fifty cal.'

'Marvellous,' said Christian. 'And the bad news?'

'The barrel is completely fucked. Rusted right through.'

'Fucking terrific. So, what do we have?'

'Apart from the fifty-cal ammo, we've got two AKs, two M16s, a couple of sat phones and a giant teapot.'

'And some fags,' added Raglan, rummaging in the glove pocket.

'Spare ammo?' asked Christian, twisting around to look at Armalite.

'None, just what's in the magazines.'

Christian sighed and accepted the cigarette from Raglan's outstretched hand.

'I never used to smoke. Come on, Dharia, so what happened to you?'

'There's nothing much to say. I was on my way to kill Sha'inti and they caught me. That's it. Nothing more. He destroyed my family and deserves to die. '

'Fair enough, love,' said Armalite.

'Complete cunt,' muttered the Beast.

'What about you guys?' asked Raglan.

'Well, you must know that I was here to hand over those diamonds to Carter,' said Armalite.

'Yes, we know that,' replied Raglan. 'But what then?'

'When Christi said the diamonds were in the back of his VW, I knew he was in trouble.'

'Why?'

'First of all he doesn't have a VW, and secondly it's what he said last time he was in the shit.'

'OK.'

'So,' continued Armalite, 'I knew anything to do with Carter would be hooky, so I brought Beasty along with me.'

'It was either this or changing nappies,' grunted the Beast.

'What? Nappies? As in kids?' said Christian.

'I'm on paternity leave. That's why I was free.'

'Is Mrs MacDonald happy with that?' asked Christian, dragging hard on his cigarette.

'Not very,' the Beast admitted. 'As for me, I'm not sure what's worse – child care or being left to die in a shipping container three feet deep in decomposing bodies.'

'Anyway,' Armalite continued, 'we got a grip on Carter and arranged the breakout with him. But once you were all out, he dumped us in it with these wankers.'

'Should have shot the fucker when I had the chance,' said the Beast.

'So that was you out in the desert?' said Raglan. 'The covering fire?'

'Yup, keeping their heads down and making sure I didn't hit Carter at the same time. Arsehole.'

'OK, folks, so things are fine except for a heavily armed mob of a hundred plus about five minutes behind us, and we're leaving tracks a moron could follow.'

'And the smell of dead people,' said Dharia, looking at Armalite.

'Listen,' Christian interrupted. 'We've got at least eight hours of daylight left and need to make those hills. Otherwise, we don't stand a chance out in the open.'

'What about using a phone to call in back-up?' said Armalite.

'We'll be dead long before anyone even gets into the air,' said Christian, rubbing frantically at the layer of dust obscuring the dials on the dashboard. 'Fuck, that's the fuel light.'

'What, the orange one?' said Raglan, leaning over.

'Do we have any fuel in the back? A jerry can or anything?' snapped Christian.

'None back here,' replied the Beast.

'Shit, shit, shit,' groaned Christian.

40

Christian eased his foot on the accelerator and changed up into fifth gear. Raglan passed around the cigarettes and all eyes darted between the needle of the fuel gauge and the grey strip of mountains on the horizon.

'Did you see when it came on?' said Raglan.

'No, I did not,' replied Christian.

'I'd rather go down fighting than in that container,' said the Beast with a shrug.

'It'll be about twenty-five to one,' said Raglan, counting the rounds in the magazine of the AK. 'Sporting stuff.'

'Armalite, go over the rifles and make sure they're OK, will you?' said Christian, glancing in the rear-view mirror.

'Sure thing, Christi.

A few moments of silence followed before Christian stubbed out his cigarette on the dashboard.

'Right, I've got a plan,' he said.

'A plan?' responded Armalite. 'Hope it's a bit better than some of your other ones.'

'Better be good,' said Raglan.

'Is it?' asked Armalite.

'Well, not that fucking good, but it's better than nothing. Probably a six out of ten,' replied Christian.

'Six out of ten sounds pretty good to me,' said the Beast. 'Must be reasonable, Christi?'

'Well, actually, it's probably more like four out of ten,' Christian admitted. 'Anyway, you can rate it later, if there is a later. Is that OK?'

'Let's hear it, lad,' said Raglan, snapping rounds back into a magazine.

'OK, we don't just drive as far as we can and run out of gas, get out, start running and get gunned down. We'll ambush the bastards instead.'

'Is that it?' said Armalite.

'No, not entirely, there's a bit more to it than that. Let me explain.'

41

Fifteen minutes later, the tyres chewed their way through loose, fist-size rocks and the mountains were no longer a distant vista of grey but a rising wall broken by a vein-like network of valleys and ridges. Christian flipped up the sun visor and peered through the windscreen. Then, his eye back on the fuel needle, he dropped down a gear and turned the steering wheel in the direction of the steepest valley.

'Still leaving tracks, I hope?' he called over his shoulder.

'Aye, big time,' grunted the Beast.

'Now, how long do you reckon it will have taken them to shift all those cars out of that cutting?' Christian continued.

'Best part of half an hour, surely,' said Raglan.

'OK, let's say twenty minutes to be on the safe side,' said Christian. 'That's probably all we'll need.'

As they approached a steep-sided, V-shaped valley, Christian was forced to slow the speed down to a fast walking pace and picked his way carefully around larger and larger obstacles of rock and landslipped earth. The terrain worsened still more and the axles groaned as they pressed higher up the central line of the valley. Finally, there was a sharp scraping noise and the pickup ground to a halt.

'Perfect,' said Christian, reaching for the door handle. 'It's amazing how far you can go on empty. Right, Beasty, I want you to find something sharp, get under the vehicle and punch a wee hole in the fuel tank. Drain out any remaining fuel into the teapot.'

'Roger that, Christi,' replied the Beast.

'Then Armalite, you crack out those fifty-cal shells and get as many as you can into the teapot. I want them packed in tight, casings and all. Plus any other sharp metal stuff you can find.

'Rags, if you don't mind, turn both those phones on and check the signal. Then scroll through the menus and get the number of one of the phones. Doesn't matter which one.

'Dharia, get up that side of the hill and let me know when you can see them coming. I want as much warning as possible.'

Christian wound up both the passenger windows and slid the glass of the rear window closed.

'Most of it's gone up my nose,' said the Beast,

reappearing from beneath the pickup, 'but there must be the best part of a litre and a half in there.'

'Good,' replied Christian, taking the teapot. 'Right, Armalite, start stuffing. Rags, got the numbers yet?'

'Yup,' answered Raglan. 'But it's not the fit Yank bird in these phones. It's some stroppy foreign cow, so I can't say how much credit there is.'

'Won't need much,' said Christian. 'Put one in here and get the other one ready to call it.'

'Are you sure it'll work?' said Armalite.

'Think about it,' replied Christian. 'A normal mobile phone can ignite petrol vapour in an open garage forecourt and they only have to transmit to a mast a few miles away. This thing has to be powerful enough to send a signal into space. It must make a load of heat.'

'They always feel hot after a while,' said Raglan, nodding.

'In a confined space, no ventilation, almost soaked in petrol, it's sure to go pop.'

'Big pop with that lot,' said Armalite, tapping the side of the teapot.

'There're coming,' yelled Dharia. 'I can see dust rising.'

'Right,' said Christian. 'Let's put the lid on, leave it on the seat and lock the doors. Now, we move uphill to four points where we can snipe. Rags, your job is to wipe out anyone on a fifty cal. We'll be able to fully triangulate them. They'll have no cover and we'll have height on our side and perfect defilade fire. Just try and leave Sha'inti out of it. We know who he is now and we don't want to have to go back to square one with someone else in charge.'

'And preserve ammo,' said Raglan. 'Even with a hundred per cent hit rate, I doubt we'll have enough. If it goes wrong, move to the ridgeline and make your way along the valley. Twelve-hour RV ten Ks north of here on the highest mark.'

Christian set off uphill towards Dharia and positioned himself behind a rock about 150 metres above the pickup. He could see Raglan a couple of hundred metres to his left and Armalite and the Beast in position on the other side of the valley. He rested the sat phone on the ground beside him and opened the action of the AK to check there was a round in the chamber.

'So what happens now?' asked Dharia.

'Well, we sit and wait until they approach the vehicle. They're sure to take a look round it. If it looks like they're not interested and head back down the valley, we leave them to it. And if they look like they want to follow us, we open up.'

'I think it's a good plan. Seven out of ten.'

'I guess we'll know sooner or later.'

Christian felt the trickle of sweat drip down the side of his shirt. He gripped the stock of the AK to stop his hand shaking. Away to the left and below, a convoy of vehicles had left the dusty white plain and snaked its way slowly through the rougher ground. Despite the thick grey cloud base, heat haze blurred his view.

'By the way, I know how we can get Sha'inti,' Dharia whispered.

'What do you mean, get him?' asked Christian, without taking his eyes off the valley floor.

'I heard people talking. Sha'inti has many brothers but one is getting married soon. In our culture, you only marry on certain days, and I know the next one is in three days from now.'

'OK, so does that mean Sha'inti will be there?'

'All the family have to be there.'

'Do you know where?'

'Yes, you get married in the village of the husband. It's always the same way.'

'So you're saying you know that Sha'inti will be in a set place on a set day?'

'Exactly that.'

'But won't there be massive amounts of heavily armed militia there too?'

'Yes. You could air-strike the whole lot at once, kill them all.'

'Dharia, good plan, but we can't really do that.'

'Why not? You could end the problem in one day.'

'But what happens when CNN turn up and they've laid out the bodies of fifty dead women and children?'

'OK. I'm just telling you.'

'And thank you. I appreciate it.'

Raglan waved his hand, pointed at his eyes and raised his outstretched fingers in the air. He then tapped his left wrist with his right hand, pointed at the ground and raised two fingers.

'What's all that about? said Dharia.

'It means he can see ten vehicles and they're two minutes away from here.'

Christian lowered his head and peered around the side of the rock. Six hundred metres away, a line of vehicles packed with militia navigated its way along the bottom of the valley. A number of men seemed to have disembarked and were walking alongside, rifles at the ready.

'Dharia, if this kicks off, which it probably will, you need to keep your head well down. These guys don't aim, they just loose off. But enough of them doing it at once can be quite effective. If I get hit, take the gun and run.'

Dharia nodded and pressed herself against the ground in the rocks next to Christian. The convoy struggled slowly up the valley. Suddenly, those on foot rushed forwards and triumphant yells and screams echoed around the valley.

'Looks like they've just seen the pickup,' whispered Christian, reaching for the sat phone.

Figures sprang from the backs of the vehicles and joined those on their feet. Pushing past one another, they stormed up the valley. The fastest among them encircled the pickup, their rifles pressed into their shoulders with the apprehension of hunters approaching the twitching body of a badly shot buffalo. Half crouching and shouting to each other, they moved in slowly, with large, exaggerated footsteps. At about five metres, the caution dissolved into a wild charge engulfing the pickup in a seething mob. People clambered into the back and swarmed over the roof and bonnet, obscuring the vehicle from view.

Christian looked to his left. Raglan lay prone on the ground, the barrel of his M16 protruding from the rocks around him. Below, the convoy pulled up behind the pickup. Third from the front, a door opened and Sha'inti stepped out of his armoured Land Cruiser. He stood beside the vehicle and waved his hand in a sweeping circular motion in the air, finishing with an aggressive forwards jab of his fist. The crowd around him roared with approval and set off running in every direction.

Christian took a breath and pressed a green button marked 'SEND' on the keypad. He put the phone to his ear, but before the voice had even started to update him on the available credit, a shot rang out. Pushing the phone harder against his ear, he raised his head sufficiently above the rock to see the body of a man toppling over the side of one of the pickups containing a rear-mounted 50 cal. Before the man's body had hit the ground, two more shots cracked almost simultaneously through the air and two men making their way up the far side of the hill cartwheeled.

The echo of the first shot raced around the valley like a jet passing overhead, only to be drowned by the thunder of the second salvo. In the tiniest of intervals before Raglan pulled the trigger again, Christian heard enough of a tone to know the phones had connected. He placed the handset upright on the ground by his knee and looked down into the valley to witness the charging mass of militiamen diving for cover behind rocks and vehicles.

The gunner on the back of a second pickup collapsed, and two more men running for cover flopped to the ground. Sha'inti darted backwards and sandwiched himself in the protected space between the half-opened door and the body of the Land Cruiser. Resting his rifle on the roof, he fired wildly in a sweeping arc. Following his example, a barrage of automatic fire erupted from the bottom of the valley. Christian pushed his shoulder against the rock and stared at the screen of the sat phone, where large digital numbers showed the length of the call reaching fifteen seconds.

The rate of fire from the militiamen finally slowed, allowing him to hear individual bullets wasping through the air above. Puffs of dust kicked up in random streaks around the valley sides.

'It's not fucking working,' hissed Christian, still staring at the screen through a film of tiny droplets of rain.

'What's not working?' shouted Dharia.

'The bomb. It's not working.'

Christian gripped the stock of his AK and eased himself into a firing position around the side of the rock. Sha'inti was calling instructions and small, co-ordinated groups of militiamen were moving uphill, some crouched, others crawling on their stomachs. Several more shots cracked from the far side of the valley and one more body fell from the back of a pickup.

Heads popped up again and a group broke cover. The leader fell and the remaining men shrank back to the ground. Christian peered down the open sights of his AK, wishing he had a proper telescopic scope. He positioned the bead on the window of the driver's door of Sha'inti's Land Cruiser and squeezed the trigger. The armoured glass resisted the impact of the bullet but shattered. Sha'inti immediately disappeared from view inside. Christian repositioned the AK and fired again.

Every couple of seconds a single round cracked through the clatter of automatic fire. Christian guessed Raglan had fired half his rounds, and the Beast and Armalite would be close behind him. He took aim and fired a round at a man crouched behind a vehicle, seemingly unaware that the shots were coming in from both sides of the valley.

'What's happened to the bomb?' screamed Dharia.

'I don't fucking know,' yelled Christian over the sound of bullets slamming into the rocks around them. 'But they've marked our position.'

Dust whirled around Christian and fragments of debris stung his face and forearms, forcing him to close his eyes. The rock shock against his shoulder and the earth vibrated beneath him. He pressed himself flat and counted the seconds, knowing that the 50-cal gunner would have to reload after twelve seconds or so of automatic fire.

He'd got to nine when the volley relented. Spitting dust from his mouth, Christian shuffled back into his firing position in time to see three gun crews manning 50 cals and a swarm of militia taking full advantage of the covering fire to advance uphill. He took a shot, dropping one member of a gun crew, and glanced left to see Raglan's position disappear in a cloud of brown dust. A fraction of a second later, the rough grunt of heavy machine-gun fire caught up. Fifty metres below, heads lurked and bobbed in the rocks. Christian steadied his breathing and blinked a mixture of rain and sweat from his eyes. He pressed the rifle to his shoulder and continued to focus single rounds on the gun crews.

Without warning, a thunderous boom shook the valley like an incoming artillery shell. The pickup flexed downwards for an instant before the back end bucked into the air. The cab disintegrated into a ball of flames, blasting a 360 degree wave of white-hot shrapnel. The vehicle immediately behind shunted backwards and the glass vanished from the windows. The swirling smoke cleared, to reveal several lacerated bodies writhing on the ground near the burning chassis and others, positioned further from the blast, screaming and pouring with blood. The driver's door, still attached by the lower hinge, hung like a broken wing. The bonnet lay several metres away, surrounded by engine parts and smouldering pieces of broken plastic.

A vehicle at the rear of the convoy jerked backwards, manoeuvred hastily through a three-point turn, and set off back down the valley. Several militiamen broke cover and sprinted after it, hurling themselves into the back. Three more vehicles followed suit, triggering a rush of men to abandon their positions and bolt after them.

On the far side of the valley, the Beast gave up his defensive position in the rocks and rested his M16 confidently over the top of a large round boulder. More militiamen sprang from the rocks below Christian and tore downhill towards the remaining vehicles. Wheels spun and engines roared as more vehicles tried to turn around and drive out; some opted to reverse. Men piled aboard or chose to run.

Christian adjusted the aim of his rifle and sent a second round into the window of Sha'inti's vehicle. There was a dull thud and the glass sagged inwards. A second later, the vehicle leapt backwards and joined the chaotic stampede down the valley. Conscious that he had less than ten rounds left, Christian counted to three and sent another round slamming into the back of the Land Cruiser. He waited another few seconds, then fired again as the convoy bounced its way down the valley to the sporadic crackle of automatic gunfire. Finally, they swung right and disappeared from view.

Raglan emerged from his position, his clothes and body caked in a sticky brown dust. He set off downhill, hopping nimbly among the stones with his rifle pressed into his shoulder.

'Careful on the way down, they won't all be dead,' said Christian, picking up the sat phone and pressing the 'End' button on the keypad. Then, wiping a film of rain and dust off the screen with his finger, he continued, 'One minute fifty-four seconds.'

A shot shattered the temporary moment of quiet. Christian's head spun round in time to see Raglan lower his rifle. On the other side of the valley, Armalite and the Beast made their way carefully downhill through sheeting rain, rifles raised.

'Come on, let's go before we get washed away,' said Christian.

By the time they reached the smouldering wreck of the pickup, Raglan was standing there, three spare magazines in his hand and a cigarette in the corner of his mouth. Around him, bodies littered the ground, encircled in expanding pools of crimson.

'Must be twenty-five dead,' he said, breathing hard.

'Easily,' replied Armalite. 'Down to two rounds.'

'Keeping one for yourself, were you?' grunted the Beast between breaths.

'Yeah,' replied Armalite. 'One for me and one for you.'

'Shitty day all round,' said Raglan, looking up at the sky.

'Well, if it ain't raining, it ain't training,' said Christian. 'Let's gather what we can and fuck off before they regroup.'

'OK, into the hills as fast as we can. Into our country,' replied Raglan. 'Good plan, by the way, Christi.'

'I may have another one. Let's go.'

42

Christian hunched his shoulders and set off uphill at a fast walk. Dharia fell in behind him, closely followed by Raglan and Armalite. The Beast brought up the rear, his M16 in his hands and an AK slung across his back. Christian picked his way among the larger stones and loose landslip which presented a slalom course to the torrents of newly formed streams. He paused by the crumpled body of a young man lying face down, arms outstretched and fingers dug into the sodden earth like crampons. Water darkened his faded blue jeans and filled a white Reebok trainer that lay beside him. A six-inch section from the upper half of his spine protruded through his T-shirt like a dorsal fin.

Keeping fifty metres below the ridgeline, they trudged the length of the valley and out across a flat-topped escarpment. The far side, the ground fell away, revealing a network of interlocking canyons filled with spikey green bushes.

'Perfect,' muttered Raglan. 'No chance of getting anything on wheels through here. Come on, Christi, so what's the big plan then?'

'Well, we get fifteen K under our belts and hole up somewhere safe. Then we call Dev and get resupplied by an air drop.'

'That'll take six or eight hours out of Cyprus,' said Raglan.

'So we sit around and freeze our butts off until they drop the gear,' Christian continued.

'Just like old times. Then what?' said Armalite.

'Then we gatecrash a party,' said Christian.

'A party?' said Raglan. 'What sort of party?'

'More of a wedding, really,' said Christian. 'Anyway, I'm not suggesting we barge on in ourselves. We'll leave that to D Squadron.'

'That's a relief, Christi,' said the Beast. 'If my wife finds out I've been partying when I told her I was helping out a mate out of the shit, she'd kill me.'

'No need to worry, Beasty,' replied Christian. 'Dharia informs me a certain Sha'inti will be at the wedding, and he'll be first rat to leave the ship once our lot hit the ground.'

'It's in three days but the clan will begin to gather at the village any time from now on,' said Dharia. 'It's Sha'inti's brother's marriage and it would show dishonour for his brothers not to be there. It has to happen.'

'Like it, like it a lot,' said Raglan. 'So, we recce the place hard, work out the obvious escape route and send in D from the opposite direction.'

'We then use the set piece Regiment ambush to grab him,' said Christian. 'D can pull out and we'll have the fucker.'

'Then what do we do with him?' asked Dharia.

'We'll have to talk to Deveral about that,' Christian answered. 'But now we have to keep going. Sha'inti may have a wedding to attend but he'll have a bunch of guys out here looking for us.'

'All he has to do is put a bounty on us and the whole country will be up here,' said Raglan.

'I think the rain's easing a bit,' said the Beast, holding out the palm of his hand.

'This may not be raining by Scottish standards, lad,' said Armalite. 'But, to normal people of balanced mind, it's pissing down.'

'But it might not rain again for two years,' said Dharia. 'We should be grateful.'

'By Welsh standards, I wouldn't call this pissing down really,' chipped in Raglan, looking around. 'It's like a downpour but not exactly torrential.'

'A downpour?' said the Beast. 'Come on!'

'For God's sake,' muttered Christian, pulling the sat phone from inside his shirt.

'What you are doing, Christi? asked Raglan.

'Calling the Met Office.' Christian pressed the sat phone to his ear. 'Hold on, this thing could well be out of credit.'

He tilted his head back and listened while Raglan passed round a sodden packet of Craven A. The digital display morphed from an image of two flashing phones with a dotted line between them into large digital numerals.

'Hello, hello,' said Christian, striding forwards. 'It's your friends from Africa calling. Your friends from Africa.'

'Hang on, hang on.' Colonel Deveral glanced in his rear-view mirror and manoeuvred his grey Vauxhall Senator across a narrow country lane and into a muddy gateway. 'Out in the sticks but I can hear you.'

'Sir, we've had a bit of a run around but have eyes on our man. The team's all together but we need a resupply, urgently.'

'Roger that, roger that,' replied the Colonel. 'Do you have coordinates?'

'No, no. We're in the hills. On a sat phone.'

'No problem. I can see the number. We'll take over the number and we can use it to find you as long as it still has some power.'

'Yes, yes. We'll need full desert kit for five. That's our three plus two.'

'Five?' enquired Deveral. 'Made some friends, have you?'

'Old friends, really.'

'So you'll be needing some kit in extra large, will you?'

'Yes, sir.' Christian looked across at the Beast.

'Very good and well done.'

'And sir, we'll need some support from D if possible. We know where our man is and will need some help flushing him out. Then we'll need somewhere to take him.'

'OK, OK. I hear you,' replied Deveral. 'First things first. Turn the phone on again in six hours. We'll triangulate off that and make the drop. I'll mobilise D and see what we can do about finding somewhere safe to take him. Might have to be a naval asset.'

'Thank you, sir. I don't think we're that far from the coast.'

'Well done, well done. Over and out.'

Christian pressed the end button and folded away the aerial.

'So what did he say?' Raglan passed Christian a half-smoked cigarette.

'Well, he seemed to get it,' replied Christian. 'Didn't seem that surprised, to be honest.'

'Don't blame him, after last time,' said Armalite.

'He knows you're here for sure,' said Christian with a grin.

'How the fuck . . . He bloody knows everything,' spluttered Armalite, shaking his head. 'He always fucking finds out.'

'And you, Beasty,' Christian continued. 'Well busted.'

'What? Me too?' blurted the Beast. 'I'm at home, for crying out loud. That's not true. Bullshit. He's just guessing.'

'Well, just wait and see what size boots turn up. Then you can judge for yourself.'

'So apart from all the guess who stuff,' said Raglan, 'what's actually happening?'

'It's like I said,' replied Christian. 'We keep moving into the hills and they'll track the sat phone signal and make a drop. Then we can think about coordinating with D and . . .'

'Gatecrashing the party,' interrupted Raglan.

43

Christian led the way downhill into the criss-crossed network of canyons. Tall pillars of eroded soil lined the sides like guards and a mixture of twigs and long white thorns crunched underfoot. Flies buzzed excitedly around them and took advantage of their soft, wet skin.

'Is it just me, or is everything in this country out to get you?' said Armalite, wiping his forearm with his hand. 'Eat you, shoot you, spike you, drench you, burn you.'

'Yup,' agreed the Beast. 'Or stick you in a box and leave you there to rot.'

'Or cut your head off with a saw,' added Raglan. 'Mind you, I've actually heard of people coming here on holiday.'

'It's not always that bad,' said Dharia.

'You left, didn't you?' said Raglan.

'That's different,' she replied.

'You know, it's weird,' said Armalite, looking at Raglan. 'You remind me of someone. Can't think who, though.'

'Could do with a brew,' Christian intervened. 'So what do they put in a resupply container? I've seen them being dropped on exercises, but they were always empty or full of old blankets.'

'All kinds of shit, really,' said Armalite. 'From a weapons point of view, normally a rifle each, a side arm of some description, grenades and some demolition gear.'

'Ration packs?' said the Beast.

'Yeah, yeah, packed out with twenty-four-hour boxes,' said Armalite, 'and I've seen fresh grub as well. Depends if it's our guys who sort it or some dumb fucks from the RAF.'

'Aye, that's it,' retorted the Beast. 'Some RAF cunts who've never set foot outside the comfort of an airbase.'

'I wouldn't get too excited, guys,' said Raglan. 'Whatever they drop, it'll probably be three miles out to sea or smack bang into Sha'inti's lap.'

'He'll think it's a wedding present,' said Christian. 'What about fags?'

'Fags, Christi?' said Armalite. 'I didn't think you smoked?'

'I don't,' replied Christian, upping the pace. 'Or I didn't until all this crap started. Like everything round here, it all boils down to Sam Carter.'

'Cunt,' croaked the Beast. 'He'll be swanning round the world now like some sort of global playboy.'

'Not that much fun,' said Raglan. 'It's not like he can settle down somewhere and grow some roots. He'll have to keep moving on like a vagrant. Always looking over his shoulder. Never a real home.'

'A terrible nomadic existence,' Christian added. 'Forever telling the captain of his yacht to up anchor and move on to the next island. Miserable for him, utterly miserable.'

'I think it is stopping,' said the Beast.

'No, it's not,' snapped Armalite, looking up. 'Mind you, at your height you're probably in a different climatic zone from the rest of us.'

'Easy, Arma,' said the Beast. 'All I've done is come along to help *you* out. Could be home with my feet up. Not getting my head shot off down here and having a hard time from you in the fucking process.'

'I've done you a bloody favour, more like,' Armalite retorted. 'You'd be at home wiping arses.'

'Wiping an arse with a tin in your spare hand would be a lot better than . . .'

'You need two hands to wipe an arse.'

'And how the fuck do you know that? How many nappies have you changed?'

'He's right,' said Raglan. 'You do need two hands to change a nappy. Promise you. Dharia, back me up on this.'

'Don't ask me. Why should I know?' replied Dharia, looking around.

'OK, Christi,' said the Beast.

'Two hands, guys,' answered Christian. 'Otherwise the shit goes everywhere. Seen it done. And the rain is stopping.'

44

Christian kept a steady pace for the next four hours, doing his best to keep heading north where the topography allowed. By mid-afternoon, the sun had control of the skies once again and had banished the protective layer of dark cloud. With no trace of streams or surface water, the parched land had locked away every drop of moisture and was not letting any go. The only evidence of the rain was a brittle, eggshell-like crust baked on the surface of the soil.

Still in the same order, they trudged through ankle-deep dust towards a tiny sliver of shade at the base of a cliff. Without a word, they flopped to the ground and sat in a row with their rifles propped beside them.

Finally, the Beast broke the silence.

'Is that the sea right over there on the horizon? Or am I just imagining it?'

'Probably some sick mirage,' replied Armalite, squinting.

'Hopefully it is the sea,' said Christian, raising his hand to shield his eyes. 'Well, if it isn't we've been heading south.'

'Which we haven't been,' said Raglan. 'That's the Indian Ocean and that's what all the fuss is about. A bit further out from what we can see is one of the busiest shipping lanes in the world.'

'Pretty much everything going from China into Europe bobs right past here,' said Christian. 'Quite frankly, I don't really blame these guys for having a crack at a few TVs. It's either that or sit around here frying your arse off in the Stone Age.'

'And the odd pair of trainers,' said Raglan, tapping his feet together.

'Fair play,' said Armalite. 'Never quite know how four blokes in a bathtub manage to storm up the side of a super tanker moving at thirty knots.'

'Our boys screw it up half the time,' said the Beast. 'And they're meant to know what they're doing.'

'Hold on, guys.' Christian produced the sat phone from inside his shirt. 'We'd better change the subject before we call Dev. He might not be so sympathetic.'

'It's not so much the piracy that bothers him,' said Raglan. 'It's al-Shabaab wankers training people how to blow up shopping centres in the Home Counties.'

Christian peered at the screen of the phone and dialled.

'If this doesn't work, we're really fucked,' he said as he pressed the phone to his ear.

'Really fucked,' echoed Raglan, passing around the packet of Craven A's. 'These are the last fags.'

'Sir, sir,' said Christian, springing to his feet.

'Come in, I can hear you,' replied Deveral. 'Now, you need to stay on the line for at least a minute while we get a decent trace on your location. The aircraft is already on the way and just needs final coordinates.'

'Roger that,' replied Christian, nodding. 'We're tucked in below a ridgeline with a clear view to our west. Tell them to dump it to the west of our position. That's west of our position.'

'Got that. Confirm. Drop will be to the west of your position. About two hours, maybe less.'

'Roger that. Will confirm safe receipt.'

'We're ready to deploy D when you need us. We'll need twelve hours' notice, but nine will do, and as much information as you can. You know the sort of thing. You can go now. We have your position. So I'm told, anyway.'

'Thank you, sir.'

'So what did he say?' asked Armalite.

'Did he ask who's here?' interrupted the Beast.

'Of course not,' Christian said. 'He doesn't give a shit. He'll love the fact you're working on your own time. It's the sort of thing he finds funny.'

'What? Funny ha-ha, or funny you're court-martialled anyway?' replied the Beast.

'Relax, Beasty, Dev's fine,' said Christian.

'Fine with you, maybe,' grunted the Beast. 'You've got the luxury of being dead. It's not so bloody easy for the likes of us.'

'Honestly, being dead isn't all good, Beasty,' replied Christian.

'It can be arranged,' said Armalite, reaching for his rifle

'OK, whoever hears the plane first, gets first crack at the water. And you only get one go. He said about an hour and a half,' Christian told them.

'Marvellous,' muttered Raglan. 'That's once you've swum three miles out to get it.'

'Can't you guys shut up for five minutes?' snapped Dharia. 'It would be nice to get some sleep.'

'He's just cross because . . .' said Christian. 'No, no, sorry.'

'What? Cross about what?' said Raglan, sitting up straight.

'Nothing,' replied Christian.

'*About what?*'

'Nothing at all. We never actually finished the game, so you didn't officially lose.'

'I cannot believe you are saying that,' said Raglan, a grin spreading across his face. 'You were the one who said it was too dark to see the pieces.'

'For fuck's sake, do be quiet. In these valleys, sound

travels,' hissed Dharia. 'They'll find us and we'll be back in that hole.'

'Hope springs eternal,' muttered Armalite with his eyes shut.

45

Christian rested his head back against crumbling sandstone and focussed on the thin blue ribbon that lay between the arid wasteland of sand and the burning brightness of the sky. Dharia lay in a foetal position with her head resting on her forearm. Either side of her, Armalite snored and the Beast breathed deeply. Raglan lowered his head to study a bright green cricket that had settled on his knee as a paper chase of tiny black birds weaved through the air above.

'Well, at least we've got a little more shade now,' Raglan whispered, jerking his thumb up over his shoulder.

'I guess so,' replied Christian with a faint smile.

'Now, I'm afraid I was a little economical with the truth earlier,' continued Raglan.

'Oh, really?' said Christian, his eyes still fixed on the horizon.

'Well, yes, I was. I do actually have two more cigarettes. Held in reserve, you could say.'

'Ah, do you now? Held back for some sort of special occasion?'

'Something along those lines,' said Raglan, offering Christian the crumpled packet of Craven A with two hands.

'Bloody marvellous, Rags,' said Christian. 'I'd been telling myself I was too thirsty to want a cigarette, but I feel differently now.'

'It was in a place just like this where it all started for me. A steep hillside, ocean in the distance and a bunch of guys out to kill me. Just missing an airbase and a few sheep, that's all.'

'What? You mean in Argentina?'

'Yes, that's it.' Raglan took back the cigarette lighter. 'Sat there on my twenty-first birthday. Most people would have been wacking down shots in some posh bar.'

'And you had people wacking down shots on you. Quite a lot of them.'

'Missed a crucial shot. Still annoys me. Can't believe how much the bullet dropped. Mind you, the quality of ammo has improved since those days. Anyway, about four thousand troops were out looking for me. They chased me halfway across South America. And I've been dead ever since.'

'Not that great, is it?'

'Hard to know. Been such a long time. Just wish

we could do some fighting in a slightly more sensible climate. You know, a little bit of grass under foot for a change. Less of the dust and sand.'

'I get it. Maybe you should talk to Dev?'

'But imagine my CV, Christi. Bit of a blank really.'

'Hold on, sorry to interrupt but . . .' Christian turned his head sideways to listen. 'I can hear something.'

'An aircraft?' said Raglan, sitting up.

'Dinner. That's what I can hear.'

'Can't hear a bloody thing. You sure, Christi?'

'Yup, listen. That way,' said Christian, pointing out towards the ocean. 'Think about it. They won't fly overland, so they'll stick out to sea and then cut straight inland.'

'I expect they'll do several dummy drops too.'

'Let's hope so. We don't need anyone gatecrashing our party.'

Christian cupped his hands around his eyes and scanned the horizon.

'There we are,' he said, pointing. 'You have to give it to Dev. He really does deliver.'

'Let's hope no one beats us to it. That aircraft will be spotted. It's hardly a common occurrence round here.'

'And the minute we get the gear, we'll need to get the hell out of here.'

'What's going on?' croaked Armalite, sitting up.

'Look,' said Christian, pointing again. 'There's the

plane. But the minute we load up, we're going to have to get out of here.'

'Mind you, it'll be dark soon,' said Raglan, standing up. 'That'll help.'

'We can handle these cunts with the right gear,' said the Beast. 'Bring it on, I say.'

'We're not here for a scrap,' Christian interrupted. 'We'd send in the Paras for that. This is much more subtle.'

'You and your bloody plans, Christi,' said the Beast.

'Shut up and start waving,' said Armalite.

The distant grey speck elongated into a rippling blur of contrast against the heat haze of the horizon. Christian raised his arms above his head and moved them slowly from side to side. The aircraft tracked towards their position, banked into turn and manoeuvred around in a circle above them at about 1,500 feet. A door halfway down the side of the fuselage opened and three cylinders slid out. They fell like stones for a couple of seconds before twitching in the air as small, circular parachutes cracked above them. The aircraft rocked its wings and the engine whined as it began to climb.

'Better not be the dummy ones,' said Armalite.

'With the way you look,' said the Beast, 'I wouldn't hold your breath.'

'Watch them and mark where they land,' said Raglan. 'We are now officially compromised. We get the gear and get out of here. Every skinny within forty miles of here is salivating.'

'Come on,' said Christian. 'Let's go.'

He led the way downhill in large steps, with his rifle in his hands. They climbed through a rocky gully and boxed around a patch of waist-high thorn bushes before looking down the valley side.

'There they are,' said the Beast. 'Well, two of them, anyway.'

'Good,' said Christian. 'Beasty, we'll find the other one. You guys get these two unpacked and sorted.'

'Roger that,' said Armalite, breaking into a run.

By the time Christian and the Beast reappeared with a long green metallic tube on their shoulders, Raglan and Dharia were spreading all kinds of military kit on the ground beside them. A hundred metres uphill, Armalite chewed on a high-energy bar whilst adjusting the sights on a Minimi machine gun. Christian carefully lowered his end of the tube to the ground.

'So, what have we got?' he said.

'You name it, Christi,' replied Raglan, passing him a tin mug of water. 'Rations, water, rifles, night sights, general desert stores clobber. Comms and maps, obviously. Oh, and a massive pair of boots for someone.'

'Thank you very much,' groaned the Beast. 'They'll be for me. So he does know.'

'I promise you there is nothing to worry about,' said Christian, tearing the top off a green packet labelled 'Beef Steak in Chilli Sauce'.

'Are you two gonna stand up for me?' the Beast demanded.

'For heaven's sake,' replied Raglan. 'It won't come to that. Do you want me to ring him right now and sort him?'

'Fuck, no,' snapped the Beast. 'Don't do that.'

'I'd be more worried about Mrs MacDonald,' said Christian.

'*I'm* more worried about a bunch of guys turning up here with fifty cals,' said Raglan.

'Just get everything we need and we'll dump the containers back in that gully,' said Christian. 'In theory, you're meant to be able to crush them flat.'

He snapped a magazine onto a Diemaco C8 assault rifle and rested it on the ground beside him on its bipod. As he pulled off his filthy cotton trousers, Armalite suddenly boomed out.

'Stand to! Stand to! Four vehicles inbound. There're four vehicles. Coming this way.'

'Fuck,' said Raglan. 'Surely they could at least let us have time to get dressed.'

'About three K that way. West, I reckon,' yelled Armalite, waving his arm.

'Right,' said Christian, yanking on a pair of desert DPM trousers. 'Get what you can into the bergens and prepare to move out. We'll get up high again.'

'No, we'll be sitting ducks on the way up,' Raglan pointed out. 'Back along the valley.'

'But there's no fucking cover once we're through that gully,' said the Beast, stuffing boxes of rations into a bergen.

'Fuck, fuck. He's right. OK,' said Raglan. 'It's time we got a grip anyway. Time we took the fight to them.'

'Armalite,' shouted Christian. 'Get down here.'

'Beasty, you take the right flank. Over there,' continued Raglan. 'Christi, you and me in the middle. Arma can take the left with the Minimi. Dharia, when I say so, I want you to run along the side of the gully and make sure they see you. The minute you hear a shot, get on the ground. I need them to follow you.'

Christian pressed a canteen of water to his lips and glugged hard. He looped his arms through the shoulder straps of a belt of webbing and fastened the plastic clip at the front. Instinctively, his hand reached for the ammunition pouch. He squeezed a brick of magazines. A moment later, he rushed forwards and crashed to the ground beside Raglan. He flipped off the dust caps and peered into the telescopic sights of his rifle. The ground fell away gently below them, flattening out into undulating scrub. A tail of rising dust led his eyes to the back of a fast moving convoy of pickups.

'These guys aren't hanging around,' muttered Raglan. 'Guess it's first come, first served round here. Must be eight of them in each vehicle.'

'And they will not stop,' gasped Dharia. 'They think it's a ransom drop; millions of dollars. Nothing else gets dropped by parachute into the desert.'

'So they're not after us, then?' said Christian.

'They will be when they find no dollars,' Dharia

replied. 'If it's Sha'inti's men, they will kill us, and if it's not, they will kidnap us for ransom.'

'Arma,' yelled Raglan. 'You take the lead vehicle. Then, anything left. Beast, you go right side, Christi, centre right. On my command.'

At a distance of about a kilometre, the convoy broke from linear formation as the rear two vehicles veered away to the left and right. One moved up the side of the valley and the other disappeared briefly from view in low-lying ground. The leading vehicles accelerated, forcing the militiamen standing in the back to cling to the bull bars.

'On my command,' yelled Raglan, pressing the stock of his rifle into his shoulder. 'Right, Dharia. Go now, along the gully then get down into it.'

Dharia leapt to her feet and darted uphill. Almost simultaneously, the two vehicles in the centre adjusted their course.

'Come on, come on, this way,' said Raglan, moving his finger from the trigger guard to the trigger.

'Closer,' replied Christian. 'We need them close.'

'Three hundred metres. That'll do,' replied Raglan.

'Three hundred,' Christian confirmed.

'On my command!' yelled Raglan, glancing left at Armalite.

A couple of seconds passed, then Raglan bellowed. 'Fire!'

An envelope of sound closed around Christian as his finger tightened on the trigger, releasing a short judder of fire into the right-hand centre pickup. In a fraction of a second, he pivoted his body on his elbows and squeezed the trigger again. For a moment, Raglan's rifle, firing in short, sharp bursts, stood out against the blur of noise from Armalite's almost continuous volley of machine-gun fire. Thirty metres over to the right, the Beast kept time with a series of coordinated bursts consisting of no more than three or four rounds.

Christian pulled his eye back from his telescopic sight to witness a ball of dust form around one of the lead pickups as it rolled sideways onto its roof. The other three vehicles continued bouncing their ways forwards with the militiamen in the back firing wildly up the valley.

'Reloading,' yelled Raglan, snapping in a second magazine.

Christian pushed his face back down against the telescopic sight and fired the remaining rounds from his magazine into the windscreen of his target vehicle. Several men fell from the back and one jumped from the side door. As the pickup to the right ground to a halt in soft sand, several figures leapt from the cab and took cover behind the bonnet. The Beast adjusted his aim and continued his percussion of fire. A second later, the pickup making its way up the valley side to the left burst into flames and came to a standstill. Burning shapes flipped and twisted on the ground around it.

Armalite lifted the Minimi and spun it through the best part of forty-five degrees. He pushed it back onto the bipod and the rough grunt sounded again over the clatter of the C8s. The gunner in the back of the only pickup still moving levelled the rear-mounted 50 cal, only to be lifted out of the back of the vehicle by a hail of automatic fire. Christian twisted his rifle sideways and snapped on a new magazine. By the time the rifle was back in his shoulder, his target was resting on its axels in the sand seventy metres away, the front tyres shot out. Still, Armalite rained down fire, moving from target to target, and the Beast continued sending carefully aimed individual shots through the soft skin of his pickup.

'Cease firing,' yelled Raglan, making a slicing movement with the palm of his hand. 'Arma, cease firing. Preserve ammo, for fuck's sake.'

Armalite pulled himself up into a kneeling position, the smoking Minimi resting in his arms. Sweat poured down his crimson face and his chest heaved. He looked sideways, his eyes wide and wild.

'Forwards,' yelled Raglan, springing to his feet.

Christian checked the chamber of his rifle and bolted after Raglan. He approached the sunken pickup and skirted around it. The outer rim of the windscreen had flopped inwards and rested around the neck of the driver like a wreath. Resting against the passenger door, a headless torso oozed with blood. A pebble-dash of blood, brains and fragments of skull lined the interior of the cab. Christian moved around to the back of the vehicle. Blood dripped from the tailgate. He took a breath, tasting a toxic cocktail of burning petrol and rubber. He moved closer, his finger on the trigger. Inside, a twisted heap of bodies took on a single form.

He jumped as a shot rang out behind him, then a second, followed by several bursts of automatic fire. He shook his head and blinked as his conscious mind resumed control of his faculties.

'Looks like a bloody pepper pot,' he heard Raglan's voice say.

'Them or us,' Christian replied, shaking his head. 'You OK?'

'Yep,' replied Raglan. 'Them or us. We need to move out of here,' he continued, looking around. 'Before the B team turn up.'

'They'll see the smoke for miles around,' called Armalite as he approached.

'It'll be dark soon,' said Christian. 'Let's see if we can't salvage one of the vehicles; cannibalise what we need from any of the others. The one that rolled will be the least shot up.'

Twenty minutes later, Christian closed his eyes and turned an ignition key. The started motor groaned and turned with increasing urgency.

'Come on, come on,' growled Raglan, bashing his fist on the dashboard.

The vehicle shuddered and the engine came to life.

Christian pressed down on the accelerator and raised the revs.

'Bloody marvellous,' yelled the Beast, leaning round from the back of the pickup to fill the frame of the driver's window. 'A Landy wouldn't do that.'

'Bollocks, a Land Rover wouldn't have rolled in the first place,' snapped Armalite.

46

'So what now, Christi?' asked the Beast.

'Well,' replied Christian, turning the pickup around. 'We can't just drive off in the direction we want to go. We'll have to follow the tracks these guys made on their way in and then veer off once we hit some hard ground. Otherwise, the next bunch to turn up will just track us.'

'Roger that,' said Armalite. 'And we've only got two hundred and fifty rounds left for the Minimi.'

'Fucking hell, Arma,' Raglan protested.

'We only had five hundred in the first place,' said Armalite.

'Whatever,' continued Christian, dragging on a Marlboro Red, 'we need to find somewhere to hole up for the night while we get a grip of where we are and how to get into position to grab Sha'inti. Think I prefer those Craven A things.'

'Dharia,' said Raglan, unfolding a map and spreading it out. 'Can you show me where this village is?'

Dharia scanned the map.

'It's a tiny place. I can't see it. It looks like only the big places are shown.'

'Bloody marvellous,' replied Raglan. 'Does it have a name?'

'Not one you could write in English,' answered Dharia. 'But I can show you where it is.'

'How's that?'

'Well, it's south of that river and to the west of this area of high ground.' Dharia tapped a blank area of light brown looped in concentric red lines. 'But the river has not flowed there since before I was born.'

'So it's not there any more?' said Raglan, looking at Christian. 'Fucking Antcliff.'

'It's a map, not a sat image,' replied Christian. 'Things move.'

'Anyway,' Dharia continued, tapping with her finger again. 'Get us to this point and I will show you the village.'

'Unless that's moved too,' said Raglan.

With the light fast fading, the tracks in the dust came to an abrupt end. The ground rose before them and the terrain changed from soft sand and dust to broken shale and shingle. Christian kept going in the same direction for a couple of hundred metres before swinging off to the left and following along the top of what he could now see was a low-lying plateau.

Next to him, Raglan fiddled with the GPS and Dharia craned over the map. In the back, Armalite and the Beast leant on the bull bars with their weapons resting on the roof.

Several hours of jolting, juddering and revving passed before Raglan called a halt.

'This'll do. If we can't see jack shit, they can't either.'

'Think about it,' Dharia added. 'If we have left any tracks, they'll need headlights to see them, won't they?'

'Yup, we'll see them coming,' said Christian, switching off the engine. 'Also, if we keep going, there's a chance we'll drive right into a village or something.'

'OK. Let's get some scoff on board and a bit of a kip,' said Raglan, pushing open the passenger door.

47

Colonel Deveral cleared his throat and pressed the 'On' switch on the side of an overhead projector. He straightened up and gripped the thick end of a snooker cue which lay across the desk that separated him from several lines of tables. Sitting there were eighteen casually dressed members of D Squadron, 22 SAS. A fan whirred inside the projector and a satellite image sprang onto a white screen that hung from the ceiling. The only giveaway that this was not a bog-standard classroom in any school up and down the country was two large posters Blu-Tacked to the wall. One, entitled 'Know your Weapon', displayed the component parts of a stripped-down M16 A2 assault rifle, and the other was an Ordnance Survey map of Northern Ireland with various coloured pins stuck in it.

'An interesting one, this,' said Deveral, slapping the

palm of his free hand with the snooker cue. 'Desert theatre, very quick in and out. Somalia.'

Except for the fan, the room was silent. Deveral pivoted around and faced the screen.

'Obviously, an airborne insertion,' he continued, jabbing at an area in the top left of the screen. 'We'll drop in here, group up and move south about six K to a point just outside this village.' Another jab of the snooker cue. 'Now, our intel tells us someone we want will be attending a wedding of some kind at this location.'

Signs of interest cracked across the faces of the assembled men and some glanced around at their friends.

'Now, I know what you're all thinking but it's not a standard hard arrest,' said Deveral, turning back to the men again. 'This time, our role is only to flush a rat out of a drain.'

'We're calling it Operation Desert Rat,' said Major Mark Day in his thick Welsh accent, getting to his feet.

'No, we're not,' continued Deveral with a smile and a swipe of the snooker cue.

'Operation Dyno Rod, more like,' muttered Trooper James Powell quietly to a ripple of laughter.

'How about Rentokil?' said someone else.

'I don't think they do drains,' said Deveral. 'Anyway, we're not going in to kill; we're going in to flush, and someone else will do the catching.'

'So, it's pretty simple,' said Major Day. 'We are not expecting much resistance, because most of the al-Shabaab militia are unknown. We expect they'll put up something of a fight while any known faces slip away. Then, once the players have bolted, they'll play the impoverished farmers defending their land card.'

'No single man is fully in control of al-Shabaab,' said Deveral, 'but one guy is as close to a leader as anyone. He's an exceptionally nasty piece of work who metes out the most barbaric forms of torture to suppress the population. He's training young British men to kill in our streets and funds the whole thing from piracy along the coast.'

Deveral paused and looked around.

'All we want is a word with him. Anyway, I'm going to hand over to Major Day now. He'll dish out briefing packs and take you through the details. But, if we're on, it's likely to be tomorrow night.'

Christian lay on his back and looked up at the stars through a haze of cigarette smoke. Raglan sat cross-legged beside him, resting his back against one of the front wheels. His fingers drummed on the screen of the sat phone. Above, the Beast sat on the roof of the truck with his feet on the bonnet doing the first stag. His night vision goggles protruded from his forehead like a giant black beak. Armalite and Dharia slept in the relative comfort of sleeping bags.

'So, we sit here till about two a.m,' whispered

Raglan. 'Then we drive to within striking distance of the village, stash the vehicle and start the recce. Doesn't sound too bad, does it?'

'Makes total sense,' replied Christian. 'We just need to make sure no one spots the truck during daytime. Otherwise, D will be reassigned to a hostage extraction.'

'More like body repatriation,' said Raglan.

'Embarrassing either way,' Christian said. 'And I doubt many people will show up to my real funeral.'

'Bit soon after the last one. You really need some sort of gap, I suppose.'

'Fifty to sixty years, I was thinking.'

'Think you might need to join a different unit, Christi. Staff College?'

'Fuck, no. You're a bloody colonel and you didn't go, did you?'

'I would have done. Well, you know what I mean.'

Christian twisted onto his side, stubbed his cigarette out and pushed the butt into a pocket on the side of his combats. He closed his eyes and focussed on the reassuringly familiar smell of mothballs which always pervaded any new Army issue clothing. In theory, he was within forty-eight of a successful conclusion to the operation. But so far, everything that could have gone wrong had done, and this last phase seemed even more high risk. The good thing, though, was that in a matter of hours D Squadron would be on the ground. That would rebalance things, along with having some proper weapons and equipment.

It was 01.45 when he felt a hand grip his shoulder. He struggled to open his eyes, despite increasingly enthusiastic shaking from Armalite.

'Come on, Christi. We need to get going. Got a brew for you.'

'Thanks, Arma,' croaked Christian, realising he had been in a deep sleep for the first time since being caught by the fat Colonel.

Raglan was hunched forwards in the passenger seat of the pickup with his head under a coat to shield the light from the torch he was using to examine the map.

'I think we could be within striking distance within a couple of hours,' he said, pulling the coat back and flicking off the torch. 'Just depends on not running into anyone.'

'Well, let's get going then.' Christian balanced his metallic cup on the dashboard and turned the ignition key.

'Why does everything sound twice as loud at night?' said Raglan, grimacing.

'Don't know, but it's going to help when D open up tomorrow night.'

'True,' replied Raglan, nodding.

Christian slipped the pickup into gear and edged forwards.

'Can't see shit,' he said, twisting around. 'Need you guys back there to keep a lookout too.'

'Roger that,' replied the Beast, tapping on the roof of the cab.

Christian peered through the dusty, fly splatted windscreen into deep, unpolluted darkness. A sliver of moon helped him avoid the largest obstacles but progress was bumpy and slow. The Beast and Dharia passed around a steady stream of biscuits, chocolate, coffee and cigarettes while Armalite checked through all the weapons. Raglan busied himself with the GPS.

Christian did not notice it at first, but he found himself driving faster and faster as the darkness took on a pink tinge. He yawned and realised that dawn was breaking. It was a good thing in some ways. Another night out of the way. But the start of a new day also brought a new set of problems and dangers. He glanced sideways to catch Raglan's profile popping out of the gloom as he lit a cigarette. Old, exhausted and drawn, he looked like a man who deserved a break. A man who needed to get back to his farm in the green hills and eat some shepherd's pie.

'We need to get this done,' said Christian. 'I'm not sure if I can face another fuck-up.'

'Fuck-up?' Raglan echoed. 'Could be a whole load worse if you ask me.'

'You think so?'

'Well, yes. But I know what you mean. The tricky bit is going to be the ambush. We haven't really got enough people to do it by the book. That's where we could fuck up going forward.'

'In theory, we have,' said Christian. 'You and I in the middle to make the snatch and Arma and Beast on each flank to cut off retreat or reinforcements. That's what we always practised.'

'I know, I know, so did we, in *my* day too. But we should be six strong in the middle and each wing ought to be four. It's a lot to ask.'

'We could swap and get D to do it? They grab him and pass him over.'

'But they won't recognise the bastard, will they? And what happens when they see you?'

'My cover's blown and I go back to a normal life. Win-win.'

'Staff College,' said Raglan with a sideways grin. 'Listen, we should be finding somewhere to dump the truck before too long.'

'Yup, just need somewhere with some topography.'

An orange glow to the East dispensed with the pink tinge of the retreating darkness. Shadows formed and a rough, undulating landscape came into focus around them. The Beast pulled off his beak and switched off the power.

'We just need somewhere with enough of a dip to break up the outline,' Christian continued. 'We don't want some bloody great valley, because they tend to be transport routes. Come on, Beasty, what can you see?'

'Keep going, Christi. It gets hillier the closer we get,' replied the Beast.

'And every metre that we don't have to drag matey, kicking and screaming, will be a bonus,' said Armalite.

'Yes, but dragging him the whole way to the coast because someone nicked the wheels isn't going to be that great either,' grumbled Raglan.

'He can walk,' said Dharia. 'I'll make him.'

'How were you planning on doing that?' said Armalite.

'Easy. Tie his hands behind his back and a cord around his balls. Lead him like an animal. It's his way of moving prisoners.'

There was a pause.

'OK,' said Armalite. 'I can see how that would work.'

'They take twenty men like that behind a vehicle. Men fall.'

'Got it. Think the Russians used to do that in Afghan back in the Seventies,' said Armalite. 'At least we know what we're dealing with.'

'Over there,' said Christian, pointing and turning the steering wheel. 'Let's try it. What's wrong with parking up in the bushes?'

A couple of minutes later, Christian positioned the pickup between two green thorn bushes. As he turned the wheel to make the final adjustment, the back of his hand brushed a lever behind the steering wheel, sending jets of soapy water onto the windscreen.

'Oi,' snapped Armalite. 'Was that aimed at me?'

'No, otherwise it would have hit you,' replied

Christian. 'Right, let's see what we can do to camouflage this thing. Can't believe I didn't try that before.'

'Beasty, I want you to sort the vehicle and keep guard here,' said Raglan, squeezing out of the door. 'Arma, Dharia, you're with me and Christi. We need eyes on this place before anyone gets up and at it.'

'They'll all be in bed pissed as farts,' said Armalite.

'Didn't think they drank,' said the Beast, tearing a branch off a bush.

'Bollocks, of course they do,' replied Armalite.

'Some drink alcohol, some don't,' said Dharia. 'Some chew khat, some don't.'

'Well, we need eyes on the place,' continued Raglan. 'Before things get active. I want an elevated OP where we can see stuff. I want to know which way to send in D and which way they'll break out.'

Christian clipped on his webbing belt, zipped up his ops vest and took a long drink of water from one of the canteens. He fastened the Velcro strap of a holster around his leg and slipped a 9mm SIG Saur inside. As Raglan repeated the coordinates of a twenty-four-hour and seven-day RV, he double-checked the primers on two fragmentation grenades. Finally, he looped a pair of Zeiss binoculars around his head and pushed them inside his shirt. Armalite humped the Minimi onto his shoulder and turned to the Beast.

'The alloys could do with a once-over.'

'If you need any rope, Dharia . . .' came the reply.

Raglan led the way at a fast walk. In one hand he

held the GPS and in the other a folded map. His M16 hung across his back. Christian brought up the rear, his rifle resting in his arms. Despite the chill of the early morning, flies immediately identified them as easy pickings. They buzzed around their heads and honed in on areas of exposed skin.

In his usual way, Raglan paused after thirty minutes or so to check his bearings. Nobody spoke, then they were off again through more low, dusty hills. They crossed a rutted track and turned directly up the side of a steep, flat-topped mountain. As they gained height, the ground turned to crumbling shale and their breathing became audible. Christian accelerated and came parallel with Armalite. He gripped the stock of the Minimi and lifted it gently onto his own shoulder. A pained expression passed across Armalite's crimson face, followed by a nod of acceptance.

Raglan maintained the pace and they gained more height. A familiar burning sensation spread up Christian's thighs. He leant into the incline and rested his rifle across the top of his webbing belt to relieve some weight from his arms. After the cruelty of a couple of false summits, they were wading through long, sharp grass on the top of the mountain. Coveys of small brown birds broke cover and called in alarm as they curled away on the breeze.

'Bit exposed up here,' said Raglan over his shoulder. 'Didn't think it would be so flat. Quickest route, though,' he continued. 'In theory, we get across here and should be able to look right down at them.'

'Hear the wedding bells,' said Armalite.

'It'll still be a couple of Ks but we'll get a good view.'

The wispy grass came to an end and they found themselves walking downhill through thorn bushes and trees with gnarled black trunks. Raglan held the GPS close to his face and wiped the dust from the screen. The ground levelled out and became a lip of hard rock. Below them, the land fell away sharply to reveal a wide open expanse of grey and yellow.

'OK,' said Raglan. 'This will do.'

'So what now?' said Dharia, sitting down.

'Well,' replied Raglan, dropping to a squatting position and pulling out his binoculars, 'it's down there somewhere.'

'Just look for the line of the river,' said Dharia. 'Every settlement in this country is on some kind of water.'

'Sure,' Raglan agreed. 'The river will be critical to this.'

'What happens now?' Dharia pressed.

'Hold on,' Raglan replied. 'You guys move back from the edge so we don't skyline ourselves. Give me a moment here and I'll tell you.'

48

Raglan reappeared a few minutes later with dust and thorns all down the front of his shirt. He lowered himself into a sitting position and unfolded the map.

'As Dharia thought,' he said, 'there is a river, well, a dry one, that runs down the middle of the plain down there. It meanders a bit and passes right by a settlement that has to be it. Looks like a hundred or so little white houses. All jumbled up with a bunch of animal enclosures around and a load of vehicles.'

'How do we know it's the right one?' said Christian.

'Because there's nothing else down there,' said Raglan, waving his hand over the map. 'Now, according to my brand-new MoD issue watch that's still set on GMT, it's nearly oh-five-forty-five local time. Christi, I want you and me to get down there and recce the area before it's fully light. Arma, you need to set up the Minimi on the edge up here, where you'll lay down covering fire if we get seen and have to make a run for it. Dharia, you're watching Arma's back. You need to make sure no one walks onto you from the rear, across where we've just come from.'

'What if they do?' asked Dharia.

'Start talking to them loudly enough that Armalite can hear,' Raglan said. 'He'll do the rest.'

'Better shout,' Armalite interjected.

'You sort that between yourselves. Now, if things do go wrong, it's the twenty-four-hour RV. Then we'll fix an extraction from there. OK? We'll be back in a couple of hours. And, Arma, I want you to get onto Deveral and give him a verbal description of everything you can see. I bet he'll be building a model of the village in the ops room.'

'Personal role radios?' asked Christian, tapping a pouch on his webbing.

'Yes,' replied Raglan. 'Come on, let's go. I'm being eaten alive.'

Raglan got to his feet and moved off, keeping low. Christian winked at Armalite and Dharia and followed him. They disappeared over the lip of rock and started a zig-zag descent through tufts of grass and knee-high thorn bushes. All around, dawn gathered momentum and streaks of cloud became visible against an increasingly blue backdrop of sky. More brown birds catapulted themselves from the grass and arced above them.

'All we need now is a herd of goats,' snarled Raglan over his shoulder. 'To really fuck things up.'

'We're too late,' Christian said. 'We should be on the way out by now.'

'I know,' Raglan replied, 'but this is just a flushing exercise and no more. Our guys just have to cause enough noise to get the bigwigs on the move. It's not like they're actually having to secure the place.'

'I get that,' Christian said. 'But what we're going to need is coordinates for an air strike to cover us as we move out. We'll need fast jets.'

'We can do that. We'll want something just behind us in the river bed. I know that's the way they'll go. Wouldn't you?'

'Why not bolt in a vehicle?'

'Because they'll be shitting themselves about drones. They know we can pick up engine heat.'

'So you would make a run for it on foot?'

'Yes, a few miles. Hole up somewhere and know full well no one's going to keep boots on the ground for more than a couple of hours. Because no one does these days. And if it goes to rat shit, we link up with D and extract with them.'

49

At 09.45, two puffs of white smoke kicked up from the wheels of a C130 Hercules as it touched down on the main runway at RAF Akrotiri on the southernmost tip of Cyprus. The aircraft taxied to the last in a row of giant green hangars and came to rest. A winch motor screeched, the rear ramp lowered and a string of men in desert combat dress emerged onto the warm tarmac. Each carried a large bergen and green kit bag. They processed through the massive metal door of the hangar and formed up in a line next to a white Gulfstream 4. Outside, a group of men in dark green overalls, ear defenders and high visibility waistcoats used a forklift to unload a series of pallets from a door in the side of the aircraft.

Armalite adjusted the settings of his binoculars to bring Raglan's face into focus. Above, the sun scorched down on the back of his neck. Flies towered above his head. Christian came into view too as they navigated their way slowly back uphill. He took a final scan of the area and pushed a notebook into the top pocket of his shirt. He rolled onto his side and crawled back from his vantage point. A couple of minutes passed before he heard the sound of thorns tearing at clothing.

'Over here,' he said quietly.

Raglan appeared, his face flushed. Dark patches of sweat stood out around his armpits and across his chest.

'OK, Arma?' he said as he approached. 'All quiet up here?'

'Fine,' replied Armalite. 'Called Deveral and he's all set. Assume it's the right place.'

'Looks like it,' said Christian. 'Well, it would be one hell of a coincidence if forty vehicles happened to be parked up in one microscopic farming settlement without something going on.'

'I told you,' said Dharia, appearing behind Armalite. 'People don't break with tradition here.'

'Dharia's right,' said Raglan. 'There is clearly something happening down there. There's a load of activity, but we didn't get too close. I'm happy to call it.'

'What do you mean?' said Dharia.

'I mean,' replied Raglan, 'I am happy to risk my government breaking international law and risking the lives of British personnel to respond to what could be described as a hunch.'

'What's a hunch?' asked Dharia, scowling.

'A glorified guess,' said Christian. 'It's when you don't know for sure.'

'I know for sure,' snapped Dharia, jabbing her finger at Raglan. 'He will be there.'

'I know, I know,' said Raglan, wiping sweat from his face with the sleeve of his shirt. 'But remember, it's my call.'

50

The rest of the day was spent on the mountain top taking turns to watch the village and pass information back to Deveral in the operations room at Stirling Lines. At last light, Raglan crawled back from the forward observation point and sat cross-legged on the ground.

'We can always abort this if something changes, but they'll be taking off about now,' he said, looking at the others. 'There's lights on down there but we don't know whether that's normal or not.'

'They will have light,' said Dharia. 'That's normal. They have generators and access to as much oil as they need from passing ships.'

'OK, sure,' Raglan acknowledged. 'But based on the number of vehicles, it's pretty clear there's something going on and we need to deploy. So, Christi, I need you to tab back over and pick up the Beast. Bring him over here, and if you can bring the truck a bit closer to the base of the mountain, all the better later on. Bring a sleeping bag too and a load of rope.'

'Sure.' Christian started to stand.

'But make sure you walk him through the ambush strategy before you get back.'

'No problem,' said Christian. 'Set piece with running skirmish and air strike. Piece of piss. It's all we ever practise.'

Armalite grinned.

'But it's different for real,' replied Raglan. 'It's not so funny when the RAF are dropping proper gear instead of red smoke.'

Christian nodded, gripped his M16 and set off into the half-light.

Major Mark Day pressed a hand against the roof of the cabin of the Gulfstream 4 to steady himself. He glanced down at the clipboard he held in his other hand.

'Fairly standard in many ways,' he commented, 'but, like always, plenty of scope to fuck up.'

With faces smeared in a brown and black camouflage cream, the eighteen members of D Squadron sat in two rows down the sides of the stripped out cabin. Divided by a line of parachute packs, they stared at their own individual clipboards, to which packs of photocopied notes and maps were attached.

'You've all seen the model,' he continued, 'but we

all know it's all a bit different when we're down there. Now, these guys may have some hardware that we don't know about, but we don't think they'll know how to use it. It's mainly for show to keep their neighbours quiet. They could have artillery of some kind, but we can't see any. So, it's up the edge of the settlement, a lot of noise, hold on, more noise and wait for the order to withdraw.'

Day took a look at his watch and continued.

'So, it's only four and a half hours' fly time to the drop zone.' There was a rustle of paper as each man turned to the next page on his pack. 'Jump oh-one-forty-five, six-K tab in and engage oh-two-forty-five. Back to the extraction site for oh-four hundred, where we RV with the PC Twelves. It's into some airbase in Kenya and back from there.'

Christian covered the distance back to the pickup in a fraction of the time it had taken to make the outward journey. Just as he looked down to see his GPS showing '120m to Destination', his sixth sense caused him to pause.

'Evening, Christi,' croaked the Beast from somewhere in the darkness behind him. 'Everything OK?'

'Hey, Beasty, good,' replied Christian, turning to see a massive outline appear against the night sky. 'Looks like we're on.'

51

Raglan's fingers ceased their drumming on the magazine of his M16 and he lifted his chin from the palm of his hand.

'It's always the waiting that kills,' he whispered in the darkness. 'But I think it's time to go. We've been through things enough times. It's thirty minutes to get into position and there's a risk being there too early.'

'Let's go,' said Christian. 'Sun Tzu would.'

'Sun who?' said the Beast.

'Chinese version of Macbeth,' said Raglan. 'Said you should never turn up late for a battle.'

'Genius, then,' said the Beast.

'Well, kind of,' said Christian. 'More like, he who arrives first in the field of battle, forces his enemy to hasten.'

'I've read that,' said Dharia. '*The Art of War*.'

'Sha'inti will have read it too,' Raglan interrupted. 'So we'd better get on with it.'

Raglan led the way down over the lip of rock. The same wind that moved the clouds nonchalantly across the night sky, allowing them mockingly infrequent intervals of moonlight, also served to muffle the crunch of their boots in the dry earth. Halfway down the gradient, they lost sight of the lights from the village and continued until they reached flat ground. They adjusted their course and took slow, careful steps through uneven scrub scattered with football-size stones.

Raglan paused, dropped to one knee and craned forwards to inspect the GPS. He tilted his head back in the darkness and looked around. They moved off again, this time a fraction slower to accommodate the noticeable drop in wind speed on the valley floor. Five metres apart, they continued across open ground before dropping down a bank.

'This is it,' whispered Raglan. 'Cut-off Point C. So, Dharia, Beast, we leave you here. Arma, Christi, come on, we're further down.'

The clouds parted above and a wide scrape of grey appeared before them with clearly defined banks on either side. Large rocks littering the river bed hinted of a once significant flow of water. Raglan took advantage of the clarity and set off across soft sand. Armalite followed him and Christian brought up the rear. They rounded a bend and caught a distant glimpse of light.

Raglan raised his hand and, like dominoes, they each dropped to one knee and raised their rifles.

Christian popped up the protective covers on his telescopic sight and pressed the button to turn on the night vision. He peered into the scope and scanned around in ghoulish electric green and white. Raglan was up again and off, stepping lightly from one large, flat stone to the next. The river took on a second gentle twist and the smell of animal manure he remembered from the recce filled his nostrils once again. Raglan continued, pausing every couple of steps to listen. They rounded the bend and the light appeared again, this time as identifiable individual houses.

'B,' mouthed Raglan, pointing at the ground with his index finger.

Armalite nodded and stepped forwards on his own. Christian watched his silhouette blend with the darkness. Admiration filled his thoughts for this man who had put his life and career on the line for him for the second time in as many months. In theory, he had retired from active duty since losing half his hand in the bomb blast in County Armagh and had been put into the less demanding role of senior Regimental armourer. He was now going to conceal himself at Point A, the closest point to the village, and let the fleeing militiamen pass right by him. He would then play the dual role of cutting off their retreat and also preventing any reinforcements entering the fray. Finally, he would make his retreat along the river bed and, if need be, call in an air strike on his former position.

Christian looked at the outline of Raglan's face and then down at the luminous hands of his watch. There was nothing to say. He turned and approached the left-hand bank. He took a couple of large steps up and settled himself at the top, lying prone on the ground. He arranged some rocks into a small row in front of him and laid the sleeping bag over them to create a rest for his rifle. If Raglan was right, any escapees would come steaming down the river bed right into their line of fire. He would knock out his side and Raglan would deal with the right. By now, D would be somewhere over Ethiopia, probably at about 45,000 feet to avoid any other air traffic. He could see the scene on board. The guys would be sitting in their rows. Some talking, some flicking through the briefing notes, some fiddling with their equipment and some just staring into space. Deveral would be in the ops room, pacing about, drinking coffee and hassling the meteorologist for more detail on the local weather conditions. A couple of hundred metres to his rear, the Beast would be lying quietly in the dark, most likely wondering why he wasn't at home with his wife and newborn child. Dharia was impossible to fathom, but Armalite would be in his element. Back on live ops and coiled like a spring.

Yellow hands ticked away time and the occasional rumble of an engine broke the rhythmical chant of insect calls. An interlude of moonlight offered temporary respite from the darkness and made Raglan momentarily visible on the opposite bank, hunched forwards, his eye against the sight, at one with his weapon.

Christian made a pact with himself not to look at his watch for at least fifteen minutes. He concentrated on listening to the sounds of the night around him – the insects and the general rustle of the odd gust of wind passing through bushes and undergrowth. At a distance of 500 metres, he would be pushed to hear anything from the village other than a shout or a scream. He adjusted the volume of his radio and pushed the earpiece against the side of his head. Nothing but a low-pitched hiss.

He caved in and looked at his watch: 01.48. A jolt of adrenalin rippled through his body. Boots were hitting the ground.

52

Christian raised himself up on his elbows and twisted his head sideways. He was sure something was going on. Then it started. The valley pinged strobe-white and then, a millisecond later, came the hammer blow of noise produced by multiple explosions. A second later followed the rough grunt of large-calibre machine guns and the zipping screams of bullets passing overhead. White light strobed again like flash photography and the ground trembled. Shouts and screams filled the airwaves between explosions and the roaring waves of echo.

Christian breathed hard and scanned around in a murky world of green and white. Raglan thought it would take between three and five minutes for anyone to grab a weapon, get out the door and cover 500 metres in the darkness. The briefest of moments in daily life and an eternity in the context of battle.

'Tap, tap' sounded in his earpiece. 'Tap, tap' again. Someone, unable to speak, was sending a message. It would be Armalite, tapping gently on his mouthpiece. They were coming.

Christian blinked his eyes and tried to normalise his focus. He stared into the sight and found his arms automatically moving his aim towards a blur of movement. Robed figures, crouching low, were running down the centre of the river bed, just as Raglan had foreseen. He counted five at no more than sixty metres. He pivoted a fraction on his elbows and toes. Sha'inti led the group, his bald head glowing white. He waved the men on with one hand and gripped a rifle in the other.

Christian made a microscopic adjustment to his aim and squeezed the trigger. The man to Sha'inti's left kicked over backwards. He did not hear Raglan's shot but a second man collapsed. Christian fired again as the remaining figures dived for the ground. He paused for a second before springing to his feet. He bolted forty metres along the top of the bank. Just as he slid down the bank, Sha'inti fired a wild burst into the air and down the river bed. There were several more individual shots and Sha'inti flattened himself into the ground again. More shots rang out from Raglan's position as Christian closed in. He leapt over two bodies and piled on top of Sha'inti, hitting him across the back of his head with the side of his rifle.

Sha'inti's body froze for a fraction of a second

before bucking up and trying to twist sideways. Christian slammed his fist into the side of his head and gripped one of his arms. He wrenched it back and tried to tuck it under his knee. Just as Sha'inti pulled it free, Raglan's knee dropped onto his shoulder and pinned him down. Christian gripped harder with his legs and pressed Sha'inti's face into the sand. As Raglan struggled with his arm and tried to slip a flexi cuff over his hand, Sha'inti managed to pull his knees up and hump forwards in the sand.

'I'll sort him,' snarled the Beast, dropping down on Sha'inti's shoulders and grabbing his other arm.

The Beast pinned Sha'inti's arms together and Raglan slipped on the flexi cuffs. A second later his legs were secured with rope and yanked up in a hog-tie through the cuffs.

'Sleeping bag and the rope,' snapped the Beast over Sha'inti's bellowing curses.

'OK,' gasped Christian. 'You hold him.'

A burst of gunfire crackled. This time close. Raglan sprang to his feet and raised his rifle.

'Come on,' he yelled.

The Beast grabbed Sha'inti, hauled him over his shoulder into a fireman's lift and started running down the river bed. Christian caught him up and held open the sleeping bag. The Beast tipped him inside and slung him over his shoulder like a sack.

'Sounds like Arma's in action,' hissed Christian.

'I'll carry, you shoot,' blurted the Beast, starting to run again.

Christian raised his rifle and scanned about, avoiding the bright white fuzz which represented a tower of swirling smoke and light glowing above the village. Bursts of heavy gunfire still barked above the backing chatter of small arms fire.

'Enemy force engaged,' called Raglan over the personal role radios.

Christian tapped his mouth piece twice in acknowledgement and kept pace with the Beast. They passed Point C, where Dharia sprang from the darkness. Pointing at the sleeping bag, she shouted.

'Make him run.'

'Of course we will,' said Christian, 'but not right now.'

They kept in the river bed for another couple of hundred metres before the Beast recognised the point they had climbed down. With a roar of exertion, he bounded up the bank and set off towards the base of the mountain. Christian and Dharia sprinted after him and caught up to find him dragging the sleeping bag along the ground behind him. As Christian gripped the bag to help the Beast, Dharia launched a kick. The muffled cry from inside was drowned out by a torrent of abuse from Dharia in her own language followed by another kick.

'Easy, love,' puffed the Beast. 'Plenty of time for that later.'

'Fucking piece of shit,' snapped Dharia. 'Rope him up.'

Behind them and now in the distance, the flashes continued, as did the gunfire. Raglan's voice fizzed against feedback with moments of hiss that sounded like some kind of reply from Armalite.

Dharia cackled with pleasure as they bumped through the patch of stones and pressed on through the thorn bushes. They slowed as the ground began to rise and, suddenly, the sleeping bag tore open, releasing Sha'inti onto the ground. He raised his head as if to speak and gasped for breath.

'Right, you're walking now or else we're going to hand you over to this lady here to make you,' said Christian.

'You traitorous shit,' snarled Sha'inti. 'I knew you were bullshit. I could have killed you a thousand times.'

'You walk or she makes you,' replied Christian. 'Russian-style.'

The Beast leant forwards and cut the rope holding Sha'inti's ankles to his wrists.

'Walk, yer cunt,' he growled. 'Or it'll be Glasgow-style.'

Sha'inti squinted up at the face of the man rumoured to be the biggest bloke in the Bristish Army and struggled to his feet.

'Aye,' snarled the Beast. 'There's a sensible chappie. It's a while since I ripped anyone's balls off with a rope.'

'It's a while since I had a smoke,' said Christian. 'Now, come on.'

As they set off, there was a whoosh in the air above them in the valley. They spun around in time to see a flash of white followed by a boom that sent shock waves through the ground. A moment later the process was repeated.

They turned and set off uphill, Christian leading the way followed by Sha'inti in his long grey shirt. The Beast was a metre behind and Dharia brought up the rear. By the time they reached the rocky lip, the gunfire had subsided to nothing more than an occasional drum roll answered tit for tat by another. Half running, half walking, they were halfway across the mountain top when running footsteps caused Christian to spin around. Raglan appeared with Armalite a few metres behind.

Struggling to catch his breath, Raglan jabbed his finger in the air.

'Come on, guys,' he gasped. 'They'll be waiting for us.'

53

The drive to the coast took two hours. Christian drove and Raglan sat beside him, turning his head from the GPS to the map like a spectator at a tennis match. Finally, the rising sun streamed through the clean windscreen and, across a hundred metres of sand, the Indian Ocean glistened light turquoise before darkening to deep blue.

'They should be just here,' muttered Raglan, shoving his cigarette end into the cassette player.

The Beast stood up in the back of the truck and raised binoculars to his eyes. Pivoting from left to right, he exclaimed.

'Can't see any sign of a boat out there. Bit of swell.'

Christian put the pickup into gear and manoeuvred onto the beach.

'There they are,' called Armalite, pointing. 'They've

pulled an RIB up onto the beach. Thought it was driftwood.'

Christian steered around a couple of washed-up oil drums and drove slowly across the beach. In the back, the Beast and Armalite stood with their arms raised in the air. What at first glance looked like a pile of seaweed, came into focus as a black RIB. Four men lay in the sand, rifles at the ready. As they drew closer, a tall, pale-faced man in a white shirt and blue jumper stood up and approached the vehicle. He held a brand-new SA80.

'Good morning,' called Christian. 'Any chance of a lift?'

'Yes, of course,' he replied, holding out a hand. 'Hankinson, Royal Navy.'

'Great,' said Raglan, leaning across. 'Where's the boat exactly?'

'Just offshore,' replied Hankinson. 'Sorry, no marines on board, so it's just us. Slightly off remit, you might say.'

'Don't worry,' said Christian, getting out of the car. 'Delighted to see you. Come on, let's go.'

Once they had unloaded their gear, the Beast hauled Sha'inti, hog-tied once again and hooded, out the back of the pickup and onto the sand. They helped pull the RIB down the beach and into the swirling surf. Hankinson started the engine and they piled in.

'Not the biggest vessel in the fleet,' he said. 'Bit overloaded, too, but should be fine.'

He opened the throttle and directed the nose of the RIB into the incoming waves. Christian looked back at the shore.

'Actually looks quite nice from here,' he said to Raglan.

'Not a patch on the Gower Peninsular.'

'No, of course not.'

'Or St. Andrews,' said the Beast.

'No, obviously not as nice as those,' replied Christian. 'But quite nice anyway.'

'Bloody hell,' Hankinson interrupted, pointing along the coast. 'Let's hope they're just out fishing.'

Raglan reached for his M16 and rested his hand on Christian's shoulder to steady himself as he stood.

'Moving at thirty knots,' said Raglan. 'I don't think so.'

'Marlin,' said Christian, snatching up his rifle. 'Come on, sir, let's speed up.'

'We'll swamp her if we go a lot faster,' replied Hankinson, increasing the revs fractionally.

'Fuck, they're coming this way,' snapped Raglan. 'Arma, get set up.'

Armalite reached into the bottom of the RIB and snatched up the Minimi. He stepped over Sha'inti, flipped down the bi-pod and rested it on the bow. A white speedboat with a cluster of men crowded on board made a beeline for them.

'Come on,' yelled Raglan. 'Start dumping kit. Everything except weapons and ammo.'

As they bashed through the waves, Dharia and the three sailors began hurling bergens, ration boxes and canteens into the sea, but still the white motor boat gained.

'Where the fuck is your boat?' screamed Raglan. 'We've not come this far to fail now.'

'On the radio now,' replied Hankinson efficiently.

'Tell them to get a fucking move on.'

Water cascaded over the front of the RIB and sloshed around inside, forcing Sha'inti to raise his head off the flooring. Static hissed from Hankinson's radio and sweat poured from his pallid cheeks.

'Come in, come in *Vanguard*,' he said.

The white speedboat closed in further and individual men holding guns in the air became identifiable. Shots rang and zinged through the air above them.

'Any moment now,' called Hankinson.

'Just warning shots, but shall I give them a burst back?' shouted Armalite over the noise of the outboard.

'Hold off,' replied Hankinson. 'Look, here we are.'

The water 200 metres before the RIB boiled white and froth fired into the air like a hot spring. Hankinson adjusted the rudder and steered them into an arcing turn. The patch of foaming water elongated into a long white line, and a black conning tower appeared at the centre. A couple of seconds later, 150 metres of shining black metal broke the surface and began to rise.

'There she is,' purred Hankinson.

'Fucking hell,' blurted the Beast. 'Not small, is it?'

'No, she's not.' Hankinson guided the RIB carefully around the stern of the 17,000-tonne nuclear powered submarine. 'Got the call-up. Nothing else around, so you got us, I'm afraid.'

'Not so hard now,' yelled the Beast at the white speedboat as it cut through a ninety-degree hairpin turn and set off in the opposite direction at full speed.

Two submariners emerged from a hatch on top of the conning tower, slid down a ladder and set up a general purpose machine gun on the gleaming hull.

'Any excuse for a bit of natural light,' Hankinson confided, lowering the revs as the nose of the RIB nudged the side of the submarine. 'Come on, I expect you could all do with some breakfast and a shower.'

They scrambled onto the deck and turned to watch the Beast hoist Sha'inti onto his shoulder.

'Better undo his legs,' said Raglan. 'You'll never get him inside otherwise.'

54

Christian had never been in an operating theatre before. In his mind, they were places on TV dramas where implausibly attractive nurses with heavy eye make-up fought for the attention of sun-tanned surgeons as they effortlessly performed life saving operations. This one was different. It was a tiny space with light green metal walls. A stainless steel operating table occupied the centre and a vast array of medical equipment was displayed in glass-fronted cabinets.

Raglan perched on a high stool dressed in light blue scrubs. Next to him, Sha'inti lay on the operating table, naked apart from the hood. A series of Velcro straps secured his body. By his feet, two doctors stood in scrubs, masks and elbow-length rubber gloves. Raglan took a sip of coffee and nodded at Christian, who leant forward and removed the hood.

Sha'inti's head jerked forwards and his eyes

widened. Tendons stood out in his arms and legs as he struggled against the straps. He saw the two doctors and blinked before letting out a stunned gasp. Raglan wheeled forwards on his stool and looked down on him.

'Ever been to Saudi?' he said quietly. Not waiting for a reply, he continued, 'No, nor have I, but it'll take us a few days.'

Sha'inti's face twisted with a mixture of rage and fear. Spit flew from his mouth.

'You – you – I saved you. You are a dog,' he spluttered.

'Yes, I probably am.' Raglan smiled. 'But you've got bigger issues to worry about.'

'What are you doing?' snapped Sha'inti, gathering a sense of control.

'Well,' replied Raglan, 'let me tell you about torture. Now back in your hole in the ground you cut people's faces off with rusty old saws. You might pelt them with small stones for half an hour before they bleed out. You might break their bones and stick them in a box to cook.'

'You don't understand anything,' hissed Sha'inti.

'The fact is,' Raglan went on, 'that traditional torture methods tend to lead to victims dying either of blood loss, heart failure, dehydration or starvation.'

He looked around the operating theatre, then continued.

'But we have the advantage of having the most

sophisticated medical equipment in the world right here.'

Raglan slid back on his stool and gestured to the two masked doctors. Without a word, they stepped forwards and positioned a small metal table next to Sha'inti. A collection of syringes and needles clattered as they were slid out of a padded sterile plastic bag. A pipe was plugged into a bag of saline fluid, which was then suspended from a metallic stand. A needle was held up against the overhead light and inserted into the other end of the pipe.

'Can't have you dying on us,' said Raglan.

Sha'inti jolted as the needle was jabbed into a vein in his lower arm.

'It's amazing really, but we can perform heart surgery down here, a couple of miles below the surface of the sea,' Raglan continued, 'Now these little pads are so we can check your heart rate.'

'What are you going to do?' wailed Sha'inti, peering forwards as a series of white stickers with wires coming from them were attached across his chest.

'You're going to experience pain in a way that you simply can't imagine,' said Raglan. 'You've dealt out enough and now it's your turn. But the difference is that you won't have the prospect of death to look forward to.'

'Why, why?' screamed Sha'inti. 'What do you need to know? I will talk.'

'It's not about talking,' said Raglan, folding his arms and looking at Christian. 'This is about payback.'

Sha'inti's stomach convulsed and a stream of thin yellow diarrhoea formed a pool between his legs.

'That's what the drip's for,' said Christian.

'Carrying on,' said Raglan. 'It's almost impossible for you to die in here. I say almost impossible, because we can't legislate for old age. But that's some way off for you.'

As one of the doctors reached for a roll of paper and began mopping up the diarrhoea, the other laid out a row of dental instruments and a small electric dental drill.

'So,' continued Raglan, 'these guys are going to get started and we're just going to sit here and watch.'

Having straightened out the instruments, the doctor produced a bright orange head brace and slipped it around Sha'inti's ears. Next, he pushed a metal clamp into his mouth and twisted a screw which slowly forced his mouth wide open. Raglan took a swig of his coffee and glanced at the screen showing a scrolling series of numbers and graphs.

'Some types of pain raise the heartbeat more than others,' said Raglan, squinting. 'But they'll know what's happening before you do.'

The doctor gripped the drill and pressed a trigger-like button on the handle. The high-pitched whir forced Raglan to raise his voice.

'They take your front teeth out, which allows access

to some of the largest nerve clusters in the human body. And, apparently, the closer to the brain, the worse it feels. So they inform me.'

Sha'inti pressed the palms of his hands against the operating table and tried to push himself even a few millimetres further away from the drill. His head pressed into the brace and sweat poured from his temples. The doctor lowered the drill and looked at Raglan over the top of his glasses for permission to proceed.

Raglan got up from the stool and looked down at Sha'inti.

'Now, you sack of shit,' he said. 'I'm prepared to offer you a deal. My colleague here will explain.'

The doctor released his finger from the trigger on the drill and stepped back to allow Christian parallel to Sha'inti.

'We'll take you back to the beach. Drop you there and you can carry on running your organisation,' said Christian. 'Life will be the same for you except one thing.'

Sha'inti stared through blinking eyes.

'You'll be working for us,' continued Christian. 'You will pass us information on every aspect of the organisation and people working with you, contacts in the UK and other parts of the world, all planned piracy and cross-border incursions, kidnappings, the lot. We'll decide what you will and will not do.'

Sha'inti's head tremored as if trying to nod in agreement.

'You'll be authorised to carry out certain activities to maintain appearances. We want you in charge and not some new jumped-up nutcase trying to make a name for himself. Now, you may be thinking you can get back home and forget all about us. Is that what you're thinking?'

Sha'inti's head tremored in a different direction.

'Well,' said Christian, 'we found you once, which means we can find you again. Of course, it will be easier now we have your full profile and DNA. And if we need to bring you in, this will happen for real. You've seen it.'

Christian leant forwards and released the clamp holding Sha'inti's mouth open. Sha'inti swallowed and spoke.

'I will work with you. I promise.'

'Words are nothing,' replied Christian. 'What else would you say? But our work is done. We'll take you back to the beach and you will never see us again. But you will be contacted.'

55

Raglan twisted the throttle and guided the RIB away from HMS *Vanguard*, leaving a throng of seabirds squabbling for access to the churning water at her bow. Christian sat on the plastic bench across the middle of the boat and Sha'inti squatted at the front, his hands secured behind his back. Assisted by a rising tide, they reached the shore. Christian looped his M16 over his shoulder and dropped into warm, knee-deep foam. He pulled on a rope and dragged the nose of the RIB onto the beach, allowing Sha'inti to step ashore.

'Right, off you go,' said Christian, releasing his hands. 'Look, the truck's just along there. You won't have to walk back.'

Sha'inti yanked his arms forwards and rubbed his wrists. He opened his mouth to say something but thought better of it, turned and walked off down the beach towards the pickup.

'Don't think you can smoke on a sub,' said Raglan, offering Christian a cigarette.

'Good point,' replied Christian, sitting down on the sand. 'Last smoke and then home.'

'Sounds good to me,' said Raglan, sitting down next to him. 'Hate subs. Always banging my head and only allowed in the shower for ten seconds. Nightmare.'

'Hopefully, we'll RV with a proper boat and they'll swap us over,' said Christian, taking a drag.

'Fuck knows,' said Raglan.

Out of the corner of his eye, Christian saw the pickup turn around and head away down the beach.

'Should have made the cunt walk,' Raglan continued.

Christian did not reply. He cocked his head to one side but it was too late.

'Don't move a muscle, either of you. Put your hands in the air,' growled a familiar voice.

Raglan ignored the instruction and twisted around. Sam Carter stood there pointing an AK-47 at their backs.

'They were fake,' he said. 'Three out of the four packets were fake.'

Christian raised his hands slowly and stood up. His cigarette smoked in the corner of his mouth.

'You're a conning bastard, McKie. I should never have trusted you.'

Raglan burst out laughing.

'Fakes,' he roared. 'Couldn't happen to a nicer guy.'

Sam's face reddened.

'Not so fucking funny for you.'

'How the fuck was I meant to know?' barked Christian.

'You shameless, murdering bastard,' continued Raglan. 'You should turn that gun on yourself.'

'Think of their faces,' hissed Christian, his finger stabbing the air. 'Jamie, Tim and Andy. And you carried my coffin. Played the big man. It beggars belief.'

'Unbelievable,' bellowed Raglan. 'You're not a soldier.'

'Shut up!' yelled Sam, pointing his AK in Christian's face. 'I'm here to kill you, not talk to you. Get on your knees. I'm going to waste you both right now.'

'But which ones did Arma give you?' said Christian. 'No bullshit, the ones I had checked out in London were real. Worth millions. Those are what Armalite brought.'

'Get down and tell me where he is now,' snarled Sam.

Raglan dropped to his knees and jerked his thumb over his shoulder. 'HMS whatever out there.'

'But I know where he put them,' said Christian, also kneeling.

'Bullshit you do.'

'Well, shoot me, but there's a whole load of them. Maybe fake, maybe not, how do I know? About sixty of them. Buried.'

'Buried where? And choose your last words carefully.'

Sam's eyes darted around Christian's face, over to Raglan and then to HMS *Vanguard* half a mile offshore.

'Come on, McKie. Last chance. Where are they?'

'Buried in the desert. About forty K inland from here. Hard to describe.'

'Not good enough,' said Sam, walking round behind them, the AK pressed into his shoulder.

'I can take you there now,' said Christian. 'Any bullshit and you kill us there. Surely, it's worth the chance?'

There was a pause. 'And how did you find us anyway?' Christian asked.

'Not very hard, actually. Followed the smell of bullshit, friends in high places and your little firework display last night.'

'OK,' said Raglan. 'It was meant to be noisy.'

'Shut up and start walking,' snapped Sam, jabbing the muzzle of the AK into Raglan's back. 'Up the beach to my truck.'

56

Christian sat in the passenger seat with his hands cuffed behind him and Raglan crouched in the back of the vehicle with his hand secured around the bull bars. Sam rested his AK across his lap, spread out a map and fiddled with a hand-held GPS.

'Here?' he said, stabbing at the map. 'That's more than forty K.'

'Do you want the fucking things or not?' Christian asked.

'It will be a lot worse for you if they're not there,' said Sam, looking sideways. 'It's a clean kill here or a gut shot there.'

'Just drive,' Christian said.

Sam clunked the vehicle into gear, the wheels spat sand and they set off inland through rolling scrub. Christian focussed on the approaching mountains and tried to think through the muddle of his physical exhaustion. Sam would kill them. He tried before back in Sierra Leone and would have done back in the fort. But what was worse? A gut shot from Sam and bleeding out in the desert, or the likely outcome of his only alternative? They picked up a track and Sam increased the speed. He glanced at Christian.

'Getting closer,' he said with a smile.

'Sure,' replied Christian. 'You'll know when we're close. You'll see a load of old buildings.'

They left the track when it swung around to the north and kept heading west. After the best part of an hour and a half, Sam lifted his sunglasses and squinted through the dusty windscreen.

'Buildings, you said?'

'Yup,' replied Christian.

'An old mining place?'

'Yup, that's right. They're in the bottom of an old opencast mine. You can drive right down inside.'

'Roger that,' said Sam, excitement evident in his voice.

They passed the graffitied buildings and slowed as they approached the cutting. Sam's expression hardened as they eased their way through the corridor of rock. The corkscrew track curled before them and the sheer drop fell away a couple of feet to the right of their tyres. Chewing his lip and craning forwards, he made minute adjustments to the steering wheel and snatched the occasional glance into the yawning cavity below.

'Down there?' he asked.

'Down there,' Christian confirmed. 'That's where they are.'

'Your funeral,' shrugged Sam.

As they reached the bottom of the track, Sam sat back and slipped the vehicle into second.

'Over there, through those rocks,' said Christian. 'By that old shipping container.'

Sam nodded and they meandered their way forwards.

'Just park anywhere here and I'll show you the spot,' Christian said.

Before they had even come to a standstill, the corrosive smell of rotting flesh assaulted the back of Christian's throat. The dark tidemark around the container glistened in the sun and feasting flies launched themselves reluctantly into the air. Sam grimaced and reached for his face.

'What the fuck is this place?' he demanded through his fingers.

As Sam elbowed the door open and stepped out of the pickup, a series of shots cracked. He spun around and raised his AK in time to clock six militiamen in ops vests appearing from the rocks. Shouting orders over waves of echo, they fanned out, their weapons levelled.

'A place to die,' replied Christian.

'Not if you know the people I know,' snapped Sam, raising a hand in greeting to the enclosing militiamen.

A couple of seconds later, Christian found himself landing on his side on the ground beside the pickup. Hands grappled at him and slapped his face as he struggled to his feet. Around the other side, Sam yelled a series of names as his rifle was pulled from his arms. Raglan looked on helplessly from the back of the truck.

Christian's chest thumped onto the bonnet and a gun pressed into his neck. Sam slammed down next to him, blood pouring from his nose. Still he protested and called Arabic-sounding names. Excited chatter broke out amongst the militiamen and instructions were replayed into a radio which crackled incoherently.

57

Christian sat cross-legged on the ground between Sam and Raglan. Ten metres away, in the shade of the cliff, four of the militiamen slobbed in deck chairs, fingering their weapons. Every few minutes, they reached into a yellow plastic bag and poked a pinch of dried brown leaves into their grinning mouths. Above, the sun had the run of the skies except for the white chalk streak of a passenger jet which served as a reminder of a faraway modern world. Christian's arms ached behind his back and he longed to wipe the sweat and dust from his face. A couple of hours ago, he'd been planning a shower and a cooked breakfast. Now, he watched Sam's eyes wander around the mine and back to the row of waist-deep pits at the base of the cliff.

Screeching brakes broke the silence. Christian squinted up to see a growing line of matchstick figures around the upper rim of the mine. They pointed and called down to the remaining militiamen, who hauled themselves out of their chairs and spat plumes of partially chewed khat onto the ground. Taking a final pinch, one stuffed the yellow bag into the netting on the front of his ops vest. A white flatbed lorry edged its way around the corkscrew. Propped up in the back, men shouted and waved their weapons. More streamed down on foot.

'It's a long shot,' whispered Christian. 'But there's no alternative.'

The closest of the militiamen heard him and spun around. With anger in his eyes but a smile still cracked across his face, he rushed at Christian, raised his AK, and clubbed him across the back. Christian toppled over sideways and twisted into a foetal position. As he braced himself for further blows, the militiamen yelled a stream of incomprehensible abuse before withdrawing to welcome the first arrivals to make it to the floor of the mine. High-spirited greetings were exchanged and four militiamen accepted triumphant high-fives. Christian shuffled back upright and fought to regain his breath. Next to him, Sam's shoulders flexed forwards and his neck bulged as he fought again his cuffs. Raglan caught Christian's eye.

An older man in a long grey shirt and circular white hat raised his hands and issued a series of orders. Instantly, they were surrounded and Christian's heels were dragging through the dust, backwards towards the cliff.

'Sha'inti,' he yelled. 'Where is Sha'inti?'

He felt the ground disappear beneath him and kicked his legs out either side of a pit. The butt of a riffle slammed into his shin and he crashed in up to his hips. Immediately, rubble was piled around him and packed down by jumping feet. Between the melee of legs around him, he caught a glimpse of Raglan a few metres to his right and Sam to his left. Both struggled hard as loose stones and earth were scraped from the surrounding area and kicked in around them.

'Where is Sha'inti?' yelled Christian again. 'Sha'inti.'

Raglan echoed his calls and Sam continued to boom a series of names. Swelling in numbers, the crowd screamed with delight and busied themselves collecting small stones which they piled into heaps. Christian blinked the sweat out of his eyes and stared up at a procession of vehicles snaking down into the mine.

'Fucking hell,' stammered Sam. 'Christi, what's happening?'

'Exactly what you think,' shouted Christian over the clamour of the crowd.

'Carter, you're a wanker,' growled Raglan, his face reddened with rage.

'Now, shut up,' he continued. 'Christi, look, that's Sha'inti's truck. Look.'

Christian craned his neck and tilted his chest sideways as far as he could. A Land Cruiser approached and a momentary gap in the crowd revealed a missing window. It swerved through the rocks, parting the crowd, and the pursuing cloud of grey merged with the dust spewed upwards by the tyres skidding to a halt.

The engine died, the door opened and Sha'inti stepped out. Christian heard the crackle of plastic teeth as he yanked up the zip on the front of his ops vest. His boots crunched and the eyes of the crowd followed him. Christian swallowed hard and tried to breathe. Time ran slow and cold. The crowd blurred and all he could see was Sha'inti's confident stroll.

'No bigger than a tangerine,' he said, dropping to one knee by a pile of stones. 'That's our rule. Maybe not quite scientific enough for you but it works for us.'

Pinching a small grey stone between his thumb and forefinger, he stood up and examined it.

'Half an hour is the average,' he continued quietly. 'It depends on the size of the crowd and the stones. It can take over an hour, sometimes just ten minutes. But, in your case, I may prefer to stop halfway through and leave you as bleeding, toothless stumps for the rats and birds.'

Christian looked up at him and cleared his throat to speak. But Sha'inti continued.

'And the first sign of a parachute or a helicopter, I'll make sure you're dead long before they hit the ground. Now, you think about all that while we give people a chance to get here.'

'Remember,' croaked Raglan. 'They'll come for you.'

Sha'inti's eyes narrowed and he stepped over towards Raglan.

'That's a risk I might be happy to take. The only shame is that I can't see you shit yourself later on.'

Raglan stared at the ground, shaking his head slowly. Sha'inti turned and walked away in the direction of his vehicle.

'I'm not with them,' bawled Sam. 'They are nothing to do with me. Let me go. I work for the Egyptian Government. This is a massive mistake.'

'For fuck's sake,' snarled Christian. 'Face it.'

He looked up into the gazing faces of the crowd. Men made mock throwing gestures and women in brightly coloured shawls sang and danced around the stacks of stones. Beyond, the corkscrew track blurred to a fluid line of motion. Other than his toes, he could not move a muscle below his waist. He breathed hard and twisted his hands around within the cuffs. Desperation built within him, brimmed over and forced boiling panic up from his stomach.

The sunlight intensified and the baying of the mob became removed to a distant place. He hauled in a breath and fought the fear. Armalite would work it out. He'd worked it out before. They had gone ashore and the only reason not to return would have been capture. Where did al-Shabaab take their prisoners? To the massive great hole in the ground. And that would be visible on any map or satellite image. It wasn't impossible. There was hope. There was.

The jeers of the mob washed over him once again. Sha'inti reappeared, raised his arms and shuffled backwards, scraping a line in the dust with the side of his boot. He called a few words and beckoned a row of armed militiamen to form up behind it. They hurried into position and scooped up stones from the piles.

'Come on then, you prehistoric sacks of shit,' yelled Raglan.

Sha'inti stared at Raglan and shook his head. He shouted an order and a blizzard of stones filled the air. Christian dropped his chin into his chest and tilted forwards as stones sliced past him. Sam let out a series of muffled gasps which, over the applauding roar of the crowd, rose in pitch to a searing scream of agony. Christian peered at his bloodied face twisting sideways in a futile effort to avoid the impact of the stones. But still not a single one had hit his own body.

The intensity of the volley increased as did the roar of the crowd. Stones glanced from Sam's head and chest, cascading onto the ground around him. Flesh hung from his cheeks and his shirt turned crimson. He bucked backwards and raised his head in a hopeless attempt to prise himself out of the ground. He screamed and choked in abandon, oblivious to the direction of the stones. Blood gushed from his head and soon his face lost human form.

Christian looked away. Raglan was unharmed too.

Perhaps they were to watch the horror that awaited them. Why rush all the fun?

Sam slumped forwards. His shirt hung around his shoulders and blood streamed over the green outline of his Para Reg tattoo. His screams subsided to agonised moans, barely audible over the ecstatic whoops from the crowd. Still the barrage rained down upon him. A second wind rushed through him and he flipped back upright, a matt layer of grit and dust dulling the glisten of the blood on his chest and face. Once more he bellowed. This time louder, longer and deeper.

58

Fifteen minutes had passed when Sha'inti stepped forwards and raised a pistol in the air. He fired a shot and waved his hands in a sweeping motion before him. The militiamen lowered their arms and the last shower of stones clattered to the ground. He snapped an instruction and one of the militiamen rushed forwards with a jerry can. He poured the contents over Sam's twitching torso and leapt back into line. Sha'nti tossed a match into the air and, with a crack, the shimmering haze of evaporating petrol became flames.

As if a puppet master had yanked his strings, Sam's collapsed frame sprang upright. A delayed reaction lasting a fraction of a second passed before he began to thrash more wildly than ever. A single, unbroken scream drowned out the crowd and reverberated around the mine. Recoiling from the heat, Christian choked as black fumes enveloped him. He tasted burning blood and skin. Seconds crawled past and still the scream held its note.

Sam finally slumped faced down in the ground. His charred arms, still bound at the wrists, arced up like a suspension bridge over his back. His blackened fingers meshed together. Fat sizzled and released a sickeningly familiar stench; part death, part cooking.

Weakened by adrenalin and half blinded by smoke, Christian raised his head, expecting to see the crowd being invited forwards to the firing line. The militiamen had turned their backs. They faced the crowd with rifles at the ready. Figures approached him and a shovel rasped into the rocks holding him. His arms were yanked upwards and then flopped free by his sides. Sha'inti dropped into view, his face shining and close.

'The people have had some satisfaction,' growled Sha'inti. 'But I will release you. We have a deal and I will continue to work with you. You can tell your people how I have cooperated so far.'

Christian was dragged roughly upwards by his arms and the rocks tore at his legs as they reluctantly released their grip on him. He fell forwards onto the ground and struggled to push himself up. The crowd bawled with disapproval as Raglan crashed down next to him and stones flew at them over the line of militia. Sha'inti jerked a thumb in the direction of a battered pickup. They staggered towards it and

Christian fumbled open the driver's door. As he turned the key, Raglan slid in the other side. The cab filled with diesel fumes and they set off through the rocks towards the start of the corkscrew track.

Christian gripped the steering wheel and, hugging the jagged wall of stone, they began the ascent. Below, the individual figures merged and vehicles became toys. The engine groaned, the tyres grappled with loose stones and burning rubber overcame the stink of diesel. Finally, the cutting came into view. They were through and gathering speed.

'That was a long shot,' gasped Raglan. 'Did you really think he would cooperate when he could have killed us?'

'Well,' said Christian, 'he's a clever bastard and doesn't want to spend the rest of his life in hiding. He's much better off taking orders from us and keeping his position. If he'd killed us, Deveral would have had him droned. He knows that.'

'Some gamble, Christi,' Raglan said. 'Mind you, fortune does favour the brave.'

'And the dead.'